Don't

Let

the Devil

Ride

Don't Let the Devil Ride

A NOVEL

ACE ATKINS

corsair

CORSAIR

First published in the United States in 2024 by William Morrow
First published in the United Kingdom in 2024 by Corsair

1 3 5 7 9 10 8 6 4 2

Copyright © 2024, Ace Atkins

A CIP catalogue record for this book
is available from the British Library.

HB ISBN: 978-1-4721-5920-5
TPB ISBN: 978-1-4721-5921-2

Printed and bound in Great Britain by Clays Ltd, Elcograf S.p.A.

Papers used by Corsair are from well-managed forests
and other responsible sources.

Corsair
An imprint of
Little, Brown Book Group
Carmelite House
50 Victoria Embankment
London EC4Y 0DZ

An Hachette UK Company
www.hachette.co.uk

www.littlebrown.co.uk

For Andria Lisle

Memphis is the kind of town where someone finds a five-dollar bill on the street and complains it ain't a twenty.

—*Porter Hayes,* Inside Detective, *March 1977*

Don't
Let
the Devil
Ride

Addison

The last time Addison McKellar's husband disappeared, it had been the night of the private Hootie and the Blowfish concert at the Overton Park Shell. That was two years ago, back in 2008.

Thinking back on it, Addison knew it wasn't technically Hootie and the Blowfish, just Darius Rucker and his new band doing some alt-country thing in sparkly blue jeans and snakeskin boots, making all the middle-aged couples awkwardly dance and clap off-rhythm, pretending they still had it. A sea of swaying sweaty arms, seersucker, khaki, and sundresses. Darius sang "Only Wanna Be with You" and his new single "Come Back Song" as the closer.

If you didn't notice the hair loss and weight gain, it could've been Ole Miss back in 1992.

Dean had held her tight, chin resting on her shoulder (they were nearly the same height even when he wore his custom-made cowboy boots) as she closed her eyes and moved with the music. Sure, he was a little on the short side, but obsessively fit, with a full head of sandy blond hair and purposeful scruff. Dean had finally relaxed when that third bourbon hit him. Not just any bourbon, but a twenty-three-year-old Pappy Van Winkle poured into red Solo cups that someone brought to celebrate Addison's brother Branch's fortieth birthday.

The idea for the Big 4-0 blowout had been hatched with her sister-in-law Libby over a three-gimlet lunch at the Brooks, not even bothering to catch a glimpse of *The Baroque World of Fernando Botero* exhibition before ordering their first of many cocktails. When Addison drank, a favorite quote of her father's always came to mind, "Suddenly, the trees had many leaves." *Poor Daddy.* He hadn't been able to stand up and make the big Hootie show for his son. When she'd asked if he'd like a wheelchair to make things easier, he'd said, "What the fuck is a Hootie?"

Dean had been back in Memphis for an extended period this past year, flying home from London via New York during some big new deal for McKellar Construction. Addison never paid attention to the details. Her husband seemed as happy as she'd ever seen him, although Dean wasn't the kind of man to show much emotion. He was constantly trying to install that stone-faced grit into their son, Preston, big on those father/son hunting trips down at their camp in the Delta. Just last fall, Preston had shot his first deer and she'd framed the photo with the poor deer's blood smeared across her son's nine-year-old face. "Get a grip, Addy," Branch had said, pontificating with one of Dean's fat Cuban cigars by their pool. "Your boy is going to be a man whether you like it or not."

She didn't like it. Addison would've liked to have kept Preston a child forever. She had treasured their trips to the Memphis Zoo and his help taste-testing at Sugar Babies, her now defunct ice cream and candy shop. Now he was ten. Soon, he'd be the same as his older sister, Sara Caroline, who was fourteen going on forty-four, sweet and vindictive, kind and manipulative, and mostly a disapproving presence in their house. Addison knew it was a phase and had bought dozens of books to inoculate her: *Decoding Your 21st Century Daughter: An Anxious Parents Guide to Raising a Teenage Girl*; *Just Us Girls: A Shared Journal for Moms and Daughters*; and *Why Some Animals Eat Their Young: A Survivor's Guide to Motherhood.* But despite collecting a neat half-read library on her bedside table, there had been a lot of slammed doors and enough eye-rolling to generate power for half the Mid-South.

The night of the birthday bash two years ago, before Dean had disappeared without a word for a whole five days, might've been the best her marriage had ever been. She'd been seeing Dr. Larry for at least a year and had started to make peace with her dead mother, her father's terminal illness, and her husband's withholding affection. Short of the obligatory and mechanical sex they'd been having for years (*Wow, that was amazing. What's on HBO?*), it was all going wonderfully. She realized Dean was an important man. A busy man. By the time he got home from those extended business trips, he was absolutely wiped out. He needed her patience and love. Not dinner conversation. Not sex. Some downtime with the boys at the Club. He seemed to be one of the few developers in the Mid-South not bankrupted by the damn 2008 recession. That took some work.

Dr. Larry had thought Dean might be suffering from PTSD after his time during the first Gulf War, his military service the bedrock of the legend of Dean McKellar.

What was it Dean had said to her, right before he walked off into the parking lot in Overton Park that night? *Oh, yeah. Keep those home fires burning.*

He'd said pretty much the same thing a week ago today, leather carryall over his shoulder, offering a thumbs-up like a World War II flyer, and she hadn't heard a word since.

It was past midnight now in their continually renovated old English Tudor in Central Gardens. Addison sat in Dean's office in Dean's big red padded chair, swiveling back and forth and watching brown liquor swish around in a crystal glass. The same chair where he held court with their friends, the men in the Memphi Krewe and on the Ducks Unlimited board who worshipped Dean with such sad devotion. The walls were filled with leatherbound books he pretended he'd read—*War and Peace, For Whom the Bell Tolls, Crime and Punishment* (Dean didn't read much beyond books on leadership and the occasional thumbed-through war history)—and a gross collection of animal heads from African safaris and hunting trips in Montana.

Addison helped herself to more of Dean's private whiskey stash, the white wine and Xanax not working anymore. She made a face while taking another hard swallow, catching an image of herself in the window's reflection. Late thirties—*okay, almost forty*—her naturally dark hair carefully bleached, warmly highlighted, and up in a messy bun. She wore an old pair of sweatpants with a tank top she bought in Rosemary

Beach. The logo read 30A (the beach highway) with a sparkling sun replacing the 0.

On top of the big desk, the antique one with eagle claws for feet, Addison played with a letter opener shaped like a bayonet, engraved with *Operation Desert Storm*, wondering just how long she was expected to wait. *Son of a bitch.* She and Dean had been together for fifteen years, but she'd been told time and again not to ask too many questions. His business was bland and boring, but if she ran the house, paid the bills from the household account Dean filled up monthly, and made sure the kids didn't drown or electrocute themselves, all would be right in the world. Still, Addison couldn't recall her own daddy ever disappearing for days on end. Not to mention, the monthly deposit hadn't been made into her account, and yesterday two of her credit cards had been declined.

She stared at her phone. No missed calls. No messages. Fifty-eight unanswered calls to Dean's cell. *Fifty-eight!*

Amanda, his secretary, hadn't helped at all, and Addison had been calling her every day since Thursday wanting to know what the hell was going on and when her goddamn husband, not Mr. McKellar, was due back in Memphis. *Just tell me where I can find him. What's the name of his hotel? What's his flight number?* It was a private flight and she didn't have the details, Amanda said, not knowing jack shit about when he'd return. Yes, she promised, she'd relay the message. No, she promised, everything was absolutely fine. Mr. McKellar had just been busy with attorneys on the Manchester project and the cell phone service in the UK was an absolute mess right now. He promised he'd return her call just as soon as possible. *Well, fuck you, Amanda*, Addison wanted to say. But she kept that bit to herself. She was, after all, a very polite Southern woman.

Addison heard the big lie in the secretary's voice. And something else, something that sounded a hell of a lot like worry and fear. Amanda had no fucking idea where Dean was, either.

Addison would call again in the morning. *And again and again and again.*

She could keep calling until she got answers.

Addison looked down at the empty whiskey glass and up at the antique clock ticking away on the mantel. *Shit.* In four short hours, she'd have to be up and pretending again that everything in the world was A-okay. Little Miss Suzy Sunshine. *Life Is Good,* right? Just like those T-shirts in Dean's closet promised.

Josefina slid their breakfast plates in front of the children, blueberry pancakes for Preston and dry plain bagel for Sara Caroline, and glanced over at Addison leaning against the counter. She shook her head again. Josefina, a serious and sturdy woman who rarely spoke, knew. She'd let herself in and cleared Dean's study of the Macallan bottle and the Baccarat glass before Addison had even woken up.

The early fall light shone hard and unrelenting through the bank of kitchen windows overlooking the pool littered with dead leaves. Addison stood there, coolly sipping black coffee in her bathrobe, wearing a huge pair of black Fendi sunglasses. When she'd bought them, she'd felt like Holly Golightly, but now she felt more like Evita Perón. *Don't cry for me, Central Gardens!*

Preston, mouth full of pancakes, studied her face and said, "Do you know you're wearing sunglasses inside?"

"I have a migraine."

Sara Caroline snorted and crunched hard on her bagel, rolling her eyes. Addison recalled Dr. Larry saying that mothers were always the safest rage outlet for adolescent girls. *Addison, you might as well have a target painted on your forehead. Don't take it personally.*

Addison needed to change into her workout clothes to give a more respectable appearance during drop-off at Hutch and Presbyterian Day. That way, the teachers and worse, other parents, would think she was headed to the gym or Pilates, not planning to go back to bed with the blinds drawn to try to sleep off this terrible week.

"Where's Dad?" Preston asked, as if just noticing.

"I'd love to know," Addison said. "Maybe he'll think enough of us to actually call today." She shouldn't have said it. It was bitchy and rude and the one thing that she had promised herself that she would never do, run down Dean in front of the kids. But by god, right now, she wanted to run him down more than anything. A week. A whole fucking week with not so much as an email or a text. What kind of father doesn't call and ask about Preston's soccer game or how Sara Caroline was doing with math or lacrosse? Or making sure the damn dog—their adorable labradoodle, ChaCha—was okay, as only three weeks before she'd had to rush him to the vet with spastic diarrhea.

Those were the days when you thank god for Josefina.

Addison marched upstairs and changed into her black lululemon leggings and oversize Ole Miss hoodie. "Five minutes," she said. "Five minutes or you miserable kids can walk to school."

It was an old lie. But a good one. The kids never called her on her bluff.

She wandered outside to warm up the big-ass white Escalade, then leaned against it and pulled a pack of Marlboro Lights from the pocket of her hoodie.

She checked her watch, furtively smoking a cigarette, as the exhaust chugged into the air and scattered into the wind.

After the Hootie incident, Dean had sworn to never disappear without warning again. *Never, ever, sweetheart. You're my one and only. Together forever. Dean and Addison.*

Addison dropped Sara Caroline first and was in line to drop Preston at Presbyterian Day—PDS to parents—when the CD player shuffled to an old Hootie and the Blowfish album, blaring "Let Her Cry" directly into her hangover. *Jesus Fucking Christ.* She turned off the song and switched it to 91.1 for the morning news, hoping maybe it would let her know where her husband had gone. *Dean McKellar, wealthy Memphis businessman, perished on a flight over the Atlantic this morning, leaving behind an indifferent wife and two bratty children.* Or maybe, *Semi-known socialite Addison McKellar, twice vice president of the annual PDS Book Fest, has been caught with her head up her ass for nearly fifteen years, accepting hundreds of excuses and seldom asking questions.*

"Mom?" She peered into her rearview mirror.

"Yeah, Pres."

"Is Granddad going to die?"

"No," she said, lying through her goddamn teeth. "Not now. Well, not today anyway."

One problem at a time, kid. One problem at a time.

"But he is sick?" Preston said. "Really sick."

"He has cancer," she said. "But he has really, really good doctors. He's taking medicine. Getting the best treatment."

"You do know cancer can kill you."

"Yes, Preston," she said. "I have heard that."

Preston seemed satisfied with the answer, turning to look out the window at the car rider line stretching out of the Presbyterian parking lot and down along Poplar Avenue. An endless snake of Mercedes wagons, Tahoes, and BMW SUVs. The parents, mostly women living in this never-ending loop, just waited for their turn and their slice of freedom, before circling back in a few hours and starting it all again. Everything was going to be all right. Everything was going to turn out great. Big smile, everyone.

Positivity can sometimes be about the convenient lies we tell ourselves. Or that's at least what Dr. Larry always said.

Instead of going home, Addison decided to keep driving west on Poplar toward downtown where Dean kept an office in the Cotton Exchange Building. She knew Amanda would continue to evade her calls and give her bullshit replies on the phone, but it would be different in person. A whole week without one word and she was supposed to be cool with this? If she asked her brother, Branch, he would say, "Yes, of course, Addison. Do you have any idea of the money we're talking here? Give poor Dean a break. While other companies are going under, he's thriving in this market." But her brother, God love him, had always been such a kiss ass and Dean devotee. The fact that Branch really wanted out from under their daddy's thumb and the barbecue business to join Dean's firm wasn't lost on her one damn bit. She was pretty sure that Branch had a crush on Dean, that he'd always been secretly gay, or at least curious, but never had the dignity or courage to admit it. *Poor Libby.* No wonder she was always drunk.

Addison found a place to park, right down the street from the Front Street Deli, and made sure that her Escalade was locked up tight. Downtown Memphis didn't get many blue ribbons for safety; all you had to do is watch the local news every morning and get the rundown of various carjackings, robberies, and murders. *Welcome to Memphis. America's Runner-Up Murder Capital!* She furtively dug into her purse for some change, but couldn't find any, and even if her credit card worked, the reader and display on the meter was broken. Oh, well. This wouldn't take long.

The daylight made her feel a little better, but she couldn't walk five feet without glancing over her shoulder, noting three homeless men gathered at a park bench. One of them broke off from the others and began to follow her, calling out, "Hey, Momma. How about a little love? Just need something to eat."

She clutched her Lanvin hobo bag tight and walked straight for the tall marble building.

Looking back over her shoulder, she could see the rolling brown water of the Mississippi and the M humpback of the Hernando de Soto Bridge. She took leggy strides toward the Cotton Exchange Building, more than well equipped for trouble. Addison had taken two years of kickboxing classes with the best instructor in East Memphis. He'd once said she had a hell of a roundhouse kick.

McKellar Construction kept offices on the third floor in a big open space for Dean and his dozen or so employees. Amanda was the gatekeeper of the whole operation, working not only the reception desk but also as Dean's personal assistant. Although Addison had never met Amanda in person, Dean was always bragging about her incredible organizational skills. She'd heard so much about Amanda that at some point, she'd grown a little jealous. *Amanda got us front row tickets to the Mumford and Sons show even though it was sold out.* Or, *I would've never gotten out of Heathrow if it hadn't been for Amanda. What a life-saver.*

The elevator opened and Addison marched toward Dean's office. She came for answers and would leave with answers. She would not stop until Amanda got her husband on the phone. She wouldn't cause a scene. But goddamn it, there were limits to how much a woman could accept. *A week.* A whole fucking week, woman. If Amanda wouldn't help, she'd go to the police. And if that embarrassed Dean, so much the better. Maybe it was time he learned a lesson. Maybe it would stop him from being so cocky, taking Addison and the kids for granted. She stopped at the big plate glass wall with the glass door and reached for the handle. The etching caught her eye and she stood back for a moment, stunned, dropping her right hand to her side and looking back and forth along the corridor. *Townsend Interiors,* the door said.

Addison walked back to the elevator. Her head was so far up her ass this morning, she must've gotten off on the wrong floor. She pushed the elevator's up button and stepped back, glancing at her reflection. A mess. She looked a goddamn mess this morning. No makeup, blond hair scattered across her eyes, and coffee spilled across her sloppy Ole Miss hoodie.

She shook her head and got onto the elevator. A heavyset white woman in a wrinkled navy business dress smiled at her as she got on. Addison smiled back and pressed the third floor again. The button wouldn't work.

"I think you've already arrived."

"Excuse me?"

"Third floor?"

"This can't be the third floor."

She continued to mash the button over and over and each time the light failed to hold.

The woman took a patient breath and pointed to the number above the doors. Addison felt her face flush and walked back out in the corridor. *What was happening? Was this how you go absolutely batshit insane?* Maybe Dean hadn't been gone a week. Maybe she'd gone into the wrong office building? Maybe this was like one of those shows where she'd walked into a parallel universe and everything had been turned upside down. *This is not my beautiful house. This is not my beautiful wife.*

"This is the Cotton Exchange?" she asked, not even sure about her own name now.

The woman offered a polite smile and nodded and quickly pressed the button to close the door between them. Addison walked back to Dean's office, or what she thought was McKellar Construction, unless either (a) they'd moved or (b) he'd gone into the interior decorating business without telling her.

Inside the office, there was no secretary, just cubicles spaced around the open floor plan. Addison flagged down the first person she saw, a hip-looking Black woman wearing jeans and a man's button-down over a tank top. "Excuse me," Addison said. "I'm looking for McKellar Construction. This used to be their office?"

The woman shrugged. "Never heard of it. Hey, Rob. You know about some construction company?"

A skinny little white guy with a wispy beard shook his head.

"Maybe ask down in the lobby?" the woman said. "Are you sure you have the right address? We've been in this space for two years."

"My husband's company," she said. "It used to be right here."

"You sure?" the woman said.

"Positive."

"And he didn't tell you they'd moved?" The woman's eyes grew wide as she cocked her head. "That's pretty messed up."

"I'm not leaving until I get some goddamn answers."

"Ma'am, are you okay?" the woman asked.

"No," Addison said. "I'm fucking pissed."

Addison found a grouping of plushy purple chairs by the glass door, sat down, and crossed her arms over her chest. She was so damn mad she could hear nothing but the blood rushing in her ears. A few more employees walked over and told her that she needed to leave, that she was causing a commotion. She told them they hadn't seen any goddamn commotion unless they told her where the fuck her husband had gone.

"Who the hell are all you people?" Addison said, her voice rising louder every second. "Where is my goddamn husband?"

Twenty minutes later, two Memphis cops walked into the office and arrested her. Addison tried to explain everything, but they wouldn't answer her back, one of them asking her if she'd been drinking—the scotch from last night maybe wafting through her pores—while the other cop said something about getting a doctor's evaluation at 201 Poplar. *Good god.* This had to be the worst, most humiliating experience of her life, until she looked back as the cops were pressing her into a squad car, and she saw a big blue tow truck backing up to her white Escalade and hooking up the cable.

"You're making a huge mistake," she said. "I just want some answers. Goddamn it. Why won't anyone talk to me?"

2

Porter Hayes

More than half of Porter Hayes's business involved preachers fucking when they should've been praying. He'd been employed by preachers' wives, jilted husbands, deacons, and assistant pastors wondering just why the hell was Head Pastor So-and-So charging a thousand bucks at the Peabody for the ultimate duck experience that included dinner at Chez Philippe and a complimentary bottle of Korbel. It was a goddamn cliché, a story as old as Methuselah's great-grandmomma. But it was a core part of Hayes Investigations, a business he'd been running out of a downtown office since early 1971. He'd developed such a talent for it that he could walk right down the middle of the big COGIC convention and the sanctified congregation would part as if he was Moses strutting down the *Soul Train* line.

Nobody wanted Porter Hayes on their tail.

But this case was a little different. Both a pastor and his wife, Reverend Frank J. Hightower and the Lady Hightower, were thieving the identity of two elders in their Orange Mound church and running up credit cards. One of the women's granddaughters had hired him, and it only took two days to connect the cards back to Lady Hightower, the woman with no shame, using one of the cards at her favorite hairdresser and for several purchases at Oak Court Mall. Hayes was back at Oak Court that morning, sitting on a bench by a fountain, next to a tarnished copper statue of white kids playing leapfrog, and sipping on a coffee from Starbucks.

Lady Hightower's arms were heavy with shopping bags from Macy's and Dillard's while she sauntered into some fancy shoe shop near the glass elevators, picking through high heels that probably cost more than Hayes's daily rate.

Not that he always earned it. A case like this, working for a nice young lady on a fixed income trying to do right by her grandmother, probably would just be an expenses-only kind of thing. The reverend and his lady were too damn thick to even try and cover their tracks. Hayes could match the credit card purchases from the last few days with clear and detailed photographs he'd been taking with one of those little Japanese cameras slipped neatly inside his leather jacket. *God-damn*. It was insulting that neither of them even tried that hard.

Hayes had just gotten out his brown leather trench coat that crisp morning, slipping it over his pair of black pants and a black silk shirt. He had both the camera and a pack of Winstons—*Real, Rich & Cool*—in the pocket, wishing he could light up in the mall like the old days and make himself comfortable while Lady Hightower ran herself deeper into the hole. He already had enough to serve them both up to the district attorney, a case so solid even that dumb SOB Fortune Jackson couldn't screw it up.

Porter pulled out the camera and thumbed through the images, shaking his head. He was no Ernest Withers, but he had some pretty clear shots of the woman trying on several items she'd ended up charging. Her husband might be a little trickier, making online ticket purchases for his own events like Men's Empowerment 2010 and Old School: Biblical Living in a New Age. But still. He had their asses.

"Can I help you?" a woman asked.

Damn if it wasn't Lady Hightower herself, slipped out from the shoe store and sliding up right in front of him. Hayes tucked the camera back inside his jacket and smiled at her. "Perhaps," Hayes said, grinning. "You taking up a collection?"

She may have been a thief, but she was a good-looking woman, somewhere in her mid to late forties, wearing a formfitting purple dress knotted on a slim waist, with strong athletic legs and a full and firm backside that had caused several passing men to nearly break their goddamn necks. She wore shiny rings on her fingers and a big gold chain around her neck with a gold cross inlaid with diamonds. Like the good reverend said on the big sign outside his church: "You Got to Name It to Claim It."

"I know who you are, Mr. Hayes," Lady Hightower said. "I saw you sitting right here, in this same place, yesterday. And I saw you this morning at the Picadilly down on EP while my husband was hosting his weekly prayer breakfast."

"Mighty fine sermon, too," Hayes said. "*Cast your bread upon the waters. For thou shall find it after many days.* Your man sure can preach."

Lady set down her bags and placed her hands on her hips. "You don't quit following me around and I'm gonna call security. They know me here."

"Is that right?"

"You too old to be sniffing around a woman no older than your daughter. Yeah, I know your daughter. Nina. Teaches English at Melrose? Just what would she think of her daddy being such a dirty old man?"

Hayes couldn't contain his smile and smoothed down the ends of his graying mustache. He took a sip of coffee. "All right now," he said. "You caught me. I guess sometimes I forget my age. But can you blame me? You sure got a lot going on, Lady Hightower."

Lady Hightower tried her best not to smile back, arms moving up off her hips and crossing her large breasts barely covered by the dress. Damn, she did smell good. Reminded Porter some of his late wife and that lilac perfume from Paris. René Lalique? He still had it. He'd kept most of Genevieve's things in her bedroom closet, where they'd remain until he was gone, too. Shirts and pants that Nina called out of style piled high on top of the boxes, years and years gone. Damn, how he loved that woman.

"Figured you weren't there for the pancakes."

"No, ma'am."

"And you ain't here at the mall for Sunday shoes."

Hayes shook his head and looked down at his classic Italian boots that zipped neatly at the ankle. Some things never go out of style. Lady Highsmith dropped her bags, sat down next to him, and let out a long sigh.

Hayes drank some coffee and watched the early traffic inside the old mall. Moneyed Black women checking out the latest styles. Punk kids skipping school. Old men like him in tracksuits walking around the food court, killing time at the Starbucks. The mall had been here since the eighties, but back then, it had been a strictly white clientele. Now, most of the shoppers were Black. Shopping downtown was long gone. No more buying your Easter suit on Beale at Lansky's or the huge old Goldsmith's on Main Street. In a few years, the mall would probably be gone, too, everything seeming to be moving farther east away from downtown where Porter still kept an office. That white flight wouldn't stop until every building downtown turned out the lights.

Lady Hightower rested her long hand with polished red nails on his good knee. She whispered a hot voice in his ear. "If you know where I shop, then you damn sure know where I live. Frankie's dumb ass gonna be gone all weekend. And I sure love to stay up late, Mr. Hayes, watching those old-timey movies."

"Old-timey movies?"

"You know, Bogart, Spencer Tracy, damn Billy Dee Williams," she said. "Real men. Like you."

"Is that what keeps you up at night?"

"I'm hell on sleep, Mr. Hayes."

Porter Hayes's mouth felt a little dry. But he had to admit it felt good to be desired as a man in his early seventies. Either that or she and the good reverend were on to him, setting some kind of trap. Porter kept lean, at six foot two and one-ninety, hit that iron from time to time, ran a few miles on the track at Booker T. Maybe more salt than pepper in his hair and his mustache, but sure, he could see a woman showing some interest.

"You'll think about it?"

Porter Hayes straightened the lapels on his leather trench. Lady Hightower used his knee to push herself up onto her six-inch heels.

"Yes, ma'am," he said. "I sure will. Long and hard."

"Mmm," she said. "I knew it."

"Man," Deacon Malone said. "That sounds like some real bullshit to me."

"Come on, now," Hayes said. "Don't be jealous. We been friends too long."

"Jealous some thieving preacher's wife trying to trick your ass with whiskey and pussy?"

"Woman didn't say anything about whiskey."

Malone stroked his goatee. "She mention Rémy and you'd be over there right now singing her some old Johnnie Taylor songs."

"'Jody Got Your Girl and Gone.'"

"What was that B side?"

"'A Fool Like Me.'"

"Sounds about right, Porter Hayes."

The men laughed, sitting at their back booth of the Gay Hawk diner off Danny Thomas Boulevard. It was Wednesday, rib tip day on the buffet, and Henry had laid out quite a spread under the heat lamps: collard greens, cornbread, mac and cheese, peach cobbler, and candied yams. Man could get diabetes just smelling it. The diner was old and worn-out, paneled wood buckling off the walls, ceiling tiles water-stained, busted, or missing altogether. The walls were decorated with faded ads, one with Fred Williamson shilling for King Cobra, a good-looking woman with her arm around Fred and holding up her index finger. *Don't let the smooth taste fool you.*

"That woman must not know who we are," Malone said. "And what we do."

"Maybe not."

"But she knew Nina?" Deacon asked, forking up some slow-cooked greens.

"Says she did," Porter Hayes said. "Probably met me at some of those things at Stax when they honor the Tonettes. Knows me for being married to Genevieve, not from being a detective."

"You don't exactly keep a low profile, man," he said. "You on *Live at 9* last week with Alex and Mary Beth, talking about school safety for the kids. Memphis's Favorite Private Eye."

The last part had Deacon doing his best to mimic the deep baritones of the anchor, Alex Coleman. Hayes shrugged and took a bite of the rib tips. Nice and smoky, cooked low and slow in the alley off a steel-drum pit.

"So," Malone said. "What's she look like?"

Hayes pulled out the little camera and slid it across to Deacon. Deacon was twice Porter's size, carrying a lot of weight that had once been muscle but now was situated mainly around his waist. But there still wasn't a hell of a lot of folks, young or old, who would fuck with Deacon Malone. He looked like a great smiling Buddha with a mean secret behind the eyes.

Deacon turned the camera around in his hands—tech wasn't his expertise. Hayes snatched it from him and turned it on, pointing to the screen on the back. Deacon pressed a button, scrolling through some of the last pictures from Oak Court this morning. "Now I know you're lying to me."

"Hey," Hayes said. "What can I say? There may be snow on the roof—"

"Hate to break it to you, man. But it's been snowing all over your ass for twenty goddamn years."

"Just saying, if I weren't an honest man . . ."

"If you weren't so honest, that woman would break you in half," he said. "The Hightowers are onto you, Porter. You come into that house and that old preacher is gonna be waiting in the closet with more than his dick in his hand."

"A hymnbook?"

"His .44 Magnum, man."

Hayes swiveled his chair around, staring out the big bank of windows overlooking Second and Madison, the stenciled letters for HAYES INVESTIGATIONS appearing a little worse for wear against the cracked-open window. He poured Rémy into an old Memphis

Showboats coffee mug and looked up at the wall and all the newspaper clippings, dusty civic awards, and sun-faded black-and-white photos. Lots of cases and lots of memories up on that wall: Porter Hayes and Elvis at a karate demonstration at Kang Rhee's dojo; a clipping from the *Commercial Appeal* after he'd saved game show host Wink Martindale from a kidnapping; Porter and Marlo Thomas raising money for St. Jude; Porter and Jerry "the King" Lawler after his stripper ex-girlfriend hired that hitman. Porter as a rookie detective at MPD. Damn, when was that, 1967?

Now people were whispering about his retirement, putting him on the prayer list at church after heart surgery, word getting out in the community that he was on the verge of hanging it all up, even though that was a damn lie. If Porter retired, what the hell would he do with himself? Move down to Florida? Start donating his time at the Boys & Girls Club? Hell, he already put in two days a week helping out the Booker T. High track team, where he'd run first place in the 440- and the 100-yard dash, hoping to make it to college or the Olympics if Uncle Sam hadn't called his number up to Vietnam. Three long years into the jungle, Long Range Ranger Patrol, hunting down Charlie for reasons he didn't understand and never would. The Soul Patrol working deep in Cu Chi.

"Little early?" Darlene asked. "Ain't it?"

Darlene had been his assistant, secretary, and all-around girl Friday for more than twenty-five years. She was a wiry little white woman from somewhere around Coldwater, Mississippi, with a country accent so thick that even locals would ask her to repeat herself. *Cain't you hear me? I'm talking with my mouth.* He'd heard that so many times. Her voice thick and hoarse from years of chain-smoking. Tiny lines around her lips.

"Wrapping up the Hightower case," Hayes said. He set the little camera at the edge of his desk and looked up. "I'm writing the report. But you'll need to develop those pictures."

"Develop?" she said. "You know you can email all that stuff now, Porter. You really want hard copies?"

He nodded.

"You're not gonna charge that woman's granddaughter," she said. "Are you?"

"Not much to it," Porter said. "Only took a few days. Expenses only. I was just stretching my legs."

"You do know your generosity is about to bankrupt us."

"You've been saying that for twenty-five years."

"How long since we had a good one," Darlene said, leaning against the doorframe. "A really good case to offset those freebies?"

"I'm not charging that lady," Porter said. "Wouldn't be right."

Darlene shook her head and picked up the camera, leaving his office but keeping the door open. He turned around and reached for an old brick to prop the window open and walked over to close the door.

He sat back down and lit a cigarette and finished the last of the Rémy. Down on the street, an idling truck knocked into first and labored forward, the shocks and suspension squeaking. He was thinking about his kids, wondering if Nina really knew Lady Hightower, and then thinking on the hard words he'd had the last time he talked with his son, Randy. His son was a grown man with a family of his own but still trying to hustle it as a music promoter, working with Three 6 Mafia and Gangsta Boo. The last time they had dinner, Randy refused to take off his hat in the restaurant. Just where had Porter failed?

The old tan landline on his desk rang, and Porter picked it up. Been so long since he caught a call on the thing he could feel the thick dust on his fingers. He wondered why it hadn't gone to Darlene's desk first.

"Remember Sami Hassan?" Deacon Malone asked.

"Sam the Sham?" Hayes said. "Sure, man. Hadn't heard that name in a long while. Thought he went straight when he started slinging barbecue out in Germantown?"

"Man was crazy," Malone said. "Only one I know to ever tell Dago Tiller to go fuck himself. And live."

"Why're you asking?"

"'Cause he called me asking about you," Malone said. "Sam was under the impression you might be dead. Ha ha."

"That's funny," Hayes said. "Real funny."

"He seemed pretty damn hot to see you, man. Says he's got some family trouble that needs attention."

"That barbecue any good?"

"Fourth best in Memphis."

"But can he pay?"

"Sam the Sham?" Malone said. "Shit. He might not keep book at the Domino Club anymore, but the man's done well for himself. If the family trouble's bad enough, this just might be the case you've been looking for."

Hayes looked up to see his office door open again, Darlene at her little desk listening in on her end.

"You getting all this, Darlene?"

"What do you think?" Darlene asked, phone pressed to her ear. "And it's about goddamn time."

3

Addison

I understand you want to file a missing person's report," the bored-looking Black woman said. She apparently had some kind of rank at the Memphis Police Department, because it took thirty minutes at the station until someone called Addison up from central holding (a fun time with two drug addicts, three prostitutes, and a woman who explained how the CIA was controlling her mind) to the third-floor offices. The nameplate on the desk said Sergeant Lantana Jones. Addison was struck by such a flowery name for a police officer. Although in her experience volunteering at the Botanic Gardens, lantanas might be the toughest flowers you could grow. Very heat resistant.

"My husband has disappeared," Addison said. "He's been gone for seven days."

"Mm-hmm."

Already the woman didn't believe Dean was missing, even after everything Addison had gone through since being arrested at Dean's office, put in a cell, and then explaining her situation to three different officers. It was barely noon and already she was craving a Bloody Mary from the Grove Grill a few doors down from her old ice cream shop. Maybe she'd see if Libby could meet her and they could just spend the next few hours not talking about Dean or fucking Branch, her worthless brother. Oh, and the kids. She did need to pick up her kids. The one single time she forgot Sara Caroline after lacrosse practice, she was called the absolute worst mother in the world.

"Ma'am."

"Yes, ma'am."

"You were going to tell me about your husband," she said. "What's his name?"

"I've already told three police officers," Addison said. "Dean. Dean McKellar."

Addison then answered a series of questions about Dean's date of birth, address, height and weight, hair and eye color, what he did for a living and when she'd last seen him.

"Um," Sergeant Jones said. "Did you say London?"

"Yes, ma'am."

"You talking London, Tennessee, or as in Merry Ole?"

"The UK," Addison said, sitting up straighter. "My husband has business in the UK."

"All right then," Sergeant Jones said. "That's new."

"Can't you just call Scotland Yard or whatever and explain what's going on?" Addison said. "Look, I know what you're thinking. Woman goes to her husband's office that isn't an office anymore. The husband has been gone for a week. You think he's got to be fooling around. But I swear to god, Dean's not like that. We're not those kind of people."

"Scotland Yard?" Lantana Jones said. "Sure thing. I got their number someplace."

"You think this is funny."

"No, ma'am," she said. "Not at all. What about your husband's family, friends? People at his work?"

"You're not listening to me," she said. "I just went to his office and it's not even there."

"Okay, then," she said. "I hate to tell you, ma'am. But lots of times men just plain suck."

"Not Dean," Addison said. "He served in the first Gulf War as a captain. He earned two medals. He runs a successful construction company. Listen, I drove downtown, and to be honest with you, I absolutely never go downtown. But I went to Dean's office at the Cotton Exchange and now it's some kind of interior design firm. At first, I thought I might be going crazy or got off on the wrong floor. But nope.

That was it. It's like he moved and forgot to tell me what had happened. Now I'm trying to call Amanda and she won't even pick up the line."

"And who is Amanda?" Lantana Jones said. "Some kind of lady friend?"

"His secretary," Addison said. "Look. I'm not crazy. We live in Central Gardens. Here's my driver's license. Everyone who is anyone in Memphis knows him. He's a member of the Chamber of Commerce. He was king of the Cotton Carnival two years ago."

"King of Cotton, huh?" Lantana Jones raised an eyebrow. She neatly folded her hands on top of her desk. She was a pretty woman, with long hair, a perfectly symmetrical face, and big green eyes. Way too pretty to be a cop, although in truth Addison had never really met many cops besides the few who'd handed her parking and speeding tickets. Maybe every other woman cop at MPD looked like Lantana Jones. Maybe they all had pretty faces and names like flowers.

Addison bent forward and put her head down between her knees.

"Look," Sergeant Jones said, leaning into her desk. "Are you sure you don't want to make a few more phone calls first? Did y'all have a fight before he left? I know this is tough, but maybe your Dean is involved with another woman. I don't mean to be rude, Mrs. McKellar, but we're stretched a little thin at the moment unless you are absolutely sure he's gone. Also, you're talking about him being overseas. I got to be honest here, it's not like I got Sherlock Holmes's ass on speed dial."

"I think he might be dead," Addison said. "Okay?"

"Why do you say that?"

"One week without a word?" she said. "No emails or phone calls. We have two children together, a big house, and a labradoodle. God. Why is he doing this?"

"A labra what?"

"A labradoodle," Addison said. "It's a dog. His name is ChaCha."

"Has he been gone like this before?"

"ChaCha?"

"Dean."

Addison waited a beat but then said no, lying through her goddamn teeth. Lantana Jones watched her in a way that made her so nervous she burst into tears right there at 201 Poplar with all the murderers, thieves, prostitutes, and god knows what else. She held herself tight for several moments and then she felt herself breaking apart. Maybe that woman back in the holding cell was right, maybe the CIA was controlling all their minds.

Jones kept a big box of tissues on her desk and handed a few over to Addison to blow her nose. The woman looked at her watch and then up at the open door. A shortish Black man in uniform walked in and handed her a Styrofoam clamshell. Without a word, he turned and left.

The food sat on the woman's desk while she continued to peck at the keys.

"McKellar Construction," she said. "That's you?"

"That's Dean."

"Y'all sure go to a lot of parties."

"Fundraisers."

"Oh, yeah?"

"Yes," Addison said, composing herself and sitting up straighter in the hardback chair. "We like to give back to the community."

"Ain't that something," she said. "A whole week, huh? Damn. I can't say I blame you for being upset. I'm sorry about what happened to you. But the arresting officers thought you might be drunk. They took you in for your own protection."

"They also said I needed a psych eval."

"Yeah," Jones said. "They said you seemed disoriented and confused."

"My husband is gone," she said. "His office doesn't seem to exist. How would you act?"

"Disoriented and confused as hell," she said. "And real pissed off."

Addison nodded. She remembered when she got called into the dean's office at Ole Miss after one of her sorority sisters was caught cheating on a French exam. He did this whole slow and silent routine that made Addison more chatty than normal, nearly giving out the information that their sorority kept exams going back to the 1970s in a filing cabinet in the basement.

"I'll see what I can do, Mrs. McKellar," she said.

"Thank you, Miss Jones."

"Sergeant Jones."

"Of course," Addison said. "Sorry."

"England sure is a long way from Memphis," she said. "If I were you, I'd be finding myself a real good lawyer."

Addison waited on the steps at 201 Poplar for Libby to pick her up from this fucking nightmare. She had called her more than an hour ago, and if her sister-in-law didn't hurry up, she'd miss getting the kids from school. How much of a loser would she be then? She'd lost her husband, her SUV, two of her credit cards weren't working, and now she was standing among criminals being brought into jail and hustled out by slick attorneys in shiny suits and two-tone shoes. While she waited, Addison tried Dean again out of habit. At least ten times. She tried Amanda again and not surprisingly went right to voicemail. Her message had been both truthful and nasty. *If you don't fucking call me back right now, I'll make sure you can't get a goddamn job cleaning the toilets at a Walmart.* Well, hell. She'd tried being polite so many times, maybe being nasty would light a fire under her ass, as Daddy would say. And then, when all else failed, she tried calling Daddy, but his caregiver said he was down for his nap until his shows came on. Daddy never missed a double helping of *Gunsmoke* and *Bonanza* in the afternoon. She wondered how he'd feel about his only daughter standing outside 201 Poplar, handing out cigarettes to vagrants, streetwalkers, and pickpockets like a goddamn Mother Teresa.

Finally, Libby pulled up in her new black G-Wagen, merrily tooting her horn. A woman in a short sequin skirt and a bright red bikini top eyed her, drawing on a cigarette, and said, "Baby, that's a nice ride. You must be doing real nice work for your mister."

"Excuse me?"

"Aw, shit," the woman said. "Don't pretend that you and me ain't both on the hustle. What you on? Meth? That's some nasty-ass shit."

Addison pulled on her big Fendi sunglasses and headed down the wide stairs. Libby had parked in front of "ASAP Bailbonds: We Put Your Feet Back on the Street ASAP." She dodged a few cars on the busy road and walked around the back of the G-Wagen and got inside. The air conditioner blew some welcome fresh air in her face. Addison peeled off her hoodie and sat in the front seat in only a sports bra, fanning her sweaty chest.

"No offense," Libby said. "But you look awful."

"Thank you." Addison sunk down in her seat and closed her eyes. "No questions. Please just drive. I have to pick up the kids in an hour."

"Where's your car?"

"Impounded," Addison said. "We'll get it later."

Libby knocked the G-Wagen in gear and made an illegal U-turn right in front of police headquarters, Addison slinking down lower in the leather seats. From the radio, a cool-voiced public radio announcer explained the last set had been a chamber piece by Rachmaninoff. His voice so smooth and calm that she wanted to punch him right in the nose.

"Where have you been?" Addison said. "I've been waiting an hour."

"I was right in the middle of an appointment with my therapist," Libby said. "We were talking about setting boundaries and how bad I am about saying no. But then you kept calling and my phone kept buzzing and I knew it had to be an emergency. Right? That's what this is? An emergency?"

"Look at me," Addison said. "Look at my face. Look how I'm dressed. I'm a goddamn mess. I guess I wasn't expecting to be arrested for disorderly conduct. Oh god. I smell like jail. My head is splitting and I need a cocktail."

"Holy shit," Libby said. "Now we're talking. My day sucked, too."

"Are you even listening?"

Libby had always been stick thin. Today, she looked so thin that you could see the collarbones sticking out of her low-cut peasant top, just like the one the little girl wore on Addison's old paperback of *Heidi*. She had a long face and huge brown eyes and hair. When she wasn't so perfectly styled and carefully made-up, she looked so mousy and plain that she could pass for a high schooler. Her trinket bracelet, baubles from all the cities she'd visited, jangled on her wrist as she drove. The radio announced they were continuing with Rachmaninoff's saddest and most haunting melody.

"For fuck's sake, can you please change the station," Addison said.

Addison remembered when she and Libby were at Ole Miss and would circle the Square in her little red car, blaring Wilson Phillips's "Hold On." Jesus. They looped around and around as if they had somewhere important to go. Addison had, for two brief years, working in the publicity office of a big publisher in New York. One year assigned to a god-awful thriller writer who boasted thirty-three books in the Richard Jones series, better known in-house as "Big Dick" Jones because the author was always pointing out the hero's manly height and weight and incredible stamina in the sack. She had a killer apartment on the Upper West Side and two of the best roommates in the world, all of it a fuzzy history after she met Dean at a Christmas party at P.J. Clarke's in 1994. "What happened?"

"Please."

Libby headed east on Poplar, out of downtown and over Cleveland, taking on the city's potholes as she weaved in and around cars, trying to make it back in time to pick up the kids. Libby's twins were a grade below Preston, and they could pick them up at the same time. Addison could grab her other car at home, her old BMW convertible, and get Sara Caroline. She'd probably be late, but Sara Caroline would get over it. She'd take them both to Ben & Jerry's by Whole Foods and maybe for sushi later. She would make it all up to them. Daddy would be home soon. All was fucking well in the world.

"Are you going to tell me what's going on?" Libby asked. "You make me drive all the way to downtown, tell me you've been arrested, and then ask me to forget about it. What about Branch? What will I tell him?"

"Branch can go fuck himself."

"Jesus, Addy."

"I'm sorry, Libby," she said. "I like you a lot. But my brother is a worthless turd and the last thing I want to hear is Branch blaming me for Dean leaving."

"Dean left you?"

"I don't know what Dean has done," she said.

"Did you have a fight?" Libby asked. "Oh god. Is he going to get the house at Rosemary Beach? Is it another woman? I bet it's that cheap whore Hannah Tracy. Son of a bitch, I knew it. I swear to god, Hannah would screw every member of the Grizzlies if they'd let her liposuctioned ass on the bus."

"Can we please not talk."

"But Hannah Tracy?" Libby said. "You'd think Dean would have more class."

Addison sat still, sunglasses on and staring straight ahead. She didn't feel sad or tired anymore, just numb and confused. "Dean is missing," she said. "He's been gone one week, and I haven't heard a word. None of my credit cards work. I can't get more out of the bank because he's the only one listed on those accounts. His secretary tells me that he's still in England."

"There you go," Libby said. "There you go. Be positive. But I bet Hannah Tracy would've screwed him in the pool house bathroom after a pitcher of margaritas."

Addison closed her eyes, her hands tightly knitted in her lap.

"It's not Hannah Tracy, for fuck's sake," Addison said. "It's something a hell of a lot worse. Something is very, very wrong. I drove to Dean's office this morning, and everything is gone."

"Maybe he really is in England," Libby said. "Branch was saying that Dean could've been a lord of a castle. That he really fit in over there with those Savile Row suits and those handmade shoes. What is that brand?"

"Like really, really gone," Addison said. "There is no office. No one there even remembers a McKellar Construction office being there. When I refused to leave until I had answers, some woman called security on me and then they called the cops. They handcuffed me and put me into a patrol car while I watched my car being towed away. It took me half the day to explain who I was and what I wanted. The police scribbled down a few notes and told me to be on my way. It's like no one can understand a fucking word I'm saying."

"Do you really want a cocktail?" Libby said, turning down the radio. "Because we should've just valeted at the Peabody."

"Jesus God."

"Let's get the goddamn kids and then let's me and you go find a nice private corner at the Grove and get completely shit-faced."

"That's a lovely thought, Libby," Addison said. "Really. I know that's the best you have for me. But please just help me get the kids home."

"And then what?" Libby said. "Just pretend like nothing has ever happened? That's what my parents did and god knows they've been married for more than forty years. Did I tell you that they just got a new dog? A sweet little puppy named Peanut."

Libby punched up a CD on her stereo and the classical music was replaced with Tracy Chapman singing, "Give Me One Reason." Libby tapped at the steering wheel and sang along as if nothing that happened that day mattered at all.

"I really need to speak with Daddy," Addison said.

"Do you think he's up yet?"

"Soon." Addison checked her watch. "*Gunsmoke* starts in an hour."

Daddy wasn't home at his condo, sitting with an oxygen mask strapped across his face as he watched Matt Dillon gun down the villain of the week. He was back at Bluff City Barbecue, hobbling through the kitchen testing the sauce, eyeing the pit, and complaining to everyone in earshot that they were turning his business into shit. He knew as soon as he saw Addison that his ass was in trouble and he waved her off, clutching his walker and heading back into his darkened office, where he'd stacked up the daily receipts by an old-fashioned adding machine, tape draping down across the floor.

He sat down in his chair, reached for his oxygen mask, and took a few pulls before setting it down and turning off the valve.

"You can't just leave when you want," Addison said. "Not now. Who drove you?"

"Lester."

"Lester?" she said. "Shit, Daddy. Lester shouldn't be driving himself. Does he even have a license? You can't leave without telling Kiyana first. She thought you'd wandered off until I told her where I'd find you."

"I'm sick, not senile," Daddy said. "Are you hungry? How about I tell Lester to make you a plate?"

"No, sir."

"It's not too bad today," Daddy said. "I didn't let him fuck it up this time. I swear to Christ this place is going to hell if you or your brother don't take over. No one else really gives a damn about quality. They can't follow simple recipes or instructions. Ain't that just Memphis as hell. How about some pie? We have coconut, lemon, and chocolate."

Addison shook her head, watching in horror as her daddy lit up a cigarette right by his oxygen tank. He kept it going in his wide fingers, taking a long inhale and then dropping the ash into an old coffee mug. Her father was a big, square-jawed man, tall, but now shrunken on his large frame. He had gray hair and wore big gold glasses. When he'd been a tight end at Ole Miss back in the early sixties, they'd called him the Bluff City Bulldozer. He had worn a blue or bright red University of Mississippi golf shirt every day for as long as Addison could remember.

"Daddy, I need money," Addison said, starting to cry and damn well hating herself for it.

"It's your brother, isn't it?" he said, taking a long pull of the cigarette. "Son of a bitch. I swear he'd fuck up his own funeral. He sent you to ask this time."

"No, sir," she said. "It's not Branch. Branch is fine. It's Dean. He's been gone a week and I can't get in touch with him."

Daddy leaned back into his mustard-colored vinyl chair, the old springs squeaking under him, as he removed the cigarette and took a piece of tobacco off his tongue. He crossed his arms over his chest, Addison always struck by how damn thin he'd gotten. He used to seem supernaturally large, six foot six and a highly unhealthy three hundred pounds. But now his handsome face had grown gaunt, white-whiskered, and bony, the radiation and chemo keeping him alive but taking a hell of a lot with it. His Ole Miss jersey had been framed and hung on a far wall of his office, along with various golf tournament awards and lacquered restaurant reviews from decades past.

"I'll pay you back as soon as Dean is home."

"How long has he been gone?"

"One week, exactly."

"Y'all must've had a hell of a fight," Daddy said.

"No, sir," Addison. "He just kind of disappeared. It's not like him. Well, it's a little like him. Shit, Daddy. I'm confused as hell."

"Huh?" Her father's hearing wasn't the best, and he leaned over the desk, straining to make out what Addison was saying over the rattling dishes and barking orders in the kitchen. "Sounded like you can't find your own husband."

Addison nodded. And goddamn, that's when she really started to cry, trying to cover her face and her eyes, and reaching onto her father's desk for some big paper napkins. Daddy just watched her, finishing the cigarette and stubbing it out in the cup. She feared what he would say, following in line with Branch, saying that Dean was an important man, busy as hell, and this thing would straighten out right quick. He'd reach into his pant pocket and thumb off a thousand dollars in hundreds as if they were dollar bills and tell her not to worry her pretty head. But he didn't do that. Instead, Daddy pushed himself up on his walker and hobbled over to her, resting one of his big hands on her shoulder, surprising the hell out of her by saying, "You know I've never liked that son of a bitch."

"Daddy, stop. I'm okay."

"No," he said. "I mean it. Something wrong with a man who lives life that uptight. I don't care for his haircut, the way he dresses, or the way he treats y'all's kids. He talks the right way to me, but I can tell it pains him to do it. Something at work behind the eyes when he runs his mouth, trying to court me into his line of thinking just in case he has trouble with you. Well. If he's gone, Addy, I say good riddance. I told your mom I couldn't stop you from marrying the man. Although two months isn't much of a courtship before an engagement. But I said I would always support you if you wanted to get free and clear."

Addison wiped her face and stood up to hug her father's neck, pulling him close and smelling the cigarettes and barbecue smoke, and hearing the raspy and rattling breathing from deep within him. "I love you, Daddy," she said. "Thank you. No one else believes me."

"That your husband is a tricky bastard?" he said. "You just never asked."

He scooted over to the door, waving away one of the hostesses who'd come to ask him a question, and moved back into the darkened little office.

"Let's talk attorneys," he said. "And then tell me how much you need."

"I don't need much," she said. "Maybe three thousand for now. And I appreciate it, Daddy. But we're not quite to an attorney yet."

"Didn't you say that little short bastard up and disappeared on you?" he said, sitting back down and lighting another cigarette. "I'll bet you a hundred to one, it's a woman. A man with an ego like that probably has a trail of them set up in all the cities where he does business. I'm sorry. I'm sorry. But I've always felt that way. I think it's his size. *Napoleon. Genghis Khan.* Can't trust those little bastards like that. Have you told the kids?"

"No."

He nodded. "But there's more," he said. "Right? You wouldn't have come to see me just for money. You could reach out to your banks for a goddamn credit line."

"I couldn't get an answer from his secretary over the phone, so I drove downtown to his office," Addison said. She took a deep breath and swallowed, ashamed of what had happened that morning and ashamed to be put into such a common, redneck situation.

"And?"

"It wasn't there."

"Who wasn't there?"

"Dean, McKellar Construction, all of it," she said. "He hadn't been there for two years. He moved everything without telling me. And when I call his secretary now, she won't even pick up."

"Call the police."

"I did," Addison said, laughing. "I wouldn't leave Dean's old office and they arrested me. And when I told them Dean was missing, they blew me off."

"Can't trust the fucking cops."

"Sir?"

"Son of a bitch."

"Yes, sir."

"If I'd gone into business with someone like that," Daddy said, "and they'd shagged ass? Boy, I'd want to know everything I could about where they've been, what they'd been up to, and where all their money was buried."

"I wish I knew," Addison said. "This woman at the police department found the whole thing kind of funny. I had to have Libby pick me up at 201 and drive me back to pick up the kids."

Daddy stood up and wavered for a moment on his walker, scooting back over the threadbare carpet and finding the oxygen mask. He took a few puffs, and then dropped it back on his old desk, the soft hiss of the oxygen coming slow and even until he turned the valve. A nameplate on his desk read TOP DOG SAMI HASSAN.

He stumbled for a moment as he tried to find his chair, Addison getting to her feet before he waved her away and took a hard seat. He nodded, collecting his raspy breath. "Okay. Okay. I know a man who can help. He's helped me out of a jam a time or two."

Daddy started to spin through a yellowed Rolodex, left hand lifting a cigarette. "I think he's who you need," he said. "That is, if he's still alive."

4

Joanna

Eight hundred bucks and a free meal wasn't too bad for two hours' work. But by god, she'd really have to earn it. All the posing for pictures and questions about Elvis. *Was he a good kisser?—It was supernatural, as if you were pulled into a vortex and shot with electricity from your head to your toes. Was he as generous as everyone says he was?—I once saw him hand the keys to a Cadillac to a beggar on Sunset Boulevard. Did you ever sleep with him?—A lady never tells but always remembers.* Elvis was the entire reason she'd packed up her life in West Hollywood and come to Memphis to live in a place where the name Joanna Grayson still meant something. Her daughter, Tippi, had been furious about the move. *We are moving where? Oh god, Mom, you must be kidding.* But here Joanna was, again holding court as she did back in 1967 as the Promising Star of Tomorrow right before she signed a contract with Hal Wallis to make two—TWO!— pictures with Elvis Presley. Even though only one panned out—the sunken treasure musical *Easy Come, Easy Go*—she'd always be connected to him. And despite making two spy spoofs in Italy after (one with Sean Connery's talentless brother, Neil) as the familiar femme fatale in a scuba gear and bikini, and then some really god-awful vampire films for Hammer, that one Elvis picture, shot in its entirety on the Paramount lot, is how she'd always been known.

"Oh god," Tippi said now.

They'd just walked into the house hosting tonight's event, a simple brick ranch with a low brick and wrought-iron fence on Audubon Drive in East Memphis, a place that Elvis himself had bought for his parents back in 1956 not long before he purchased Graceland. Joanna had been told the current owners were huge Elvis freaks and had turned back the clock to that same period, the wife telling Joanna that she'd painstakingly removed five different layers of wallpaper to find the correct pink poodle paper from a *Life* magazine spread about Gladys Presley.

Tippi had made some hors d'oeuvres for the VIP Elvis Fall Fan Event only to now discover her puffed pastries would share a table in the historic kitchen with macaroni salad and what looked to be chili spooned over Fritos. *The horror.*

"I don't know how you stand it," Tippi said.

"This appearance pays our rent for a month."

"But, Mother," Tippi said, "these people make my skin crawl. There's something ghoulish about all this. Elvis has been dead a very long time."

From the kitchen window, Joanna watched the fans who'd paid three hundred dollars each to attend a pool party with one of Elvis's leading ladies. A large, pale man with dyed black hair and a belly swelling over a pair of Hawaiian swim trunks performed a cannonball off the diving board, splashing several geriatric fans holding margaritas. A DJ played the soundtrack to *Clambake* and asked everyone to sing along.

Tippi made an unpleasant face. The girl was twenty-six and soft. By the time Joanna had turned eighteen back in London, she'd already been in a wrestling match with Otto Preminger and had been drugged by and fought off Roman Polanski. Twice!

"Any chance you might tell different stories tonight?" Tippi said. "You know, just to spice it up a little."

"I always tell different stories," Joanna said.

Tippi frowned and began to make a plate, arranging mini beef *tourtieres* beside a hideous slab of lasagna. Joanna found it odd that Tippi had been so critical of the food and then went straight for the most obvious and American item on the kitchen island. Private school in Switzerland had not affected her appetite. Of course, they hadn't eaten all day. Their apartment refrigerator had grown a bit bereft lately, several weeks past Death Week in August where she had a paid appearance every day, sometimes two.

Joanna could feel her stomach grumble a bit from hunger. But she was used to it. Lemon water and cigarettes for days when she'd made that picture with Richard Harris in Martinique. When she arrived on the set, she could barely fit into that yellow string bikini, and three days later she'd looked amazing. She stacked a fat dill pickle on her plate, recalling long, drunken nights with dear Richard.

"Excuse me, ma'am?" a man asked.

It was the fat man from the pool, dripping wet in a gold terrycloth robe. His dyed black hair was plastered against his giant head. So black, she expected the trickles of pool water to run the same color.

"Lord," he said. "I can't believe it. The real Joanna Grayson. I used to clip pictures of you and hang them in my bedroom ceiling when I was a boy. That scene with y'all doing yoga. *Whoo-wee.*"

"'Yoga Is As Yoga Does.'"

"That old woman singing, what did she say to Elvis, *I can see you can't get settled.* Ole Elvis struggling like hell trying to do them poses."

"Elsa Lanchester," Joanna said. "She studied dance under Isadora Duncan and later married Charles Laughton."

"Lady," he said, "no offense, but I don't know any of those folks. But I sure laugh every time when Elvis says back to her, *How can I, twisted like a pretzel?* Haw. Haw. I don't care what folks say. I sure love that picture. That tight black turtleneck you was wearing sure woke me up in the middle of the night."

"Oh," Joanna said. "That's, um, kind of you."

Joanna tried her best to look modest, thanking the man and turning her back. Tippi leaned against a red vintage refrigerator, biting her lip and nearly convulsing from trying to stifle her laughter. The hefty man's eyes looking to her daughter now, noting the same thing everyone else did. Tippi looked identical to Joanna's younger self despite her darker hair and all that god-awful eye makeup.

"And who is this little lady?"

"This is my daughter," Joanna said. "Tippi."

"Like the actress?"

"Tippi Hedren is a dear friend," Joanna said as she had countless times. "We met while on safari in Tanzania. I was the first to introduce her to the majesty of the lions."

"Ain't that something," the man said, standing there dripping black dye across Elvis's original checkerboard linoleum floors. "The woman had lions living with her without getting killed."

"A male lion did maul and try to eat her daughter," Tippi said.

"Good lord," the man said.

Joanna looked at Tippi and winked. "So there were some advantages," she said.

"Well," Tippi said. "That was both enlightening and lovely."

"Must you be so catty?"

It was dark by the time they left the little party, Joanna's daughter zipping in and out of cars along the brightly lit interstate in a hideous Ford Fiesta that they'd borrowed from a fan. Memphis was such a small town in so many ways. She'd only been here for a little more than a year and already had a lovely network wrapped around her little finger. Like poor Omar, who was impatiently waiting for her at the antiques mall even though she told him it could be nearly ten o'clock.

"That man dripped his hair dye all over me," Tippi said. "Yuck."

"Once you've made a film, you belong to the public," Joanna said. "Hal Wallis told me that. Your private life is over whether you like it or not. It's really more of a responsibility than anything."

"You appeared to be having a ball."

"Would you rather for me to behave like a spoiled old bitch?" Joanna said. "Besides, you looked pretty content by the craft service table."

"You mean the kitchen?"

"That was a large portion of lasagna," Johanna said. "A moment on the lips, darling."

"Top form, Mother," Tippi said. "Talking like you'd never even been kissed before you came to America. I mean, come on. You totally shagged Elvis."

"Elvis was special," she said, checking out her lipstick in the visor mirror. "More like a brother to me. We had a spiritual connection that no one will ever be able to understand. Did you know we both shared Natalie Wood's spiritualist?"

Tippi turned off an exit ramp, a drive-in theater glowing down below, four gigantic screens lit up with those lovely faces larger than life. Joanna didn't go to the shop at night and it was her first time noticing the drive-in, thinking how wonderful it had been the first time seeing herself so incredibly big. Her eyes so very blue and hair so blond it was nearly white. She'd never gotten over it. There was something God-like about being on film.

"But the virgin act," Tippi said. "You do know I read your diary when I was twelve."

"You were such a naughty little girl."

"Not as naughty as you, Mother," she said. "I never shagged Terence Stamp and his flatmate at the same time."

Joanna stifled a smile, Tippi damn well knowing all about the cocaine orgies with Bowie and Bolan, too. A kind of a movable feast in London of delicious debauchery, Joanna Grayson making the rounds in that wonderful velvet top hat, Soho parties in kitten heels and little else. Wondrous white linen tables with smoked salmon, Beluga with loads and loads of good toast and champagne. Her second husband, Tippi's father, had an entire garage filled with pink Veuve Clicquot that he'd bought on the black market.

"Mother," she said. "I love you . . . but I want to go home."

"Back to Hollywood?"

"England."

They traveled along Summer Avenue, far away from the cloistered green-lawned neighborhood where they had been, entering an endless stretch of pawnshops, check cashing businesses, used car dealers, convenience stores, and secondhand churches. So very American. *Finger Lickin' Good. Jesus Saves. Yo Gotti: Product of the Public Schools.*

"England isn't your home, darling," Joanna said. "You've barely spent a season there. Not since your grandmother did the right thing and finally died."

"You're so hard on her."

"Am I?" Joanna asked. "You didn't really know her. Not the real her. She showed you a side that wasn't exactly accurate. Tea parties and teddy bears and all that rubbish."

"But this isn't home. This is purgatory in gold lamé."

Joanna should have never involved Tippi in her personal appearances. If Tippi hadn't been so insistent on driving after Joanna had those two drunk-driving incidents, her daughter could be at home right now watching some mindless reality show instead of handselling *One Night with You: The Joanna Grayson Story* along with signed 8x10 glossies of Joanna with Elvis and a few skimpy bikini shots she had from her time in Rome. Joanna truly had the most delicious little figure back then.

"I'm doing the best I can."

"I know, Mother."

"And I'd like you to stay."

"I know, Mother," Tippi said. "But this Elvis business is so beneath you. Beneath both of us."

"Remember, I had to make do during the Blitz. And we can make do now."

"You were born after the war, Mother."

"So much you don't know, Tippi," Joanna said.

"Please promise me this business with Omar won't take long."

Tippi wheeled into the lot of Summer Antiques and Oriental Rugs, the plate glass windows glowing a dim grayish blue through the security grates. It was nearly ten and Joanna hoped that Omar had waited for her.

She had something very special to show him.

It took three different keys but she was finally inside the antiques mall, after knocking and knocking for Omar, who had promised to stay up and wait. He was usually so vigilant, always concerned for her safety late at night. *These people here will kill you, Miss Joanna. You are too beautiful a flower to be on the streets at night. Come walk with me, I have a big gun and will hold your hand.*

Joanna hit the bank of switches and the overhead fluorescents tripped on across the endless ceiling as she walked over to the front desk, where Omar eyed the whole operation on a bank of small black-and-white TVs when he wasn't devouring pornography. She'd once caught him transfixed by some intense sadomasochism, whips and chains, maybe a donkey somewhere, and she knew she had him. He was so embarrassed, shutting down his computer and standing up with a very noticeable erection. *Omar, you bad, bad boy,* Joanna had told him, wagging her finger.

Where the hell was he? She could see his tiny blue Honda parked right outside the front window.

She opened her purse and pulled out the item she hoped would get them through the next few months, a string of pearls she'd nicked at the Audubon House. No one had seen her go in the room that had been Gladys Presley's, and no one had seen her come out. Only she and Tippi, and that stray fat man, had been allowed inside during the pool party. Joanna wasn't exactly sure if the pearls were real or synthetic, but it was clear that they had indeed belonged to Elvis's mother, GP initialed on the sterling silver clasp.

She hadn't noticed it at first but now she saw Omar's desk was a real mess. An overturned coffee cup, papers scattered across the floor, along with a broken VCR of some sort. Through the plate glass windows, she could just make out Tippi behind the wheel of the car, headlights shining into the mall. It appeared Tippi was waving for her to hurry up.

That girl would be her undoing, she thought, as she held on to the filing cabinet to step up onto Omar's chair and reach up to the air vent where he'd often leave her cash after hours. The dear little man so helpful when she'd fallen behind on rent a time or two.

She lifted out the vent cover and was about to set the pearls inside when she found a thick envelope that she hoped was stuffed with the cash he'd promised. She took it and slipped it into her shirt and under her bra as she climbed off the chair, now noticing all the wires to

Omar's monitors had been cut and the desk drawers ransacked. Two security cameras lay on the floor and appeared to have been pulverized with hammers.

Oh god. Someone had broken into the place.

She ran down a long corridor with dozens of open booths, the attic smell of old furniture and soured upholstery strong. As she turned the corner, she spotted the sprawled figure of a man, crooked and mis-shapen, on a short stack of Oriental rugs. Joanna's heart felt like it would stop, her mouth dry as she inched toward the figure and knelt down.

It was Omar, very dead and horrid-looking, with a gaping mouth and wide-open eyes. Blood was seeping out of him from god knows where, soaking the rugs he advertised as SPECIAL DEAL. BIG DIS-COUNT.

She covered her face with her hand, trying to block that sickly, wet coppery smell, and nearly gagged. Joanna had absolutely no idea what had happened but didn't want to be there if these thieves were still around, nor did she want to wait all hours of the night to speak to a bunch of nosy policemen. She daubed the sweat from her face and checked her makeup in case she was arrested on the way home. The words of the immortal Liz Taylor in her ears, "Pour yourself a drink, put on some lipstick, and pull yourself together."

Joanna made her way to the back door, wiping off the light switches with Kleenex as she shut them all down. By god, she'd been in enough awful BBC procedurals to know how to behave. She let herself out the back door, deciding at the last minute to lock up, feeling like some kind of grave robber who'd entered a great, giant tomb.

Joanna walked across the lot, climbed into the passenger seat, and shut the door. She pressed the locks and they snapped shut with a hard snick.

Tippi backed up and then turned around, the headlights shining bright onto the darkened stretch of Summer Avenue as they headed back to the interstate. How did one get here from having one's own se-ries in France, roving about the countryside in a new, forest-green MG?

The It Girl, the loveliest face in all of Britain, scrounging for pearls among swine.

"Oh god, Mother," Tippi said. "Check your face. You're such a mess."

Joanna pulled down the visor and looked in the mirror, seeing a bright smear of red across her cheek. It wasn't lipstick. She jabbed into her purse for the Kleenex to wipe it away, her stomach tumbling.

"Are you sure you're all right?"

"Lovely," Joanna said. "Just lovely. Do we still have any good gin at home?"

"Unfortunately."

As Tippi drove, Joanna reached down into her bra and pulled out the envelope. She used her nail to slit it, but instead of a wad of cash, she found a neatly folded stack of official-looking documents. It appeared to be a shipping manifest of some sort from Turkey. Omar's beloved home country.

"What's all that?" Tippi asked, glancing down.

"Darling," she said. "I have absolutely no idea. But Omar certainly went to some trouble to keep it hidden."

Gaultier

Gaultier didn't want to tell the One-Armed Man about the helicopters. He'd already promised them to the Jordanians, who wanted at least six US-made Cobras with 20 mm rotary machine guns. Beautiful surgical instruments for a coup was the way he'd spoken of them at their last meeting in Paris. The men were set to meet on the upper terrace of the Cairo Four Seasons with a fantastic view of the beach along the Nile, old wooden sailboats floating along the edge of the city, shapely women down by the kidney-shaped pool shaded by the palms. It was all very European and very cosmopolitan. The best thing about the violence in Egypt these last few years is that it scared off all the tourists.

The waiter asked if he wanted another Stella. Of course. *Why not?* It had been a long flight from London and he planned to stay at the hotel until tomorrow morning. He had checked in only thirty minutes before and changed into a fresh white linen suit, navy shirt, and leather sandals. After relaying the unpleasant news on the deal, he would treat himself to an early dinner at the hotel restaurant. Stuffed grape leaves, grilled lamb chops, and an entire bottle of Obelisk Rosetta Red. As a Frenchman, he'd been a little skeptical, but he'd learned not to fear Egyptian wine. He'd take it ten times over anything made in California. Perhaps even buying a few bottles as a novelty for his girlfriend back in Paris.

Gaultier checked his watch as the waiter brought him his second Stella. *Merci. Non, non. Rien.* He was more than fine, enjoying the coolness of the Nile and watching the women by the pool. One caught his attention with such a wonderful sinewy body and slick black hair wetted against narrow shoulders. A few years ago he'd have made himself known to her, back when he'd been with the Legion in Sarajevo, Rwanda, and the Congo. So much fighting and blood. He tried to dismiss it from his mind, watching the young black-headed beauty dive into the pool again and disappear under the cool turquoise of the water.

"Monsieur Gaultier?"

Gaultier nodded. The One-Armed Man towered over him, dressed as you might expect an American to be in Cairo. Military-style pants, a black T-shirt reading RANGER JOES overlaid with a Tac vest. He believed he had said the Four Seasons in his communique with the man, but despite his best efforts, all Americans were barbarians at the core. The One-Armed Man had an oversize, scruffy head and a thick neck, thick chest, short legs, and half of one arm topped with a hook.

"Welcome to Cairo," Gaultier said. "Won't you please join me?"

"Where's the shitter?" the One-Armed Man said. His real name was Jack Dumas, but he often was just called Sarge by those who worked with him. Gaultier preferred "the One-Armed Man" because it sounded more Graham Greene, and in Cairo, at the Four Seasons and dressed in a white linen suit, what could be more fitting?

The man disappeared for a moment and Gaultier scanned through some images on his tablet to show Dumas. He may not have helicopters today, but there were plenty more items to broker for whatever little adventure Dumas and his mercenaries had planned. The last he'd heard, there had been some security work against pirates in Djibouti, good work and high wages from oil companies.

The One-Armed Man finally returned to the table up along the empty expanse of the terrace. It was too late for lunch and too early for dinner but a perfect time for cocktails. The man mopped his face with his good hand and plopped the wet towel onto the table.

"I have bad news for you, my friend," Gaultier said. "All the helicopters have been sold. *Whoosh.* Very fast. But I do have some lovely Panzerfausts from my supplier in Germany. They could make quick work of your pirates."

"What pirates?"

"I thought you and your team were off in Djibouti."

"There ain't no pirates," the man said.

"Oh?"

"Not no more."

The man stared at Gaultier across the café table. A warm wind blew off the Nile and ruffled his hair as Gaultier took a drink and watched the flat, cool expression on the One-Armed Man's face. He had the appearance of a man suddenly awake after a long, disturbing dream. Apparently the helicopter issue had really thrown him. There had been talk of Libya, some assistance in finally ousting that madman Gaddafi.

"I don't give two shits about no helicopters," he said. "I'm looking for Peter Collinson."

"Your partner?" Gaultier said and shrugged. "I have no idea. I imagined that he would be joining us today as always."

The man shook his head. "Nope," he said. "But I think he came to you about some shipping problems. He checked into his fancy-ass hotel yesterday and now they're saying he's gone. Don't tell me y'all didn't cross paths."

Gaultier shrugged again. It had been some time since he'd done any business with Peter Collinson. The arrogant American always wanting to have a *concours de penis*, a dick measuring contest with him. Wanting to know just how bloody it had gotten in Rwanda, as if the man had missed some kind of sporting event.

"There were two Conex containers sitting at Haydarpaşa Port," the One-Armed Man said. "You know damn well what I'm talking about. He needed passage back to the States."

"I'm sure Collinson was more than adept at finding his way home."

"With the containers, you French fuck," the One-Armed Man said.

"No need to be unpleasant," Gaultier said, waving to the waiter.

"Please. Let's have a drink. All right. The helicopters being gone was unfortunate. No need to discuss business."

The man leaned into the table. "Everything is business, Pepé Le Pew."

Gaultier understood the reference, the man calling him a little cartoon skunk. *Zee cabbage does not run away from zee corn beef.* There'd been a time when he'd choked a man to death for such an insult. But at his age, it was just too much work. Gaultier checked his Rolex, growing weary of this American prick.

"I think we are done." Gaultier stood and fished some Egyptian pounds from his pocket, finished the beer, and set the glass on the table. He looked down to see his lithe, tan beauty emerge from the pool and find a chaise lounge under the shade of a crooked palm. Such a small swimsuit in a Muslim country.

As Gaultier turned, the One-Armed Man flipped over the table and lunged for Gaultier. He clasped his arm with his hook and pushed Gaultier backward toward the railing facing the Nile. Gaultier tried to catch his balance as the world turned and he found himself hanging upside down. The One-Armed Man held him by the legs as he looked down upon the sand and the rocks, the lovely sailboats floating by as if captured in oil on canvas.

"Collinson."

"He's gone."

"Where?"

The pounds and loose piastres fell from his pocket and out into the open air. The One-Armed Man was stronger than he could have imagined, holding Gaultier up with little effort, a firm grip on his crocodile belt as he fluttered loose. A quick drop would surely kill him. He held on to his tablet for dear life, everything personal and business was on it.

"Home," Gaultier said. "He flew home two days ago from London."

The One-Armed Man said nothing, but within seconds yanked him up over the railing and set him down on his feet. The man didn't even appear to be sweating. But for a brief moment, he smiled, smoothing down Gaultier's lapels and clasping that cold steel hook on the back of his neck.

"Where is home, Pepé?"

"Memphis."

"Memphis?" the man said. "You sure?"

"The one in America," Gaultier said. This was no business of his. "Once when we were very drunk, he told me he had a family. In the town of Memphis."

6

Porter Hayes

The address was along Belvedere out in Central Gardens, a big old English Tudor mansion, not two blocks away from where Porter's mother worked as a maid for more than thirty years. His momma had been so loyal to that family, the Vances, that sometimes he wondered if she loved them more than her own kids. Not until he was grown did he understand why she'd been absent every birthday, every Christmas and Thanksgiving, not coming home until dark, dead on her feet, to make a late supper for Porter and his little brother. But he'd always had nice clothes, mostly hand-me-downs from the boy his age. *Jonathan Vance* inked in the collars and old underwear, something he didn't think much of until he'd once run into the boy outside the house, the kid believing Porter had stolen his jacket and calling him a thieving little nigger. Little things like that a man didn't forget, not even twenty years later when that boy, now a man, came to him and asked Porter to peep into a window to see if his wife was doing the deed with his business partner. Porter laying the black-and-white photographs on his desk, some real fine 8x10 shots of the partner's bald white head between the thighs of young Mrs. Vance at the Holiday Inn. *Damn.* He'd never heard a man make a sound like that, wailing something horrible down deep.

Hayes parked his old black Mercedes sedan on the curb and headed up four different sets of concrete steps cut into the hill up to the mansion. The front door looked to have been taken off a castle, polished old wood adorned with heavy iron fixtures and a big square peephole. He knocked twice and took a step back, remembering that his mother never was allowed to enter the front door, only the back entrance by the garage and straight into the kitchen. He still could see his mother's thick winter coat set on a hook by the door, her back to him as she rustled through the refrigerator to make the Vance family breakfast, Porter left to sit at their kitchen table reading through the funny papers.

The door opened and a small, youngish white woman appeared. He figured her to be Addison McKellar, but she sure didn't look a thing like Sam the Sham. This woman was thin, blond, and pretty, missing big ole Sami's heft and hawkish nose. She wore a set of large blue silk pajamas, so big the sleeves covered her hands, and greeted him with a nice toothy smile, inviting him inside. Her hair was done up in a bun and she carried a lit cigarette in her right hand.

Hayes had to check his watch to make sure it was indeed ten o'clock in the morning.

"Jesus," she said. "Thank you so much, Mr. Hayes. My dad already told me so much about you and I can't believe you came over so quickly. It's a mess. A fucking mess. Oh god. Sorry to cuss. But it is, isn't it? My husband is missing and I can't find him and now I'm not so sure where my husband goes every day or if he's dead or alive or left me for some other woman. But Christ, I'm only thirty-nine, you'd think he'd wait until I got a little older to start sleeping around?"

"Good morning, Mrs. McKellar," Hayes said. "You have a beautiful home."

"Would you like some coffee?" she said, smiling as if the preamble had been a bit of a joke. "Please excuse the kitchen. It's a mess, too. The contractor has been working on it for two months now and still can't seem to finish the job. We had the cabinets put in three weeks ago, everything painted, but the countertop guy keeps on making excuses. Marble. I figured the white marble was the way to go. The old countertops had gotten so dull and dirty. I figured time for a change."

A curly-coated brown dog wandered up and smelled Porter's crotch and then tried to run its head and ears up under his hand. "Oh god,"

Addison said. "Don't mind him. So sorry. That's ChaCha. He's sweet but dumb as a box of rocks."

"Some dogs and many people are like that."

"Our previous dog was awesome," she said. "We called him King. A Malinois that would've taken a bullet for this whole family. God, I miss that guy. But at least ChaCha doesn't shed."

Hayes patted the dog's head and followed Addison McKellar into the kitchen that was, as promised, a complete goddamn mess. Most of the cabinets were covered in plastic sheeting while a Hispanic woman at a large sink ran dirty plates under the faucet. He thought about the Hispanic woman and his own momma, wondering just how much of her life she spent scraping plates and leaving the dishes up to dry.

"This is Josefina," Addison said. "Josefina, would you please bring some coffee into Mr. McKellar's study? None for me. Thank you. I've already had three cups this morning and feel like I've just finished a line of coke."

She stopped and then held up a hand, her face coloring. "Only a joke," she said. "I don't do cocaine. I'm only a little jumpy. I know that's what you do, look at the little things, the small details to look at a larger picture? And surely a wife who is a coke addict would be a clue. Right?"

"I'm not what you might call a literal person, Mrs. McKellar," he said. "I know that when things get tight, you better laugh or you might just start crying."

The woman hugged her arms around herself, the legs of her pajamas pooling thick around her ankles. The pajamas had the initials SH on a breast pocket, a dark blue piping around the cuffs and down the buttonholes. "I'm sorry," she said. "I didn't ask how you like your coffee."

"Plain is fine."

"Just black?"

Hayes smiled. The woman's face colored again. The old Memphis divide would never go out of style.

Addison McKellar was only four years younger than Nina. He hoped like hell that Nina's husband never up and did a boneheaded move like Dean McKellar. Ninety-nine times out of a hundred in these cases, the man has gone and pulled a damn Bobby Harris, although explaining the Bobby Harris case to a nice young woman like Mrs. Mc-Kellar might not be the best idea. Harris had just up and disappeared one day, gone to Cincinnati to find a new name, a new job, and new woman, and soon a new set of kids. Without any indication, the man simply picked up his coat and hat one morning, kissed his wife on the cheek, and moved on to the new version of himself that was all just a brand-new lie.

"No sugar?"

"Just plain," Hayes said. "Thank you."

She pulled back one side of two giant sliding doors and ushered him into a wood-paneled study. The whole house felt as austere and staged as a tour of the Pink Palace. Porter half expected to be blocked with a velvet rope before he was able to enter. Leatherbound books lined the walls around a big-ass desk with carved eagle talons for feet. A bar held whiskey in crystal decanters and a big glass-topped humidor. A framed American flag hung on the wall and some kind of bronze cowboy statue balanced on a pedestal.

Hayes sat down in a green leather chair with brass nailhead trim. He crossed his legs and prepared to hear Mrs. McKellar do a hell of a lot of talking. He'd let her just flow. He'd always found that letting a client get it all out, first and foremost, sometimes worked a hell of a lot better than him trying to come on too hard and ask a grocery list of questions.

"My daddy speaks very highly of you."

"Your daddy said he thought I was dead."

"Sounds about like Daddy," she said. "You know, he's not doing too well himself."

"Sorry to hear that," Hayes said. "He's a good man."

That was a big ole fat lie but that's what you said when you heard a daughter talk about her sick daddy. Hayes crossed his legs, resting his left ankle across right knee. A sharp pain shot up through his spine, reminding him that none of the old Memphis crew was getting any younger. Over these decades, they were just lucky to be hanging on. Addison sat at the edge of the desk, nervously playing with a letter opener in the shape of a sword—actually, a bayonet. "Okay," she said. "I got arrested yesterday. Just for showing up at my husband's office and asking where he'd gone. Only he wasn't there and it wasn't his office anymore and the police had to escort me out of the building."

"Happens sometimes."

"Have you ever been arrested?"

Hayes smiled, smoothing down his mustache with his thumb. "Oh, yes," he said. "Many times. Goes with the job."

"It sucks," she said. "It made me feel dirty. They stuck me in a cell and towed my car. When I talked to the sergeant in charge, she thought the whole thing was a joke."

"What was her name?"

"Lantana something or other."

"Lantana Jones?"

Addison nodded, still fiddling with the letter opener. A fidgety little thing. The maid slid open one of the partial doors and brought a small cup of coffee on a fancy tray. Porter helped himself and leaned back into the sofa, trying to get a feel for this man, Dean McKellar, who'd up and disappeared. He'd already done some digging. White male, forty-six, five foot eight, hundred and seventy pounds, blond hair and blue eyes. CEO of McKellar Construction.

"How long have y'all been married?" Hayes asked.

"Fifteen years."

"And has your husband ever been gone like this?"

Addison nodded and sat up straighter in the chair, pulling her legs up under her and leaning toward him in a conspiratorial way. "A year and a half ago," she said. "After my brother's big birthday party at the Overton Park Shell. He never told me he'd be leaving town but then showed up five days later as if nothing happened."

"And never did try and explain it?"

"Dean said he'd had an emergency in New York," she said. "And there were some issues with his cell phone."

"Does he know the old landlines still work?"

"Just what I said."

"And what did he say?"

"Same as always," she said. "Turned it all back on me. He found a way to make it my problem, said I never understood about his work. The deadlines, the people trying to screw him, the unions and the politicians, always having to watch everything on the construction site. He said he was buried with work and knew I'd be fine taking care of the kids."

The woman talked as if everyone in Memphis must've heard of the motherfucker but in truth, the name meant nothing to Porter. Besides what he'd dug up online with the help of Darlene.

"Do you have access to his credit cards?"

"No," she said. "Only my own. Although he pays the balance. Or did."

"You know where he gets his statements?"

"I assume his office," she said. "Wherever the hell that really is."

"Your father said you were worried for his safety," Hayes said.

"You mean, I think he might be dead?"

"Yes, ma'am."

Addison hopped up and began to pace the floor, old hardwoods overlain with some real rich-looking Orientals. Hayes studied the art on the wall. He was no critic but recognized some good oil work when he saw it. Scenes from the Old West, cowboys riding the open plains, bustling seaports and old-timey big sailboats. One scene looked particularly interesting, a big sprawling valley of pine trees at the golden glow in late afternoon, the hint of a blue stream meandering through it all. Addison stopped pacing.

"We got that one in Wyoming," she said. "Dean and I have another house there."

"Any chance that's where he's hiding out?"

"Wyoming, Rosemary Beach, New York, Hot Springs," she said. "You name it. We have places everywhere. It's disgusting, really. I sometimes can't keep track."

"This is a fine old home," Hayes said. "My momma used to work at a house right around the corner. Ever heard of the Vance family?"

The young woman shook her head. The Vances had probably sold out long ago, moved farther on out of Memphis, the old relic of a house now inhabited by a new family, new kinds of people to cook and clean, manage the upkeep of such a big property. It didn't appear much had changed around Central Gardens.

"I'll need a list of Dean's close friends and associates," he said. "Your father mentioned a secretary."

"Amanda," she said. "Did I give you that number?"

Hayes nodded. He already had Darlene running it. But chances are it was just a burner.

"What about other people who work there?"

"I almost never went to his office," she said. "I knew his old partner, Alec. But they split off about six years ago. Alec went back to work at his dad's company."

"What's Alec's last name?"

"Dawson."

"And do you think he's still in town?"

Addison nodded. "Dawson-Gray Construction. They had a place at the White Station Tower."

"Friends?"

"My brother, Branch," she said. "Some people at the Club."

"Memphis Country Club?"

"He served on the Ducks Unlimited Board, too," she said. "Dean had his drinking buddies and his own life away from the family. I didn't really care if he came home a little ripped, so long as he came home and spent time with the kids. He's a good father. He takes Preston hunting and fishing. Plays catch with him. And he's so proud of Sara Caroline and her lacrosse. I swear."

Addison nodded a few times to add some emphasis to it, Porter thinking this man kept a real tight circle of family and friends. If he was really a big swinging dick in the construction business, he should have contacts all over town, although this woman kept on mentioning places far from Memphis. New York. London. She talked about some stuff in the Middle East on the phone.

"Sounds like we need to find Amanda."

Addison nodded.

"This is Dean's office?"

"Yes, sir."

"You mind if I take a look around and through your husband's personal papers?"

Addison shook her head and Hayes made his way behind the desk, fiddling with two drawers to find them both locked. He looked up at Addison, who marched on over, grasped the letter opener and jammed it into the edge of the drawer, prying it open until there was a sharp crack. "Help yourself to anything, Mr. Hayes," she said. "You have my complete and total permission to make as big a goddamn mess as you like."

"Appreciate that, Mrs. McKellar."

She smiled. "Call me Addison."

They took the I-240 loop to I-55 and down to Southaven, Mississippi, to an interchangeable gathering of Walmart, Target, Home Depot, and a dozen or so car dealerships. There was a Cracker Barrel, a place that Porter Hayes had never wanted to visit based on the name alone, and a few Starbucks along the way. The address from Darlene was in a strip mall right off Goodman; "Turn at the Olive Garden," she'd said. Porter had done his damnedest to go it alone but Addison had come down dressed and ready to come along while he was still snooping through the study.

"Did Dean ever mention Southaven?"

"Nope," she said. "Only times I visited Dean's office, it was always downtown."

"At the Cotton Exchange Building?" Hayes said. "That lease expired two years ago. What do you know about this woman Amanda?"

"Besides that she's a fake and a liar?" Addison said, seated in the passenger seat of Porter's Mercedes. "I feel like a total fucking idiot. I've spoken to her a million times. I know this sounds stupid, but talking about Amanda was almost like talking about family. Dean talked about her all the time. *Amanda this. Amanda that.* Now to know she was just some lying bitch."

"Well," Hayes said. "I got to warn you, but it sure smells like some honey hooch situation."

"Honey hooch?"

"Pardon me," Hayes said. "Another woman living situation."

"That's what people call it?"

"It's what I call it," Hayes said. "Although I just may have coined the phrase myself."

"You think Dean might have another family?" she said. "Wow. He could barely keep ours going."

Hayes checked out the addresses as they drove west on Goodman, past a big movie theater and a Chevy dealership, before finally taking that turn at Olive Garden, a sign boasting unlimited breadsticks and pasta bowls. Redneck heaven.

"How exactly do you know my father?" she said. "If you don't mind me asking."

"He didn't tell you?"

"Nope."

"Then he might not want me to say."

"Oh," she said. "I've heard that before."

"Sure you have." Hayes grinned as he drove into an industrial park, passing a strip mall filled with a pizza joint, two accountants, a few massage therapists, and a chiropractor. The suite number they had looked for was wedged right between a Vietnamese restaurant and a Mexican ice cream shop.

"I used to own an ice cream shop," Addison said. "Everything went great for the first few months but then I couldn't give a cone away. It started costing Dean five thousand a month."

"Hard running a business," Hayes said. "My son's in music management. That seems to be even worse. But what do I know? I stopped listening to the radio when disco was on the way out."

"Who's he work with?"

"Ever heard of the Ying-Yang Twins, Gangsta Boo?"

Addison shook her head as Hayes turned in to park. Addison stared straight ahead at suite number 8, Book Endz. Used Books, Paperbacks, and Hardcovers. *Buy, Sell, and Trade.*

"Heard anything about this?"

"Probably just a waste of time," she said. "Like the Cotton Exchange."

"Maybe," Hayes said. "Only one way to find out. This is where this Amanda, or whatever her name is, gets her bills. You want to come in with me or wait in the car?"

"What if I told you I wanted to wring that bitch's neck?"

"I'd advise you that assault isn't a good conversation starter," Hayes said.

"But if you need me to assault her," Addison said, "on account of her being a woman and you don't want that on you, I'd be glad to."

"Damn," Hayes said. "You are Sam's daughter."

"Are you ever going to tell me how y'all met?"

Hayes reached for the door handle and turned to Addison, smiling. "Maybe," he said. "One day. Once we get to know each other a little better."

The door was unlocked but the shop seemed abandoned, rows and rows of homemade bookshelves painted a base white, signs marking the coves of Fiction, History, Self-Help, Mystery, and Gardening. The shop had that particular odor of musty old paper and moth-balls. He and Addison moved through the stacks of books, bringing Porter to mind of the shabby old paperbacks that Genevieve used to ship to him in Vietnam along with bubble gum, cigarettes, and mag-azines. *The Complete Works of Langston Hughes, The Maltese Falcon, The Strength to Love* by Dr. King. Porter would never forget seeing Dr. King step off that tarmac in 1968 and coming face-to-face with him at the gate. He was assigned to protect King during his first visit for the sanitation workers' strike. In his black suit, starched white shirt, and tie, King had brought the word *resplendent* to Porter's mind. King called him Detective Hayes and Porter always called him Dr. King, although his people had taken to calling him "Doc."

What happened to King at the Lorraine still tore Hayes up inside and haunted all of Memphis.

Hayes picked up the yellowed paperback on the dusty shelf, King's smiling profile in grainy black and white. *Goddamn.* More than forty years ago. Addison moved past him into the section of the store where the fluorescent lights flickered over countless cardboard boxes of unsorted books. He set down the King book and followed her into a narrow opening toward a rear fire exit. The hallway was long, with scuffed white walls and threadbare industrial carpet. Addison popped out of an office and raised her hands with exasperation. "Nothing."

Hayes passed her and walked into a small, simple office with a desk, computer, and walls lined with blue plastic bins. Several cell phones had been lined up on the desk and along a well-marked blotter. Each phone had been marked with a different color tape. Just as Hayes motioned to Addison to follow him inside, they both heard a toilet flush. After a few seconds, a heavyset white woman in a long maroon top and black slacks sauntered in drying her hands with a paper towel. Her body looked as round as a barrel, and a helmet of dyed brown hair framed her bulldog face and tiny eyes. She looked to Hayes and then back to Addison. "Store's closed," she said. "Didn't y'all see the sign?"

"I'm looking for a copy of *Ben-Hur*," Hayes said. "The one with the erratum on page 116."

"Are y'all fucking high?" the bulldog woman said.

"That's her," Addison said. "That's Amanda."

When the woman heard Addison's voice, her crinkled face folded in an *oh-shit* kind of expression. She glanced to Hayes and then back to Addison, before picking up one of the cell phones and saying, "Y'all have two seconds to get your dang asses out of here before I call the fucking cops."

Porter Hayes smiled. "You know what?" he said. "I was about to do the same."

"Who the fuck are you?" the woman asked. "Miss Daisy's driver?"

Hayes crossed his arms and glanced down at the dozen or so phones.

"You know my voice," Addison said. "But who are you? Really."

"I don't know you from bubble gum, little miss," she said. "This is a private goddamn business and the both of you have no right to be in here. If you think I'm bluffing, then y'all just stick around until South-aven's finest come to cart y'all out by your ear."

Hayes eyed a well-worn leather purse on a nearby table and walked over and turned it upside down. "Shit," the woman said. "Put that down. Who the hell do you think you are?"

"Aren't you gonna call the cops?" Hayes said. "Or is your big ass just whistling 'Dixie'?"

Hayes found her wallet in the pile and flipped through until he found a Tennessee state driver's license with the name Maude Herron. Two *R*s and one *N* and a picture of a face that only a momma bulldog could love. The woman's deadpan look reminded Porter of someone who was used to getting their picture made. He called Darlene and it didn't take but a minute for her to start to run down Maude Herron's previous charges and convictions, Darlene connecting her to a man named Lunatti who ran most of the strip clubs south of I-240.

Hayes slipped the wallet back into the purse and tossed it to Maude, who caught it like a tight end, clutching it to her chest. "How long have you worked for Dean McKellar?"

"I don't know what the fuck you two want or why you're threatening and intimidating a decent Christian woman," she said. "If you want my money, go on and take it, but leave me the hell alone."

"Miss Herron," Hayes said, "we don't give a good goddamn about the books you cook or the folks you do business with. We're looking for this woman's husband and know you've been manning the phones here."

Maude Herron gave him a hard look and then glanced back over at Addison. She shook her head and then shrugged. "Don't get your pant-ies in a twist," Maude said. "It's just a damn job, Cinderella. Hope the kids are okay. Did Preston ever shake that cold?"

"He did."

"And Sara Caroline?" she said. "That boy still calling up y'all's house at all hours?"

Addison slowly nodded as Hayes heard the soft click of a door clos-ing and the brushing sound of footsteps in the hall. He motioned for Addison to stand behind him and for Maude to sit her big ass down. He pulled out his .38 from his jacket and stood on the right side of the door. A white man entered with two sacks from Popeyes. Hayes stepped up, stuck the gun in his back, and told him to drop the chicken and raise his hands. The man did as he was told.

The man was thick, big bellied, and baldheaded, with a dark mus-tache and goatee. He had on wide-legged saggy blue jeans, orange Crocs, and a T-shirt that said SALT LIFE with a marlin flipping free from the ocean. Porter checked him and found a shiny new Glock slid up into his front pant pocket.

"Come on, man," the bald guy said. "Our chicken's gonna get cold."

"Your fat ass is gonna get a lot colder you don't do what I say."

"Go ahead," the man said. "Money's in the file cabinet. Shit, it ain't even locked."

Maude threw a slap at the fat man's face so quick and hard that Hayes barely saw it coming. It ended with a sharp *thwack* and the man dropped down to one knee, stroking the red cheek. "Goddamn it, Momma."

Addison stood up next to Hayes now, both of her hands over her mouth, watching Maude pick up one of the cells, one with a red band, and twirl it in her hands. "Baby," she said. "I don't know your husband. I ain't never met him. I get money wired into my account twice a month for answering calls from you and telling you just what you want to hear. I don't think I've spoken to your man more than a half-dozen times. I don't know what he's doing or his shuck and never even considered on asking."

"Bullshit," Hayes said.

"You think so?" she said. "You know who I am. And who I do the books for. Someone asked me if I'd like to make a little money on the side, and I'm not the kind of lady to turn down an offer like that. I got to feed Junior's stupid ass, and that kid eats a lot of chicken."

Hayes smiled. "That true, Junior?"

"I don't see why you got to bring fucking Popeyes into this shit."

"How does he contact you?"

"Through telepathy," Maude said. "How the fuck do you think?"

"Which number?"

"My own line."

"Which is?"

Maude closed her eyes and inhaled deeply through her nose and then picked up one of the cells without a color mark on it. She wiggled it at him like she was teasing a dog with a bone. She scrolled through some numbers and then showed him the one with the 212 area code. "Give me your palm and I'll write into your hand."

"Nope." Hayes snatched the phone away.

"Me and Junior got a lot of friends," she said. "You mess with me and they'll come for you."

"I hang my hat downtown at Madison and Second," he said. "Third floor. Porter Hayes Investigations. Y'all come anytime. Who introduced you to Dean McKellar?"

"Wouldn't you like to know," she said, setting her purse on the desk and then strutting over to pick up the fried chicken. She searched through the sack and then looked over at her son. "Goddamn it, Junior. You forgot my fucking biscuits."

"Who was it?" Hayes said. He could feel Addison creeping up on his right side. He could hear her breathing.

Maude shrugged and set about opening up the sack and pulling out the boxes of chicken and setting down what was left of the jumbo sweet teas. Her gaze moved off Porter and over to Addison. She smiled. "Honey," she said, "I always loved talking to you until you said that thing about me cleaning the damn toilets at Walmart. I know you're not the Walmart type, but I tell you that's a hell of a cruel statement to make to any human."

"Was any of what we talked about true?" Addison said.

"Some of it," she said. "I sometimes got y'all dinner reservations. Maybe a concert at the Pyramid. I think it was Prince. Lord, that wasn't easy."

"And you never met him," Hayes said.

"I wouldn't know Dean McKellar if he walked into this old bookshop buckass nekkid with an ID tag hanging from his pecker."

Maude reached for a hot chicken breast and took a big bite, her son still on the floor soothing his reddened cheek. Sipping on the jumbo tea, she smiled at Addison. "If you tell him I said it, I'll deny it. But you may want to ask ole Jimbo Hornsby a question or two. I'll tell you, whatever I get paid ain't worth goddamn Cinderella and Samuel L. Jackson coming in and fucking up a family supper."

"You really think I look like Sam Jackson?" Porter said.

"You favor him a bit," she said. "But you got hair on your head and a lot more miles."

"And who the hell is Jimbo Hornsby?" he said.

The woman slurped on her tea and then handed over a drumstick to her son, who'd gotten off the floor, hands still up and keeping a wide berth from Porter's gun. "Wouldn't be no fun if I gave y'all all the answers."

"Come on," Addison said, her hand shaking on Porter's elbow. "We've been friends with the Hornsbys ever since I moved back to Memphis. He lives in Chickasaw Gardens."

"Oh, yeah?"

"He's our lawyer and my son's godfather."

7

Joanna

Seeing Omar dead didn't bother Joanna nearly as much as the idea of someone seeing her leaving the antiques mall. Maybe there was another set of security cameras, or someone passing along Summer Avenue had pointed to their little borrowed car and said, *Isn't that Joanna Grayson, the famous British film star?* Believe it or not, she'd slept soundly, perhaps on account of the three gin and tonics she'd downed out by the apartment community pool. If she closed her eyes and shut out the sound of the interstate, she could've very well been in Monte Carlo or along the Amalfi Coast. The Amalfi Coast always made her think of Tippi's father, such an outrageous little raconteur, a tour manager for every brilliant band that no one could remember anymore. That was the seventies, and he'd worn those ridiculous tiny yellow bathing shorts while rubbing coconut oil on her back, their sandy transistor radio playing Italian versions of pop tunes. Caterina Caselli singing "Tutto Nero," a fun little upbeat version of "Paint It Black." Skinny cigarettes and copious amounts of red wine.

When Joanna awoke later that morning, Tippi was absent from their hideous one-bedroom flat, gone to do whatever Tippi did during daylight hours. It certainly wasn't work. The girl had been completely dependent on Joanna since she'd emerged from the womb wearing a contemptuous grin and pointing to an open mouth. Joanna always asked her and Tippi would just reply, "I've been out."

Most surely Omar had been killed, because who ends up with that much blood from a heart attack? Perhaps he'd had an aneurysm?

Blood pouring from the nose and eyes, something satanic and awful like the Hammer film she'd made a million years ago, *Dracula's Mistress.* The blood such a deep red, made of golden syrup, red food dye, cornstarch, and water. What the prop men used to call Kensington Gore. No, someone had stabbed Omar several times and left him there to die sprawled across a thick stack of the carpets he'd imported from freighters out of Turkey. She knew he had a wife and a plonker for a son, Omar always slapping him in the back of his curly black head like something out of a Benny Hill skit, calling him something awful in Turkish. *Salak! Salak!* Omar didn't come home last night, and someone had most surely found the body.

Joanna poured herself a little espresso and added a large amount of sugar, taking the tiny cup and dry white toast to the living room. The television was already on and she flipped through the morning news stations for anything on poor Omar. Her hands were a bit shaky, waiting for a furious knocking on the door, the police coming for her as a suspect in the killing. They'd take her into a shabby little cinder block room and men would shout at her and pound on a desk with their fists, until she'd be charged with murder. Maybe a big trial with lots of news cameras and a suitable setting for her best dresses and hats.

Joanna ate a bit of toast and set her teacup on top of Tippi's new copy of Italian *Vogue,* an extravagant purchase for twenty-five dollars filled with clothes she could never afford or ever own. Why did the poor girl torture herself? A move back to London. Why? Their life was here.

Joanna sat back, slipped her cheaters up from the beaded necklace, and leafed through her daily calendar. It appeared she'd already missed a useless call with her agency that morning. Her longtime agent Maury Feldstein had died in Palm Springs in 1981 from a supposed heart attack but actually from a virtual Matterhorn of cocaine. She was being represented by a twenty-four-year-old Harvard girl who'd never heard of either Vivien Leigh or Shelley Winters. Over a particularly awkward lunch in Beverly Hills, she'd asked Joanna if David Lean wasn't that old man who used to sell sausage on the telly. The horror.

We have breaking news for you this morning. Memphis police are investigating a homicide in the seven hundred block
of Summer Avenue at Summer Antiques. Police say they were
called to the business early this morning to discover the body
of a fifty-six-year-old man. Police have not yet released the
name of the victim. We will keep you updated as more details
become available.

Joanna's mouth was agape. *Unbelievable.* Omar was only fifty-six!
She'd figured him for his early seventies. She could tell he'd been dyeing
his hair for years—she'd spotted the ink up under his fingernails—and
that potty little stomach aged him considerably.

If only she hadn't left that stupid necklace inside the air vent. She'd
been so worried about what Tippi might think that she'd tucked it up
inside not twenty meters from Omar's body. If the police weren't complete dullards, they'd search every little crevice and find the pearls and
soon connect them to the Elvis party last night. All she ended up with
in exchange was some kind of useless shipping manifest from Istanbul.
Omar got shipments from Turkey almost every week. Why on earth
was this one so important that Omar had hidden it away like a daft
squirrel?

Joanna picked up her phone and spotted five missed calls from one
of her best clients. Please let me take you to lunch today, dear Joanna.
Thank you and God bless.

Joanna choked on the espresso and set down the cup. *My god, where
was Tippi and their damned car when she really needed it?* She dialed
Tippi from their house phone and listened to the cell ring and ring and
ring until her daughter picked up.

"I'm shocked you're up this early," Tippi said. "Don't tell me. The
building is on fire?"

"I need you to come and pick me up," she said. "I have errands."

"What kind of errands?"

"I don't see why that matters," she said. "Where did you go anyway?"

"If you must know," Tippi said, "I'm at the zoo making a sketch of a male and female lion. The male is lazy but rather proud of his equipment."

"They should call him Richard."

Tippi didn't answer, such a prude, and Joanna started to pace, holding on to the phone and looking outside to the pool where she'd fallen asleep last night, now occupied by a half-dozen unemployed twentysomethings who spent their days boozing and having sex. A muscular young man drifted aimlessly on a silver float, a beer can held loosely in his hand. Ten years ago, she could've made him get on his knees and bark like a dog.

"You want to go back for the necklace," Tippi said.

"What necklace?" Joanna asked.

Tippi didn't answer.

"If you must know, I have an important luncheon."

"With whom?"

"I'll explain on the way," Joanna said. "And, oh, by the way, Omar is quite dead."

Leslie Grimes had a horsey face topped with a whoosh of thinning white hair, bright white veneers, and the most outlandish jug ears. He wore a purple dress shirt with a purple striped tie, braided leather braces, a gold wedding band, and a simple gold wristwatch. No one would've paid him a bit of attention if he weren't worth billions of dollars. Grimes was founder and CEO of a Christian gift shop and bookstore chain with more than eight hundred stores in forty-seven states. He also did a bit of chatting on cable news about family values and political nonsense while maintaining a rabid fascination with high-end antiques.

"You sure are lovely, Miss Joanna," Grimes said. "I bet you take after your mother."

"I certainly hope not," Joanna said. "My mother was a mean, self-centered bitch. She only worked to please herself and treated me like an unnecessary appendage. Like some kind of tumor growing out of her arse until I turned sixteen, moved to London, and liberated myself. Everybody who was anybody was there. It was as they said. *A happening.*"

"I'm afraid the sixties never came to Arkansas," he said. "Although a fella did once offer me some pot at a Glen Campbell concert." She and Grimes had been sitting in the upper section of Chez Philippe at the Peabody for nearly twenty minutes now, making small talk—mainly him talking about growing his little ole shop in Blytheville to an empire—as he sipped sweet tea and she drank weak mint juleps that did little to nothing for her hangover.

"Well, Miss Joanna," he said, "how about we get down to those sharp brass tacks. I figured you've heard already that our ole buddy Omar is dead. Someone stabbed him and left him to bleed out on a stack of his finest carpets. Antiques from Afghanistan."

"I know," she said. "So tragic."

"Memphis sure is a dangerous city."

"But it does have its charms."

"Does it now?" Grimes said. "He sure was a funny little fella. Didn't understand half of what he was saying. But, boy, did he deliver. He was a fine man with lovely tastes. My wife and I were saying just this morning that he furnished half our house. With your help, of course."

Joanna forced a smile. "Of course."

Chez Philippe was pretty if a bit stagey for her taste, with marble columns and marble steps, white linen tablecloths, and black-suited waiters buzzing about to refill glasses. The Peabody wasn't exactly the Dorchester or the fucking Ritz but it absolutely beat her little flat where she'd been living for nine hundred dollars a month for the past year. The dreaded "Village," where she just waited for that big white bubble to follow her one day out to the parking lot and envelop her into nothingness.

"Hope you didn't mind us meeting like this," he said.

"Meeting like what?"

"A married man with a pretty woman like yourself," he said. "I've made it my business to never have a one-on-one meeting with a woman unless some more folks are present. That not only cuts down on tongues wagging but also protects me from any of those frivolous lawsuits that come up from time to time. A man in my position can be prone to flattery."

"I'm sure a great number of women just can't keep their hands to themselves."

"You have no idea, Miss Joanna," Grimes said, pushing back a few strands of stringy white hair from his long, florid face. "Did Omar tell you what he'd been doing for me?"

Joanna looked over her shoulder and then back to little Leslie Grimes and said, "Of course," she said, lying. "I have to admit poor Omar told me everything. He was a great flirt."

"Is that right?" Grimes said, leaning back. "I figured. I wasn't trying to cut out the middle man or anything. This was just a very private arrangement and I didn't want too many folks to know about it. Not that I in any way would doubt you."

"Heavens, no."

"Are you a spiritual woman, Miss Grayson?"

"Well," she said, brightening her eyes. "Faith is what bonded me to Elvis. We often spoke of matters of religion. Sometimes he and his boys, what they called the Memphis Mafia, would sing old-fashioned songs while Elvis played piano. I never felt closer to Jesus Christ and his father, too."

"Well," he said, "it's all pretty much the same. Do you read the Bible?"

"Constantly."

"And you believe it is the true Word of God?" he said.

"Oh, yes," she said. "Absolutely."

Thankfully the sad waiter, a slump-shouldered Black gent with a bald head and shaky hands, brought more drinks. She took a sailor's swig, as her old father might say, of the fresh julep. A bit weak on the bourbon. Joanna always felt she was best at lying when she was a bit sloshed. She could bat her eyelashes at the most horrid-looking producer, telling him that his hair plugs looked just marvelous.

"My family has been very blessed," Grimes said. "I started my business with a two-thousand-dollar loan from my momma and the crazy idea to sell art supplies and custom frames to regular people like myself. Silk flowers, Christmas decorations year-round, and paints and glitter to help people express their God-given talent."

"I met Salvador Dalí once in Barcelona," Joanna said. "He told me my eyes were made of flames and my breasts were made to suckle."

"Isn't that something?" Grimes said, pausing to drink some sweet tea. "I never understood all the melting clocks and crazy eyes sort of thing. I'm afraid Dalí was a bit extreme for this ole country boy from Blytheville."

The waiter set down a Cobb salad before her and a salade Niçoise for him. Neither of them touched it, Leslie too preoccupied with poor Omar's death. *Who would rob a sad little antiques mall in such a shabby part of town?* Joanna thought of the methadone clinic next door, recalled commenting to Tippi that it was only a matter of time. Omar had wanted to protect her, calling her "Miss Joanna." What a joke. Where was Omar when Otto Preminger slipped a liver-spotted hand up her miniskirt and asked her how badly she wanted to play a gogo-dancing hippie in *Skidoo*?

"This was a very special project to both me and the Grimes family," he said. "Ole Omar came through in a pinch and did exactly as he was asked. Of course, he was paid handsomely for his services. But his dying has just left a few mysteries for me."

Joanna played her best unconcerned poker face and picked up her salad fork. She began to furiously rake around the salad, concentrating on holding a smile. "Really? What would that be?"

"Well," he said. "You both had been so wonderful about getting those old statues for us without trouble with customs. So I thought I might impose upon him again."

Joanna looked up from her salad. She held the fork and stared at his dumb little face, now knowing exactly why he'd texted her so many times. She wanted to scream *aha!* but instead held a steady smile. The julep was working wonders. "I imagine this has something to do with Peter Collinson?"

Grimes grinned with his big veneers and plucked a thumb inside one of his braces, looking for all the world like Big Daddy in *Cat on a Hot Tin Roof.* Joanna never met Tennessee Williams but she had met Truman Capote once in London at some big shindig at David Bailey's warehouse. He looked content and perverted in a white suit and swinging wicker chair while watching two male models wrestle for a silver plate of cheese and sweets.

"Mr. Collinson assisted me with this very special purchase."

"More trinkets from the desert?"

"Much more than that, Miss Joanna," Grimes said, suddenly turning very serious. "Omar promised to usher my purchase all the way back to Memphis. No questions asked. But a little over a week ago, Peter stopped returning my calls, and now poor Mr. Omar got himself killed."

"And now you can't find where he's hidden your prize," Joanna said, setting down the fork and staring right at ole Leslie Grimes, the third richest man in the state of Arkansas.

"You do know."

"Of course I know," she said. "Like I said, Omar confided everything in me. He trusted me more than he did his own wife."

"Oh, thank god," he said. "Then all is not lost."

"Don't be silly," Joanna said. "But I don't think it's proper to be meddling in Peter's deal without first speaking with him."

"Peter Collinson has disappeared," he said. "With half of my money."

"How much did you pay him?"

"I'd rather not say."

"You not saying means that you paid Peter quite a handsome sum," she said. "You must've been really hot for some old relic. Why not allow me to barter for you? Like last time?"

"This isn't just some relic," he said, face turning a bright red. "What Peter promised me might just change the course of this godless country."

"Goodness," she said. She hadn't heard such theatrics since listening in on O'Toole and Burton after their fifth whiskeys. Was the poor man about to sing a hymn to her? "All Things Bright and Beautiful" and that sort of thing.

Grimes closed his eyes for a moment and took a deep breath before reaching for his sweet tea and staring right at Joanna. "You do realize my position affords me to write you a blank check," he said. "For what would be your considerable assistance."

"Changing the course of this godless country?"

"It's best you don't know all the details."

"I might know a few," she said. "All of this is coming out of Istanbul?"

"That rotten son of a bitch," Joanna said. "That awful, awful deceitful man."

"Which one?" Tippi asked. "You always say that all men are wretched."

They'd left the Peabody and wandered over to the newish shopping mall next door, a big project that was supposed to bring scores of shoppers to downtown but had instead grown into a fatted white elephant. All but two of the shops had closed, a sad little fountain trickling in the center, as she walked with her daughter in solitude past what had been a Victoria's Secret, an empty Gap, and a defunct restaurant that had sold hot dogs and A&W root beer. She couldn't think of anything more awful. She'd heard there had been a shooting on the sidewalk the day the mall opened. She couldn't imagine anyone braving this part of Memphis for a fucking hot dog and cheap lingerie.

"If it hadn't been for me, Peter would have never met a fat cat loony bird like Leslie Grimes," Joanna said. "I've been grooming Leslie for years and years. Long before we came to Memphis. Before all this Arabian nonsense, he'd been interested in buying anything that Joan Crawford had ever owned. Apparently, he'd met her as a young man outside a theater in Little Rock and had supposedly become taken with her. This fascination he has now is a beautiful sickness."

"What is it?" Tippi said.

Her daughter wore a sloppy Von Dutch sweatshirt, ragged blue jeans, and bejeweled ball cap. Dreadful pink sandals that made smacking sounds as they walked together.

"I don't know," Joanna said. "He wouldn't say. I was not fool enough to ask."

"How was lunch?"

"It was a salad at a hotel restaurant," she said. "How do you think?"

"I haven't eaten all day," Tippi said. "I'd even fancy a hot dog at the moment."

"Tippi."

"Well," she said. "Not much time to eat while playing chauffeur, Mother."

"This"—Joanna said, stopping by a row of faded movie posters for the derelict movie theater—"this is really something. A true stroke of luck. We haven't had this kind of luck in a long while."

"Omar being dead?"

"Yes, yes," she said. "Poor, poor Omar, that backstabbing little pervert. Who gives a damn about Omar. He should've locked up better. He and Peter. God."

"I've never met your Peter Collinson," she said. "You've told me stories. At one point he sounded too good to be true."

"A charming scoundrel," Joanna said. "And your mother is a curator of scoundrels. He might have topped them all."

"Can you find him?"

"Of course," Joanna said. "Because now I have something he wants."

"And what's that, Mother?" Tippi asked. She wasn't even looking at her mother, studying a ragged poster for a film called *The Duchess* with that preening little twat Keira Knightley.

Joanna had chosen to wear a silk pantsuit, with an abstract print of black, white, green, and gold brushstrokes. Very Klimt. Tall white strappy heels and the set of pearls (much nicer than the ones she'd nicked last night) layered over a golden necklace she'd borrowed from Twiggy during eight days of frozen debauchery in Saint Moritz. She was pretty sure she'd seen Peter Sellers launch a stuffed olive off his erect penis, a demonstration he offered after a lengthy discussion on the cliff divers in Acapulco.

"Mother."

"Yes."

"What does this Mr. Collinson want?"

Joanna stepped back and waved her hands over herself like a magician presenting a wondrous act. "Me," she said. "What else?"

"Oh, course," Tippi said. "Joanna Fucking Grayson. What else."

8

Addison

Thank god she'd had time to pick up the kids at school and get them settled before meeting up with Mr. Hayes again that afternoon. Addison felt terrible about lying to Sara Caroline that she had a late hot yoga, and then sneaking out the garage and down to the street to slip into this private investigator's black Mercedes. The car was an older model, but the interior was clean and cool and smelled vaguely of cigarettes and aftershave. He had on some old-school soul, something from an era that wasn't hers, and she thought she recognized Otis Redding. But when she'd asked as they made their quick getaway, out from Central Gardens and headed to the Country Club, he told her it was one of Johnnie Taylor's best albums. *Taylored in Silk.*

"I never heard of him."

"What?" Porter Hayes said, shaking his head, turning the car down onto McLean. "The Wailer? Johnnie Taylor?"

"Sorry."

He turned the music up slightly, and she noted the car was old enough to still have a cassette player. She hadn't seen one of those in ages. She'd been raised on mixtapes of her favorite bands back in high school and college. R.E.M. INXS. And god help her, some Hootie as well. Everywhere she went, there was fucking Hootie.

"Tell me more about this Jimbo Hornsby."

"More than he's just some high-paid attorney and on the Club board?"

"Yeah," Mr. Hayes said. "Need to know a little more as we're going to be getting all up into his personal business. Maude Herron and all that."

"He's got a lot to explain," Addison said. "But I really think he'll be a huge help. He and Dean are really close. Jimbo and his wife, Chris, are very active on the social scene. I don't think they miss a fundraiser. Le Bonheur. MISA foodbank. Dean and Jimbo are both in the Secret Order of Boll Weevils."

"The secret what of what?"

"It's a men's club in the Cotton Carnival," she said. "Every spring, all these doctors and lawyers and business guys dress up as boll weevils. You know, the insect?"

"Sure," he said. "My daddy grew up picking cotton."

Addison's face flushed, but she swallowed and tried to keep straight on the story. "Jimbo and Dean have these insect costumes with crazy green legs and antennae and stuff. They have an old fire engine and drive around to these poor neighborhoods to hand out toys and food. It's pretty crazy, and they do stay more or less drunk all week, but it's for a really great cause."

Mr. Hayes didn't seem to be impressed, nodding along to her story before asking, "You and your husband go to lots of these fundraisers?"

"I know it sounds ridiculous," she said. "But it makes me feel like I'm doing more with my life."

"And Dean?"

"I think he likes giving back, too," she said. "He also thinks he looks like hot shit in a tuxedo."

Mr. Hayes nodded and turned down Southern and on toward the Club. Her stomach felt a little funny about the idea of her strolling into the clubhouse with Porter Hayes. It wasn't because he was Black or that the Club had just admitted women into the bar ten years ago. It had more to do with the shame that people already knew about Dean. Maybe they'd been gossiping and talking about some love nest Dean had and how poor Addison McKellar was dumber than dog shit for being so late to catch on. Maybe she'd find Dean sitting right there in the dining room sharing an afternoon cocktail and a steak sandwich with his new girlfriend, already introducing her around. No. Dean wouldn't do that. He was too concerned about his image and reputation as a family man. That was on brand for Dean McKellar. To him, that image meant about as much as his time in the army. A captain in the first Gulf War. His work for a Fortune 500 firm in Manhattan. Coming to Memphis to build a major company.

"There's a few things you should know, Miss McKellar," Mr. Hayes said. "McKellar Construction doesn't exist."

"Not now?"

"Not ever."

Addison felt all the breath go out of her and her mouth go dry. She just stared straight ahead at the road as she listened, trying to think how pretty Memphis could be in the fall. All the leaves sprinkled across the road, the late golden light across the old houses with barrel tile roofs and thick iron gates promising twenty-four-hour security. Her mind was a rush and completely blank. What the hell was Mr. Hayes even saying?

"As far as I can tell, your husband hasn't had a contract for nearly seven years," Mr. Hayes said. "He and his partner worked on a shopping mall in Collierville in 2003 and then an office building in Nashville. After that, one of your husband's companies filed for bankruptcy. I also don't think y'all have paid your taxes for years."

"None of that make sense," Addison said. "He gets up. He goes for a five-mile jog. Every damn day. He shaves and showers then goes to work or flies to a job site. He makes money. We have a lot of money, Mr. Hayes."

"Did you know he's listed as a principal of at least four different corporations in the state of Tennessee?" Hayes asked. "And three in Florida."

"The only business Dean has in Florida is when we take the kids to Disney," she said. "And he really hates Disney. Especially Epcot. He spends half his time checking his phone and excusing himself to take a call. He'd much rather take our annual trip to Mustique where he can really relax without so much noise."

"He also owns a lot of property in the Panhandle."

"Well, we do have a home in Rosemary Beach."

"This is rural property north of Pensacola," he said. "Three hundred acres. Give or take an acre."

Addison let out a long breath. This was a lot of information to process in one day. She'd wanted to find Dean and get him home safe. She had never given a crap about Dean's business. As long as she kept the home fires burning, he did what Dean McKellar was always good at. Making money and providing for his family. Cadillacs, trips to the Caribbean, Christmas card pictures in khakis and white dresses along the beach dunes.

"I'm sorry, Mrs. McKellar," Mr. Hayes said, turning into the parking lot by the clubhouse. "I know this is a hell of a lot to take in."

"I just want to find Dean," she said. "I don't really care about all this other stuff."

"But, ma'am," Hayes said, "this other stuff is how I get to the center of the Tootsie Pop, if you get what I'm saying."

"I do," she said. "The wise old owl and all that."

"Yeah," he said. "That wise old owl sure knew his shit."

Mr. Hayes parked his Mercedes and Addison crawled out and took a deep breath. The big oaks shed leaves that flickered down onto the asphalt. Out on the eighteenth hole, three men stood on the putting green in visors and sunglasses, laughing about one of them missing an easy shot. On first glance, she thought one of them might be Dean, he looked so goddamn interchangeable with most middle-aged white men in Memphis. Same sandy brown hair, stubble on his jaw. The polo shirt, the stock golf pants, the easygoing cocky mannerisms.

When she walked around the back of the Mercedes to join up with Mr. Hayes, she saw Jimbo Hornsby loading his clubs into the back of his massive Expedition. *Son of a damn bitch.* He'd promised to meet her and Mr. Hayes at the bar and talk about Dean's disappearance. Now his chunky fat ass was trying to hop in his SUV and ghost her. *No fucking way.* Addison called out his name, and Jimbo turned, a friendly grin on his pudgy face. Yes, you had to be fat with a name like Jimbo Hornsby.

He was on the requisite fried-chicken-and-bourbon diet that old frat boys seemed to love.

She and Porter Hayes walked up to the Expedition.

"I thought we were meeting for drinks?"

"Sorry, Addy," he said. "Something real important came up."

"More important than Dean going missing?"

She looked to Porter Hayes, standing next to her in his vintage leather jacket, high collared with big leather buttons. Mr. Hayes raised an eyebrow as Jimbo started to laugh. "Let's not get dramatic," he said. "Dean's in Europe. He told me he wasn't going to be home until the end of the month."

Addison felt her face flush. She shook her head. "That's complete bullshit," she said. "Why would you say something like that? And by the way, who the fuck is this Maude Herron woman who cooks your books and answers phones for you? I bet Chris would like to know what you've been up to while she's out trying to raise money for kids at the Ronald McDonald House."

Jimbo smiled and laughed some more, putting up a hand like he was signaling to a dog. He looked to Mr. Hayes like *Can you believe this crazy woman?* "Down, girl," he said. "Down. Come on. I knew you were going to be like this, and that's why I wanted to go the hell home. I can't get involved in one of your and Dean's fights. I've been there before, Dean sleeping on my couch, you crying to Chris. We both agreed we want no part this go-round."

"What the fuck are you even talking about?" Addison said. "Who are you?"

"Addy. Addy."

Mr. Hayes stood there stock-still, checking out Jimbo's silly-ass madras pants and orange UT golf shirt. His brown hair was still wet, either from a shower or sweat, and combed straight off his florid and bloated face. Jimbo looked to Mr. Hayes and just sadly shook his head. *C'mon, man. You know what it's like dealing with women.*

"Mrs. McKellar filed a missing persons report with Memphis Police yesterday," Mr. Hayes said.

"You did what?" Jimbo said.

Hayes held up the flat of his hand to shut up Jimbo, and Jimbo did as he was told, that stupid cocky grin fading off his face. The madras pants were even more ridiculous up close, reminding Addison of the cover of *The Preppy Handbook* she owned as a kid, thinking that kind of dress was completely normal and cool. Maybe back in 1985, but now it looked like some kind of Halloween costume.

"You and Mr. McKellar share an off-the-books answering service down in Southaven," Mr. Hayes said. "It's run by an ex-con named Maude Herron. She said you'd set up Mr. McKellar with the service. That woman has been posing as Mr. McKellar's personal secretary for the last year."

"Last two years," Addison said.

"I have no idea what y'all are talking about," Jimbo said. "This is harassment and trespassing. Who the hell are you anyway?"

Mr. Hayes stepped up and got nose to nose with Jimbo Hornsby, blowing out a stream of smoke as he did. "Me?" he asked. "I'm goddamn Porter Hayes."

"Ha," Hornsby said. "You're Porter Hayes? *The* Porter Hayes?"

"The one and only, Jim-bo," he said. "And you're supposed to be a friend to this fine couple. How about you man up and tell the woman what she needs to know? Where is her husband?"

"Man up?"

"Yeah," Porter Hayes said. "You heard me. Or do you want me to pass on the news about your little answering service to the detectives looking for Dean McKellar?"

"Oh, come on, both of you," Jimbo said. "No one is looking for Dean, because he's not missing. This is another one of Addison's stupid mental breakdowns and she wants us all to be pulled into it. I'm sorry, Mr. Hayes. This isn't what you think. This is a domestic situation that has gotten out of hand. You also might want to consult with her shrink. It appears she's out of her pills. If you check with the management of the Club, you'll find out they're on strict orders not to serve her alcohol."

Addison had never, ever heard Jimbo talk like this. It was like meeting a completely new person. He was always fun and gags, hands full of big sloshy bourbons and dirty jokes and asides about his crazy legal cases. He was looking at her with scorn and mock pity, shaking his big, fat head like he was so sorry for her. She couldn't even look up at Mr. Hayes. Addison could hear her blood rushing in her ears and had to clench her hands together to stop herself from slapping the ever-living shit out of Jimbo. How the hell did he know that she talked to a therapist or took medication?

"Addison, the only reason you're still a member here is because I fought for you when the board wanted you kicked out," Jimbo said. "You assaulted a member during his own birthday party."

"The fucker grabbed my sister-in-law's tit by the bathrooms," she said. "*He* assaulted *her*. Does me mashing a piece of goddamn birthday cake in his face constitute assault?"

"In the state of Tennessee?" he said. "Yes. It does."

She looked to Mr. Hayes. Mr. Hayes shrugged.

The day was so goddamn pretty and golden, with the smell of the freshly cut grass, the ticker tape of oak leaves through the soft, hazy light. This was the kind of day where Addison should be poolside with a tall cold drink, gossiping with Libby or, god forbid, Chris Hornsby. But instead, she was being insulted, called crazy, and listening to a bunch of half-truths and outright lies about her own marriage.

"Jimbo," she said, jabbing an index finger into his fleshy chest above his big stomach, "Dean has not called home in an entire week."

"That's on you, Addy," he said. "Maybe you should treat him better."

She couldn't clench her hands this time and slapped the ever-living shit out of him. It was a hard thwack across his face, leaving a sweltering mark on his jowls. It felt good and a little terrifying. She raised her arm to do it again, but Mr. Hayes gently held her hand back.

"You saw that," Jimbo said. "You saw that. She attacked me. She jumped me here in the parking lot and assaulted me."

Mr. Hayes let go of her hand and then took a long, hard look at Jimbo Hornsby. A group of three of four members had gathered by the entrance to the Club to watch. Two of them had those same fucked-up madras pants on and one of them wore a silly-ass visor. As her dad always said, either wear a hat or don't. A visor is completely noncommittal. *God.* Daddy would hate these fucking people. There had been a time that he'd wanted to be a member here, and he tried. But year after year they'd turned him down. The Club wasn't a place for a man whose parents were born in Lebanon and had the last name Hassan.

"What's your real name?" Mr. Hayes said.

"Jimbo."

"Christian name."

"Melvin James Hornsby."

"Yeah, I'd probably go by Jimbo, too," Mr. Hayes said. "Here's what I think, Melvin. I think you definitely know where we can find Dean McKellar, but you're refusing to tell his wife."

"You don't understand the situation here, man," Jimbo said.

Porter Hayes glared at him. "Mr. Hayes."

"Huh?" Jimbo said.

"I'm not your man," he said. "Call me Mr. Hayes."

Mr. Hayes turned to Addison, who had her arms wrapped around her midsection, fighting hard against the urge to slap Jimbo again. He smiled at Addison.

"I know my client," Mr. Hayes said. "How about you?"

Jimbo didn't answer. He turned to the open hatch of his Expedition and pushed the close button, the hatch slowly locking down into place.

"I know you and your reputation," Jimbo said. "I'll warn you. If you want to keep it, I'd keep far away from this woman. She's not mentally stable or in any condition to talk about her husband. Who, by the way, is an honest-to-God American hero and one of this city's most successful businessmen."

"Even after three bankruptcies?" Mr. Hayes asked.

Jimbo's fat cheek twitched a bit. The men from the canopied entrance to the Club started to walk to where they stood by the SUV. One of them called out to see if Jimbo was okay. "Fine, fine," he said. "I'm just leaving."

The little white man in the visor announced he was calling the police and pulled out a cell phone, staring right at Porter Hayes as he talked. Addison heard the words, *Black male in leather jacket.* Mr. Hayes just shook his head and smiled.

Jimbo Hornsby crawled in behind the wheel and started to back out. As he did, Porter Hayes knocked on his window with his knuckles. The SUV stopped and the glass went down.

"Tell your friend, client, butt buddy, whatever he is, that I will find him," Mr. Hayes said. "And while you're at it, you might explain the legal context of abandonment."

"This isn't your world, Mr. Hayes," he said. "You need to realize. No one, and I mean no one, here will talk with you."

"Oh, yeah?" Mr. Hayes said, glancing back at Addison and winking. "One thing you need to realize, Melvin. To quote the late, great Joe Tex. *One monkey don't stop no show.*"

The backyard pool used to scare the hell out of Addison when the kids were small. Just the thought of them wandering the edges and toppling down into it made a pit form in her stomach. The pool, the stairs, the electrical outlets, the front door, the bathtub, an uncut grape—death lurked in everything with toddlers. Now that they were older, and she prayed less reckless, she didn't need to stand guard every damn second and could actually sit on her ass with a drink. It was dark now, the Chinese takeout long gone, and she was poolside with Libby, both reclined in loungers. Addison leaned up and offered her big empty wineglass to Libby. Libby refilled.

"What a dick," Libby said.

"I know," Addison said. "And here I thought Jimbo was our friend. He told Mr. Hayes I was mentally unstable and that I was always causing problems at the Club."

"That's bullshit," Libby said.

"I know," Addison said. "We only occasionally cause problems."

Libby raised her wineglass and clinked it with Addison's.

It seemed like every room in her house was lit up, a giant glowing box that deceptively implied a lot of activity. But inside it was cold and silent, only the television playing the new season of *American Idol*, Sara Caroline curled up on the couch. Preston was upstairs doing whatever it was that Preston did at night. Playing Nintendo, working on Legos, checking out naked pictures of girls on the internet. She'd already caught him twice after checking his browser—women with ginormous breasts and shaved privates—and now he was afraid she could read his mind.

"It was like I was talking with a completely different person," Addison said. "Do you know he's Preston's damn godfather?"

"That's a mistake right there," Libby said, taking a big pull on a joint. "I wouldn't let Jimbo and Christie take care of goddamn ChaCha. No offense, ChaCha."

ChaCha trotted up after hearing his name and pawed at Addison's leg. She rubbed his ears. Content, the dog went back to sniffing around the pool, seeking stale potato chips or old charred meat that had fallen off the grill.

Libby tried to pass the joint to Addison, but Addison waved it away. Not that she was a prude or anything. She had too many problems to figure out, and being high wouldn't help. The last time she and Libby had gotten high down at Rosemary Beach, Dean had been so fucking pissed. He called her an unfit mother, which led to a mournful late-night walk on the beach, lots of stupid tears, and a half-hearted apology from Dean the next day. All had turned out well with a brand-new pair of diamond earrings.

"Fucking Jimbo knows where Dean is," Addison said.

"Maybe," Libby said. "But why would he make up that stuff about you? You are crazy. But only crazy in the best of ways."

"Thanks," Addison said. "Men do stupid things for their so-called honor system. I'm sure it's some woman. How dumb do I look for not noticing?"

"You're not dumb," Libby said. "You're the smartest person I know."

"Really?"

"Well, I don't know many smart people," Libby said. "Still. You're top of the list."

"I agree," Addison said. "I have to be honest with you, Libby. I'm not weepy about it. I'm over it. I'm over Dean. I'm over this marriage. I'm over the whole goddamn thing. I just want to know where we stand so I can get on with the rest of my goddamn life. I feel like I've been in some fucked-up limbo since college. Jesus. I can't believe it's been almost twenty years. Fuck. It seems like the kids were just born."

"Like sands through the hourglass."

"Ha ha," she said. "Especially when every day feels pretty much the same. Take the kids to school. Have just enough time to work out and maybe do some shopping. Lunch with you if I'm lucky. Pick up the kids, run them all over town to whatever activity, make sure they're fed, make sure they do their homework, make sure they take a bath and brush their teeth and go the fuck to sleep and then wake up and repeat."

Dark clouds bloomed far in the distance, grumbling with thunder. The wind picked up, blowing about her magnolia trees and little Japanese maples at the edge of the backyard. Everything was arranged so perfect and lovely in the elegant landscape lighting. The grand old Tudor with all the stately stonework and the beautiful pool. The playhouse she'd always wanted, set up high on the hill. The old house had been a mess when they'd first bought it, the property tied up in a bankruptcy. Dean got it for a steal. She recalled running up the hill and inside like Natalie Wood in *Miracle on 34th Street*, half expecting to find old Kris Kringle's cane by the mantel but instead finding a bottle of Dom that Dean had bought. Sweet, sweet heroic Dean to the rescue, knowing her deepest darkest childhood desire, to live in Central Gardens in a grand old house with so many ghosts.

"Can you really blame him?" Addison asked.

"Excuse me?"

"For walking away from all this," she said. "The house, the wife, the bratty kids, the constant renovations, the stuff, all of it, when you could just leave and start over. You get married and then all you do is start collecting shit. You buy a big house and then need to fill it. You have kids and start needing lake homes and beach homes. And then the right dress clothes to make sure you look the part at Second Pres on Sunday morning. You get the right bracelets and earrings. Did you know Dean collects vintage watches? He must have a dozen of them, and every single one costs a fortune. It's sick. We'd need a goddamn dumpster to get rid of all the crap we don't need."

"You really believe Dean just wants to start over?"

"You should've seen Jimbo's fat face," she said. "I'm absolutely sure of it."

Addison looked up at the clouds starting to blossom with lightning and then back at the empty house. She pushed herself up from the lounge and passed her empty wineglass to Libby.

"Listen, I probably shouldn't mention this, but be careful what you say to your brother," Libby said. "He's been acting even more strange than normal. I've been checking his phone to see if he's heard from Dean, but there was nothing. That doesn't mean they don't talk. So I just asked him straight out and he denied knowing anything. He just made a bunch of excuses for Dean being AWOL."

"Sounds like Branch."

"But two days ago, Branch wired ten thousand dollars from our account into a bank in the Cayman Islands," she said. "When I confronted him about it, he stormed off and accused me of spying on him."

"Branch doesn't know shit about the Cayman Islands."

"I know," Libby said. "But Dean sure does. Watch your back, Addison. Don't trust anyone."

"Not even you?"

Libby drank down the last of the wine and then looked to Addison. "You can always trust me," she said. "I'm the most trustworthy bitch in this whole damn city."

By the time Addison walked back inside the house, the television over the mantel was off, and only a few lights remained on in the kitchen. She set the empty wineglasses and bottle in the sink to find a handwritten note tucked just below the window. *We can smell your stinky weed all the way in here.*

A little of Sara Caroline's handiwork. Addison removed the note, tore it up, and tossed it into the trash. The floors and cabinets were still draped in plastic sheeting and crinkled as she walked. Thunder outside rattled the glass in the bay window as she watched Libby's G-Wagen heading back down the long driveway. Addison locked all the doors, checking the front door twice, and took the grand staircase from the foyer upstairs. She knocked three times, but Sara Caroline refused to answer her door although Addison could hear her giggling on the phone. She then tried Preston, and he was already tucked into his bed, the twinkly Christmas lights that covered his bookshelves glowing in the darkness. Dozens of action figures lined the shelves, Godzilla and Transformers, *Star Wars* figures, and the little matchbox cars that she used to buy at Kroger every time they made it through the aisles without toddler Preston throwing a fit.

Leaving her without a word was bad enough. How the hell could Dean leave the kids too? There had always been something emotionally remote about Dean that she'd chalked up to him being in the army. He never really showed a lot of joy or a lot of sadness. Dean used to say Addison's excitement over everything was enough for one household and that he'd been brought up to keep things to himself. He said his dear old dead dad always said emotions were a feminine trait, and Addison responded that she was pretty sure he meant "human," but that had started a whole thing.

She sat down beside Preston and smoothed the hair from his closed eyes. She wondered how long she could keep all this from the kids. Sara Caroline was hardened enough to catch on quickly and would most definitely blame her mother. But Preston would be crushed, finding a way to blame himself for Dean disappearing.

There was more thunder outside, the big old house shaking and the windows rattling from the incoming storm. Preston stirred as Addison stood up and walked into her bedroom, again checking her phone for any messages. She changed into some oversize sweatpants and one of Dean's old army tank tops, ChaCha whimpering from the thunder and trailing behind her into their deluxe bathroom. All marble with a tub that was more like a small pool and a walk-in shower with four different types of heads.

As she stared at herself in the mirror and began to brush her teeth, ChaCha started barking and ran off downstairs. Stupid dog. He'd already been out two times and had been sitting by the pool with her and Libby for the last two hours.

Now he was downstairs barking loud enough to wake the dead. *Good god.* When would this day end? She thought about that old Calgon commercial from when she was a kid, the woman sighing *Calgon, take me away!* and soaking all her troubles away in a big bathtub, transporting herself to an acid dream of the Garden of Eden.

Addison was halfway across the bedroom when she heard ChaCha yelp.

She reached for her phone and then went straight into Dean's closet for the shotgun on the top shelf. Dean was insistent that it be kept there, loaded, all the time, even against her protests. He was always getting on her about arming the alarm system and not going off their grounds during the night.

She rooted up and around a folded stack of Dean's work pants and T-shirts and found the stock of the shogun. If this was Dean's idea of a homecoming, she could scare the ever-living shit out of him. He couldn't just disappear and then waltz back into their home in the middle of the night. She checked the shotgun load, snicked it closed, and then descended the staircase around the great chandelier and down onto the cool of the marble landing.

ChaCha had stopped barking and trotted in to see her as if nothing had happened, panting heavily and trying to get up under her legs. Addison didn't say anything, but followed the hallway, switching on the lights as she went, past Dean's study and into living room, heading back toward the kitchen. She could see the dull gray glow in the kitchen and the rippling of the plastic sheeting against the floor. The sound of the dry wind got louder and she could hear the screen door slamming over and over against the frame.

Addison took a deep breath and lowered the shotgun.

"Goddamn you, ChaCha," she said.

That's when she felt a thick, sweaty arm reach around her neck and heard a voice whisper into her ear. "Drop the gun and do as I say and no one gets hurt."

Not very original, but she did as the voice told her. Dean's shotgun clattered to the floor. She felt her heart race and her bladder went a bit loose.

"Will you be a good girl?"

Addison tried to nod with great difficulty. She felt her oxygen being cut off.

"What the fuck is all this?" the man asked.

"A renovation," Addison said, croaking and barely audible.

"Renovation?" the man said. "Huh. Just countertops or the whole deal? How much is that going to set y'all back?"

"Fifty thousand."

"Fifty thousand," the man said, his voice very rough and rural. "Whoo-wee. Ain't that something? It's no business of mine. But someone sure is cornholing you folks. You can do synthetics that look just as good. There's this shit I used at my place called Silestone that looks amazing. Y'all should check it out."

Addison attempted to nod. ChaCha wandered into the kitchen and stared directly at them both. The damn dog tilted his head, and the man loosened his grip on her neck.

"Don't make no noise."

"I won't."

"Is your husband upstairs?"

"Yes," she said. "He's got a big-ass AR-15 ready to blow your fucking nuts off."

"Ha ha," the man said. "Bullshit. You really know where he's at?"

Addison didn't answer.

"I've been tracking his sorry ass halfway across this godforsaken earth," he said. As the man stepped back, she noticed he had a hook for his right hand. He was a big, brushy-bearded guy with a ruddy face and greasy hair.

"If you play straight with me and get his ass on the phone," he said, "me and you is straight. There's no need for me to snatch you up, take you with me, and do the whole kidnapping shit show. I seen it before and it ain't of any interest to me. I don't care at all for your husband, but he does know an ugly situation when he hears one."

"Mind if I sit?"

"Be my guest."

"Please don't harm my kids."

"Oh, come on, now," he said. "I don't mess with no kids. What kind of man do you think I am?"

"A man who broke into my kitchen and tried to strangle me?" she said. "Why are you here?"

"To get straight with your husband."

"Oh," Addison said. "Did he screw you over too?"

She sat down in the dark at the head of their breakfast table. The man walked over to their big Sub-Zero fridge and started rooting around. He pulled out a loaf of French bread, some turkey she'd had cut at Whole Foods, sliced Swiss cheese, and a squeeze bottle of country-style mustard.

"You have a name?" Addison asked.

"Yep."

"Are you going to tell me?"

"Nope," he said, standing against the kitchen island. He began to slice through the bread loaf with her longest and sharpest knife. "You said he done screwed you over too? What's that mean?"

"It means he disappeared."

"From his wife and family?" he said. "Ha ha. Don't that beat all."

"No, it doesn't."

"Doesn't what?"

"Beat all."

"Well, I ain't no marriage counselor and don't give two horse-size shits about your problems, lady," he said. "I come here for your husband and to get straight and see if we can't come up and make a deal. If not, I'm going to make y'all's life a true and authentic living hell."

"You're too late," Addison said. "He's fucking gone. You're going to have to stand in line."

The man didn't answer. His ugly, paunchy bearded face was shadowed in the soft light of the kitchen while he ate the enormous sandwich. They were silent for a good long while, with Addison at their breakfast table and the man at the island until Preston walked in rubbing his eyes. He stopped cold and looked at the big man and then his mother. His eyes grew wide and he froze with fear.

"It's fine," Addison said. "It's all fine. Please go back to bed."

The man set down his sandwich and walked over to Preston. He got down on one knee like an understanding Little League coach. "Did we wake you up, big man? Sorry about that."

Addison looked to the kitchen floor where she'd dropped the shotgun. She started to stand and make her way toward it. The man got to his full height and picked up the long knife he had used for the bread. It shone bright as he twisted it in his hands. "Made in Japan. Damn. I bet this is as sharp as a samurai sword."

"Go back to bed, Preston."

"Naw," the one-armed man said. "He can stay right here."

"Mom."

"Go to bed," she said, nearly screaming it, and Preston turned and bolted from the room. The man shrugged, put down the knife, and picked up the sandwich. As he ate, the mustard spilled across his shirt.

"Don't y'all have any cold beer?"

"Get the fuck out of my house."

"Guess that means no."

The man swallowed and wiped his mouth on his shirt. "Here's the situation," he said. "You call the police or make yourself a pain in the ass and I'll be back. But I don't think that'll happen. I think you'll call up your husband on his secret phone and tell him I was here. He'll know exactly who I am and what he's dealing with and we can straighten out this raw deal man-to-man."

"Dean would never work with a man like you."

The man twisted his head, set down what was left of the sandwich, and tossed a piece of turkey up in the air. ChaCha snatched it and gulped it down. Addison felt like she couldn't breathe. Her heart was up in her throat somewhere.

"Who the fuck is Dean?"

"Dean McKellar is my husband."

"Dean Mc what?" he said. "Come on, lady. Your fucking husband is Peter Collinson, or didn't he tell you that on y'all's wedding night?"

The house alarm started blaring and the outside security lights flashed on. The man looked about, shook his head, and gave a long, hard stare at Addison. "And here I come to you being a man of reason."

He used the pinkie of his good hand to pry something loose from his teeth and brushed past her, knocking her flat on her ass, and went straight out the back door to the pool.

She called 911 and then called Mr. Hayes. "Hold on," he said. "I'm comin'."

9

Gaultier

Gaultier flew back to Paris to make a deal with the Serbians, spend time with his mistress, and perhaps even warn Collinson of trouble with the One-Armed Man. The night before, there had been much drinking and celebration with the Serbs, crates and crates of AK-47s that would ship from Marseille, and an odd assortment of used pistols he'd won in a card game in Martinique. The money wasn't much to speak of, but the Serbians had offered him a night of Jack Daniel's shots and champagne and prostitutes at a tourist club off the Champs Elysées called the White Stallion. All the women were from Ukraine and Russia and very intent on separating Gaultier from as many euros as they could, whispering in his ear all types of acts that held no interest for him. Still, it was fun and festive, and he'd gotten back to his flat and his mistress at a respectable time, finding himself up and showered early the next morning and reading *Le Monde* at Le Fumoir by midday.

He had a lovely Liga Privada going in a large ashtray, sitting outside and facing the Saint-Germain-l'Auxerrois and the back of the Louvre. His mistress, Valerie, sat with him, smoking a skinny cigarette and drinking black coffee while thumbing through an enormous fashion magazine. She would bend back the pages to show him a list of where she wanted to shop after lunch. Almost always the Triangle d'Or.

"I'm afraid you'll have to go alone, my dear," he said in French. It sounded much more heartfelt in French. As most things do. "I have to see a friend."

She gave him a mock pout before returning to her magazines. She was just a girl, only now twenty, and perhaps even loved him a little. He'd done much work with her father some years ago and had been stunned by her beauty—properly curvy with devilish lips and short, curly brown hair—when she'd visited the south two years ago. He promised to take her to dinner the next time he was in Paris—a private table at Le Train Bleu laden with pâté and steak tartare—and a short time later they'd worked out an arrangement. Of course, there were others. But he didn't ask. He only asked that she was available to him when he visited. And the whole charade had worked into a very sensible arrangement.

"Who is this friend?"

"Someone your father knew quite well," he said. "He's in some kind of trouble and I must warn him."

"Oh," she said, placing the phonebook-size *Vogue* down face-first on the glass-topped table, nearly knocking over his cigar. Her father had died in a most tragic auto accident that she didn't realize hadn't been an accident at all. "That sounds exciting. Is someone trying to kill him?"

Valerie was young but not exactly ignorant of her family's business.

"Yes," he said. "I think so. A man came to me in Egypt and threatened to cut off his penis."

She threw back her head and laughed. "Does this man deserve it?"

Gaultier picked up the cigar, considered the question and Valerie, and nodded his affirmation.

It was such a lovely time of year in Paris, a slight chill in the evening, the leaves falling from the trees along the Seine. The most wonderful golden light over the bridges and across the city. Lovers and tourists strolling the Pont Neuf. Everything was the same as when he'd been a child in his short pants and shirts with Peter Pan collars. Everything the same as when he'd been a student in 1968 with the riots. Levi's and dirty black T-shirts. His mother had called him a revolutionary, a Communist. Perhaps she was right. A little revolution time and again was quite healthy and very good for business.

"Would you like to make love after lunch?" Valerie asked.

"I wish there was time."

"And tonight?"

"Whatever you wish, my lovely," he said. "But after all your shopping, won't you be tired?"

She shook her head and laughed. The wonderful outline of the church spires over her shoulder looked almost like a charcoal sketch in the midday light. Collinson wasn't much of a friend, but Gaultier knew favors facilitated favors. This was more of an issue of mutual respect than anything. If the tables were turned, he'd expect Collinson to do very much the same thing. And the pesky issue of him telling the One-Armed Man where Collinson lived in America. He'd felt a gnawing sense of guilt since that indiscretion. Even upside down and staring at the Nile, he shouldn't have told that secret.

"Where exactly is Peter Collinson's flat?"

"Pardon?"

"Please," Gaultier said. "Let's not waste a lovely day arguing. I am quite aware you have another life."

Valerie shrugged. She picked up Gaultier's large cigar and took a long draw. She eyed him and placed her bare feet, separated from her Christian Louboutins, into his lap and wiggled her toes in the proper places.

"Oh," she said. "You meant a friend of my father's. I should have known."

"And?"

"I need a new handbag," she said. "A Birkin."

"Of course."

Gaultier reached into his jacket pocket, removed his wallet, and tossed an American Express Black card onto the glass table. He raised his eyebrows. She ran her hands through her short hair and bit her lip. She stifled a little laugh and scooped up the credit card.

"Does this help you remember the address?"

"Peter has a lovely apartment in the ninth," she said. "On the Haussmann Boulevard. A fourth-floor walk-up with a stunning view."

"Of course."

"If you must know, he's a bit of a timid lover," she said. "I had to teach him many new magic tricks."

"My dear," Gaultier said, plucking the cigar back. He respected Valerie. They were both prostitutes in their own ways. "I would expect nothing less. You are a born sorceress."

He took the Metro to the station at the Gare Saint-Lazare and walked the rest of the way.

Gaultier wore a gray-checked three-piece suit with a custom white dress shirt, black silk tie, and black handkerchief. His shoes were black Hermès crocodile and calfskin slippers and his cuff links, small enough to go largely unnoticed, were ivory and shaped like human skulls.

What a lovely day. And the promise of a lovely night. He didn't care in the least that Valerie had been with Collinson; however, his pride did resent that she'd taught Collinson some well-guarded tricks that Gaultier had learned as a young man in Hong Kong. *What a waste.* The double-crested dragon was his go-to performance, and much too intimate and sensual for an American to perform. Despite her bravado, he doubted Collinson had the stamina and suppleness to actually pull it off. Valerie had probably lied, trying to puncture his nonexistent ego because Gaultier had been spending so much time away from Paris. The double-crested dragon was what tied them even more deeply than his black AmEx. *Dragon a double*, she'd whisper to him, hands clenching the headboard as if she were an animal in a zoo.

He strolled past the Galeries Lafayette and crossed over the bustling hub where Haussmann met the Rue de Halévy and la Chaussée-d'Antin, filled with luxury shoe shops, newsstands, and brightly lit lingerie stores. More shops and outdoor cafés, mostly empty in midmorning. He followed Haussmann into a quiet stretch lined with trees and bicycle racks, where he saw the apartment entrance beside the Flores café. Tall blue doors opened into a marble lobby with shabby old furniture, dying plants, and a row of copper mailboxes tarnished bright green.

He found the staircase and took his time making his way to the fourth floor and Collinson's apartment. He wondered how many times Valerie had walked up these same steps, meeting Collinson in her black lingerie under her Burberry overcoat, letting the coat drop to the floor with a giggle as if unwrapping a very special gift.

Gaultier knocked on the door. An old woman passed him in the hall, offering a bonjour, an ancient dachshund in a knitted sweater trailing behind. She didn't even glance at Gaultier as she passed, calling out to the dog. "Saucisse."

Gaultier knocked again and waited until the woman had gone into the stairwell.

He slipped his hand into his suit jacket and brought out a small lock-picking kit. Within seconds he'd opened the door and closed it behind him.

Instantly he was greeted by a familiar and horrid smell. The thick old door must've masked it from the hall. The great windows facing Haussmann had been opened wide, long white curtains billowing in the brisk wind. Gaultier reached for the silk handkerchief in his breast pocket and covered his mouth, nearly gagging.

He spotted a pair of overturned leather chairs, cushions splayed on the floor, and an empty bottle of wine in a red puddle. He got down on his haunches and looked at the bottle without daring to touch it. *What a shame.* A bottle of '99 Petrus Gran Vin.

He followed the buzz of the flies to two bodies on the floor. Both men, both dressed in black and wearing hoodies, their guns fallen close to where they'd been shot. Very slowly and very carefully, Gaultier moved toward them, waving away the flies. He reached for a Mont Blanc pen in his suit jacket and pulled the hoodie from one of the men's faces. He was Pashtun and young, with wide, empty brown eyes and a wisp of a beard and mustache. The other had a shaved head and cleanly shaved face, lying flat with his head twisted at an ugly angle, a hole in the center of his forehead. Gaultier kept walking, moving into the apartment hallway. A third man had been shot dead in the kitchen. He also appeared to be Pashtun, only much older, with closely cropped gray hair and a bulbous nose. He lay on his back and had been shot many times in the center of his body. The blood had pooled and congealed near the humming refrigerator. *The Taliban in Paris?*

Collinson. Collinson. Quick and efficient work with a handgun, most definitely a suppressor, in order not to gain the attention of the old woman and Saucisse down the hall. Saucisse would've probably not liked the gunshots.

In the large bedroom, with its tall windows looking down upon Haussmann, sat an open leather grip on an unmade bed, half filled with dress shirts, pants, and socks. Inside, he discovered an unused 9 mm clip and a combat knife still in its black leather sheath. A pair of black lace panties lay loose under the sheets, along with a used condom and a pair of men's undershorts.

After a quick search, Gaultier found the closets nearly empty, with only two suits and one pair of black lace-up shoes. A quick look around and under the bed revealed a cell phone that appeared to have been dropped and lost.

Gaultier slipped the phone into his pocket and was making his way to the exit when someone began to knock on the big apartment door. He stopped walking and listened. The knocking was forceful and rude. He heard the jangling of keys and pressed his back against the wall. He pulled out his pistol, a nifty little SIG P series that was small enough not to ruin the perfect cut of his suit.

Did he really want to kill the proprietor? Or the cleaning woman? It would give him absolutely no pleasure, but neither would being caught by the police and connected to the murder of three men in an American's apartment.

Soon the knocking stopped. Gaultier let out his breath.

He pushed off the wall and walked back into the living room and kitchen, again covering his face from the congealing blood, feces, and all the hungry flies. It reminded him of digging all those graves in the Congo, the smell never really leaving him. A horrid, bloody time that he wished he could forget forever.

He slipped out the front door, wiped the prints off the knob, and made his way into the stairwell and out into the fresh air of Haussmann. He strolled as he watched a patrol car arrive, blue lights flickering, in front of the café. A short, bald man in dungarees met the police and pointed up to Collinson's apartment. Gaultier waited until they'd disappeared into the building before he walked in the opposite direction, coming to the busy intersection and ducking down into the Metro.

The three men couldn't have been dead more than twenty-four hours. Either the One-Armed Man had neglected his information and come straight to Paris, or a completely new crew was after Collinson. Either way, Gaultier was done. The American had done the double dragon to himself.

10

Porter Hayes

Sometimes Vietnam came back so clear it was as if only a year or two had passed since he'd been on patrol with his unit, deep in the boonies, skin stained red from the dirt and his feet eaten up with jungle rot. This morning, Porter was back on his proper routine, around the corner from his office at the Bon Ton café, a *Commercial Appeal* in his hands, sitting in his favorite booth and drinking coffee when he heard Joe Tex singing, "I Believe I'm Gonna Make It." And right then, Porter Hayes was back in it, a foot solider up on a mountain near Dalat. He could hear his platoon sergeant, a good man, a big fella named Ellis, leading the way through the vines and monkey piss, only two days out from flying home and whistling Joe Tex nearly every minute. *And you can believe, I'll be home before you can say, Jackie Robinson.* They were coming down the mountain to the fire base, the whole unit dragging ass, when one of the newbies hit a trip wire. The mine spared the kid but sure took out Ellis, blowing his goddamn intestines outside his body. It looked as if the sergeant had been turned inside out, dead before he hit the ground. Porter always thought he'd go to North Carolina and meet Ellis's family one day and explain what the man had meant to him. Without his sergeant, he could've been dead long ago.

"Damn, you early," Deacon Malone said, having difficulty with his increasing girth as he slid into the booth. He picked up the menu out of habit, although he and Porter had been eating at the Bon Ton for more than twenty years. "Biscuits and gravy," he said to the waitress, the woman pouring out his coffee. Porter could've told her that with-out even asking. Deacon rarely ordered anything different.

"Lady Hightower got a message for you," Deacon said.

"Oh, yeah," Porter said. "Hand it over."

"For your ears only," he said. "See, I'm the royal-ass messenger. She says that you'd promised to let her work off those indiscretions you may have heard about."

"Say what?"

"She says she'll give up some booty in return for you not tying her to her thieving-ass husband."

"I never said that."

"But I know you," Deacon said. "And maybe you said something that might have caused her to believe something like that?"

"I told her I'd think long and hard about coming over when the pastor was away."

"*Long and hard*," Deacon said. "Shit, man. You see what I'm saying?"

Porter shook his head, folded the newspaper, and leaned back into the booth while the waitress brought his ham and eggs with buttered wheat toast. Malone asked for some prune juice after she'd told him his biscuits and gravy would be up shortly.

"You need to keep on the Hightowers," Porter said. "This business with Sami's daughter might take a while. I'll need you to document more of the good rev's lifestyle. That big-ass house on South Parkway. The clothes, the jewelry. What kind of car the preacher driving these days?"

"Brand-new pearl-white Escalade."

"See?" Porter said. "The preacher and the good lady aren't even trying."

"And what do I tell her?" Deacon asked.

"About what?"

"About you making that booty trade."

"*It's too late, baby*," Porter said, singing.

"Carole King?"

"By way of the Isleys."

The Bon Ton wasn't the best in town, but it was close and convenient. The blue-and-white checkerboard floors and old dark wood booths had gone through a lot of owners over the years, and most of the café's clientele had moved on or died. Sam Phillips used to sit in that very booth, telling folks about his days making records with Elvis and Jerry Lee. Porter had done some work for Jerry Lee and his people a few years back but didn't feel really good about it. One of those cases where nobody, absolutely nobody, got out looking clean.

"So what's up with Sami Hassan's daughter?" Deacon asked.

Porter told Deacon about his day yesterday and the break-in last night. Deacon didn't say a word until that plate of biscuits and gravy came and then made a few grunts of affirmation.

"Was the break-in connected?" Deacon said. "Or just Memphis?"

"Connected," Porter said. "A one-armed man was asking her questions about her husband or a man named Peter Collinson."

"Which one was it?"

"She didn't find out," Porter said. "Motherfucker threatened her and then made his ass a turkey sandwich before the police showed up."

"A turkey sandwich?"

"On a French baguette," Porter said. "Or at least that's what I've been told."

"Devil lives in them details."

Dean McKellar's old business partner, Alec Dawson, kept an office in East Memphis on the fourteenth floor of the White Station Tower. The building was blocky and ugly, with a big cylindrical top that used to be one of those revolving restaurants back in the seventies. Porter wanted to say it was called the Embers, but then the name Top of the Tower came to mind. The tower was a long, lasting monument to the city's eastward white flight.

Alec Dawson ran a company called Dawson-Gray Construction, which according to Darlene, had been around about forty years. Dawson took over the business from his father after a few years of going out on his own with Dean McKellar and then splitting up. She was able to find a lawsuit from six years ago when Dawson had sued Dean for two million bucks for improper distribution of assets and corporate waste. Darlene printed out the suit for him and Porter read it in his car before heading east. Looked like Dean had created a backdoor account for his personal finances, including purchasing land in Florida, a few vehicles, and repairs to the house in Central Gardens. All this while the company was showing annual losses.

Dawson didn't hesitate when Hayes had called him up. Old business partners and jilted wives sure loved to talk.

It wasn't nine o'clock yet and Hayes was kicking back in Alec Dawson's huge office with comfortable leather chairs and antique bookshelves filled with stuffed ducks and vintage shotguns. The plate glass window behind his desk commanded a view of commuters fighting around I-240 and down along Poplar into Germantown. "On a clear day, I bet you can see all the way to Nashville," Hayes said.

"Or at least Collierville," Dawson said.

Alec Dawson was a tall, skinny but fit white man in his early forties. He had dark brown hair and blue eyes and a shadow of a beard, although he appeared to be clean-shaven. He wore a white button-down dress shirt without a tie and gray flannel pants with immaculate leather lace-up shoes. Hayes hadn't been in the office but two minutes when he asked, "Okay, then. What exactly did Dean do now?"

Hayes nodded. "I'm not real sure," he said. "But he hasn't been in touch with his family for more than a week. His wife is pretty worried."

"Poor Addison," Dawson said. "I don't know how she puts up with his shit."

"If you don't mind me asking, Mr. Dawson," he said, "just what kind of shit are you talking about?"

"Dean was a horrible business partner but an even worse husband," he said, leaning back in a brown leather and chrome office chair. "He cheated on her their entire marriage. But he always finds a way to lie right out of it."

"Do you think she knew?"

"Of course, she knew," Dawson said. "Everybody knew."

"But never mentioned it."

"Maybe she prefers to keep that private," he said. "If she doesn't think about it or talk about it, then it never happened. But I can't imagine she'd be surprised if Dean just up and left her and the kids one day. You know he's pulled this crap before?"

Hayes nodded. "He always comes up with a good excuse."

"Always," Dawson said, spinning right to left in his chair. "Dean is the most confident son of a bitch I ever met in my life. He could steal, lie, and cheat you and then try and convince you that it was all your fault."

"Is that what he did to you?"

"Unfortunately," Dawson said, standing up and then walking over to the window. "I bought into the bullshit and trusted him like a damn brother." It was cloudy and slick outside, the cars backed up all along the interstate and onto Poplar. Rain ran down the glass as Dawson frowned and shook his head, looking disappointed not with Dean but with himself.

"Did you ever settle up with him?"

"Yep," he said. "But it took a while. For a few months after we filed, I kept on having heavy equipment sabotaged. Hydraulic lines cut. Sand in the gas tank. That sort of thing. I got the cops involved. And then, I get a call from my attorney that Dean wanted to settle for one point five million. How's that for timing?"

"He didn't like questions."

"Nope." Dawson laughed. "He paid and we never spoke again."

The office was spacious, but felt a little like a high-end hunt club with all the dead ducks and photos of Delta hunt camps on the wall, recent images of old white men in waders with shotguns and an older photo of a fluffy white-and-brown dog sitting proudly beside a pile of dead birds. One photo featured an older man who resembled Alec Dawson in the middle of a cleared construction site holding up a blueprint.

"Mrs. McKellar didn't know Dean had quit the construction business."

"Who told you he'd quit?"

"His company was dissolved," Hayes said. "When Mrs. McKellar visited their offices downtown, she found they hadn't been there for two years."

"Well, it may not be called McKellar, but Dean is definitely still in the game and into some big-time projects," Dawson said. "I've been keeping tabs on him after all the trouble he caused. I heard he got into some overseas work for the government. This was some post-9/11 money, to rebuild roads and hospitals over in Iraq and Afghanistan. We're talking about big, big bucks. I think because he'd been in the military, he was able to jump through the hoops faster than most of us. DOD clearance and all that. I applied for a lot of the same things but got nowhere."

"Makes you wonder why he wouldn't explain all this to his wife?"

"Because Dean McKellar never has and never will be able to keep his pecker in his pants," he said. "Wherever he has an office, he has a girlfriend. Even with me, a guy who was his partner and supposedly a trusted friend, he was very secretive. Within just a few years, he was able to swindle me out of almost everything. It nearly ruined my name and my career. For Dean it's all about ego. He can't help but be a liar, be deceitful. I mean, look at Addison. She's one of the most beautiful, sweet, and genuinely funny women I've ever met. They have two great kids. But I guarantee Dean has found a way to royally fuck that up while giving pep talks to the Jaycees about his family values. He is a dishonest and deceitful piece of shit."

"Well," Hayes said, rubbing his jawline and smiling. "No need to dip it in sugar. If you were me, where would you start looking for him?"

"Where does Addison think he is?"

"London, but I'd rather keep my investigation to the 901," Hayes said. "Do you know some folks here who may have worked with him recently? Someone who's more acquainted with his business with the government?"

Dawson shook his head. "I'm sorry," he said. "I try to stay as far away from that man as possible. But there are a few workers who might have stayed on with him. Might give you a place to start. Give me a second."

Dawson disappeared and Hayes stood up and walked over to the big window to get a closer look at the slick streets and backed-up taillights. Dawson seemed all right and to be shooting straight, but Porter had learned long ago to watch his ass in white Memphis. Although Porter didn't have a problem working with white people. A few years back, he'd gone down deep in the rabbit hole with a white reporter for the *Commercial Appeal* named Sawyer. What they'd uncovered together was a conspiracy that few people knew about or would ever believe. Sawyer had ended up at the *Washington Post* and Hayes made a mental note to give him a call. Maybe he'd have some insight into these government contracts Alec Dawson was talking about.

"Here you go," Dawson said, handing Hayes a page of printed names and contacts. "Hope this helps. And please give my best to Addison and the kids. How old is Preston now?"

"I believe she said ten."

"He's a good kid," Dawson said. "Too bad his father is an asshole."

"Last night, someone broke into the McKellar home," Hayes said. "Preston was the one who tripped the alarm and scared the man off. The intruder was a big man with a beard. Only had one arm. Ever hear of anyone like that?"

"Big man with one arm?" Dawson said. "No. *Jesus*. Is she okay?"

"Yeah," Hayes said. "I think so. But this man seemed intent on doing Dean McKellar some harm."

"He'll have to get in the line," Dawson said. "I don't have names, but I guarantee I'm not the only person Dean has fucked over. He just can't help himself. It's in his nature."

Hayes stopped by 201 Poplar on the way back to the office, finding an open parking space behind Liberty Bail Bonds. 201 was the epicenter of law enforcement for Shelby County. The sheriff, the police, the county jail, and the criminal courts all resided in the twelve-story building with mirrored windows—one-stop shopping for lawyers, reporters, and bondsmen. Porter went through security and took the elevator up to the third floor to find Sergeant Lantana Jones. Jones was the daughter of his former partner Eddie Lamont, who'd proudly served MPD for more than forty years before retiring to a farm out in Paris, Tennessee.

Her glass office door was open but Hayes knocked anyway.

Lantana looked sharp in her blue uniform, sergeant stripes on her left arm and gold shield pinned on her chest. He remembered when she was just a little girl in pigtails out in Bartlett, running around backyard barbecues while he and Eddie smoked and burned ribs, swapped war stories, and drank cheap beer. She hung up the phone and turned to him. "Mr. Hayes," she said. "I haven't seen you in a week. Last time, you were complaining about parking tickets. And before that, you were telling me about one of my officers hanging up on your old girlfriend. The esteemed former Councilwoman Frank. You do realize I have more work than just tending to your personal business? No disrespect."

"None taken," Hayes said. "How's Eddie?"

"Oh, you know," she said. "Complains about every damn thing. If it's not his back, it's my momma. And if it ain't my momma, he's trying to explain to me how to do my damn job."

"Looks like you're doing just fine for yourself," Hayes said, walking on into the small office. There was a huge stack of blue files on her desk and full bin of overnight reports. It never stopped raining in District 1.

"Desk sergeant beats checking meters," she said. "Again, no disrespect. But Mr. Hayes, what brings you to darken my door this rainy morning?"

"Addison McKellar," he said. "Rich white lady from Central Gardens looking for her missing husband."

Lantana Jones nodded and smiled. "Yeah, I thought that woman was crazy at first, her running around saying that folks had taken over her husband's office and didn't have a right to be there. She told two of my officers that she wasn't going anywhere until she got answers. You know, demanding some fine customer service like we were Shoney's or some shit. What's that got to do with you?"

"Addison McKellar is my client."

"Oh, no."

"But the good news is that she's not crazy," he said. "And her husband is really missing."

"Said he was missing in London," Lantana said. "I told her that I didn't have Sherlock Holmes's ass on speed dial. But if I knew she was working with you, I might not have made that joke. You being the Black Sherlock Holmes and everything."

"Your daddy used to say that," Hayes said. "More of an insult than anything after I went private."

"That sounds like Daddy," she said. "So you came by to see if we have anything for you? Right? Before you ask, I'll have to stop you right there. Last night, we had two murders, eight car jackings, and seventeen robberies. Not that I don't shed a tear for some nice white lady and her poor rich husband over in swinging ole London. But you've been a cop, Mr. Hayes. I don't have time for all this mess."

"Did you know a man broke into her house last night?" Hayes asked. "And threatened her with a knife?"

"Excuse me if I haven't gotten halfway through the overnights," she said. "You want me to send out a unit?"

"Y'all already did," he said. "I just wanted you to be aware that something really funky is going on with this man Dean McKellar. The man with the knife said he was looking for her husband, but that her husband was actually someone named Peter Collinson, which I think is another identity for Dean McKellar. You know I'm good. *Real good.* Memphis's own Sherlock Holmes and all. But I don't have access to the NCIS. Figured you might want to take a crack."

"I said the Black Sherlock, not Memphis's own," she said. "There's a difference."

"Oh, yeah?" Hayes said, grinning. "Who else does what I do in the city?"

Lantana smiled back and leaned over her desk, shuffling through the overnight reports. She asked the address in Central Gardens and Porter told her. After a few minutes, she found the report she was looking for and went through two sheets, nodding along.

"One-armed man?" she said. "What the fuck is this, Mr. Hayes? The goddamn circus come to town?"

"Figured he'd be easy to spot," he said. "But in the meantime, you might want to cross-reference those McKellar files and add that name I told you about."

"Okay, okay," she said. "How about some coffee?"

"Already had some," he said. "And I don't ever, ever drink coffee at the 201. It's part of my personal code."

"Yeah," she said. "Can't say I blame you. But I got to tell you something, Mr. Hayes. Not because you're Daddy's best buddy and all that. Just one professional to another."

Hayes smoothed down his mustache and widened his eyes. The cubicles in the next room bustled with energy and chirping phones. Things looked a lot different from when he was one of the only Black cops working out of the cold basement of the original station over on Adams.

"And?" Hayes said.

"I just happened to meet a fine Black man early this morning," she said. "Dressed way better than you. Sharp suit and spit-shined shoes, flashing me his badge. You see, the feds are interested in Mr. Dean McKellar or Peter Whosis or whatever the hell that man's name is. Seems like he did something really wrong and really bad, and this man who came to me—" Lantana looked down at her notebook and back to Hayes. "Carson Wells. Mr. Wells said folks better pray to the good Lord that the government gets to this McKellar before some other folks do."

"Did he say why?" Hayes said. "Or who?"

"Did you miss the part where I said he was a goddamn fed?" she said. "Those boys wouldn't say shit if their mouths were full of it."

"Ain't that the truth."

"Better stick close to your client," Lantana Jones said, picking up a ringing phone but not saying hello. "Looks like she's about to earn every bit of those diamonds she had on her."

11

Joanna

Once a month, the King's Keepsakes hosted a reading and signing by the legendary Joanna Grayson, award-winning actress and Elvis's costar in *Easy Come, Easy Go*. (The award-winning part was a Golden Globe nomination for a trashy Jackie Collins miniseries in which she had to wrestle Suzanne Somers in a swimming pool.) The souvenir shop wasn't owned by the Presley estate, which was one of the reasons Joanna preferred holding her *One Night with You: The Joanna Grayson Story* book-signing events there. Over the years, there had been a few squabbles and threats from Elvis Presley Enterprises that she wouldn't even dignify with a response. She only agreed to nonsanctioned events during Death Week and had even attempted to launch a rival event at the Motel 6 by the airport called "Intimate Close-Ups: Elvis's Favorite Costars." It was almost a runaway smash if not for the petty money-grubbers with the estate who slapped Joanna with an injunction for breaking copyright laws.

It was raining that afternoon and Tippi had driven Joanna, per usual, to the shop on Elvis Presley Boulevard, where she was disappointed but not shocked to find only the dirty dozen regulars who always showed without ever buying the book. *Was forty-two dollars really too much for a nicely bound paperback?* If a fan wanted to know the full and complete story about the making of *Easy Come, Easy Go*, they'd have to buy the book.

"Call me when you're finished," Tippi said.

Joanna leaned back inside the clunky Ford Fiesta to retrieve her lucky black umbrella. Would this rain ever let up? She felt as if she were back in London.

"And where will you be?"

"Running errands."

"Please," Joanna said. "You're meeting up with that tour guide again. The one with the tattoos and the greasy hair."

"His name is Mark, Mother."

"I don't want to meddle in your affairs, but there's no future there."

"I know," Tippi said. "That's what makes him such a dish. Oh, and please make it at least an hour this time. Anything less is just a waste."

Joanna shook her head and closed the creaky car door. She'd made Tippi pull up deep into the parking lot so no one would see the horror of a car they'd arrived in. But it was too late, the dirty dozen had already spotted her and clapped and whistled, to her mortification. A pimply-faced little young man named Fritz who bused tables at Pete and Sam's held the door, saying "How are you today, Miss Grayson?" as if he'd been the concierge at Chateau Marmont.

A card table covered in a blue cloth had been set up by the cash register with two dozen copies of her tell-all biography. Joanna filled her lungs with air, brightened her smile, and greeted the store owner with a warm hug. He asked if she'd noticed the marquee outside advertising her appearance and said he was sorry about the weather, surely dampening the big crowd he'd been expecting at noon on a Thursday.

"I have you a comfortable chair and a microphone, Miss Grayson," he said. "Unless you'd rather just keep it informal?"

She watched as the dirty dozen and a few new faces filled a smattering of folding chairs. Most of them elderly or morbidly obese. One haggard fellow in a Grizzlies tank top had parked his red Rascal scooter directly in her path to the table. "Excuse me," she said, grinding her teeth into a smile.

"Getting there is half the fun, baby," he said.

She tilted her head.

"It's from the movie," he said. "You remember? That sexy girl had her arms around Elvis's neck while he tried to make his way through that beatnik party. *Easy Come, Easy Go.* You were in it."

"Yes," she said. "Of course I was. I'll never forget the beatnik scene. Pure magic."

Joanna took her place by the card table to a smattering of applause and instead of starting with sordid tales of Hollywood decided to go straight into autopilot, using the event as more of a therapy session than presentation. She talked of the untimely death of her dear father (the war hero turned abusive alcoholic), her mother (cold, manipulative, but a natty dresser), and then finding herself living in swinging London at sixteen and lying about her age. She lived off fags and thickly poured beer from the pubs, sleeping on the couches of David Bailey and Terence Stamp, who thought she was at least twenty.

"My mother had such an acute dislike for me," she said. "We didn't speak for years. She was jealous of the way men threw themselves at my feet, once telling me she wished I'd died in childbirth."

The room grew very quiet as the rain tapped against the windows fronting Elvis Presley, Tippi probably already shacked up at some horrid motel with that greasy tattooed Mark. Tippi was like a finely tuned Italian automobile that everyone took for a spin.

Feeling the temperature in the room chill, Joanna added, "I think that's what connected me to Elvis. He had such a strong bond with Gladys, and maybe that's why he could never understand the relationship I had with my misguided mother. When I told him this after a very tough day of shooting the comedy bits with Frank McHugh as Captain Jack, he held my hand and wept. I will never forget what he said to me, looking deep at me with his wonderful, soulful blue eyes. *Little darlin', your momma may not have been there for you, but deep down you got to know she loved you.*"

Joanna smiled and looked at the group hanging on her every word. A few of the women were crying, blubbering really. The horrid man on the scooter slipped on a pair of big gold glasses like Elvis wore in the seventies and glanced around like a confused buffoon. A few hands shot up, the crowd knowing it was time to ask the most inane and ridiculous questions that sprang into their tiny minds. Surely the Chinese or Russians had developed a similar torture.

Do you think Elvis was murdered? Was that really you scuba diving, or a stunt double?

What can you tell us more about Elvis's monkey, Scatter? What was he really like?

That's when she'd give the cat with the canary grin and pick up the nearest copy of *One Night with You: The Joanna Grayson Story.* "Darlings. Darlings. It's all in the book. Even the King's chimp."

As they laughed, even those who'd heard that little joke a million times, she noticed a man who hung back at the far edge of the shop who did not seem to belong with all the outcasts and Elvis Presley acolytes. He was much younger, perhaps early thirties, and extremely handsome. A trim Black man who appeared to be impeccably dressed in a black suit and black tie, wearing mirrored sunglasses despite being indoors on a very gray and rainy day. All she could think about was Sidney Poitier in *Guess Who's Coming to Dinner.*

After Joanna wrapped her talk and took a few photos, the handsome man wandered over and picked up a book as if inspecting a piece of rotten fruit. He flipped it over and read the back copy. "You really go out with Jerry Lewis?"

"Unfortunately," she said. "He was as clumsy in the bedroom as he was on-screen."

The man set the book down, removed his mirrored sunglasses, and tucked them into his jacket. "You do know it says the exact same thing on the back. *He was as clumsy in the bedroom as he was on-screen.* Ain't that something?"

"I pull few punches." She looked into the handsome man's brown eyes, giving him the same look she had given Richard Harris, Jerry, and Elvis all those years ago. She lifted her eyebrows, took in a deep breath, and smiled. She patted the edge of his face, noticing a nasty little scar right below his right eye. "Aren't you a dish?"

"Is there somewhere else we can go," the young man said, "and talk?"

"Why not?"

Tippi wasn't the only one who got to have a little fun. She whipped through several more copies, scrawling out her quickie signature. Even though only two people bought the book, scores of people would be in and out of King's Keepsakes and see the pyramid display.

Joanna stood up and smoothed down the hem of her dress. It was a well-fitting slim pink number she had bought at Saks in New York during more heady times. "And who might you be?"

"Carson Wells," the man said. "I've been wanting to meet you for a good long while, Miss Grayson."

Joanna joined the man at the Blue Suede Diner, a sad enterprise across from Graceland that sold little else but burgers, peanut butter and banana sandwiches, Coca-Cola products, and three flavors of shakes. From the window, she watched a line of white tour buses that ferried the devout across the busy boulevard. Even though lunch hadn't been offered, Joanna took the occasion to order a club sandwich and a chocolate milkshake. He had invited her, and she was absolutely famished.

"Do you live here in Memphis?" she asked, eating a neat quarter of the sandwich. "Or are you visiting?"

"Guess you could say I'm here on business."

"And what kind of business are you in, Mr. Wells?" Joanna asked.

"I work for the federal government."

"How exciting." Joanna leaned forward and sipped from her straw. "Doing what, may I ask?"

"I'm with the FBI," Wells said, reaching into his jacket pocket and flipping open a gold badge and ID. "I investigate major crimes."

She wanted to do a spit take but instead swallowed while keeping the easygoing smile. "And yet you had time to attend my book event," she said. "I'm flattered."

"The pleasure was all mine, Miss Grayson," Wells said, reaching out and grabbing a french fry without being asked. "Joyriding with Elvis in that dune buggy sure sounded like fun. Sounds like he and his boys were all just a crew of goofy peckerwoods."

"Elvis was so much more," Joanna said, trying to calm down a little bit. Surely this man, Carson Wells, was here looking into Omar's death. There must have been another security camera at the antiques mall, catching her standing over Omar's lifeless body atop all those lovely rugs.

"This may be blasphemous, being where we are and all," Wells said, "but I never really gave a damn about Elvis."

"The man or the music?"

"Both," he said. "I guess it has something to do with him ripping off Black folks, doing his little minstrel show thing, and then acting like he was the one invented it."

It had been some time, actually decades, since she'd heard anyone say anything remotely bad about Elvis Presley. Especially being in the Memphis Elvis bubble where everyone flat worshipped the man.

"I promise Elvis's love and appreciation for Black artists was quite genuine, Mr. Wells," she said. "I know for a fact that he praised many Black entertainers. I remember him calling Sammy Davis a dear and personal friend."

"No shit," Wells said, flashing that beautiful grin. "Ole Sammy D. This all coming from you knowing Elvis—what—a few weeks? He told you all about how he really felt about Black folks back in sixty-nine?"

"Sixty-seven," she said. "And it was much more than a few weeks. We remained friends until his untimely death."

Wells leaned back into his chair and showed the palms of his hands. "No need to get testy," Wells said. "Just making a little conversation, Miss Grayson. I got nothing against ole Elvis the Pelvis. I just was feeling you out, trying to get to know you a little better."

Joanna hadn't touched the second half of her sandwich. Thinking you might be the target of a murder investigation tended to sour one's stomach.

"Mr. Wells, I worked in Hollywood for a great many years," she said. "And to put it kindly, I'm quite familiar with the smell of bullshit. Is there something you want to ask? My work with the Presley family puts me in contact with a great many attorneys."

"And how do you expect to pay them, Joanna?" he asked, snatching up another fry. "You're living on the edge of the American dream in some shithole apartment with your grown-up daughter. Barely eking out a living. But it's cool. I'm not here to grill you about that poor dead son of a bitch at the antiques mall on Summer Avenue. We both know his dumb dead ass was just collateral damage."

Joanna stopped breathing and offered a most impassive expression she'd picked up from dear Judy Geeson.

"I came to talk about your close and personal friend, Jonathan Devlin."

"Devlin?" she said. "Who on earth is that?"

"Peter Warwick?"

She shook her head.

"Dean McKellar?"

Again, she shook her head. She was beginning to think Carson Wells was as mad as the fans who claim to communicate with Elvis. She motioned for the waiter to please bring her a to-go bag. *No use in wasting a perfectly good club sandwich*, she thought as she fumbled in her bag for her phone.

"*Peter Collinson?*" he said.

She stopped fiddling. She looked up at him.

"*Ding, ding,*" he said. "I do believe I have a winner."

"I honestly have no idea what or who you are talking about," she said. "I should have never accepted an invitation from a complete stranger."

"This is no free lunch, lady," he said. "This is a federal goddamn investigation and I'm looking for your Peter Collinson. If you don't assist me, you may be writing a sequel to your book behind prison walls."

"Surely you're joking," she said.

Joanna looked back out into the portico lined with buses, their windshield wipers slapping back and forth. She searched for Tippi but only saw a snaking line of tourists waiting to take a photo in front of a Graceland facade.

"I don't give a damn what he calls himself," Wells said, tossing a business card onto the table. "His ass is burnt. You need to come clean with everything about y'all's little import/export business before this shit hits the goddamn fan. Nobody in his world will come out smellin' clean."

"You can go to hell."

"And here I thought we had a little thing going," Wells said. "Some spitfire cougar action. If I weren't on the job and you were a little younger, I sure wouldn't mind us sliding under the sheets."

"Ha," Joanna said. "Do you really know who I am and the things I've done? I'd leave you in the corner calling out for your dear mother and sucking your thumb."

"Whew," Wells said, standing and leaving the bill on the table. "I sure like the sound of that. Catch you later, movie star."

Joanna paid the bill and walked into the adjoining welcome center to find the phone booths, Graceland one of the last places that still kept working pay phones in their shabby lobby. Her hands shook as she removed an international calling card from her change purse, but she found the first phone as dead as Marley's doornail. Moving onto the next, she heard a ringtone and carefully dialed the number Peter had made her memorize, quizzing her from time to time during their furtive lunches in Memphis, discussing her latest business with the mad Leslie Grimes. The sound cacophonous, almost underwater, the slow droning buzzing of European telephone service. She counted ten rings, deciding on twelve to hang up, when she heard the voice of a very groggy Peter pick up and ask, "What time is it?"

"Thank god," Joanna said. "Peter, is it really you?"

"I told you not to call me."

"Unless it was an emergency."

"Yes," he said. "I must have fallen asleep. What is it?"

"Something horrid is happening."

Peter didn't answer, just the underwater buzzing of the foreign connection.

"Don't worry," she said. "I'm on a secure line at Graceland."

"Graceland?" he said. "Christ. What do you want, Joanna?"

"Omar is dead," she said.

"Yes," he said. "I heard. Is that it?"

"A federal agent just came to my book event," she said. "He was a horrible arrogant man and said he'd put me in jail if I didn't help him find you."

"Calm down," he said. "Jesus. I'm sorry about Omar but that doesn't have anything to do with you. Okay? Everything will be fine. What exactly did you tell this supposed agent?"

Joanna took a deep breath and glanced about the ticket lobby. She felt as if everyone was staring directly at her. Perhaps that old woman in the bedazzled tank top was an undercover agent, watching her every move. Joanna turned her back.

"Damn it," she said. "Just what on earth have you concocted with Leslie Grimes? He's my client. Not yours."

Peter didn't answer, but she could hear him groaning as if lifting himself from a bed. He heard a woman speaking French and he said back to her, *Rien. Ce n'est rien.* So now Joanna was absolutely nothing.

"I cultivated Leslie when I ran the gallery in Beverly Hills," she said. "I must insist on being a part of any deal that you've forged with Leslie Grimes or his wife, Roberta."

"It's nothing."

"You just said I am nothing."

"I said this is nothing," he said. "I have to go, Joanna. We don't know who is listening."

"No one, Peter," she said, answering her name with his name. "Or should I call you Jonathan Devlin? Or Dean McKellar?"

"Have you been drinking?"

"I've never been more clearheaded in my life," Joanna said. "But please don't force me to talk to this horrid FBI man."

"Wait," he said. "Why do you say FBI?"

"He said he was a federal agent," she said. "I was giving a presentation and he was following me. I can't have that."

"What's his name?"

"What does that matter?"

"What was his name, Joanna?"

"Carson Wells," she said. "I thought him quite handsome before he turned on me."

"Jesus," Peter said, laughing. "Let me guess. This Carson Wells was Black. About six feet, slender, with a small scar below his right eye?"

"You know him?"

"Yes," Peter said. "Only his name isn't Wells, and he's no federal agent."

"Who is he?"

"A business competitor," he said. "I want you to stay away from this man. If he approaches you again, tell him you're going to call the police. He's not who he says he is."

"And what about Leslie?" she asked. "I want in, Peter. I actually insist on it. You poached my client. And people are intruding on my personal appearances. Do you understand I found my dear friend Omar face down in a pile of Persian rugs? What kind of mess have you made?"

Peter didn't answer. The Frenchwoman again calling to him. Joanna could hear a hand cover the receiver and then Peter returned. "Yes," he said. "Everything is such a goddamn mess. I need to think and get my head right. I'll explain everything to you tomorrow."

"You will call me?"

"No," Peter said. "I'll see you. I'm flying home."

The line went dead and double-clicked over to a very hollow American dial tone. Joanna cupped her hand over her mouth, knowing she could never ever trust Peter Collinson, and hoped to God that no one would be coming for her the way they came for Omar.

She composed herself and headed out from the little alcove, running right into Tippi. Her heart nearly stopped and she gasped. "Good gracious," she said. "You nearly scared the life out of me."

"Mother," she said, looking stoned and disheveled, "why are you using a pay phone?"

"I had to make a quick call."

"You do realize you can do that on your cell," she said. "We've been over this."

"Yes, yes," Joanna said, taking Tippi's arm. Tippi absolutely reeked of marijuana. In that very moment, Joanna recalled long motorbike rides with Steve McQueen up and around Mulholland and Laurel Canyon. "Shall we go? I am truly exhausted from my appearance, darling."

"And the event?"

"A smash," Joanna said. "An absolute smash. The loveliest people. The most intelligent questions. I could've talked for hours."

"Why must you always lie, Mother?"

"Everyone lies, Tippi," she said. "Some of us just do it much better than others."

12

Addison

Even with two police cars parked along Belvedere, she'd barely slept. The morning came and went. The same old routine of Josefina arriving at six thirty sharp and making coffee and starting breakfast while Addison woke the kids. The old house seemed larger and even more empty in the daylight. Last night, Preston had slept in her bed worried that the one-armed man would return. She didn't blame him. She'd held Preston tight and lied, saying everything was okay and he'd been a hero by setting off the alarm. But in truth, the man had both scared the hell out of her and confused her. *Who the hell was Peter Collinson and what did he have to do with Dean's disappearance?* Mr. Hayes had shown up last night and talked with the police, but he insisted on searching for Dean today on his own while she got a rest. That's funny, even with two Klonopin, she could barely close her eyes. She sat in Dean's study, curled up on his manly leather couch that reeked of cigars and whiskey, when the phone rang and a caller ID showed Sara Caroline's school was calling. *For fuck's sake, what could it be now?*

"Mrs. McKellar?" a woman said. "This is Miss Perry at Hutchison. Sara Caroline is here with me in my office. I wonder if you might be able to pick her up early? There's been a small incident."

"A small incident?" Addison said, throwing her head back on Dean's leather couch and staring at the ceiling. "Is she okay?"

"Sara Caroline is fine."

"I'm so sorry," Addison said. "But can you handle this and we can talk later? At the moment, I'm juggling some very complicated personal issues."

"I'm sorry to hear that," Miss Perry said. "But your daughter assaulted a member of her lacrosse team this morning. I've had a nice chat with both girls. But we feel it's best if you could come and pick her up."

"What happened?"

"Sara Caroline says her stick slipped and she accidentally broke Bailey Carlisle's nose."

"But you have your doubts?"

"Mm-hmm."

"How bad is it?" Addison asked.

"We feel Bailey may be out for some time," she said. "There was a lot of blood. Plastic surgery has been discussed."

Forty-five minutes later, Addison was out of her silk pajamas and into her uniform of leggings and a black T-shirt and sitting in Miss Perry's office. This wasn't the first time she'd been invited into Miss Perry's office. In the spring, Sara Caroline had decided to call her geometry teacher a bitch, denying the whole thing but later admitting that she'd said it, but under her breath. "There's no freakin' way she heard me," Sara Caroline had said, pleading with her and Dean not to be grounded.

"Sara Caroline said there's been some problems at home," Miss Perry said, which Addison thought was a rude comment as it was absolutely none of her business.

Miss Perry—only the DMV and God knew her first name—was in her late fifties or early sixties but seemed to have been at Hutchison since the very founding of the school after the turn of the last century. She wore her stark white hair in a blunt bob and had the calm, irritating voice of an NPR announcer.

"We are looking at suspension," Miss Perry said.

"For how long?"

"That's up to the administration."

"Christ," Addison said, looking to Sara Caroline, sulking in her black-and-gold lacrosse uniform. "Can you just please hold off on that for a while? Like I said, I have some very complicated personal issues I'm juggling."

"And we are very sorry to hear that," she said. "Has there been a death in the family?"

Sara Caroline looked over at her, her long blond hair obscuring most of her face. Her eyes looked red and puffy from crying.

"Not yet," Addison said. "But I wouldn't be surprised."

"How terrible," Miss Perry said, fingering the white hair away from her glasses. "I don't mean to pry, but is someone ill?"

Miss Perry seemed to delight in having the upper hand this morning, probably still nursing a sore ass from the argument she'd had with Addison last year about the whole "bitch" incident. She'd just love to suspend her daughter for as long as possible, even though Bailey Carlisle probably would've gotten a nose job anyway. Half of Bailey's mother had been redone in the shop, from her overinflated lips to her massive breasts that she loved to show off in tight little sparkly tops.

Addison said nothing. She smiled.

"Sara Caroline's father is out of the country," she said. "It's added a lot of pressure in the house."

"That's bullshit, Mom," Sara Caroline said. "I heard you and Aunt Libby last night. Dad is missing. You don't know where the fuck he's gone."

"Sara Caroline."

Addison was pretty sure she saw a smile on Miss Perry's face. Why is it that people with the smallest offices and the tiniest amount of power like to complicate other people's lives? If Miss Perry could just get out and get some perspective, she would realize there was more to the world than the revolving soap opera of teenage girls at Hutchison. Real-world problems like one-armed burglars making goddamn turkey sandwiches in her unfinished kitchen late in the night. Or a husband who flew off to London only to completely go off the grid. So sorry for little Bailey Carlisle and her busted nose. But she did not have time for this.

"The headmaster will be calling later," Miss Perry said.

"That's it?" Addison said.

"I'm afraid so," Miss Perry said. "And I'm sorry to hear about your personal issues."

Addison stood up and motioned for Sara Caroline to come on. Sara Caroline, still in knee socks and cleats and wielding the offending weapon like a staff, walked with her to the door.

"I do know a number of family therapists that might help," Miss Perry said.

"That's so very kind of you, Miss Perry," Addison said. "I bet you can't wait to pass along to the staff and all the other parents that the McKellars' perfect little family has turned to dog shit."

"Everything we say here is private."

"As it should be."

"But we can't have our girls assaulting each other," she said. "Several girls said Sara Caroline used her stick as a weapon."

"It slipped," Sara Caroline said.

Addison closed her eyes and held up the flat of her hand.

"Come on," she said. "Let's go home."

As they walked through the halls and toward the front offices, Addison muttered under her breath, "Why'd you do it?"

"Bailey Carlisle is a supreme bitch," she said. "She told everyone that Dad had left us because you were dating some old Black pimp. And that you and this Black man had shown up at the Club yesterday making a big scene."

So this is how fast it all starts.

Addison walked past the school secretaries and toward the front door to the parking lot. She held the door for her daughter. "How much blood?" Addison asked.

"So much," Sara Caroline said. "What's going on, Mom?"

Out in the school parking lot, Alec Dawson was standing by Addison's Escalade.

It had been some time since she'd seen Alec. When their business partnership split, Dean had forbidden her to even talk to Alec's wife, Susan, who was now Alec's ex-wife. And even worse, he wouldn't let

Sara Caroline have anything to do with Alec's daughter, Ellie, despite them being friends since preschool. The whole business breakup had been worse than any nasty divorce. Addison hadn't seen Alec since the Cotton Carnival two years ago, where they caught each other's eye across the banquet floor and Addison offered only a slight nod. She'd felt like such a bitch.

"Hello," she said.

Sara Caroline, dirty and disheveled, cut her eyes at Addison, knowing how her father felt about Alec Dawson. She and Sara Caroline stood shoulder to shoulder under a big green-and-white golf umbrella.

"Picking up Ellie," he said. "Orthodontist."

Alec had on a navy raincoat over his suit and held up a black umbrella. The rain had settled into a slight drizzle, dappling the puddles. His dark hair was wet, slicked back from his forehead. His light blue eyes seemed to go soft, something like sympathy in them, and Addison thought, *Holy fucking shit, he's heard something, too.*

"Mom," Sara Caroline said.

"In a minute," Addison said, pressing unlock on her key fob. Sara Caroline walked ahead and placed her stick inside the SUV. "I need to talk to Mr. Dawson."

"Mom."

"In a minute."

Sara Caroline crawled into the passenger seat and slammed the door. Alec smiled and reached out to Addison's shoulder. "I met with Mr. Hayes this morning," he said. "I told him everything I knew about Dean. I'm so very sorry for you guys, Addy. Shit. I wish I could do something, but you know I haven't talked to Dean in a really long time."

"Did you hear that I made a big scene at the Club yesterday?"

"I haven't been to the Club in years," he said. "I hate that damn place."

"What did you tell Mr. Hayes?"

"I told him about Dean embezzling from the company," he said. "I told him about the lawsuit. And I told him about all the affairs. I'm sorry, but I figured you'd want me to be straightforward and honest."

"What affairs?"

Alec laughed. Not in an asshole-ish way, but as if something was genuinely funny.

"I'm serious, Alec," she said. "Jesus. What are you saying?"

"I said I wasn't surprised that Dean had disappeared," he said. "He has girlfriends all over the place. You know that."

"Sure." Addison reached up with her free hand and grabbed a hunk of hair, trying to stifle a scream. "Fuck," she said. "Fuck, fuck, fuck."

"I'm sorry," he said. "I figured you knew."

Alec rested a hand on Addison's shoulder. He continued to stare at her with his clear blue eyes. The dark outline of a beard on his jawline. He looked as solid and steady as she was wobbly on her feet. She recalled a time back in college when she'd been trashed and he'd hoisted her over his shoulder, carried her into her apartment, and tucked her in bed. She awoke the next day in her cocktail dress, a small trash can positioned thoughtfully next to the bed.

"I didn't know," she said. "But I suspected. Where do you think he is, Alec?"

"Mr. Hayes said you told him London."

"It's been more than a week," she said. "Nothing. The kids are scared. Preston ran off a lunatic with one arm from our house last night."

"I heard."

"And today Sara Caroline broke Bailey Carlisle's nose with her lacrosse stick," she said. "Because apparently people are saying that Porter Hayes and I are a hot item because we showed up at the Club to ask that son of a bitch Jimbo Hornsby what he knew."

Alec shook his head, water beading off the top of his black umbrella. The rain picked up and slanted sideways in the lot. "I could've saved you the trouble," Alec said. "Jimbo Hornsby would eat dog shit if Dean told him to. He's been protecting his dirty deeds for years."

Addison bit her lip. She could see Sara Caroline pouting behind the windshield, occasionally looking at her mother and shaking her head.

"Dean said you were the one who stole from the company," she said. "He called you a pathological liar."

"Of course he did," Alec said. "Dean does for Dean."

Addison looked straight at Alec, who was still so comforting and familiar, a huge part of her life going all the way back to Ole Miss. He'd been a KA and she'd been a KD, and after a million frat parties and late nights off the Square, they'd become really great friends. Then they'd both ended up in Manhattan, and Alec worked at the same firm as Dean. *A really cool guy you just have to meet.* Dean had arrived early to a Christmas party and Alec was late . . .

"I think he's dead."

"Don't say that, Addy," he said. "I hate Dean's guts more than anyone. But I don't want that on my conscience."

"I'm serious," she said. "He wouldn't disappear like this. For the last two years I thought Dean got up and went to his nice office downtown. Wrong. There's no fucking office. I thought he had a nice secretary who took care of all his business. Wrong. It was some big redneck woman down in Southaven who does dirty work for Jimbo Hornsby. And now you're telling me that he's been fucking everything that moves."

Inside the Escalade, Sara Caroline had scooted over in the driver's seat and started to mash the horn. Just when Addison thought they'd developed a nice mother-daughter bond, up walks her husband's archenemy to spotlight Sara Caroline's true loyalties. A daddy's girl to the last.

"Can I call you?" she said.

"Anytime," Alec said. "I want to help."

He offered another sympathetic smile but she didn't mind it at all. She smiled back and opened the driver's door, watching Sara Caroline scoot over.

"Dad hates that man's guts."

"I know."

"I don't trust him, either."

"Maybe we should," Addison said. "You're old enough to understand exactly what's been going on."

13

Leslie

The rain had let up long enough in Hot Springs for Leslie Grimes to welcome Pastor Randy out onto his sprawling back deck overlooking Lake Hamilton. The good pastor came to talk to Leslie about his work as an entrepreneur, a philanthropist, a father, a husband, and most importantly a Christian. Pastor Randy's faith segments were viewed by millions of people across the globe on YouTube and translated into sixteen different languages, according to Leslie's wife of forty-three years, Roberta, and their grandson, Leslie III.

The sunset behind the Grimeses' Mediterranean Revival house was nearly perfect, spreading a lovely orange light across the lake like a scene out of the Old Testament. The two men were seated at a table, very low-key and conversational. Pastor Randy, dressed in all black like Johnny Cash, beamed with health and charity as he congratulated Leslie on his latest million-dollar gift to Oral Roberts University. A crew had set up a small camera on a tripod and looped a lapel mic up under Leslie's navy blazer with gold buttons.

"Your generosity is overwhelming," Pastor Randy said. "Just where does that come from, Mr. Grimes?"

"Probably my mother," Grimes said, closing his eyes. "Mother thought of her family and her community before she ever thought of herself. My daddy was a door-to-door Bible salesman, and we got by day to day, week to week. He was a good man who drank a lot. Mother kept us all straight. I don't remember her owning more than two dresses at a time. I can still see them hanging on spindly wire hangers in her closet, threadbare and faded from drying in the sun. She instilled a love of hard work, generosity, and Christ in all of us."

"And it was your mother who loaned you and your wife two thousand dollars to start up Tomes and Treasures?"

"Right in downtown Blytheville by the seed and feed," he said. "My momma had been saving that money for years. We began with Easter gifts and then moved into engraving Bibles and selling silk flowers, inspirational gifts, and such. And over the last few decades, we've grown it into a multibillion-dollar business with over nine hundred stores across this great nation."

"Incredible," Pastor Randy said. "Just incredible."

"We are truly blessed."

"Amen," Pastor Randy said.

"Amen," Leslie said. "I couldn't have done it without Roberta. We've been married more than forty years. We have a brood of grandkids and even great-grandkids now. We met through our church where we were both helping with the Christmas pageant and recognized our mutual love of arts and crafts. Our first enterprise together was selling Easter baskets and then sugar eggs with dioramas inside. She had a talent. Not only would you see the Easter bunny and chicks cavorting about the tulips, but Jesus as well, high atop of Calvary. Folks came from all over Arkansas for them."

"Some might wonder how a person can be both a Christian and a billionaire," Pastor Randy said.

"Well, I'm a Christian who just happens to run a billion-dollar business," he said. "But Tomes and Treasures belongs to Him. Not to me. Me and Mrs. Grimes are just the stewards. We all are on this earth for just a speck of time, but some things are everlasting, like God's holy word. Finding a way to explain the concrete evidence of the Bible and its message for all people has been my calling."

"Sounds like a major announcement from the foundation."

Grimes offered a sly grin and nodded. "An awful big announcement is coming. It's taken some time, but I feel it will be my legacy."

He was about to tell more about the impending gift from the Leslie and Roberta Grimes Foundation for the Family when everyone heard a tremendous ruckus down by the docks. A man was yelling profanities and threats over the chugging of a boat motor. Pastor Randy told the videographer to stop and Grimes untangled himself from the microphone, winding his way down the marble staircase to find two of his security people and his publicist arguing with a bear of a man who appeared to have only one arm. He figured they'd gotten into him about fishing too close to his dock, but when he turned to Grimes, Grimes darn well knew this was something else entirely.

"Mr. Grimes, I've come a fur piece to talk to you."

"Talk to my assistant."

"Sure thing, Leslie," the one-armed man said. "But I figured you'd rather talk about the whereabouts of Peter Collinson with the man's partner."

"You work with Peter Collinson?"

"Every damn day since 9/11," he said. "Now let me tie up this fucking boat and let's get to gettin'."

"Please," Leslie Grimes said. "Won't you come inside?"

"What's wrong with this fancy-ass porch?" asked the one-armed man. "It ain't raining no more."

"I thought we could speak in private," he said. "About Peter."

"Peter Collinson is a fucking liar," the one-armed man said. "He cornholed us both and I'm the only chance you got to getting square."

"I don't care for that kind of language," Grimes said. "This is my family's home."

"I don't give a good goddamn what you want, Mr. Grimes," the man said. "I'm not here to teach fucking Sunday school. I'm here to talk about business. Your business. Did you, or did you not, have Peter put a foot up my ass and move heaven and earth to get you some Conex container direct out of Istanbul and on the night train to Memphis?"

Grimes shushed him as he held one of his French doors wide open and ushered the man to follow him into the kitchen. A place that Roberta always referred to as Grimes Diner, where they fed the grandkids pancakes and hot dogs on a long granite bar top adorned with ice-cream parlor stools.

"Please sit down."

"I'd just as soon stand up," the man said, pushing past Grimes. He was a brute of a fella, a bull of a man, as Leslie's dear mother would've said. He looked like a defensive tackle for the Razorbacks or maybe a mountain man. That was it, he looked like an even larger version of that Dan Haggerty on *Grizzly Adams*. A man so big and bearded he could wrestle bears up in the mountains even with his obvious physical defect.

"Took a long time to get here," he said.

"You said you came from Memphis."

"I didn't start in Memphis, Q-Tip," he said. "I barely got out of Istanbul with my nut sack. Ended up on a cargo ship that smelled like ass crack and feet all the way to Cairo and then flew to London and then back to Atlanta. I have to admit, the Atlanta airport was the worst of it. Folks talk about Dallas–Fort Worth, but Atlanta is the real asshole of this country."

The man had opened his refrigerator and started to rummage through the inside as if he were a member of the Grimes family. Leslie had seen his second-youngest grandson, Broderick, aka Scooter, do the very same thing. But little Scooter searching for last night's chocolate pie was endearing. This man searching through the contents of his refrigerator felt as invasive as getting a colonoscopy with a garden hose.

"Damn," he said. "That's a good-looking porterhouse."

"My cook said it's enough to feed the whole family."

"She must be stupid as fuck," the man said. "Y'all got some seasonings? Dale's sauce or some of that Tony Chachere?"

Grimes pointed to the cabinetry above the Viking stove. The man rummaged around until he hooked out a container of garlic salt.

"Did you get my messages?"

"Is your name Jack Dumas?"

The one-armed man smiled. He removed the hunk of beef, roughly the size of an Asian elephant ear, and poured the garlic salt out on the meat. "In the flesh," he said. "How come you didn't call me back?"

"You didn't mention Peter Collinson," he said. "You told my assistant you needed to talk business with me. I run a very large company, Mr. Dumas. I get calls like that every day."

"But you remembered my name," he said. "That's good."

"Well," Grimes said, "I guess I should've recognized you. I was told you used a great deal of profanity. And used the Lord's name in vain a number of times."

Dumas pulled out a large cast-iron skillet and set it on the stovetop, clicking the gas up to high. Leslie wanted to tell him there was a much better way to cook that steak, outside on the propane grill set into the Italian marble. But instead he took a seat at the kitchen bar where Roberta served him a boiled egg and a slice of gluten-free toast each morning. Gluten didn't agree with him at all. Since he'd gotten on that new diet that Roberta found in *AARP* magazine, he'd dropped fifteen pounds in the blink of an eye. He might even fit back into his old swim trunks come springtime.

"Why are you here, Mr. Dumas?"

"Well," he said, adding some oil to the skillet, "don't you want to get your shit back?"

"Excuse me?"

"You're acting like some confused old man who's just walked into the picture show late," he said. "If you haven't figured it out yet, Peter Collinson is dead. I worked for the man for ten fuckin' years. I know him better than I knew my own daddy, who was a worthless piece of shit, by the way."

"Perhaps you should forgive him."

"Peter?"

"Your daddy."

"Who the hell cares?" he asked, setting the meat into the skillet. The meat started to sizzle. "Yesterday's news. They're both dead, Leslie. And here's the deal. As Peter's right-hand man"—Dumas held up his right hook and smiled—"I am your best goddamn chance in the world of getting your treasure back."

"Mr. Dumas," Grimes said, surprised by the sound of his own voice, "please. My wife will be down any moment and won't stand for that kind of talk."

"You're awful calm for a man who's put so much effort in hauling a load of junk from the other side of the planet only to let it all slide down the shitter."

The kitchen had started to fill with smoke and the fire alarm started its high-pitched beeping. Dumas grabbed a broom and beat the stuffing out of the alarm, shattering it onto the floor.

Grimes walked over to the French doors and closed them with a sharp click. His staff had left them alone as instructed, but Pastor Randy and his crew had remained on the Italianate patio watching the last of the sunset.

"Thank you for your concern," Grimes said. "But Mr. Collinson is alive and well. A trusted mutual friend has been in touch and told me everything has been worked out."

"A trusted mutual friend?" he said. "Ha. Peter Collinson doesn't have any friends."

"Would you like to take that steak with you?" Grimes said. He was feeling back in charge again, knowing this was just a simple redneck shakedown. "Maybe a doggie bag? I'm sorry you traveled all this way."

"I'm the only one who knows about this fucking Conex," he said. "I know what's in it and just what it means to you. And I know how and when it will arrive in Memphis. Why don't you ask this trusted friend all that?"

"I most certainly will."

"Because when you figure out you've been double cornholed, don't come crying back to me," Dumas said, flipping the steak. "The price of delivery only gets higher by the hour, Leslie. And now that Peter is taking a goddamn dirt nap, I feel I'm free to offer the contents to other parties."

Grimes felt himself sweating a little bit and rubbed his brow with his fingers. The sun was nearly down, and shadows had fallen across the wide patio and out into the lake.

"You said you know the contents?"

Dumas ambled over from the Viking range and stared across the bar at Grimes. He looked back over his shoulder at the smoking skillet and outside to the gathering of Pastor Randy's crew and some of Leslie's personal staff. He'd told them all to give him a minute, but now it had been far longer than a minute. The lights had cut on out on the deck, lighting up the fig and fruit trees, a special time of day that made him think of the Garden of Gethsemane.

Jack Dumas leaned across the bar, Leslie recoiling as he felt the scratchiness of the man's stubble against his cheek. The man whispered two very important words in his ear. The man spoke Greek.

"Did I stutter?"

Leslie's mouth had gone dry. "I need to make some phone calls."

"And so do I," he said. "My patience is being strained."

The man walked back to the range and turned off the gas, pulling the steak off the hot skillet and setting it in the center of the kitchen island to cool.

"How's your faith, Mr. Dumas?"

"Oh, you know," he said. "Folks say there are no atheists in foxholes."

"And in your experience, is that true?"

"Don't know," he said, mulling over the question. "Never been in one. My combat's either been staring down the looking glass or hand to hand. I once killed me a hadji with a Coca-Cola bottle."

"Can you give me a few hours?"

The man didn't even ask for any cutlery, only picked up the big, bloody piece of meat and started eating right off the bone. "How about I come back around in the morning," Dumas said, chewing with his mouth open. "If you're not interested, Peter gave me a list of other folks who'd be glad to put out."

"This man came into my home and ate a porterhouse over my sink," Grimes said.

It was an hour later, Jack Dumas had disappeared, and Grimes had spent the last half hour making excuses to Pastor Randy about the intrusion. He'd barely been able to compose himself and talk fifteen minutes more about the Leslie and Roberta Grimes Foundation for the Family, the one-armed man's foul words still echoing in his ears.

"I never heard of a Jack Dumas," Joanna Grayson said. "And Peter confided in me every small detail. It sounds like some kind of poor shakedown artist. I think you'd do best to stay away from him."

"But he knows."

"I doubt it," she said. "I'm the only one who knows. He may have heard something, but trust me, Leslie. I've been importing valuables from all over the globe since I left the film business. I've worked with both Sotheby's and Christie's. I once handed over a pair of ruby earrings to Liz Taylor that were as big as golf balls. You are more than welcome to check my credentials. *My god.* You wouldn't have even heard of Peter if it hadn't been for me. As far as him being dead, that's an absolute fabrication. I just spoke to Peter this morning. He's been overseeing every detail of the shipment and will be in touch shortly."

"He smelled awful."

"Pardon?"

"This man smelled like the inside of a horse barn," he said. "He used language and manners that were horrific. He called me Q-Tip and attempted to push me around in my own home. He ate a bloody steak with his bare hands."

"Well," Joanna said, sounding as if she was walking and talking at the same time. Her breathing sounded a little labored over the phone. "I would increase security at your home and stay close to the phone. I promise we will be arranging final details once your shipment clears customs."

"*If.*"

"Yes, yes," Joanna said. "I know there were a few issues before, darling. But every, and I mean every, consideration has been taken. The devil lives in the details."

"The devil is everywhere, Miss Grayson," Grimes said, looking down at the empty blackened skillet. Nothing left but the porterhouse bone and fat congealing white and purple. "I don't like people knowing my business."

"I don't know this Jack Dumas," she said. "Let's just all calm down and take a deep breath, and soon your lovely home will be filled with all the treasures of Ali Baba."

The comment about Ali Baba caught Leslie off guard. He looked to the skillet again and then the empty patio, "Ali Baba was a thief," he said. "I'd like to think of us as crusaders."

"Yes, yes, love," she said. "Crusaders. Absolutely. Ta-ta."

14

Porter Hayes

The work wasn't sexy. Never had been. Being an investigator involved a lot of phone calls, long nights in motel parking lots, and getting to know the courthouse clerks' favorite brand of cigarette or booze. A few things had changed, as Darlene was quick to point out. You could find stuff online in seconds that used to take days. Property records, arrest reports, and tracking known associates. At the moment, Darlene was trying to expedite Dean McKellar's service record while Porter dialed his old friend Sawyer who used to work for the *Commercial Appeal* before being called up to the big leagues in D.C. He and Porter kept in touch, connected forever by one big-ass case they worked together in '93 that changed both of their lives.

Hayes leaned back into his cushioned leather chair and placed his zip Italian boots on the window ledge, looking out at the fire escape. He spotted a dead spider plant in a coffee cup and an empty bottle of Rémy that his ex-girlfriend had given him two years ago. That Rémy had lasted longer than the relationship. "Hey, man," he said. "It's Porter Hayes in Memphis."

"As opposed to Porter Hayes in New York City?" Sawyer said. "Or Porter Hayes of San Francisco? Could Porter Hayes exist anywhere else?"

Sawyer had been a young, white hipster who found the world funny when Porter first met him. Now he was an aging hipster who still seemed to find the world a little bit humorous. Man had shaken a lot of trees in Memphis and uncovered a lot of dirty deeds during his time here. Back then, he was the kind of dude who lived on a busted-ass houseboat and wore ironic T-shirts with his sport coats. Old Chuck Taylor sneakers to funerals. Porter wondered if he still dressed that way.

"I need a favor."

Hayes laid out what he knew about Dean McKellar and the current situation. He gave Sawyer the man's date of birth and that he'd been told McKellar served as an army lieutenant in the first Gulf War and was honorably discharged as a captain. "His wife said he's from Upstate New York," he said. "She met him in New York City and then brought him back to Memphis where they married. Central Gardens. Country Club. Two kids. You've seen the movie."

"But never lived the dream," Sawyer said. "Is McKellar a bad guy or a good guy?"

"If I thought he was a good guy, why would I waste a favor?"

"Because I haven't heard from you in a few years?" Sawyer said. "Not even one of your famous Christmas cards."

"I quit on those Christmas cards, man," Hayes said. "Folks complained about me wearing a Santa hat and holding a Smith & Wesson. Listen, I heard this man got hooked up with some big-time DOD contracts. Figured with all those bylines from Baghdad and Kabul, you could find out if that's fact or fiction."

"You have a deadline?"

"PIs don't have deadlines," Hayes said. "But this case does have what I call urgency. I'm working for the wife and she's getting some external pressure."

"That meaning?"

"Some one-armed motherfucker broke into her big-ass house and made some threats."

"Yep," Sawyer said. "That's pressure. How 'bout I call you back when I have something?"

The connection dropped and Hayes stared out the window at the old facade of the bank across the street. The building was a big block of pebbled concrete with mirrored windows and gold trim. He recalled when the bank was bustling, men in suits and ladies in hats coming through the glass doors that now had been shuttered and covered over in graffitied plywood.

Darlene walked in and placed a handful of message slips on his desk. He stood up and followed her into the anteroom, pouring out some coffee, and shuffling through the slips. Darlene sat back at her post, hammering away at a big blocky keyboard, reading glasses down on her nose. Lots of framed photos of her grandkids on her desk. Church functions and fishing trips down to Panama City, Florida. *The World's Most Beautiful Beaches!*

"I've found five of those associated persons," she said. "Three of them are still in town. Ran a Lexis-Nexis on all of 'em. Figured that's what you'd want."

Hayes added a little sugar to his coffee as the printer hummed to life and started riffling through multiple pages. When it quit, he picked up the hot sheets and ambled back into his office, searching for his own pair of reading glasses and settling in with what Darlene had found out. *Jackson E. Kelly. Wilson R. Gregory. Aron T. Taylor.*

He dialed up Kelly first. It went straight to voicemail, and he left a message.

He called Gregory and a woman answered. He left his name and number. The woman wasn't friendly or helpful and hung up quick.

Third time was a charm; a man picked up on Taylor's phone.

"Mr. Taylor."

"Yeah, this is Aron." The man's voice was guttural and countrified.

"Aron," Porter Hayes said. "You used to work for McKellar-Dawson."

Hayes said it just like that, not asking the man but telling him the information right in front of him. The man didn't answer but he could hear Taylor breathing on the line.

"Mr. Taylor?"

"Yeah, I heard you."

"My name is Porter Hayes," he said. "I'd like to ask you a few questions about Dean McKellar."

The line went dead quick. A loud hollow ringtone sounded in his ear before he set the receiver down on the cradle. The silence and hang-up told Hayes all he needed to know. He checked his slim Hamilton watch—five twenty-two—and stood up, walking over to his hat rack to pick up his leather jacket. The address showed a neighborhood way the hell out in Cordova. *Shit.* Traffic would be rough, but maybe he could get to the man before dark. Not to judge, but the man sounded like a genuine redneck and might greet a Black man with a certain skepticism.

On the way out, he told Darlene where he was headed.

"Aron Taylor expecting you?"

"Nope," he said. "But I thought I'd lay down the Porter Hayes charm anyway. Want to walk out with me?"

"Why?" Darlene asked. "You don't think a woman from Coldwater can hack it in the big city after twenty-five years? What the dang hell? You gone soft, Porter?"

"Okay then," he said. "But do me a favor. Run a background check on that man I told you about earlier. Alec Dawson."

"Why Dawson?" she said. "The man who helped y'all out?"

"Yes, ma'am," Hayes said, sliding into his jacket. "Remember what I always say."

"Don't trust no one?"

"The other one."

"Everybody got a side hustle in Memphis."

Hayes snapped his fingers. "That's it."

Ever since his last girlfriend, the esteemed councilwoman Harriet Frank, moved out, Porter did his best to not spend a lot of time lying about at home. Randy and Nina still came over for Sunday dinner, trying to convince him to sell the ranch house he and his late wife had bought in seventy-one and paid off in eighty-two. He resisted not just because it was stocked full of memories, 'cause there sure was a lot of that shit piled high in sagging boxes in the garage and up in his attic. But where exactly did they think he was going? Move into some sad Midtown apartment or go ahead and put a down payment on some retirement center? Go fishing in the damn Ozarks? He knew the kids loved him and were thinking of him, but Hayes damn sure wasn't ready to ride off into the sunset. Not now. Not yet.

Hayes punched in a cassette of Syl Johnson as he eased the old Mercedes out of the parking space and made a quick turn on Second. He spotted the tail before the car even started to follow him. At least he figured it for a tail, a young brother in mirrored sunglasses behind the wheel of a silver Ford Taurus (a rental for sure), and not bothering to turn on his lights until Hayes turned out onto the street.

Hayes glanced up into the rearview, Syl singing his damn ass off on "Any Way the Wind Blows." On the fly, Hayes decided to change things up and head toward the river instead of Danny Thomas, trying to see if he was right or just getting edgy. He found his way onto Front Street and down the cobblestones to the river, the Mississippi stretching far and muddy over to Arkansas. He did everything slow and deliberate, the man hanging two, three car lengths back, rolling south along Riverside at sunset, while Hayes took a cool and casual pace along the bluffs.

Hayes headed up into the bluffs toward the old Rivermont Hotel, the fancy hotel now some kind of sad-ass apartments (man, that place used to gleam!), and then made a slow and easy U-turn into a parking lot before heading across Riverside and into a stretch of new condos just being framed. Used to be nothing but crackheads and abandoned warehouses up there, now people were paying top dollar for a sunset view of the Mississippi.

When he glanced back, he appeared to have lost the tail. No need to keep the son of a bitch riding close all the way to Cordova.

Hayes took a few turns before he headed up South Main and was driving back toward downtown to hook up with Union and the interstate, when he saw the Taurus coming up fast and hard behind him. *Son of a bitch.* The man not even trying now, knowing he'd been spotted. Hayes didn't pay him any mind, grooving along with his open windows and letting Syl do his thing. He passed the empty and boarded-up Hotel Chisca, the Orpheum with its flashing marquee. "The Sound of Music Live." Syl's music always taking him back to

Genevieve after she'd stopped touring, a long time before the cancer, and the days when they could enjoy what all they'd built. A family, a home, backyard parties with the neighbors, crazy-ass Rufus Thomas doing the funky chicken at a Fourth of July cookout. Willie Mitchell, the master producer himself, trying to convince Genevieve to get back into the studio, offering his new sound that ultimately went to Ann Peebles, Genevieve finding more meaning with Randy and Nina than hearing her voice on the radio or seeing her face on an album cover. She was kind and generous, infuriating and opinionated, cold and passionate, and damn, how he missed her. There had been other women since, but none could even come close.

He wound his way down Beale and over to Union, the man now two car lengths back as if that would make everything right. There was little doubt this man had been sent by the good Reverend Hightower, maybe one of his young deacons, to put the fear of God into him. Hayes crossed Union and drove past the Redbirds' stadium and then made a quick turn without a signal onto Madison, planning to head on up to Danny Thomas, where he knew he could lose the tail on the interstate. He glanced back again, now seeing only a pickup truck between them at a stoplight.

There were two other cases that might bring on a tail. But he sure didn't figure this to be connected to Addison McKellar, her missing husband, and some one-armed white man. Her story of the break-in reminded him of Spencer Tracy in *Bad Day at Black Rock*. He'd watched the whole thing as a young man at the old Palace on Beale, knowing the whole theater understood what that one-armed man was feeling, an outsider trying to find justice in a corrupt world. He believed in all that shit until he got shipped off to Fort Benning after graduation and the real world came into focus. *Vietnam. The department. Dr. King.* All of it. Helicopters beating overhead with the National Guard invading his city.

When the light turned green, Hayes drove up toward the Wonder Bread factory, the big neon sign glowing red and yellow at twilight, the windows down and the air smelling of freshly baked bread.

It was after five, and this section of town was an empty swath of cleared lots with commercial realty signs. He pulled up in front of a vacant lot across from the bread factory, knocked his car in park, and looked in his side mirror.

The Taurus slowed twenty or so yards away and came to a full stop. Hayes could barely make out the man's mirrored sunglasses, the fella probably thinking Porter's ass was on the phone and might pull back out onto the street to wherever the hell he was going. Best to stop things when they started. No need to get this man tied up in the McKellar case.

Hayes pushed in the lighter and fired up a Winston, keeping an eye on the Taurus.

Halfway through the cigarette, the sedan pulled out and raced around Hayes. Before the smoke had floated away, the man was gone. As he noted the plate, Porter knew he wasn't working for the Hightowers. The Taurus was a government car.

The damn feds. What the hell did they want with him now?

15

Addison

Addison's father had flat refused to go to the hospital.

Now it was nearly four and she was back at his town house in Germantown, Sara Caroline was at Libby's, and Preston was in the living room with her dad. Dad reclined in a hospital bed in the center of the room with the television tuned to *Have Gun Will Travel.* His caregiver Kiyana had called Addison not long after the meeting with the counselor at Hutch as Addison was winding into PDS to pick up Preston. (She'd have to return in a few hours for a soccer game.) Her father had chest pains, but wasn't making a big deal of it. Kiyana told Addison something she'd heard a thousand times: *Your father is a very stubborn man.*

"Would it hurt to get checked out?" Addison asked.

"My heart is the last thing I'm worried about," Sami Hassan said, shooing away the thought with an open hand. "That's like taking a car with a blown transmission in for a tune-up. It's probably Kiyana's food. She's trying to kill me with indigestion. How many times can a person fix beans and rice?"

Kiyana had worked for the family for more than two years, but Addison knew almost nothing about her life in Memphis or back home in Jamaica. The most intimate conversation they'd ever had was Addison telling her she'd listened to a lot of Bob Marley in college and smoked a little pot. Kiyana wasn't impressed, and Addison was rightly embarrassed for saying it, knowing that's exactly the kind of clueless crap the Hassans faced when they'd first arrived from Lebanon. Her grandfather and his brother opened up rival diners on Union Avenue, their kids born Americans but always struggling to assimilate. Her father had been bullied at Central High, although he'd never call it that, fielding jokes about being a camel jockey, that kind of thing. Dad always told them to suck his camel's pecker. Being bigger, tougher, and smarter than the bullies certainly helped.

When Addison was growing up, people would always tell her things like "you don't look Lebanese." Sorority sisters would compliment her tan with a meaningful look or say that her nose job looked wonderful. Which yes, she'd had, but never, ever admitted. So much shit she put up with as a blond Hassan until she married Dean and officially became a McKellar. Now the only thing she worried about was dyeing her roots.

"You look tired," her father said.

"Me?" she said. "What about you?"

"It's nothing," he said, waving his hand in dismissal. "A bunch of bullshit. I said I felt a tightness in my chest and she wanted to call the damn paramedics. Kiyana wants to be a hero so you and Branch will give her a raise. She spends half her day watching soap operas and calling home to talk to her sisters. She thinks I can't understand that patois. But I do. I took French in college. And yesterday, I know she called me a son of a bitch."

Addison used the remote to raise the back of her father's bed. The living room had taken on the feel of a triage, all her mother's knick-knacks moved into a spare bedroom. The only decor remaining from their old house was hanging on the wall: a tacky print of her father's Ole Miss football coach, Johnny Vaught, alongside a framed oil of St. Charbel that he'd bought on a family trip to Lebanon. She hated this new house, hated the memories of watching her mother die here, and then watching it become some kind of museum to her and Branch's childhood. An entire guest room was filled with cheerleading outfits, prom dresses, and various sparkling numbers from her formals at Ole Miss. Branch's baseball and soccer uniforms, his letter jackets. She'd told her mother to trash it all when they moved into the town house, which was only two miles away from the spacious four bedroom/three bath she grew up in. Addison explained that getting rid of all that junk was the point of downsizing, but her mother wouldn't hear it. Now, she was gone, her cancer diagnosed before they ever even took that long vacation to Hawaii. The town house stuffed with a million pill bottles, two hospital beds, walkers, IV drips, and stacks and stacks of newspapers and magazines, her father saying he hated to read on the computer because you couldn't take it to the toilet. The entire house had taken on the same antiseptic, sickly smell as it had with her mother.

"The doctor said six months," her father said. "Now it's been eight. Maybe I should ask for my money back?"

"Daddy."

"I'm just trying to make you smile," he said. "I haven't seen you smile in a long time. How are things with Dean?"

"Don't you remember?"

"Of course, I remember," he said. "I have cancer, not dementia. Did you talk to Porter Hayes? What did he say?"

Addison told him everything since Wednesday, the run-in with Jimbo Hornsby at the Club, the phony secretary in Southaven and her stupid son, and what she knew about Mr. Hayes's meeting with Alec Dawson earlier that day. However, she decided to skip over any mention of the break-in and the one-armed man making a turkey sandwich before threatening her and his grandkids. Her father was listening but staring intently at the black-and-white image on TV, a man in a smoking jacket named Paladin sitting in his suite at a fancy San Francisco hotel and complaining about his salad to his waiter. *A miser with the vinegar, a spendthrift for the oil . . .*

"When are you going to file?"

"For what?"

"Divorce," her father said. "Did you make sure to get the police report?"

"Yes, sir."

"Can Porter establish a trail of all Dean's bullshit?"

"Yes, sir," Addison said. She still always addressed her parents and older people as sir or ma'am. Her father wouldn't settle for anything different.

"Okay, then," her father said. "What else do you need?"

"I would like to know whether the father of my children is alive or dead."

Her dad waved away the notion, continuing to watch this hero Paladin run down not only his hotel waiter but now a long-suffering Chinese worker named Hey Boy. God, this was all so terrible. *Hey Boy?*

"It's not what you think, Dad."

"What do I think?"

"That Dean is having an affair."

"Baby," her father said, turning to smile at her. "I hate to break it to you. But men are terrible creatures."

"You've said that all my life."

"They can't be trusted," he said. "They lie, cheat, and steal."

"What about you?"

Her father shrugged, a commercial coming on about the benefits of a reverse mortgage. Happy white-haired people talking about how draining their lifetime investment had worked out so well. They played a lot of golf and walked on beaches into the sunset where presumably they'd turn to dust and float out into the crashing waves as if no problems would remain. Getting old was such a fucked-up business. She thought she'd grow old with Dean, maybe selling off their big house when the kids were grown. But now what?

Addison stepped away and into what was once a dining room. She remembered celebrating just one Christmas there before it turned into floor-to-ceiling boxes and two different exercise bikes. Thank god it still contained her mother's lovely rolling bar cart filled with an array of booze in crystal decanters and colorful bottles. She lifted the plastic lid on her Chick-fil-A lemonade and poured in a good amount of Hendrick's gin, swirling it around the slushy ice. The first few sips were a relief, like letting go of some imaginary weight.

"Addison?" he said.

She walked back into the living room. "Yes, sir."

"If Dean isn't screwing around, then what is he doing?"

Before he launched into a coughing fit, Addison was about to explain to her father that Mr. Hayes was beginning to think that Dean wasn't exactly Dean and that everything about him seemed to be constructed on one massive lie after the next. Sort of like Preston's Jenga set. She wasn't even sure she knew what Dean did or where he went to make the money while she kept the kids pampered and fed and darting around East Memphis in her spandex and running shoes like the road warrior of Poplar Avenue, white-knuckled on the wheel, between Hutch and Presbyterian Day School. Stopovers at the soccer fields and consistent exercising. She'd turn forty in a month, and wasn't this whole exploding shit show a grand and glorious birthday gift?

Her father began coughing, almost gagging, before Kiyana ran into the family room and raised up the back of the bed more while she handed him a water glass. Preston looked up from his PlayStation Portable and watched open-mouthed as Kiyana whacked his grandfather hard on the back, helping him cough up something that might've very well been part of his lung. She wiped it off his chest and off the corner of his white-whiskered mouth. "Well, shit."

Addison grabbed Preston and walked him out the front door of the brick town house telling him that Grandad wasn't feeling well and to wait in the car. "Give me a second to say goodbye."

"Can't I say goodbye?"

"Later."

"We will see him again," Preston said. "Won't we?"

She felt a huge stone form in her throat just as her brother, Branch, decided to make a heroic appearance in his brand-new Land Rover, pulling up behind her Escalade and hopping out. Although it had been raining like hell, he looked as if he'd come straight from the putting green, wearing a bright blue golf shirt and stretchy gray pants, eyes wide and out of breath, as if he'd run all the way there. He'd never been able to keep hours at the restaurant as he'd been taught. "How's Dad?"

"Hard day at work?"

"Fuck you, Addison," he said, then glancing over at his nephew hanging out of an open window, "Oh. Sorry, Preston."

"He's inside," Addison said. "Don't worry, Branch. Dad hasn't changed his will. Not yet, anyway."

She could do this.

She could balance a rage-filled teen, a dying parent, and a missing husband all at the same time. Dr. Larry told her to just keep on her routine, keep to the same patterns of behavior where she found the most comfort. It was nearly six now as she fought through traffic to get back home, and she knew she needed to stop off at Fresh Market and grab something to eat. She could keep her head above water—the gin had definitely been a huge help with her perspective—but she damn sure wasn't about to go into her half-finished kitchen, tie on an apron, and play Martha Stewart.

"Why do you and Uncle Branch argue so much?" Preston asked, catching Addison's eye in the rearview from the back seat.

"Your uncle is older and thinks he knows more than me," she said. "I won't have him talking down to me. He can be a real jerk."

"When you went back inside to check on Granddad, he asked if you'd been drinking."

"What did you say?"

"I said we got lemonades at Chick-fil-A."

"Good boy."

"But I saw you adding liquor from Grandma's cart," he said. "Are you sure you should be driving?"

"I'm fine," she said, gripping the wheel tighter. "But I appreciate your concern."

"Uncle Branch also asked about Dad," he said. "He asked me if I'd heard from him."

"You?"

"Yeah," Preston said. "He thought maybe Dad had called home from London."

"Dad isn't coming for a while," she said. "And Preston, I have to be honest with you. You're a young man now. I'm not sure that when Daddy comes home that he'll be living with us anymore."

Preston was silent. Addison weaved in and out of the narrow three lanes along Poplar before taking a left, crossing the train tracks, and wheeling down into the Fresh Market parking lot. She pulled into an open space and killed the engine.

"Are you okay?"

"Yes."

"You're very quiet."

"Dad told me the same thing," he said. "Before he left. About not living at home anymore."

Addison didn't say a word, feeling her cheeks flush. She took a long breath in and tried to let it out slowly. A return to breathing like in her yoga classes, be still and at peace as a river flows past. "He said he might be moving away," Preston said. "For a long time. But that he'd always love me."

"You never told me that."

Preston unlatched his seat belt and reached for the door. "Because I promised," he said. "Dad said men don't go around talking about people behind their backs or getting all emotional over stuff."

"That sounds like Dean."

"You mean Dad?"

"Yes," she said. "Of course. Dad."

The hardest part was the waiting. Waiting to find out what happened to Dean. Waiting to find out the latest prognosis on her father. Even waiting around to see if any new sociopaths would be showing up in her kitchen, even though the police had offered to check on their house throughout the night. To be honest, the least thing that concerned her was Dean. Whether he decided to show up or not was on him. She couldn't control his actions. Another Dr. Larryism. She could only do the best she could for her children and for herself. That's why she was paying Mr. Hayes to do her checking for her, open up Dean's dirty little closet of deceit and misdirection and return to her with a nice, typed-up report that she could hand over to her attorney. (She didn't have one yet, but once the word was out that she and Dean were divorcing, the bloodsuckers from the Club would be calling nonstop.)

Addison picked up a roasted herb chicken and placed it in her cart, tossing in a container of mashed potatoes, and then doubling back for a salad. The least she could do was make a salad, although Preston wouldn't touch it. She thought she still had a bag of green beans in the freezer for him. "Preston, will you at least try to eat a salad?"

Preston was pushing the cart as mournfully as Sisyphus through the aisles of Fresh Market, classical music playing overhead and the store smelling of smoked bacon, coffee beans, and chocolate. The poor kid was being tortured.

"Who's that man?"

"What man?"

"The Black guy in the suit," he said. "The one pretending to be looking at the cheese."

"Don't say Black guy," she said. "Just say the creepy guy with the cheese."

"Who is it?"

"I don't know," Addison said. "Why should I know?"

"He keeps on staring," Preston said. "Maybe you shouldn't wear gym clothes to the grocery store."

Addison had forgotten she still had on leggings and a black tank top that boasted 30-A, (LIFE'S BETTER AT THE BEACH!), wanting everyone to know she and Dean had a delightful little place on Rosemary Beach. Even her hat was a brag: TELLURIDE in green collegiate font. What was she? A fucking walking billboard? No wonder the man was staring. She was practically inviting it.

She told Preston to march on, moving on to the cereal aisle.

Preston turned to her, shoulders lowered, pushing the cart. "He's behind us," he said, under his breath.

Addison didn't answer. She just kept on looking for some homemade apple juice from Vermont and maybe some organic granola bars. She had to admit, there was something strange about the man wearing mirrored sunglasses inside the grocery store. But maybe he was handicapped. Maybe he was partially blind or something. Or, after the last few days, maybe she was just being paranoid and ridiculous.

"Mrs. McKellar?" the man said.

The man rolled his cart up to hers. There was nothing in it. Not even a block of cheese.

"I'd like to talk to you about your husband."

"And who are you?"

Preston looked up at the man and then back to his mother. She was pretty sure he'd also noticed the man hadn't picked up any cheese. He was smart like that.

"Sorry to roll up on you like this," the man said. "But this is of national importance."

If Addison had been drinking, she'd have spit halfway across the aisle. "Excuse me?"

"Can we speak in private?"

"This is my son," she said. "He can hear anything you have to say."

"First off," the man said, removing his sunglasses and then taking a deep inhale, "you both have my deepest condolences."

"Preston," she said. "Go get us some milk."

"What did he say?" Preston stared at the man in the suit, his voice starting to shake a little.

"Now," she said, raising her voice and gripping Preston by his shoulders, pushing him forward. Preston did as he was told. When he was out of earshot, she turned back to the Black man in the suit. "Now who are you and what the fuck are you talking about?"

"My name is Carson Wells," he said. "I'm a federal agent investigating your husband's business. I tried to find you at home, but—"

"Instead you decided to follow me to my father's house."

"How did you know that?"

"You drive a silver Ford sedan?" she said. "You're not very discreet."

The man didn't answer. He pushed away the shopping cart and stuck his right hand into his pants pocket, very casual against the rows and rows of healthy cereals and boxes of granola. "I need your help," he said. "Your husband was a very bad man."

"Was?" she said. "Why are you talking about him like he's dead?"

"Because he was killed four days ago in Paris, Mrs. McKellar," he said. "I'm so sorry. I thought you knew."

But she could tell by his sly little grin that the man wasn't sorry one bit. She left the cart, hot roasted chickens, cold mashed potatoes, Healthy Os, all of it, and rushed to find Preston, grab him by his little arm, and race out of the fucking Fresh Market.

"What about dinner?"

"We'll order pizza before your game," Addison said, suddenly feeling her voice cracking and tears run down her face. *Goddamn it.* "Pizza sounds good to me. How about you, buster?"

In her walk-in closet, Addison changed into a fresh pair of black leggings and looked for a hoodie that wasn't an advertisement for every damn vacation she'd ever had. Mustique. Vail. The ranch in Wyoming. Finally, she found her ancient bright blue Ole Miss hoodie, frayed at the cuffs, and slipped it on along with a trucker cap from Bluff City Barbecue. If the other PDS mothers didn't like her modified look, they could go straight to hell. She might very well be a grieving widow for all she, or they, knew. She'd cried a lot in the shower, composed herself with a Klonopin, and then made herself a tall thermos of gin and grapefruit juice and called up to Preston that they were running late for his soccer game.

A half-eaten Domino's pizza remained on the sad little island, the last part of the kitchen that hadn't been completely disassembled. She checked the doors to the patio twice and set the alarm before closing up and rolling out to the soccer game.

She didn't remember much of the game. There was a red team and a blue team. Preston was on the blue team. *Go blue!* And she sat off by herself, texting back and forth with Libby about picking up Sara Caroline on the way home.

Branch said you were drunk . . .

Branch is an asshole.

Are you?

I am half-drunk. Trying to get there.

Can Sara Caroline stay the night? She's worn out after what happened today.

I think Dean is dead.

. . .

OMG.

A federal agent stopped me at Fresh Market and gave me his condolences.

WTF? Does Preston know?

Apparently, no one knows.

And you went to his game?

Super Mom. I'm drinking gin and juice and trying to steer clear of Hannah Tracy. You were right. She did have her tits done.

I'm so sorry, Addy. I'm so sorry. I'm coming to you.

Goddamn it. The last thing she needed was a teary-eyed shit show. Addison poured out a little more gin and juice from her thermos and clapped at something that was happening on the field. Go team. Go Preston. Go Addison. *Fuck. Fuck. Fuck.*

She sat through the halftime in her folding chair under her dad's trucker cap and in her dark sunglasses. The night was already coming onto the soccer fields and bright lights clicked on overhead. The advantages of paying high-price tuition for PDS.

Hannah Tracy had gathered with three of the other moms down the field and they all waved to her. Hannah all smiles and pointy bosoms, holding up a fancy thermos of her own. Addison toasted her with her cup and watched as the kids retook the field. After an eternity, the game was over, and Preston had to come over and shake her awake from where she'd dozed off in her chair. Maybe with the sunglasses, no one noticed.

"Did you see my goal?"

"I saw all of them."

"I only had the one."

They walked back to her Escalade and she loaded her chair and her now-empty thermos into the rear. She hadn't eaten almost all day but didn't feel hungry in the least. Maybe she'd have the half-eaten pizza at home and fall asleep. They could do it all again tomorrow. All the fun and the laughs. She'd have to call someone. Who did you call when a federal agent told you your husband was dead? Porter would know. She needed to talk to him badly.

The house on the hill in Central Gardens seemed more ominous to-night, set up high with a patchwork of lights on. Hadn't she turned off the lights? Or had Libby already brought back Sara Caroline? Surely Libby wouldn't leave Sara Caroline there alone after the break-in. Maybe she was there, too, with Branch, ready to have a family meeting about what she'd heard about Dean. Even now, riding up the slant of the hill up to the garage, she had a hard time imagining Dean dead. Maybe it was better that way, everything Dean had kept secret for years remaining a secret forever. She'd be the Widow McKellar now. That's how they addressed women on her dad's old Westerns. She'd be poor Addison McKellar, so brave and strong, raising two kids on her own. At least she had money. She still had money? Right?

She punched the garage door opener and Preston scooted on inside, letting out ChaCha into the side yard, ChaCha barking and looping round and round. That crazy fucking dog. Addison didn't see Branch's or Libby's car and didn't give the lights much thought. Maybe Josefina had turned them on earlier and she hadn't noticed.

She left everything in the Escalade and headed upstairs to take a hot bath. A hot bath would make everything much better. She visited the bar in Dean's office and searched around for a good bottle of red. On Dean's desk sat an empty whiskey glass, still cold, with condensation running down the side, nothing left inside but a few melting ice cubes. She smelled cigar smoke.

"Preston?" she said, yelling upstairs. "Preston?"

She took the wide staircase upstairs, finding her son on top of his covers with his PlayStation in hand. "Are you okay?"

He didn't answer as she headed into her bedroom to look for the shotgun she'd aimed at the one-armed man. The bathroom door was closed and she heard the water running. She was about to call 911 when she saw a black leather carryall on the bed. The DRM monogram near the handle. She pushed the bathroom door and walked inside the steam. The water shut off and she watched, frozen in place, as Dean emerged from the shower, wrapping a towel around his waist.

She was suddenly a teenager, lying in front of her console television with both of her parents watching the season finale of *Dallas*. Patrick Duffy scrubbing his back and turning to his wife, Pam, or whatever her name was and saying, *Honey, what's the matter? You look like you saw a ghost.*

Jesus Christ. All she could think to say was, "You fucking asshole." And then she slapped him hard across the face. She tried to slap him again, and he reached out and grabbed both of her wrists and yanked them downward, motioning with his head back to the shower. Blood spattered across the white tile wall and circled down the drain.

Dean had horrible punctures all along his side, as if he'd been stabbed by a pitchfork. A bloody bandage lay by the shampoo bottles.

"Stop it," he said. "Just stop it. You need to be quiet and listen to me, Addison. I was in a terrible accident."

16

Gaultier

Gaultier was in Dubai.

Gaultier detested Dubai. But when your business was selling illegal arms and mercenaries by the dozen, this was the new Casablanca. His clients didn't come for the waters; they came for the endless pockets of the sheiks, the indoor ski slopes and surfing pools, the camel rides and torch-lit Arabian feasts at the edge of the desert. And even though the faithful were called to prayer five times a day by a muezzin and just a simple kiss on the cheek might lead to an arrest, the whores were plentiful. Gaultier had just bargained with a lithe blonde from Minsk calling herself "Lisa" for a thousand dirhams to pleasure a retired American general looking for companionship in *Sodom-sur-Mer*.

He was seated in a large white leather booth at a club called SNOW (all crystal icicles and fluttering flakes floating from the ceiling) on the second floor of a brand-new hotel with an expansive window view of the Burj Khalifa. He himself was staying at the Fairmont, but the general and his two friends wanted to see the place a manicurist they'd met at the Dubai Mall had told them about. The woman indiscreetly left her phone number on a business card if they needed anything at all. The general, a grizzled man in his late fifties from Indiana, had the arrogance to think she was flirting with him. While at dinner, Gaultier had offered to find him a guide for the evening. The general, well along on his eighth Johnnie Walker Blue at one hundred dirham each, slapped

Gaultier on the back and called him brother in arms. *What happens in Dubai damn well stays in Dubai.*

The general was off with Lisa, and Gaultier was alone now, drinking a glass of muscat from Frontignan. The taste recalling happy memories of home, so pleased to have found it on a wine list as large as a telephone book. But the nightclub held absolutely no interest for him as he waited for his last client meeting of the evening. At an enormous dance floor in the center of the club, a DJ dressed in a white *kandura* and red-checked *shemagh* played Arabic rap and made it rain with a handful of countless bills.

Gaultier checked his Rolex. The client, a go-between for the prince of Bahrain, was late as usual, and he signaled the waitress for one more muscat. A long line of waiters emerged from a side entrance holding aloft champagne topped with blazing sparklers. The seated guests started to clap and shout in unison.

He stifled a yawn. He'd barely slept since leaving Paris two days ago. All the blood in Collinson's flat an unpleasant but distant memory.

As he glanced about SNOW, he spotted a group of Western-looking men seated with women who he presumed were whores accepting the endless bottles of champagne. *Russians.* Gaultier detested Russians as much as he did being in Dubai. A man with Stalin's gray haircut and jet-black mustache stared in his direction and lifted a glass to Gaultier. The man wore a black silk T-shirt with large gold chain under a suede fringe coat like an American cowboy.

Gaultier looked away as the waitress arrived with a fresh glass of wine.

"Compliments of the gentleman," the waitress said.

"That's no gentleman."

"He's paid your tab for the night," she said. "And would like you to join their party."

Gaultier lifted his eyes to the woman. She smiled apologetically.

He looked at the drink and back to Anatoliy Zub.

"Please take the glass away."

"But, sir . . ."

"Take the wine and bring me the check," he said. "Please don't ask me again. I am not on the menu."

Gaultier was tired and said the last bit of it in French, sending her away with a flick of the wrist. But the waitress understood his tone and took away the muscat. He'd have a drink at the Fairmont bar before doing the whole thing again tomorrow, agreeing to take his prized general to a falconry exhibit at a desert preserve. The things he did to feed and clothe his six children, his wife, and two mistresses. Sometimes he thought of changing his name and grabbing one of his many passports and flying off to a nice little shack in Bora Bora. Perhaps Gauguin had the right idea.

Gaultier paid his tab and walked to the elevators, noting Zub's icy stare from his banquette. Zub's usual entourage of muscled bodyguards and prostitutes cavorted about him, the champagne bottles still popping and sparkling. Gaultier rode the elevator down to the lobby and walked out into the brutal heat of a Dubai night. The doorman flagged down a black car for him.

A black Lincoln pulled up and the doorman held the door wide. Gaultier tipped him again and climbed inside. "Fairmont."

He'd just pulled out his phone from his suit jacket when he noticed there was another man up front with the driver. The man in the passenger seat turned to him and politely pointed a gun in his direction. The lack of sleep and alcohol had made him stupid.

"Mr. Zub is offended you turned down his hospitality."

"I don't drink with men like Mr. Zub."

"Mr. Zub disagrees."

"*Bordel del merde.*"

Anatoliy Zub was the kind of man who gave arms dealers a bad name. He was a gunrunner who'd crawled out of the old Soviet Union and made billions off its relics. A friend of Vlad's, he'd bought and sold arms from his fleet of old Antonov An-8s for years and years. *Air Anatoliy.* Gaultier had known the man since they'd fought on opposite sides in Angola and later Liberia. Zub had so much blood on his hands, he was practically dripping.

"Where are you taking me?"

"The airport," the man said. "We've already collected your luggage from your hotel."

"And may I ask where we are flying to?"

"For that, you will need to ask Mr. Zub," he said. "Perhaps you should have accepted that drink?"

Zub had a Gulfstream G-70 painted a slick and shiny black with a tan leather interior touched with gold. His people had forced Gaultier inside and offered him some champagne as they waited outside in their SUVs (all black of course) on the tarmac for Zub to arrive.

Gaultier finally relented and helped himself to a bottle of '96 Dom Rosé and a tin of Beluga, searching the galley for some toast. He was, after all, Mr. Zub's guest, and if Mr. Zub wanted to toss him out at eighty thousand feet, then he figured he might as well have a full and healthy stomach.

Two Russians resembling bears ambled into the plane and took a seat at a round table without so much as a glance. They knew Gaultier was unarmed and not a threat as they joked with each other in Russian, one showing photos of an unconscious naked woman to the other. Gaultier slipped the spoon back into the Beluga and spread it onto some dry toast. It was quite good, and the Dom Rosé was fantastic.

"Gaultier, Gaultier," a voice boomed. "Where is my slippery little Frenchman? Did he give you boys any trouble? Did you check his boot? He sometimes likes to keep a knife in the shaft."

It was true. But sadly, Gaultier hadn't worn boots tonight. He had on a pair of Gucci alligator loafers he'd bought earlier that day at the Dubai mall.

Zub was trying his best to look like an American cowboy, but he couldn't hide being an impossibly ugly Russian. The Stalin brush cut, the thick black mustache, the cold blue eyes that had a hint of Siberia in them. He removed his fringe jacket and tossed it onto one of the bear's heads. The bear grunted and Zub made his way to the back of the plane, where Gaultier sat with a half-empty flute of champagne, the bubbles drifting to the top.

"The rosé?" he said. "You have excellent taste. So very expensive. But of course. You are French. The French are such snobs. The last time I was in Lyon, I ate at one of your bouchons and became sick from the feet of veal. Even my stomach isn't that strong. Ugh."

"I appreciate these little games as much as anyone," Gaultier said. "But I have clients and much business to conduct. You might have just called."

"I offered you a drink," Zub said. "And you tossed it in my face."

"Metaphorically."

"What does that mean?"

"It means your English is not so good," Gaultier said, lifting the flute and taking a sip. "Is this about the prince? You can have him. He likes to be wined and dined, but his orders are paltry. You'll find out."

"What prince?" Zub said, taking a seat opposite Gaultier. His black silk T-shirt was skintight, showing off a hammer and sickle tattoo on his right bicep. If the man was any more Russian, he'd have a scrawl of Khrushchev's face on his penis.

"I thought you were going to retire," Gaultier said. "I heard you opened some kind of cowboy store in New York where you sold ten-gallon hats and lassos."

"A western wear store," he said. "Yes, yes. We also sell saddles and boots. It was my dream. You should come. I will give you ten percent off a hat. You would look good in a hat, Gaultier, like Depardieu in *La Chevre*. The goat."

"I detest Depardieu."

Zub shrugged and reached for the bottle of champagne. He snapped his fingers at one of the bears and he went to the galley for a glass, pouring it for Zub and topping off Gaultier's. Gaultier took a long sip.

"Shall we cut the bullshit, partner," Zub said. "I know you saw Jack Dumas in Cairo."

Gaultier shrugged and sipped some more.

"He hung you upside down over the Nile?" Zub said. "Ha ha. I would have loved to see this. You, the dapper little Frenchman, dangling by your ankles."

Gaultier leveled his eyes at Zub. He wasn't proud of the memory or being mocked, but now he knew that all roads led back to Peter Collinson. Did Dumas work for Zub? Surely not. The one-armed man was a brute but not a moron. There was a limited life expectancy to working for Anatoliy Zub, something that Dumas would've understood.

"How is the caviar?"

"How is all Beluga?"

"You sent Dumas to Memphis, Tennessee," Zub said. "*Help me information, give me Memphis, Tennessee.* You know that song? Chuck Berry. Wonderful."

Again, Gaultier didn't answer. He watched as one of the bears left the plane, leaving just him, Zub, and the single bear. He felt the cold bit of the knife against his forearm. A butter knife wasn't exactly an old school KA-BAR, but it would do.

Zub held out the palm of his hand and nodded toward the knife. "Go on and give it to me," he said. "Dimitri was watching you on the camera. He was more worried about the Dom. But I told him you were my guest. Such an important man. The great Gaultier. Legionnaire. Leader of armies. Defender of Africa."

"What do you want?" he said. "My stomach is starting to turn."

Zub leaned forward into his seat. He shrugged in that way that all Russians do, the thick gold chain hanging from his thick neck. "Ten days ago, I spared Dumas his life. He had brought me container upon container of junk brought from the US military in Afghanistan. I was promised Javelins, PHAR rifles, Reaper drones. But no! Worn-out M4s, old grenades. Boxes and boxes of useless ammunition. *Why?* Why had Collinson sent a man like Dumas to bestow such an insult?"

"Because he wanted Dumas dead?"

Zub snapped his fingers and pointed at Gaultier, smiled, and drained his glass. The bear, confused over the snap, rushed over to refill his glass, but stopped short seeing Gaultier hadn't touched a bit more. Zub told the man to sit.

"The transaction had already been made," Zub said. "After so many times with Collinson. Same accounts. Same Bahamian banks. Of course, you know this. As I had my gun in Dumas's mouth, I wondered, Why would Peter do this to me? What could be worth making such a deal for absolutely nothing? To rob from Anatoliy Zub? Why would he do this?"

"And so you sent Dumas to me."

"Then I sent Dumas to Memphis," Zub said, draining the glass again. "To make things right. And now I am no closer to finding my money or finding Collinson."

Gaultier took in a deep breath, stood up in the private plane, and straightened his skull cuff links. "Well," he said. "You have no need of me, Anatoliy. That's all I know. Thank you so much for the hospitality."

The second bear entered. Gaultier glanced out the window as the jetway was rolled away. Nothing but the tarmac and bright blue lights and an endless desert beyond. It was a lonely site, the entire space around them an endless void.

"You," Zub said, smiling. "You know so much more, my friend. We will go to Memphis together. Tonight. You will make this right for Anatoliy."

"I won't be of any help," Gaultier said, wondering if Zub's goons had found the mobile phone he'd taken from Peter Collinson's flat.

"Dumas said you assisted Peter getting some cargo out of Istanbul?" he asked. "I think that cargo is rightfully mine."

The plane began to move. The bears up front put a movie onto a flatscreen, two naked women taking the clothes off a famous American billionaire sprawled on a luxury bed. As they started to spit and urinate on him, Gaultier turned his head in disgust.

"Do you remember General Mombu?" Zub asked.

"But of course."

"Good," Zub said, standing and walking to fetch a humidor and a lighter.

The lighter was the size of a grenade and wrapped in a thick, oily leather. Zub opened the humidor and Gaultier selected a cigar, reaching for the lighter and flicking on the flame. The leather felt rough against his hands.

"That lighter is made of Mombu's . . . *how you say?*"

"'How you say' what?"

"Nut sack."

Gaultier set down the lighter and wiped his right hand on his suit pants. Zub bellowed out a deep laugh as he sat down again and buckled his seat belt. The Gulfstream began to taxi and Gaultier, understanding his position, did the same. Zub helped himself to what was left of the caviar, spreading it thick along the toast.

"We stop in Amsterdam and New York," Zub said with a full mouth.

"I know nothing about Collinson or any of his cargo."

"I've always wanted to see Memphis," Zub said, brushing the caviar off his brushy black mustache. "Have you been to Graceland? I'd very much like to go. Elvis could be a cowboy. He was very good in *Charro*. *You've turned your back on yesterday. Betrayed a man who swore he'd make you pay.* That is Elvis. You like Elvis, no?"

Gaultier knew this was going to be a very long flight.

17

Porter Hayes

Porter Hayes stood up and looked out his office window facing Madison. And there he was: the same motherfucker in the same silver Taurus with the government tag. He thought about just walking down the street and tapping on the window, *Hey, man. Who are you and what the fuck do you want, youngblood?* Before he could, Darlene returned from lunch. She'd gone down to the Front Street Deli and brought Hayes a slice of their blueberry pie, a nice treat for a slow Wednesday.

"He still there?" Darlene asked.

"Sure is," Hayes said, sitting back down at his desk and setting the pie in front of him.

"That man is going to give you a crick in your neck."

"Got to be a man named Wells," Hayes said. "Lantana Jones told me about him. He'd been looking into Dean McKellar and now he's on my ass."

"Even though Dean McKellar is back home," she said. "And his wife fired your ass."

"Appreciate that, Darlene."

It had been a week since Addison McKellar had told Porter she no longer required his services. Three days ago, he'd received a handwritten note on monogrammed stationery thanking him for his time and interest in her family along with a check written for a thousand dollars more than the invoice. Hayes was a good detective, what some folks called a dogged detective, but he sure as hell wasn't about to stay on the McKellar case pro bono. Didn't matter if she was Sam the Sham's daughter or not. He did his job until she fired him. Only a fool would keep working for free.

"We ever turn up anything on that land in Marks?"

"You said you didn't care," she said. "Said it didn't matter anymore."

"Humor me," he said.

"Because of what you heard from that crazy Aron Taylor?" she said. "I wouldn't take the word of some peckerwood with a felony record as gospel. GI Joe training compound? Shoot houses? Sounds like a lot of horseshit to me."

"Maybe."

"Why do you give a damn?" she said. "The check cleared, Porter."

"But I still got a damn crick in my neck from that fed," he said. "And I'd like to know why."

"I say if Mrs. McKellar invited that son of a bitch back home, then it's her own goddamn problem."

"Aron Taylor told me some other things."

"Like what?"

"Two Mexican workers tried to shake down McKellar," he said. "And they just up and disappeared."

"You're not her daddy," she said. "You did your damn job."

The whole case was fucked-up and full of holes. His buddy Sawyer at the *Post* couldn't find any contracts between Dean McKellar or McKellar Construction and the DOD. Hayes had made his own inquiries, too, looking into McKellar's service record and hitting a wall; the only Dean McKellar who came up was a man from New York who died in 1992. Either McKellar was lying about his service record (a truly despicable act to a vet like Porter) or he'd come back from the dead. Then there'd been that one-armed man who'd busted into Addison's house looking for a fella named Collinson. Who may, or may not, be Dean McKellar. But connecting McKellar to Collinson had gone nowhere real fast, too.

Darlene set the thin file on his desk: a Lexis-Nexis report on both Dean McKellar and Addison, typed-up reports of his interviews with

Alec Dawson and Aron Taylor, and a short expense report for mileage and four cups of gas station coffee. He flipped open the file to find the property records on a forty-acre parcel down in Marks. Porter recalled that Marks had been the place where Dr. King and Reverend Abernathy wanted to kick off the Poor People's Campaign in the spring of '68. They picked Marks because of its extreme poverty, the poorest pocket of America right at the edge of the Mississippi Delta.

The property report stretched back decades, but all Hayes cared about was the most recent owners. He ran his finger down the sheet until he got to 2004 and saw the land had been purchased by the Devlin Group. The report listed a suite address in Virginia Beach, Virginia. He reached for the background report on McKellar to see if there was anything listed about an associated company called Devlin Group. He found nothing but McKellar Construction LLC and something called SugarBabies Ltd., which he knew had been that candy shop Addison ran in East Memphis. Even rich white ladies like having a side hustle, although it hadn't made any money.

He called out to Darlene's office. "Can you get Sawyer on the phone for me?"

"Thought you said he didn't know shit."

"I said he didn't know shit about Dean McKellar," he said. "I just got an itch is all. Damn, Darlene. Can you call him up for me?"

"You forget how to dial the phone?"

"Damn it, Darlene."

Hayes used a pen to highlight the property record and wondered how long it might take to drive down to Marks. Maybe an hour, hour and a half. He'd burn up a tank of gas and his whole afternoon for a client who had fired him. Not to mention things had heated up on the Hightower situation, the righteous reverend filing a cease and desist on his ass, saying that Porter Hayes was trying to slander his good name.

"Sawyer's not in," she said. "I left a message."

"All right then," Hayes said, standing up and doing a little pacing.

Hayes's karate certificate from Kang Rhee was crooked and he walked over to straighten it. Hung by its side was a picture of Elvis, grinning wide, in happier times, with his arm around Porter's shoulder. Sometimes he felt like Elvis was still around. Same thing with his late wife, like maybe the ghosts of some bright souls walked with you, watching your back when things got tight. Or maybe his ass was getting old, a little more religious in his later years. Always telling his daughter she'd see him in church one Sunday, although that Sunday never seemed to come.

"I'm going out," he said, reaching for his leather jacket and tossing it over his right shoulder.

"Where?"

"Gay Hawk," he said. "Almost forgot they had fried catfish today."

"But you just ate a piece of pie," she said.

Porter Hayes looked down at his secretary of nearly thirty years and offered his best smile. She shook her head and smiled back.

"No crime in having your dessert first."

Hayes returned an hour later with a full stomach and a toothpick hanging from the corner of his mouth. Darlene looked up and told him Sawyer had called him back. "You want me to try him?" she said. "Figured you may be worn out from eating all that catfish and cornbread."

Hayes gave her a thumbs-up, walking back into his office, not even taking a seat before he saw line one's flashing red button. He picked up.

"You sitting down?" Sawyer asked.

"Working on it, but my knee's giving me hell."

"Darlene gave me the name and address of the company out of Virginia Beach."

"And . . ."

"What's it to you?"

"Do we really need to discuss balancing them scales?"

"Last time you sent me a nice bottle of Rémy," Sawyer said. "And I don't even drink Rémy."

"Man's got to have class to drink brandy."

Hayes could hear a lot of talking and typing and general newsroom chaos on the other end of the line. He pictured Sawyer, unshaven with uncombed hair, the phone cradled up to his ear.

"This Devlin Group's nothing but a shell," Sawyer said. "But I assume you already knew that."

"That's why I was relying on your infinite knowledge of folks who make their dime sucking on Uncle Sam's tit."

"Graft is my business."

"And trouble is mine."

"See, the thing is that Devlin connects with two other shells before it hooks up with Warlock."

"Like a fucking witch?"

"A male witch," he said. "But yes, a witch."

"All right then," Hayes said. "You gonna lay on the good stuff or you just going to keep up the suspense, bullshitting until I drop dead at my desk?"

"Oh," Sawyer said. "You never heard of Warlock?"

"Only Warlock I know was the one Paul Lynde played on *Bewitched*," he said.

"Uncle Arthur."

"Yeah," Hayes said. "Uncle Arthur."

"So let me lead you through this mess," Sawyer said. "Warlock is a beast of a contracting company."

"Dean McKellar builds shopping malls and office buildings."

"You're not hearing me, Porter," he said. "Warlock is a major *military* contracting company. You said they own some kind of training compound in the Delta? Didn't you read about the slaughter in that bazaar in Kabul a few years ago?"

"Yeah," Hayes said. "Some dumbass security guards opened up on a bunch of women and children. Said there was a suicide bomber and then tried to cover it all up. Wasn't there supposed to be a big hearing about it?"

"The esteemed congressmen lost interest fast," Sawyer said. "This is a huge multinational group. You want to tell me how all this is coming out of Memphis?"

"Just a missing person case."

"See, I can't find anything about a Dean McKellar or a Peter Collinson connected to Warlock," Sawyer said. "Not that these are the kind of people that throw up a website or send out press releases. They have offices in London, Paris, and Dubai, but I couldn't get past an answering service. I called up a guy I know at the *Times*. He'd been doing some reporting after the bazaar massacre and he said he couldn't even find that so-called office in London. I did find out the company was started back in the nineties by a guy named Whitman Chambers. Nasty piece of work. Ex-SEAL, soldier of fortune type. He died in a plane crash in Sierra Leone back in '95. Sierra Leone's president took credit for blowing up the plane."

"Well, goddamn."

"Listen, Porter?"

"Yeah."

"This isn't your regular old trouble in the 901."

"No shit, man."

"Things don't work out too well for folks checking into Warlock," he said. "One of the men set to testify in the hearing just up and disappeared one day. Two other guys responsible for that bazaar incident ended up dead up in Kandahar a few weeks later. Another helicopter accident."

"I'll promise to watch my ass," Hayes said. "Besides, I hadn't been up in a helicopter since February of sixty-six back in Nam."

18

Addison

t's been a while since our last appointment," Dr. Larry said. "How have you been?"

"I've been better," Addison said. "To be honest, my life is a complete and total fucking mess."

Dr. Larry nodded. He was a great nodder, letting Addison continue with whatever thoughts she wanted to get out. She recalled one session when the only words Dr. Larry said were *Nice to see you* and *Well, when would you like to meet again?* Addison had a whole lot to say today. "I'm sorry, but things are worse than a mess. My life is a total train wreck."

"How so?"

Dr. Larry kept a neat little office on the fourth floor of the Poplar Perkins building, a run-down slice of old East Memphis with a Relax the Back store and a kitchen remodeler fronting the parking lot. He had a small waiting room with two chairs and a radio on a side table playing 91.1. Classical music with NPR breaks. *The US military failed to investigate the mistreatment, torture, and deaths of insurgents captured by Iraqi forces according to . . .* A series of Debussy string quartets, somewhat relaxing Addison as she anxiously flipped through *Psychology Today* until the office door opened and it was her time, a nervous couple not making eye contact as they left the office, the woman blotting her eyes before they continued into the hall.

"Dean left me."

"I'm so sorry."

"And then he came back," Addison said, legs crossed with her right foot rocking back and forth. "Like a bad penny. Isn't that what people say? But this was more like the return of a dumpster fire. Everything about us—everything about our family—is a goddamn lie."

Dr. Larry didn't ask a lot of questions. He took a lot of notes. He was an older man in his sixties with a dark ring of hair around a bald head and a long, drawn face. He wore comfortable clothes, wrinkled checked shirts with chinos, and sensible shoes. She'd met with him regularly for the last four years, starting with the first hints of trouble with Dean. Dean had called her both paranoid and jealous, blaming many of her issues on her late mother. Dr. Larry didn't think that was the case at all, although she never shared that with Dean.

"Addison?"

"Yes."

"Tell me about the lies."

Addison told Dr. Larry about Dean disappearing, about finding out his office was a fake, and the absolute humiliation of having her Escalade towed and being arrested. She said she'd gone to her dad, feeling like such a little girl, and then meeting Porter Hayes. She told him a little about Mr. Hayes and the run-in with that crazy country woman who faked being Amanda. (Dr. Larry knew all about Amanda. Once they'd had a complete session about how she believed Dean thought more of his secretary than he did his own family.) She told him about these long business trips to London and how he'd hoodwinked poor Alec Dawson, a good and decent guy, out of millions. "Do you see this watch?" she said, pointing to the Cartier. "Dean brought it back from London. And what do I do? I'm such an idiot. I'm wearing it."

Dr. Larry took a long breath. He removed his reading glasses and clamped his teeth on the temple. "Are you now separated?"

"No."

"But you've asked for a divorce?"

"Not exactly."

Dr. Larry slipped the glasses back on and took some more notes. His hand moved furiously across the legal pad. She wondered what he was writing. *Paranoid schizoid. Daddy issues. Spoiled bitch.* A man with such sensible shoes would never write something like that. Would he?

"And he was gone a week?"

"A week and a couple days," she said. "He wouldn't answer my calls. He'd lied to me for years about his office. He lied to me about Amanda. You ever meet anyone stupid enough to wake up one morning and realize they've been sleeping with a stranger for years?"

"All the time," Dr. Larry said, giving one of those knowing Dr. Larry smiles. "It's practically my bread and butter." *Bread and butter.* Again, prime Dr. Larry. He tilted his head. "So," he said. "Where exactly was Dean? Did he explain this to you?"

Addison took in a deep breath through her nose. She rested her hands in her lap and stared across to the other wall at the macramé hangings and a small Buddha statue that was new from last time. Was Dr. Larry a Buddhist? She always thought he was Jewish. She knew he put in a lot of hours at the Jewish Community Center working with the elderly. He would sometimes brag about So-and-So's wonderful blintzes.

"Dean said he was attacked."

"Where?"

"In the stomach."

"I mean, where did this happen?"

"London," she said. "It was always London. He said he'd been at Paddington Station and two guys asked him for money. When he told them to get lost, one of them stabbed him with a knife and the other kicked him in the head. They stole his new leather jacket, a really nice one I gave him for Christmas, and his wallet and passport. He said he woke up in the hospital two days later and drifted in and out of consciousness after that."

"Why didn't he call you when he woke up?"

"He said he had to sort out a lot of business at the American embassy and police reports and he said he was both ashamed he'd been beaten and thought I'd only be more worried."

"More worried than him disappearing?"

"That's what I said."

"And what did Dean say?"

"He said he wasn't thinking straight," she said. "He said that he only wanted to get his clothes and his new passport and take the first flight home. He said it was much easier to explain all this in person. He's done a lot of sulking since he's been back, just sitting in his study and drinking. He's been making a lot of phone calls, talking for hours to God knows who, and then he goes out, coming back up for air with me and the kids later as if nothing has happened. When I tried to get him to tell me more about it, he said it was too fresh for him. We ended up sitting for two hours out by our pool and not saying a goddamn word."

"Your pool is still open?"

Oh, Dr. Larry. Nothing escapes you!

"No," she said. "It's just a place where we usually sit and talk. It has comfy furniture out there and I kind of like looking at it. I guess it's a place where I go and think. We just sat out there in silence and I drank a bottle of wine and god knows how much scotch Dean had. He'd bought a nice bottle in Duty Free. He told me how much he loved me and apologized for scaring me. And that he hoped we could put the whole mess behind us."

"And you told him you couldn't live that way?"

It was one of Dr. Larry's hopeful questions. Addison took another deep breath and changed her crossed leg, dangling her left foot over the knee, pumping it up and down.

"Addison."

"No," Addison said. "We ended up having sex."

Dr. Larry looked down to the page, more scribbling. She waited what felt like an eternity before the scribbling stopped and he looked up again. He removed his glasses as if the scribbling had taken all the energy out of him. She looked for some kind of sign of disappointment in his eyes but didn't see it. So well trained, Dr. Larry. Never passing on any judgment, although he'd worked for years with her about establishing boundaries. Outside his window was an old stone Baptist church, a lovely building where she used to go with her grandmother the mornings she didn't go to Our Lady of Perpetual Help with her parents. Developers were about to tear the old church down to make way for a Walgreens.

"I guess it was a mistake," Addison said.

"Why do you feel that way?"

"Ever had a one-night stand?"

Dr. Larry smiled. "I went to college," he said.

"It felt like that," Addison said. "Like screwing a goddamn stranger. Yesterday, I told him I couldn't live with him anymore and that he had to get out."

"Did he?"

"No," Addison said, swallowing. "He said I was having a nervous breakdown and that I needed to see you. He thinks I need to up my meds."

"You said he leaves the house during the day," Dr. Larry said. "If he doesn't have an office or a job that you know about, where do you think Dean goes?"

Nothing is lost on Dr. Larry. *Nothing.* Addison opened her mouth but for the first time didn't have an answer.

19

Joanna

Peter had come to her flat that afternoon, Tippi out running errands, doing whatever it was that Tippi did during daylight hours, with strict instructions not to come home until after five. Joanna prepared a lovely meal of coq au vin in her Crock-Pot, along with a salade Niçoise and a decadent bottle of red she'd bought with the paltry advance from Leslie Grimes. Grimes would've been horrified to know she'd spent his advance on the demon alcohol. Even at their Peabody lunch, he'd stared at every sip of her julep as it was one more step on the road to hell. As she prepped, she watched the telly about thirty-three men trapped in a mine in Chile. More than sixty days underground. *Oh, well. Things could be much worse.*

Joanna greeted Peter at the door in a pink silk kimono, a lovely gift from Richard Chamberlain after they'd become friends during *Return of the Musketeers* (long before his coming out), her first film in years after shooting one of those horrible *Carry On* films at Pinewood. *Carry On Girls. Carry On Abroad.* Carry On My Ass. The most miserable winter of her life, cast as a French maid who had a habit of tipping her bosoms down to horny old goats like Sid James and Bernard Bresslaw. *Sugar or milk, monsieur?* "Oh, Peter," she said. "You naughty, naughty little boy. Do you fancy a spanking?"

Peter had taken her into her bedroom where he'd made love to her for almost an entire hour. He did things to her in the first twenty minutes that she'd only imagined. His flexibility, delicate fingers, and knowing mouth. Later, both of them lying naked under her pink silk sheets, she'd asked him what on earth he had just done to her. Her ash blond hair over one eye, dizzy and wild from the whole experience, her breathing quick and her heart still racing. He leaned into her ear and whispered, *Double-crested dragon*. Oh god, she thought, blowing the hair from her eye. Double-crested dragon! This man in his midforties— nearly twenty years her junior!—might be the death of her yet. Where had he learned such a wonderful and impressive trick? It seemed like something one could only pick up in the Orient. A Shanghai whore- house perhaps? She'd never ask.

Joanna slipped back into the kimono and set the table with antique silver and lace as if they were lunching at the Savoy instead of a shabby apartment with a view of the parking lot and expressway. She uncorked the bottle and poured a glass of the red as Peter appeared shirtless in only his trousers. He'd grown a slight beard since she'd last seen him, looking for all the world like a shipwrecked ruffian with his tousled blond hair and impish smile. Joanna heard her mother's Yorkshire ac- cent in her head: *such a charmer, that one.*

They were both ravenous from the sex and barely spoke during the meal, Peter asking only once for a bit more wine. She knew he was mar- ried, but that didn't really bother her much. Darling Richard Harris had been married with three children, but the chemistry had been undeniable. Although Peter didn't offer Richard's considerable assets, he made up in enthusiasm and technique. Joan Collins always said a younger man was better than any colonic at Enton Hall.

"I really wish you hadn't gone to see Leslie Grimes."

"He called me, darling," she said. "He was an absolute wreck when you disappeared. We lunched at the Peabody and he told me about some arrangement you had. I was covering for you more than any- thing. More wine?"

"No, thank you."

"You're upset?"

Peter shook his head. Such a roguish and passionate man. She hoped that Tippi would find one like him for herself one day. There had to be someone much better than the Graceland tour guide she'd been seeing, with his horrible greasy hair and cuffed blue jeans, wallet chain, and tattoos up and down his arms.

"May I ask how you got shot?" she said, pointing to the wound along his right flank.

"There was a misunderstanding in Paris."

Joanna shrugged. Such things had happened in Paris.

"How is your family?" she asked.

Peter shook his head. Talk of his wife and his family were strictly off-limits. They'd first met back in January, a handsome American in a Savile Row suit working with Omar to unload four containers languishing at the Mississippi docks full of rugs, paintings, and ancient curiosities. Even before he mentioned that the antiques were from the Middle East, she knew he'd been a military man like her father. She'd been right, Peter making vague references to his time in the army and the Gulf War, maybe with a little hint that his work with the government hadn't ended. She made him for some type of spy with enormous worldwide contacts. He spoke passable French, decent German, and they both shared a passion for skiing in Switzerland, a love for winter sports in Interlaken.

"Are you in pain?" she asked.

Peter shook his head. What was going on in that handsome skull of his? She watched him scrape up a bit more salad and the rest of the coq au vin. He appeared to not have eaten for days, so scruffy and wild-eyed. She reached across the table to trace the cleft in his chin. He could've been an actor, so short, but with an enormous and handsome head on his shoulders.

"You've got to stay away from Leslie," he said. "He can be very temperamental."

She started to speak, but Peter gave her a look that would've wilted a hedgerow.

He held up his hand and shook his head. "That man, Jack Dumas?" Peter said, swallowing and wiping his lips with a napkin. "He came to Memphis to kill me and wouldn't think twice if you got in the way."

"Did he kill Omar?"

"Apparently."

"May I ask why?"

"Because he's pissed off and crazy," Peter said. "He believes I double-crossed him. In truth, he's the one who fucked up. And he nearly got himself killed back in Istanbul."

"And why would he kill Omar?"

Peter shrugged. He tossed back the rest of the wine and looked at his watch. "I need your help, Joanna."

"Well, you certainly didn't today," Joanna said, offering her wicked smile. The kind that brought Hal Wallis to his knees, panting like a frustrated old dog.

"Can you get me back into Omar's place?"

"Today?" she said. "Right now?"

"Tonight."

"I'm sure his family has changed the locks and the security code."

"I can take care of all that," he said. "I just need you to show me where you found him and help me look around his office."

"Omar didn't have much of an office," Joanna said, now knowing exactly why Peter Collinson had brought along his wonderful double-crested dragon from Paris. "Only two little desks, file cabinets, and some cubbyholes."

"A safe?"

"Yes," she said, tapping at her teeth with her index finger. "A very old one. I don't think you could get it open."

"We'll see about that," Peter said, getting up from the table and walking around behind her. He leaned down and kissed her cheek. "I'll pick you up at eight."

"So, Mother," Tippi said, "tell me about this mystery man of yours. What is this Peter Collinson really like? *Who is he? What does he do?* You're practically glowing."

"Only on the inside, darling," Joanna said, dipping her feet into her flat's community hot tub. She and Tippi were the only ones inside the pool area near the grills, Ping-Pong tables, and some game the younger people liked called cornhole. A banner spread across the fence read "Boo to You! Halloween 2010 Move-In Specials." The heavens wept that Joanna Grayson had to live in such a wretched place like The Village.

"I did have to wait in the car for nearly an hour," Tippi said, popping the cheap champagne Peter had left and filling a tall plastic cup. "I saw his poor shirttails flying during his escape, carrying his dress shoes. I know you're dying to tell me all about it."

"You saw him?"

"Of course, I saw him," Tippi said, gulping down the champagne. "Handsome. Although a little short for my taste."

"Tippi."

"Mother," Tippi said. The hot tub's water was foaming about her daughter's rather thick calves. "You're so wicked. He could be my brother."

"He's many years older than you, my dear."

"You've always called me a late and unexpected arrival."

"I was only twenty-eight."

Dear Tippi couldn't help herself, the theater in her blood, and she spat out a mouthful of the André Brut into the hot tub. "Twenty-eight?" Tippi said, laughing. "Mother. Are you trying to have some fun?"

Tippi was right, but Joanna so hated doing the math. There was her age during her coming out in London, and then her age when she arrived in Hollywood, and then take back two years for when she did press for the Hammer films, and then the period that her agent called her "return to normalcy," then moving ahead four years to when she did some erotica in Italy in the late '70s and early '80s with darling Sylvia Kristel. Soft focus, skinny dipping, untrimmed pubic hair that resembled a poodle caught in a headlock.

"Peter arrived with some wonderful news, Tippi."

"Let me guess," she said. "He's leaving his wife and I'm about to have the father I've always wanted. *Goody*. Even though he really could be my brother. If any of us were actually inclined to do the math."

Joanna snatched the cheap plastic cup from Tippi and poured it half full of the so-called champagne. "I never told you about finding poor Omar's body," she said. "Did I? And what he'd hidden away?"

Tippi shook her head.

"Omar made arrangements to bring over a new container from Istanbul," she said. "And only dear Omar knew those ten little numbers that would identify the right one. Without it, it would be a bit like looking for a grain of sand in the Sahara. Do you understand?"

"I know," she said. "The papers you found. But what's inside?"

"It must be something very big and very valuable to have been shipped halfway across the world and worth poor Omar's life."

"And Peter Collinson knows that you know how to find it."

"Of course not," Joanna said. "Not yet. I'd much rather play the heroine than the victim."

"Since when?" Tippi said. "You've always played the victim. Like when Elvis had to rescue you from those frogmen or pirates or whatever in *Easy Come, Easy Go*. I have to admit, you did look very scared. I believed you."

"This is our lucky ticket out of this god-awful purgatory," Joanna said, looking down at the gold watch Peter had given her earlier, its braided band glinting in the sunlight. *Fake*. A good fake, but not a true Cartier. "I won't trust our future to an extravagant lay, no matter how young and dashing he is."

Joanna wondered how long Peter would go on searching and searching for something that Joanna found so easily that first night. If he knew she had the shipping ID numbers, he'd just leave her in Memphis and take the truckload direct to Leslie Grimes for his Christian Crusade. Like the idiot former American president said: *Fool me once, shame on you. Fool me . . . you can't get fooled again.* The very idea of Peter leapfrogging over her and using her long-cultivated relationship with Grimes to move his container of goddamn trinkets he'd found shooting about the sand dunes. Just what was Leslie into now besides rugs and magic golden lamps?

Peter's flashlight shone down the path and across love seats covered in moth-eaten velvet and hand carved wooden chairs pulled up to ornate dining tables, one with a little porcelain doll sitting at the head. The doll's empty black eyes and slack jaw nearly gave Joanna a fright.

"Can you really open a safe?" she asked.

"Of course I can."

"Are you going to use explosives?" she said. "Because if you are, I'd much rather wait in the car. They used so many explosives when I was working in Italy that my ears rang for years and years. *After the Fox* with Peter Sellers. It was my first picture and Peter was madly in love with me."

"You must have made that before I was born."

Peter Collinson. So very cruel tonight.

He turned on the lights in Omar's back office, and for the first time, she noticed Peter was wearing gloves. Of course, he was wearing gloves, skintight black leather, and Joanna worried perhaps she should have worn them, too. But then she remembered her prints must be all over the bloody antiques mall after working with Omar for the better part of the year. Omar's own personal "English Rose" with all her mysterious contacts in Hollywood. (Beverly Hills really, but she never corrected him.)

Peter handed her the flashlight and asked her to shine the beam on the dial as he donned a stethoscope. Within a few seconds, he popped the door to a safe so old that it could've been used in a Cagney film. He reached inside and began to toss the contents on the floor, stacks of money, handfuls of loose silver dollars, and some glittering diamond necklaces. She bent down and scooped up what she could in her arms, the flashlight wavering over the empty safe and Peter's reddened face.

"What are you doing?" he said. "Hold still. Hold still, goddamn it."

She pressed the jewels and a roll of cash into her pant pockets, doing her best to compose herself. Peter spread a big ledger onto the floor and flipped through it for what felt like an eternity. He finally got to his feet and walked over to Omar's desk and began emptying drawer after drawer until he punched at the wall and left fist-size holes in the sheetrock.

"Peter," she said. "Quit acting like a child. What on earth were you hoping to find?"

Peter gave one last swift kick to the desk as he snatched up Joanna's arm and marched her from Omar's office, the light of the flashlight bobbing up and down and along the walls and tile ceiling. Joanna wasn't able to catch a breath until they made it outside and Peter slammed the big metal door behind him.

He tossed her the car keys and said, "You drive."

"I don't see so well in the dark, darling."

"Don't worry," he said. "I'll tell you where to go."

When he brushed past her, she noticed he'd torn his wounds, the side of his shirt blackened with blood.

Peter's directions were complex and paranoid. He told her five times that they were being followed by a man in a silver Ford Taurus but not once did she see the car. They hopped on 240 and circled the city in an entire long lap before exiting and heading south on Germantown Road. Joanna had been behind the wheel quite some time, wearing her smart tortoiseshell glasses, waiting for Peter to compose himself and tell her exactly where they were going.

"What was he like?" Peter asked.

"Who?"

"Elvis."

"You've never asked me that."

"I'm asking now," he said. "I was always curious. Maybe I'd like to know if he and I shared a thing or two."

"Wondering how you might compare, Peter?"

"Just keep driving," he said. "I have to meet someone. Then I want you to take my car back with you. I'll call you when I get settled."

"Will I see you again?" Joanna asked. But truly not really caring either way.

"Son of a damn bitch," he said. "Why did Omar have to be so damn stupid and get himself killed like that?"

"How did he get himself killed?"

"Just drive, Joanna," he said. "Don't make trouble."

Joanna leaned forward, the night traffic a bit of a blur. She turned on the windshield wipers as a little rain started to sweep the road. "If you must know," she said, "I was never with Elvis. We were dear friends. More like brother and sister."

"Come on," he said, smirking. "You?"

"He did invite me to his home in Palm Springs one evening," she said. "We spoke of things a man like you could never understand."

It had all happened that way. Hadn't it?

The drive out to Palm Springs in '66 where Elvis had rented a home for the duration of the shoot. *Easy Come, Easy Go.* A perfectly dreadful film, one critic calling it "a tired little clinker that must've been shot during lunch hour." But the connection they'd had. That had been real. The all-night talk of destiny, the afterlife, reincarnation, and astrology.

There had been attraction without touching. Chemistry with only a good night kiss. You could see it all in the picture. So many fans had told her so. The way that Elvis so lovingly untied her from the mast of the ship and knocked out the frogmen who'd bounded onto the deck with spearguns. They trusted each other. Elvis believed they'd known each other in another life. If he hadn't been engaged to Priscilla, perhaps things would be different now. He held her hand and stared into her eyes as the sun came up across the desert. Just thinking of it now made her feel his strength.

She would get through this.

But that wasn't it, was it? Not all of it. There was their last meeting, the one she'd never talked about. Not a word about it in *One Night with You: The Joanna Grayson Story.* Three years after the picture bombed, after patching up the mess of her career and life back in London, she found herself back in the States with, of all people, her mother. *You are not beautiful, Joanna. But you are striking . . .*

Mum wanted to see Elvis. *Your dear friend?* And so they flew from New York to Las Vegas to watch him perform at the new International Hotel in the fall of 1970. Everyone was there. Sammy Davis Jr. Cary Grant. George Hamilton. Lovely Juliet Prowse. Mother had worn a blue gown to cover her expanding hips and hefty bosom. Joanna was resplendent in a white silk tunic, very Greek, her blond hair worn up, tendrils falling down her neck.

The show was transcendent. She'd never known Elvis as alive as he'd been onstage. (He'd been so sad back in Hollywood, a bored kid playing with motor scooters and water balloons.) Like her, Elvis wore all white, a contoured jumpsuit with conchos that were surely inspired by the necklace Joanna had once favored. *Did he know she was coming? Was this a subtle message that she was the girl that could have been?*

She could hardly breathe watching him, drenched with sweat, singing "Suspicious Minds," squatting into a side bend (muscles flexing in his legs, so very tan and limber), a move she knew he'd developed in yoga training for their film. His blue eyes set on her, snarling and smiling, so playful and so fun. Joanna could barely contain herself after the curtain fell as the casino manager took them through security and up through the tunnels behind the stage.

"He's quite handsome," Mum said. "Reminds me a bit of that fella Tom Jones."

"No, Mum," Joanna said. "Tom Jones reminds you of him."

A throng of fans surrounded Elvis. Elvis kissing and hugging them all. Touching hands, laying hands on shoulders. He patiently signed autographs and posed for photos. One of his Memphis Mafia boys handed him a white towel to dab his brow and a woman snatched it away and buried her face in it, inhaling his sweat. He and Joanna locked eyes. She had smiled at him.

And Elvis had smiled back.

"You always said we'd find each other again."

"Excuse me?" Elvis said.

"So many years," she said. "You were wonderful. *Spectacular.* God. You seem to have finally found your purpose."

"Yeah?" Elvis said. "Okay, baby. My purpose? You got something for me to sign? Or you want a picture or something?"

She'd never felt such humiliation. Made ever so the worse by the little smirk on Mum's disapproving Yorkshire face. Joanna couldn't speak or move. Elvis reached over her shoulder to snatch up a child's autograph book.

It was the worst kind of insult. To be forgotten. To be a nobody.

And now, so lost in her life, arriving to a destination of nowhere with a man she barely knew, she wondered if anyone would even know she had existed. *We all have our purpose, Miss Joanna*, Elvis said that night in Palm Springs. *What's going to be yours?*

"We're here," Peter said.

"Here?" she said. "We're nowhere."

It was a lonely service road somewhere in Shelby Farms, an endless stretch of power lines snaking between electric transformers across the hazy landscape. Peter was out of the car before she even turned off the ignition, a good distance away from a fall carnival lit up in neon and flashing lights, barely able to hear all those happy screams. "Why are we here?"

"I'm meeting someone," he said. "Then you can go."

"What's going on, Peter?"

Peter had his back to her, watching the carnival from under the huge transformers. When he turned around, a change had crossed his face. He no longer looked like Peter Collinson, dashing young man, but instead a stranger, a master stroke of acting as if he had picked up a reset scene, taking over for the stand-in and then coming on magically with the character. Peter's new character wasn't a hero. His eyes were dead and his mouth cruel. He reached out for Joanna's hair, twisted it roughly in his hands, and brought her down to her knees, pressing a gun to the side of her head. "What did Omar tell you?"

"My god," she said. "My god."

"What did he say, Joanna?"

"He was dead," she said. "He was dead. I swear to you."

He let go of her hair and dropped her in the dirt. She caught herself with her hands and turned to him to spit. He just shook his head and smiled at her, the headlights of another car bumping down the road. She stood up and ran to it, waving her hands and screaming for them to please stop. As the car slowed, she saw two figures emerge. Two large men who slammed the doors behind them and walked directly past her to Peter. They were dressed in dark stiff clothing like soldiers.

"She's a tough old bitch," Peter said. "Take her and see what you can get."

20

Libby

Libby would never ever talk about Addison behind her back.

However, Addison had been acting very weird since Dean left on his trip to London. She'd actually gone downtown to his old office and become convinced that he'd been lying to her for years instead of the likely explanation that he'd rented a new space and she hadn't noticed. She'd gone too far when she got herself arrested and then later showed up at the Club with some Black detective she'd probably picked right out of the phonebook to interrogate Jimbo Hornsby. Libby thought Addison at least would've calmed down with Dean safe and back home—how tragic that he'd been mugged on his trip—but instead she'd only grown more paranoid and weird, so damn chatty after they'd dropped the kids at school and met up at the walking trails at Overton Park.

"You've been through some real shit," Libby said.

They walked at a nice, fast clip. Libby hoped she'd burn off the generous slice of cheesecake from last night, regretting it as soon as Branch had brought it home to her.

"It's not every night that you walk into your kitchen and find a one-armed man raiding your fridge."

"Right," Libby said. "I'd forgotten about the one-armed guy."

"And then Dean decides just to show up in our shower."

"Where else would he have shown up?"

"Duh," Addison said, walking nearly shoulder to shoulder with Libby. "How about you call first? He had to have woken up, been discharged from the hospital, met with the people at the embassy like he says, and then flown all the way home. Somewhere along the line, maybe he would've thought to check in with me?"

"Branch saw where he was stabbed," she said. "He said it was really nasty."

"Branch would want to see that."

Libby ignored the dig, Addison obsessed with the idea that Branch was secretly gay. She loved to tell the same story at Thanksgiving about how Branch used to pretend he was the Bionic Woman when he was just five, making the bionic noises when he practiced tennis and acting like he had super hearing.

"I've been drinking since I woke up."

"Ha ha," Libby said.

"No," Addison said. "I'm serious. I had a double Bloody Mary before I took the kids to school. I thought it was bad when Dean was gone, but my nerves are totally shot since he got home. He's on the phone constantly and then leaves for a big part of the day. I have absolutely no idea where he goes and he won't tell me."

They walked up and over an old stone bridge, the faint smell of the nearby zoo in the air. Elephant shit and all that. The leaves crunched under their feet as they walked, Libby and Addison looking like twins in their black Patagonia vests, black leggings, and black baseball hats, being passed by joggers and the occasional asshole on a mountain bike. *On your left!*

"He's a businessman," Libby said. "He's doing business. I'm sure that horrible thing in London really set things back. Not to mention, getting new credit cards and filing reports. You know all about that. You filed one on Dean when you believed he was a missing person."

"He *was* a missing person," Addison said. "Just not in Memphis. In London. He was missing in London."

Addison didn't believe her own husband. Dean had nearly dragged himself back from England, had come straight to his home after being attacked, and instead of welcoming him with open arms, Addison decides to doubt every word he said. This coming from a woman who claimed a one-armed man made a turkey sandwich in her kitchen before trying to kill her. It wasn't just the drinking (although the drinking with the kids wasn't good), it was the pills, the paranoia, the constant obsession that Dean was lying to her. Dean McKellar was a good man and wonderful father and husband and Libby had absolutely no idea what Addison was trying to prove.

"He's hiding something," Addison said, looking at her watch as they walked, a lovely gold Cartier from Dean. "I'm sure of it. When I get back home, I'm going to call back Porter Hayes and ask him what he found out. Could you live like this? I can't live like this. Christ, I can barely sleep."

"Who's Porter Hayes?"

"The private investigator."

"Just some random guy?"

"He's a friend of my father."

"Oh."

"Dean said the one-armed man was just a nut ball who broke in," she said. "But he asked me about Peter Collinson."

"So?"

"Peter Collinson is the name of Dean's grandfather," she said. "On his mother's side. It didn't come to me until later, but then I knew I'd heard that name before. I'd seen some letters addressed to his grandfather on his desk. That's not a coincidence."

They passed by a young mother running with her baby in a jogging stroller. Libby looked to Addison and rolled her eyes as if saying, *Yeah, that dumb bitch thinks she's gonna keep it all tight a few months after giving birth. Wait till the next one.* They had shorthand like that. Always had. That telepathic connection that had only grown staticky in the last few years.

"Wouldn't you want to know?" Addison asked, pumping her arms around the next bend on the Overton trail. The leaves scattering across the path after a hard, cold wind. "If Branch was keeping something from you?"

"Honestly," she said. "I wouldn't. He and I have our own lives."

"Libby."

"It's true."

"Well," Addison said. "I'm going to find out. I'm going to find out exactly what Dean's been up to. This is too damn much."

Addison stopped, tipping back the water bottle and looking ahead at the winding trail as if it would go on forever. Libby snatched the bottle away from her and took a drink just to see if she'd been right. Yep. Addison had made goddamn mimosas for their morning walk.

"Addy."

"It's been a tough week."

"I know," Libby said. "I know. But come on."

"I'm calling Mr. Hayes," Addison said, grabbing back the bottle. "Today."

"Even if it ruins your marriage?" she asked. "And tears apart your family? Because whatever it is, Dean's keeping it a secret for a reason. Probably to protect you."

Addison didn't answer. She just turned and started walking again, Libby nearly out of breath before she caught up with her.

"Does you running into Alec Dawson the other day at Hutch have anything to do with this?" Libby asked.

"Of course not."

But Libby saw something in Addison's eyes and the slight way she bit her lip. She'd been obsessed with Alec since college—Libby was convinced Addison only married Dean because Alec had just married that uppity bitch from Texas. Now as she was starting to slowly unravel her relationship with Dean, she looked at newly divorced Alec Dawson as a fucking rock in her swirling river of shit. Alec was like Dean, only better. There had been something between them long ago, but then Alec introduced Addison to this guy he worked with—Dean.

"When is the last time you saw Dr. Larry?"

"Yesterday."

"And what does he say?"

"He used a fancier term . . ." Addison said, smiling for the first time in a while. They found a straightaway on the trail, a glorious fall cavern of light and falling leaves. A Hallmark card in motion. "But basically, he said I was an absolute fucking train wreck."

Branch was behind the wheel of his beloved new Land Rover, nearly identical to Dean's, darting in and out of cars on their way back to their house in Chickasaw Gardens. Their twin boys, Samuel and Ernest, were insulting and punching each other in the back seat. It was late afternoon and Libby hadn't eaten a thing since her breakfast smoothie.

"I am worried about your sister," Libby said. "She's having some kind of nervous breakdown."

"I hate to break it to you," Branch said, punching his CD player. *Dave Matthews.* Branch bobbed his head to "What Would You Say" as he drove. Branch had always been a huge Dave Matthews fan, nearly as big as he'd been of Hootie. "But she's always been kind of nuts."

The constant hum of improvised sound effects had erupted into howls from the back seat. Samuel had punched Ernest in the arm and now Ernest was hammering his brother's leg with a closed fist. The boys, who just turned eight in June, were having a hell of a time. Samuel called Ernest a booger-eating asshole.

"Hey," Libby said. "Hey. Stop it. Just stop it."

Branch was home early for a change, and they'd decided to get a babysitter later and meet a few friends at the Grove. She'd asked about inviting Addison and Dean, maybe an act of good faith to help out, but Branch said absolutely not. He seemed to know something that Libby didn't and was holding back. But then again, she knew more about the situation than he could ever know. She felt like Addison was set on getting a divorce.

"You went walking with Addy today?" he asked.

"I did."

"And?"

"And what?"

"What the hell did you guys talk about?" Branch said.

"Oh, you know," she said. "The usual. She believes Dean might be an international assassin. Crap like that."

"Was she drinking?" Branch asked.

"Who?"

"Who are we talking about?" he said. "Shit, my sister."

"What would you like for dinner?" Libby had already said too much. She'd been friends with Addison since Ole Miss, much longer than she'd been married to Branch. They'd been legends for a time in Oxford, dancing on bar tables together and smuggling Ziploc bags of bourbon in their bras on game days, dressed to the goddamn nines.

"Libby," he said, glancing over as he stopped at a traffic light. "Was she drinking?"

"I don't know," she said. "Maybe a little."

After a long moment, the light turned green and he was off, heading down past the library and turning into Chickasaw Gardens, where they had a simple yet ridiculously expensive two-story brick colonial. They were so far in debt on the house and the new Land Rover and her G-Wagen that she hated to even think about it.

"I may have seen some pills in her purse," she said. "Damn it. I hate this. But Addison is losing it. She told me that a federal agent was after her in the Fresh Market."

Dean came over that night.

The kids were already in bed and Libby was upstairs, fast asleep from trying to read *The Help* for book club (she couldn't get through a chapter without dozing off), when she was awakened by their yellow lab—Buddy—going batshit crazy at the door. She slipped on a cardigan over her tank top and Christmas pajama bottoms and headed down the steps to hear Branch and Dean in the living room. Their voices were muffled and hard to hear over *SportsCenter* blaring from the TV. But she could make out Branch's voice as he laughed at something Dean said and then added, "So sorry, man. My sister has always made shit up."

Libby waited a beat, just out of sight. Her left hand rested against the doorjamb, the massive diamond on her finger twinkling under the hall light. She heard Branch uncork something, some type of super rare bourbon, as they began to discuss Addison's many mental and addiction issues.

She could see Branch in profile but only the back of Dean's perfectly coiffed head as he sat in a leather armchair facing the fire. Her decorator said it was a perfect place to read, as if Branch would reach up onto their color-coordinated shelf of antique books and find a copy of Dickens to enjoy with a pipe. The only reading Branch did was on the toilet. The same book all the time, *The 500 World's Greatest Golf Holes*. Every time she tried to banish it from the bathroom, he complained. He once confided in her that it relaxed him while he sat on the toilet, thinking about the gorgeous holes of the world.

"Libby and I are committed to helping you and the kids."

"Appreciate that, Branch."

"This has been a long time coming," Branch said. "The smallest thing could've set her off."

"You know I got home as soon as I could."

"I know," Branch said. "You're not the one who's been making a fool out of herself. Libby told me tonight she'd found a goddamn pharmacy in Addy's purse."

Son of a bitch. That was supposed to stay between her and Branch. Branch couldn't see her, looking straight at Dean as he nodded along with something Dean was saying, most of it being drowned out by some asshole dissecting every fucking detail of last week's Alabama game.

"How much do you think she's been drinking?"

"Put it this way," Branch said. "While you were gone, she drank down half a bottle of gin while checking on Dad. I know, because no one else touches the Hendrick's but Addison."

"And she had the kids with her?"

"She had Preston," Branch said. "I'm sorry, man. I'm so sorry about this. This whole thing just sucks."

The men didn't speak for a while. Branch turned to the ridiculously large new flat-screen TV mounted over the fireplace. His decision, not hers. She'd bought a lovely oil landscape that the Geek Squad from Best Buy removed for that massive eyesore.

"Did Addison say anything else?"

"What's that?"

"Did Addison say anything else to Libby?"

Libby wanted to march right into her living room and pull Branch's sorry ass off her Restoration Hardware couch by his ear. She closed her eyes and gritted her teeth, knowing there wasn't a fucking secret that Branch could keep from his idol Dean.

"Not much," Branch said. "Only that Libby said Addison thinks you're some kind of international man of mystery. And that she's being followed around East Memphis by a federal agent."

Dean laughed. It wasn't a good laugh. It sounded hollow and forced. "A what?"

"She told Libby that she's going to go back to that Black detective," Branch said. "She says he has something incriminating on you. God knows what he'll come back with. People like that are always looking to extort money from people like us."

Dean stood up, and Libby shrank back behind the door. When she peered back into the living room, Dean had the remote in hand and turned off the television. "Tell me everything she said about this detective."

"I wouldn't worry about it," Branch said, rattling the ice in his whiskey glass, and looking up at Dean, who was now standing. "Just a bunch of crazy talk. Even Libby thinks she's nuts."

Dean moved over to the front window and glanced out to the street. His back was turned to Branch, who looked a little rattled as he gulped down half the bourbon on ice.

"There's a nice place right outside Oxford," Dean said. "Good doctors who offer a highly recommended treatment. I'll need your help talking her into it. But it's the best thing."

"You're a good father."

"Appreciate that, buddy."

"Hey, Dean?" Branch asked. "Those are some nice gloves you've got on. What are they? Calfskin?"

21

Porter Hayes

Deacon Malone had Reverend Hightower's routine down cold, enough that he could take an extra minute or two to stop off at a Dixie Queen on Airways for coffee and egg with bacon sandwiches before parking on a residential street in Orange Mound. Hayes had let Malone drive his Mercedes that morning so he could take the photos of Hightower's comings and goings from the home of one of his girlfriends, a woman named Constance who was married to Hightower's assistant pastor. "The man has no shame," Malone said. "Anointing the husband one minute and laying his hands on his wife the next. I never seen a man with a more restless pecker."

"A what?"

"Haven't you seen those commercials about people having that restless leg syndrome?" Malone said, unwrapping his sandwich from the foil. "This man got himself a restless pecker."

The men laughed. Porter picked up one of the coffees, tore open a single sugar, and stirred it in. The house was a simple one-level brick box with a tall spiked wrought-iron fence topping a brick border wall. Behind the open gate, the reverend's black Escalade was parked big and bold behind an older green Accord. The license plate read TRUSGOD.

"I don't see why we need more pictures," Malone said, half his mouth full. "He'll just say he was giving the good news to Miss Constance this fine morning. And you know damn well Lady Hightower don't give a damn."

"Might matter to the reverend," Hayes said. "I'd say he'll be highly invested in keeping the truth from Constance's husband."

"And why's that?"

"Oh," Hayes said, blowing the steam off his coffee. "Didn't I tell you? See, this Constance woman is married to a fella named Vontre Hubbard. And you've got to understand that Mr. Hubbard didn't get to be in the ministry by accident."

"All right," Malone said, laughing. "All right then. Go ahead."

"Mr. Vontre Hubbard studied the good book down in Parchman after choking out his daddy over a matter of twenty dollars," Hayes said in his deep preacher voice. "Vontre claimed it was just an accident, his hands just slipped around his daddy's old throat before he lifted his ass off the floor and broke his neck."

"Off the damn floor?" Deacon said, taking another bite, and shaking his head. "Must be a big man."

"Funny you ask, Deacon," Hayes said. "Only about six foot six and three fifty."

"Got damn."

"Yep," Hayes said. "Just about the right size to make the Rev come to Jesus and make right with those old women. The difference between justice and compensation."

"Heard you say that a time or two," Malone said. "If the preacher got charged, he'd just lawyer up. Drag this thing out longer than those women got."

Porter drank some coffee and they watched the house. They'd parked next to a big oak and behind two other vehicles, a decent buffer in case anyone was watching them from the house.

"Still don't know how a man that little satisfying six different women," Malone said.

"Five."

"Only five?"

"Way the Lady Hightower came on to me, I don't think they got much going on," Hayes said. "Seems like a strictly financial relationship."

"Maybe an opportunity for you?"

"For five minutes of pleasure?" he said. "Hell, no."

"That all you got, Porter Hayes?" Malone said. "Five minutes? Seems like you could give that woman at least ten minutes of your valuable time."

"Maybe," he said. "But then I'd be just like all the rest of them. I wouldn't do it. And you wouldn't, either."

"Shiiiit."

"She stole from two nice old ladies," Hayes said. "Drained their life savings. Used their money to buy designer dresses, high heel shoes, and fancy-ass perfume. Why? Someone like that doesn't feel a goddamn thing."

"Woman like that could make me feel a lot," Malone said. "Woman got more curves on her than the International Raceway. Known you a long while, Porter Hayes. You're a hell of a detective, but I know you ain't no saint. Don't tell me I finally got you coming back to the Cross."

"It ain't religion."

"Then what is it?"

"I guess I'm trying to respect myself more," he said. "I've done some things over the years I'm not proud of. Ran a little wild after Genevieve died. Partying and drinking all that mess. Shit. You know that story. You the one got me out of the mess, young man."

"Not so young anymore."

"Funny how that works."

Reverend Hightower walked out in a blue tracksuit, wearing a ball cap and sunglasses as if the big-ass Escalade and the TRUSGOD plate didn't give him away. Miss Constance was nowhere to be seen as he shut the door behind him. Porter mashed the button on his camera, catching frame after frame of the reverend's cocky-ass walk. Hightower looked up the road and lifted his chin to get a better look down the street before he hustled for the keys out of his pocket, jumping behind the wheel and backing out fast. Must've been a glint off that camera lens.

"You want to follow him?" Malone said.

"Naw," Hayes said. "I think we got all we need."

Porter set down his camera on the floorboard and was about to reach for his coffee when his phone buzzed.

"You taking the day off?" Darlene asked. "Or are you planning on showing your pretty face at the office?"

"Apologize if my detective work is interfering with your schedule."

"More stuff from Sawyer hot off the fax," she said. "Even though we're not getting paid, I know you'll want to check this out."

"More on Dean McKellar?"

"I don't rightly know, Porter," Darlene said. "I can't make heads nor tails of what I'm seeing. Looks like your old client up and married a dead man."

Hayes's office had grown warm and muggy, a cool breeze shooting through the open window a welcome change, rattling the paperwork on his desk. He used his Showboats mug to keep the fax sheets from the *Cortland Standard* and *Syracuse Post* from flying away, obits and news items about the death of Dean Russell McKellar on January 4, 1992.

Army veteran McKellar, 26, was decorated twice for his service during the Persian Gulf War. State troopers say he lost control of his GMC Yukon on I-81 after hitting a patch of ice. The vehicle then struck a tree, according to reports, killing McKellar on impact at about 1 a.m. His mother, Dorothy McKellar, said her son was an avid hunter and fisherman and a member of Memorial Baptist Church . . .

Hayes picked up the phone and dialed 411 and asked for Cortland, New York. There was only one D. McKellar listed in the area and he scribbled the number on one of the obits. The phone rang several times before a woman picked up. He asked for Dorothy McKellar and he heard the woman say, "Mom, it's for you."

He wanted to stop the younger woman but soon got, "This is Mrs. McKellar."

"Mrs. McKellar," he said. "My name's Porter Hayes. I'm a private investigator in Memphis, Tennessee. I know it's been a long time, and your son's death still has to be filled with a lot of pain for you, but Dean's name came up in a current investigation."

"Mr. Hayes," she said, "my son died eighteen years ago. Thank you."

The line went dead. Darlene walked in, closed one of the windows, and snatched the empty coffee mug off his desk. He called the number back. After another long series of rings, the younger woman picked up. Darlene returned and set down a mug of hot coffee, steam rising from the lip.

"I don't know who you are or what you want, but calling about my dead brother is about as low as it gets."

"Ma'am," Porter said. "Ma'am. Let me stop you right there. I'm not calling to inflict more pain on y'all. I'm calling because I believe an individual down here might be currently using Dean's identity."

"This sounds like a scam," the woman said. "Who the hell is this?"

"Did your brother have friends in Memphis?"

"No."

"Was he involved in any type of military contracting service after the first Gulf War?"

The woman let out a long breath. And then she sighed. "No," she said. "My brother did his time in the army and had just graduated from Syracuse. He wanted to go to Manhattan and work in finance. I don't know why you're asking me all these questions. I really need to go."

"Ma'am," Hayes said, "if you'll do me a favor, I'm going to give you the number of a woman named Lantana Jones who's a sergeant with the Memphis Police Department. You can call her and she'll be able to vouch for me."

"How about I just call the Memphis police on my own?" she said. "And ask who you really are?"

"Even better," Hayes said. "Let me leave you with my phone number."

Thirty minutes later, the woman called back. The real Dean McKellar's sister's name was Beth. This time she was polite and understanding right until she said, "Okay, now. Just what in the hell is going on, Mr. Hayes?"

"I need you to verify a Social Security number that I've gotten from my client."

"You mind me asking who is your client?"

"Mrs. Dean Russell McKellar."

"You've got to be shitting me."

"I shit you not, Beth."

He heard Beth and her mom go back and forth and then Beth picked up the phone again and said she had it, waiting for Porter to call out the nine numbers.

Porter spoke slowly and carefully.

"Son of a bitch," she said. "How's that even happen? This person just stole my brother's identity and is living it up in Memphis. Who is this asshole?"

"I'm working on it."

Porter looked through the doorframe to Darlene where she'd been listening in and nodded at her. He picked up the phone by the cradle and walked over by the window, the cord trailing behind him. "I'm going to send y'all a photograph of the man using your brother's identity. Can you give me a good address?"

"You think we know him?"

"I don't know," Hayes said. "But at this point, nothing about this case makes a lick of sense."

22

Addison

She had sixteen missed calls from Porter Hayes. And six voice-mails. *Mrs. McKellar, this is Porter Hayes. We really need to talk . . .*

Since her walk in Overton Park and her confession to Libby, Addison had been too much of a coward to call Porter Hayes back. If she did call Mr. Hayes, she knew it would blow up everything she'd built these last fifteen years and create a whirlwind of shit for the kids. Dean had pretty much promised as much in his office the other night, asking her all kinds of questions about her fragile state of mind and saying he was really worried that she'd been drinking too much and taking too many pills. All this delivered in Dean's dry, condescending tone, what she liked to call his army voice, speaking down to her as both the head of the household and the true voice of reason. Of course, she denied everything and said she had absolutely no idea what he was talking about. Sure, she took a daily Zoloft (doesn't everybody?) and on the rare occasion took a Klonopin. She'd started taking them when she first got those horrible panic attacks after scuba diving in Cancun (diving into a cenote with Dean and not knowing which way was up or down, lost in a swirl of bubbles).

But Addison damn well knew how that game of telephone went. From Libby to Branch and then direct into the ear of Dean. In the last week, Dean was now more present in his family's life than he'd ever been. She'd wake the kids for school and there was Dean in their incomplete kitchen, flipping pancakes and frying bacon. The other night, he'd stayed up late with Sara Caroline on the couch to watch those awful *Twilight* movies. A girl in love with a vampire and in some kind of triangle with Teen Wolf. *Jesus God.* And then there was Dean again, driving the family to Preston's soccer game, cheering and clapping from the sidelines and gladhanding the other parents. Dean McKellar, Superdad! No one seemed to know or ask about his horrific accident in London as he helped pack up the soccer balls and took the family for a big pizza at Mellow Mushroom.

And now it was late afternoon on Friday, Dean casually mentioning the fundraiser at the zoo tonight, just an offhand comment about maybe both of them dressing up this year. Wouldn't that be fun? All forgiven and forgotten for the annual Zoo Boo, an event that McKellar Construction always sponsored. Dean and Addison would be expected to be at the opening wine mixer just outside Primate Canyon, where you could guzzle cheap pinot noir to the smell of ripe gorilla shit.

"What are you going to be this year?" Dean asked, coming in from wherever he'd been and kissing her on the cheek. "Everyone is dressing up. It'll be fun."

"No, thanks," she said. "You take Preston."

"What about Sara Caroline?"

"Sara Caroline is fourteen," Addison said. "She hasn't dressed up for Halloween in three years."

Dean sorted through the big stack of mail while he explained exactly why she had to go to the Zoo Boo. It was one of his company's biggest charitable events and everyone would be expecting her. Addison grinding her teeth, wanting to ask the obvious question: *What fucking company are you even talking about?*

Dean disappeared upstairs to change out of his business suit, Addison left alone in the half-finished kitchen. The cabinets had been installed weeks ago but she couldn't store anything in them until the countertops arrived. They were useless, open, and exposed. She rested her elbows on a piece of plywood set over the island until Preston walked in, pissed off that he was just being told about Zoo Boo. Horrors of all horrors, he hadn't picked out a costume.

"You have a playroom filled with them," she said. "Just pick one out."

"They're old," he said. "They don't fit."

"Preston," she said. "I don't have time for this crap. Just find something that fits and put it on. No one is going to judge you."

"The only thing that fits is Pikachu."

"Okay," Addison said, already dreading every moment of this night, playing happy and content as she made small talk with the people from the Club and Second Pres. "Pikachu's perfect."

Preston ran his hands through his hair as if the whole world had conspired against him. He was still in his blue polo and khakis from school, his hair sticky and wild after a side trip to Ben and Jerry's, which she considered a second-tier ice cream shop to her own dear and defunct Sugar Babies. "I'm ten, Mom," he said. "Kids will laugh."

"Pikachu is awesome," she said. "He can electrocute people with his tail. I wish I could do that. Don't you?"

She could get through this. She'd have to get through this for Preston. She wouldn't wear a costume, but she'd dress up just the same. All smiles and laughter. Those McKellars. *What a wonderful family.*

"Are you okay, Mom?"

"Just thinking."

"Can I get Sara Caroline to paint my face?"

"Sure," she said. "Sure. Whatever you want."

"What if Pikachu was dead," he said. "But then came back to life? Wouldn't that be cool? Like a zombie."

Two and a half hours later, Addison and Dean were walking into the wine mixer at the Gorilla Grillz pavilion at the Memphis Zoo. Most of their friends had dressed up. Even Branch and Libby came as characters from *Pirates of the Caribbean*, Libby as Jack Sparrow and Branch as a lusty wench, with big balloons up under a puffy blouse and a red scarf tied around his head, which everyone found funny as hell. Addison didn't look for anyone's approval as she accepted a glass of red from Hannah Tracy. Hannah, *oh boy Hannah*, going full-out as the Little Mermaid in a bright red wig, wraparound sparkly green skirt, and purple bikini top.

"Preston looks so cute," Hannah said. "What exactly is he?"

"He's Zombie Pikachu," Addison said, taking down half the wine. "Sara Caroline painted his face."

"So creative," she said.

"I know," Addison said. "Zombies are so fun. Always coming back for more."

Dean was encircled by several men she knew, including that son of a bitch Jimbo Hornsby. Jimbo, appropriately dressed like Shrek with his fat face painted green, sipped from a big red Solo cup and laughed at a joke Dean had just told. She figured everything over the last two weeks was just some big goddamn joke. Ha ha ha. *Sorry, babe. Just a little accident in England, got stabbed and lost my passport. But it's all cool now.* Ha ha ha.

"Addison?"

Hannah Tracy was still standing there, dressed as half woman, half fish. Who wears a bikini top out in the middle of October? Her husband, Ward, one of Dean's best friends from an old-money Delta family, had probably talked her into it. Dean wanted Addison to show off the gold and diamond-encrusted Cartier. Ward wanted Hannah to show off her new tits.

"Are you okay?" Hannah said, placing a hand on Addison's back. "Do you need to sit down?"

"I'm fine."

"You're as white as a ghost."

Addison finished the wine. "We're all as white as ghosts," she said, walking to the bar, shooting Dean a hard look. Preston ran off with his twin cousins, asking if they could go and play in the House of Glass down by the giraffe exhibit. Why the fuck not? Have a ball, Zombie Pikachu. Bring chaos and disorder to us all. Devour the meek.

Dean intercepted her before she got to the bar, reaching for her hand. His hand so cold on the back of hers, gripping her fingers. He had on a navy cashmere sweater vest over a checked shirt, a pair of six-hundred-dollar custom-made jeans with crocodile cowboy boots that added two inches. "I thought we talked about slowing down."

"I'm only getting a glass of prosecco."

"Do you think that's a good idea?"

"How do I know what's a good idea, Dean?" she said. "You've been telling me that since you reappeared like magic in our shower."

Addison couldn't stand it anymore, everyone dressed up as pirates and pimps, mermaids and superheroes, getting tipsy and making small talk. She could've recited from memory almost every word of it. All of it sounding the same. *30-A, Montana, Thanksgiving in New York, the brand new G-Wagen, Presbyterian Book Sale* . . . "Please let me go," she said. "You're hurting my fingers."

Hannah Tracy was with Libby now, Addison not speaking to her supposed best friend and sister-in-law since they arrived. Libby nodded along with whatever bullshit Hannah was telling her but also glanced at Addison with what might've passed as apologetic regret. Why did she have to start all this? How was Addison now the bad guy in this whole melodrama? A large banner flapped in the breeze over the bar, cocktails provided by McKellar Construction. *"The Mid-South's Most Trusted Name."*

Dean returned and handed her a plastic flute of prosecco before pivoting and greeting more friends from the Club and the Cotton Krewe.

Addison took a big sip, and another. How could anyone get through these events without something to drink? She knew she was glowering at Dean but didn't care a goddamn bit, her face flushing and her knees weak. She felt almost weightless, not remembering the last time she ate, the fucking stuff going straight to her head. She leaned against a support beam, Hannah Tracy laughing and laughing, looking like the bow of an old ship, her artificial breasts pointing due north. Addison closed her eyes and wobbled a bit. *Fuck. Fuck.* What the hell was wrong with her? She was feeling lightheaded as hell.

"Are you okay, ma'am?" someone asked.

So many people staring at her. All the vampires and witches wanting to take a bite of her neck. For a moment, she thought she saw that federal agent from the Fresh Market standing beside a row of singing pumpkins. The one who said Dean was involved in something of international importance and then told her Dean died in Paris. He was dressed as a scarecrow, watching her and lifting a hand to beckon her to him before she realized it was a goddamn skeleton robot with red, glowing eyes laughing at her.

"Mom, Mom!"

A dead little yellow rat was tugging at her sleeve. "Come on," he said. "You've got to see this."

"Please get me out of here, Pres," she said. "Please."

"Have you ever been in a glass house?" he said. "Ernest ran into a wall and got a bloody nose. It's freakin' awesome."

He'd drugged her. The bastard had drugged her.

That was the only explanation that made sense as she followed the little yellow rat, aka Preston, down the winding path with inflatable black cats and spiders shuffling in the wind. Preston held on to her hand, taking her down past the construction signs for the Zambezi River and past the African Veldt. She spotted the glass house in the distance, surrounded by tons of kids and their parents. A safe place where she could hide from Dean and his friends, clear her head, and maybe get calm until she could figure this whole thing out.

"Come on," Preston said, walking up onto the metal platform.

They stood in line up a metal ramp, Addison glancing back to see if Dean or Branch was behind them. She felt safe among the costumed kids and parents. Buzz Lightyear, a human hot dog, Britney Spears, and Beetlejuice. The line moved slow and easy up to the glowing glass house flashing with string lights and neon. Preston pressed a ticket into Addison's hand as they got close to the maze entrance. Kids screamed and laughed inside, floors seeming to crack under them like ice. The ramp tilted beneath her feet as she walked, but the guardrail under her left hand kept her steady. Someone touched her shoulder and she turned and stared right into the face of a Flying Monkey, Addison nearly coming out of her skin.

"The line's moving, darlin'," said a woman behind the mask.

Addison reached out and patted the monkey on its dear little red hat as if it were ChaCha. "Good boy," she said.

She placed a hand over her mouth but kept walking, knowing Dean had done this to her. Back in college this god-awful KA from Texas cornered her at The Gin and bought Libby and her Jack and Cokes that went right to her head. The KA had held her upright and carried her out to his jacked-up truck before shoving her inside, Addison as loose and wobbly as a rag doll, when Libby came running out with two friends from the football team who helped Addison out of the truck and then took the KA behind a dumpster and beat the ever-living shit out of him. That's what she needed now. Someone to pummel the shit out of her husband.

"Come on," the little yellow rat said. "Follow me. I know the way, Mom."

And just like Alice, she was down deep in the rabbit hole, only the rabbit hole didn't look like a rabbit hole, it looked like the inside of a disco with flashing lights and awful music. Preston felt along the passageways with his little hands, being blocked at every corner until he'd put his hand through a glass wall and motioned for her to come on. Addison closed her eyes and felt her way through the glass maze, feeling the walls, knowing she could do it all by touch, when she ran smack into the glass, falling on her ass.

Preston laughed and helped her up. What a good kid. She followed. She took slow baby steps now, wondering where all this would lead. Maybe she and Pres could keep on twisting and turning until everything was far behind them. The zoo. Central Gardens. Dean and his boll weevils. She glanced down the path she'd just followed and through row after row of glass walls and saw Dean standing outside watching her. She felt all along the next wall and the next until she touched nothing at all and hustled through. He'd never catch them. Ever.

In New York, he'd made so much sense. Addison about to hit twenty-five, absolutely ancient in her mind at the time. She'd already been a bridesmaid in six weddings. *You're next, Addy. You're next.* The only thing she got out of the weddings was getting laid twice. The publishing world no longer held her interest. How many times could she write a crappy press release for another crappy thriller. *This is Richard Jones's most personal mission ever. From the all-time bestselling master of suspense* . . . Flapping thousands of books for the author's scrawl at Barnes & Noble and Borders and then ending up with him at a book expo in Amarillo with his liver-spotted hand moving over her knee. Addison pressed on and kept on following the rat, ramming her head into three different walls like a stupid goddamn bird. Why Dean? Why had she chosen Dean? He'd appeared like something both new and familiar. Then it came to her. Dean McKellar was goddamn Big Dick Jones, former soldier turned world traveler, a guy who talked about backpacking across Europe and all the vineyards he'd visited. The son of a bitch even knew how to sail.

She turned and saw Dean, or who she thought was Dean, waiting outside the glass house, just a shadow, a ghost, or maybe a blot of ink running down from the pages of a book. Had she made him all up? Was he even real? She began to pound on the glass, "Let me the fuck out of here. I'm locked in."

"Jesus, Mom," Preston said. "Calm down. It's just a fun house."

Addison didn't recall the ride home, only coming to in the front seat of the Escalade, Preston shaking her awake and telling her that there was a man inside their house.

They were parked right in front of the guest cottage, lights off, both garage doors down and the security gate to the street closed. Her head felt like a goddamn balloon as she flipped down the illuminated mirror on the visor. Her face was a mess. Mascara smeared across her cheek. "What happened?"

"Mom," Preston said. "You need to call the police. Dad's been in there more than five minutes and he told me to call the police if he wasn't back."

"Who's in the house?" she asked, her voice echoing inside her head.

"The one-armed man," Preston said, shaking her shoulder. "Dad saw him in the window. He said for us to stay here and he'd take care of it. But you need to call the police now. Call them."

Addison reached into her purse but she couldn't seem to find her phone. She felt along the receipts, stray coins, and business cards, a tube of lipstick and her change purse. She pulled out Preston's Pikachu cowl and a ring of keys. Outside, the trees shook in a cold wind, the only light coming from a security light on the corner of their guest cottage.

"Are you sure he saw someone?"

"Dad said he thought he saw someone."

"But you said the one-armed man?" Addison said and reached for the door handle, telling Preston to stay put. "Everyone will be fine. I'm sure Dad is just turning on all the lights."

Thank god Sara Caroline was still over at Darby Saunders's house. She said they were going to do homework, but Addison knew Darby's parents were out of town and they'd probably invited some boys over. Not her main concern at the moment. Her main concern was looking like a drunken idiot in front of half of Memphis and now facing a killer in their house.

"Stay."

Preston tried to argue, but Addison shut the door behind her and raised a finger in his direction. *Stay, good boy, stay.*

And where the hell was ChaCha in all this? Their curly-coated friend and companion should be barking his goddamn head off if there was someone inside. As she walked along the stone path behind the home, the wind kicked up a bit, scattering more leaves into the empty pool and across their stone deck. She heard thunder in the distance and blooms of lightning, bad weather rolling in.

Keys in hand, she walked toward the back door.

As she passed the big bank of windows in the living room, she saw Dean arguing with a much larger man. Yes, it was the same man from the kitchen, the fucking one-armed man. Dean yelled something and the man yelled something back, all of it framed like a silent movie, until the man rushed Dean but didn't get two feet from him when Dean raised a pistol and shot the man three times in the chest. The dimly lit room bloomed with flashes of bright light, almost no sound except the thud of the intruder dropping hard.

She felt herself trying to scream, something ticking the back of her throat. But instead of coming out, the scream drew back inside her. She held a hand to her mouth and started to shake. Whatever she'd taken, it had paralyzed her. She couldn't scream, she couldn't move. Oh, fuck. Preston was in the car and she didn't have a phone.

Addison walked closer to the windows and watched Dean drag the big man by his feet out of their living room, past her antique hutch filled with her mother's crystal figurines, knocking a few framed pics of the family from a side table onto the floor. Each year with the McKellars in white linen and khakis by the dunes and seagrass. Most years she used the photo as their Christmas card, running down all their travels and milestones. Preston lost four teeth. Sara Caroline made it to the play-offs. Dean is the hardest-working and bestest husband on the planet.

She hurried back toward the SUV just in time to see Dean running down the front walkway. He had a casual, confident smile on his face as he looked at Addison and watched Preston climb out of the car. "All clear," he said. "Just being extra careful."

She mouthed, *Are you fucking kidding me?*

Dean shot her a look. "Give me a second, and then you guys use the back door. I'm headed out. Some business just came up."

Addison just stared at him, absolutely frozen. Her husband had just shot and killed a man in their living room and now planned to calmly go out for a quick drive, probably to drop the body into the Mississippi. They both watched as Preston hustled around the corner of the house to wait at the back door, leaving Addison standing there with Dean. A light rain started to pat the asphalt.

"You know you made a real scene tonight, Addy," Dean said. "Christ. I had to carry you out over my shoulder."

"Me?" she said. "You just fucking killed a man."

"What?" Dean looked at her and slowly shook his head. The bastard had the audacity to look hurt. "Oh, Addison. Why don't you go up-stairs and sleep this one off. You're not thinking straight."

23

Gaultier

They had landed in Memphis the night before and immediately drove south in four shiny black SUVs to Tunica, billboards along the cotton fields inviting them to Sam's Town, the Horseshoe, and the Fitz. *Welcome to the Gateway to the Blues. All You Can Eat Crab Legs. $10,000 slot tournament. Weekly Chevy Truck Giveaway. Snoop Dogg and The Charlie Daniels Band.* If Gaultier wasn't convinced he was on the last leg of his final voyage, he might've found the trip amusing.

"I thought we were going to Memphis?"

"They know me at this casino," Anatoliy Zub said. "I go to Vegas every Christmas. Spend lots and lots of money and get the points. So many whores and poker games. And the Charlie Daniels this weekend. How could I pass up such a trip?"

"Are you joking with me?"

"You don't know Charlie Daniels?" he said. "You don't know the *Urban Cowboy*? That ass of Debra Winger in her blue jeans. So fantastic. 'The Devil Who Goes Down to Georgia.' He plays the fiddle. Very good. Like the devil himself gave him this. Like Faust. You understand?"

"I'm tired, Anatoliy," Gaultier said. "I haven't showered or changed my clothes in two days and the meal we had in Newark was horrible. Even by American standards."

"Don't worry," Zub said, punching him in the arm. The SUV bucking up and down over potholes in the highway. "Don't worry. We have your luggage and all your Italian suits, black silk underwear, and so many watches. Why so many watches, Gaultier?"

"Why am I here?" he said.

"I need you as the, how you say, *go-between*."

"Go-between."

"See," Zub said, punching him in the arm again. This time even harder. "You understand. You must make everything clear to your friend Jack Dumas. Collinson left him in Istanbul alone to die. Standing there with his cock and balls in his hand. Like a goat tethered to the tree. A sacrifice."

"Jack Dumas is not my friend," Gaultier said. "The last time I saw him, he dangled me over the Nile by my feet."

"Ha ha," Zub said. "You really don't know Charlie Daniels? Come on. He is real country western music. He sings like my way of living or leave this long-haired country boy alone. *Ha ha.* You know it. I know you do."

The headlights cut through the dirt swirling across the road and endless flat land. It reminded Gaultier of taking the high-speed train across the farmland of Provence, but instead of rolling hills of lavender, it was flat dirt and cotton. He could see the flashing neon of a city far in the distance.

"You brought me all this way to kill me."

"Please, please," Zub said. "You are Gaultier. The great negotiator. You brought Peter Collinson to me. And now I bring you to Peter Collinson. I know you both will make things right. I will be compensated for everything. Perhaps more. And maybe we play some blackjack, meet some women, and see the Charlie Daniels. You will love him. He's legend."

"I'll ask again," Gaultier said. "When we make things right, are you going to kill me?"

Anatoliy Zub didn't answer and stared out the window toward the bright flashing lights of the casino town. An entire city rising from the cotton fields. Gaultier twisted and straightened his skull cuff links. "People say those are made of human bones," Zub said.

"Is that what they say?"

"Is it true?"

"They were made for my father," Gaultier said. "Crafted of ivory in Botswana. *Memento mori*."

"You and me," Zub said. "We are the same. We sell death. Once we make things right with Dumas and Collinson, we put all this in the past. Yes, me and you finally have that drink, Monsieur Gaultier. Won't that be nice? Do you like the tequila?"

"I would rather drink gasoline."

The four SUVs wheeled in front of the neon-lit portico to the Sam's Town casino hotel, door popping open, hatches rising. All of Zub's muscle and luggage being deployed with a sharp, efficient military energy. The valets barely had time to hold open the doors for the Russian bears, who pushed them aside and headed into the lobby.

Gaultier looked inside the glass doors where Jack Dumas stood with four of Zub's guards, pulling luggage with his hooked hand from a wheeled rack. He hefted up one of Gaultier's Louis Vuitton leather bags—Gaultier held his breath, waiting for the hook to slice right through the delicate leather—and tossed it over his shoulder.

"We don't need him," Gaultier said. "He is a detestable human."

"But he knows things we don't," Zub said.

"Like what?"

"He knows why Collinson would be so foolish as to double-cross Anatoliy Zub," he said. "This treasure he has brought to his secret home must be incredible."

"I have absolutely no idea what it is."

"You know what I think?" Zub asked.

Gaultier ran his hands over his wrinkled pants. He looked at Zub and shook his head.

"It is a bomb," he said. "Boom! I think Collinson has brought his war home."

"Then why would you care?"

"Maybe I like to be the good guy," he said. "Save many lives."

Gaultier shook his head. "You would sell it."

"Yes, of course," Zub said, laughing, slapping him hard on the back. "I sell the shit out of whatever it is."

When Gaultier got to his room on the fourth floor, the Huck Finn Suite as promised, he found every piece of his Louis Vuitton set arranged by the door. He grabbed the leather duffel bag and began to pull out socks and underwear, reaching deep inside for the cell he'd found at Collinson's flat. Before he'd been propositioned/abducted by Zub and his thugs, he'd charged the phone at his hotel.

He sat on the edge of the bed, the curtains drawn back on a plate glass window looking deep into the cotton fields, past more casino lights, and onward to what must've been the Mississippi River snaking down from the north. He'd read about it in books, but Gaultier had never seen it. The muddy water shone nearly white in the moonlight and he was taken by the entire scene. A simple man born in the south of France and now deep in America like Champlain or Cartier, out to seek his fortune . . . He pushed the power button on the cell.

The phone immediately started to ring and buzz in his hands. He answered.

"Is this Peter?"

"Yes."

"Peter, what the fuck did you do with my mother?" a woman said. "I know all about Omar's and this pile of shit coming in. I've gone to the police. I told them everything."

"You told them everything?" Gaultier said. "I hope not. Perhaps you and I can conduct some business."

"Why would I trust you?"

Gaultier took a breath. "Because I'm not Peter Collinson," he said. "Even Peter Collinson is not Peter Collinson, my dear woman. I'm afraid your mother, whoever she is, might be dead. My name is Gaultier, a fixer of sorts. And you have the most lovely voice."

"Fuck you."

"Ah," he said. "So young and full of life. We must meet. You tell me about this Omar and his pile of shit and I'll tell you how you might find Peter Collinson and your mother. *N'est-ce pas?*"

The door to the suite rattled open and Jack Dumas stumbled in. Gaultier shut off the phone and slipped it back in the leather bag. Dumas slapped Gaultier on the knee before eyeing a sofa by the large window. "Don't get your fucking panties in a twist, Frenchie," he said. "I'm here to watch you. Not cuddle with you."

Dumas pulled out a SIG Sauer from his belt and made a circular motion with the barrel. "But go head and get into your jammies," he said. "Daddy's got some serious work to do tomorrow. I can't wait to see fucking Peter's face when I walk into his goddamn kitchen."

24

Addison

She'd slept most of Saturday nursing an epic hangover from whatever had been slipped in her drink. On Sunday, Dean refused to let Addison leave the house. He'd slept in the guesthouse but had conspicuously taken her car keys off the rack, leaving a Post-it that it would be best if she stayed at home until she felt better. "Felt better" being not-so-secret code for her acting like a crazy drunk in front of their so-called friends. All day long she'd done her best to check on the kids and take care of some laundry, not speaking to Dean but often being spoken to by Dean, who kept going back and forth from the guesthouse. She wouldn't answer him, just stared in his general direction until he was done talking. On Monday, the keys had miraculously returned to the rack and Dean was nowhere to be found, Superdad obviously finding better things to do than make pancakes on a busy Monday morning. Thank god Josefina was there to keep the family rolling along. *You no look so good, Mrs. McKellar.*

Addison had dressed in her supersuit, the black leggings, black cashmere hoodie, and Seaside ball cap, and worn her enormous sunglasses as she drove into the rising sun to drop off Preston first and then Sara Caroline. No small talk that morning. Both the kids sensed a seismic shift in the McKellar household that no one wanted to discuss. Sara Caroline only answered questions with a grunt and then moodily exited the passenger seat, opening the rear hatch for her lacrosse stick and slamming it shut behind her. Addison wondered what kind of stories were being passed around among her Hutch friends.

By 8:30, she was pulling into CK's Coffee Shop across from East High School. Porter Hayes's black Mercedes was parked in a handicapped space, its wheels with conspicuously heavy theftproof lug nuts on the rims. When she walked inside, she found him sitting in a booth facing Poplar and reading a copy of the morning's *Commercial Appeal.* The headline above the fold read: "Expected GOP Victory Could Help Obama in 2012" with a smaller headline below: "Elvis Costar Reported Missing. Daughter Seeks Answers."

"Okay," Addison said. "I'm ready, Mr. Hayes."

He looked over the edge of the paper and folded it twice, setting it by his coffee.

"So glad you came around, Mrs. McKellar."

"Addison," she said. "Just Addison. So what in the fuck is going on?"

Hayes leaned back into the booth and glanced over his shoulder. He looked every bit the part of the cool seventies investigator in his brown leather jacket over a cream-colored turtleneck.

"You sure you're ready?" he said. "Because once that cat's out of the bag, it's gonna run loose and free."

"Who is my husband?"

Porter Hayes reached down beside him and slid a manila envelope across the table.

"Mr. Dean McKellar," he said. "Once was lost but now he's found."

"Clever," she said, slitting open the top with her nail.

"Happens when you grow up in the church," he said. "My mom sang in the choir. Most beautiful voice I'd heard before I met my late wife. Say, you sure you want to open this here?"

"You want me to go back home to Dean with it?"

Hayes didn't say a word, only reached for his coffee.

The first page was an invoice from Hayes Investigations for an additional six hundred and twenty dollars and ninety-eight cents. The other pages were lengthy reports of where and when. *Investigator spoke to . . . Investigator then consulted . . .* "Want to give me the short version?"

"Yes, ma'am," he said. "Been trying for a while."

"I wasn't ready then."

"But you are now?"

"My husband drugged me on Friday night and made me look like a drunken idiot in front of all our friends," she said. "And then he topped off the night by killing a man in our living room."

"Then what happened?"

"When my son and I came back inside, the body was gone," she said. "Dean left for a few hours and acted as if nothing happened."

Hayes raised his eyebrows. That was it. Just an eyebrow raise while he smoothed his mustache. Addison figured Porter Hayes wasn't exactly shocked by another murder in Memphis, or a man as deceitful as Dean McKellar. The letterhead on his invoice proudly reading *Serving Memphis Since 1971.*

"Your husband is not Dean McKellar," he said. "He took the name of a dead man from Cortland, New York. That's upstate, right below Syracuse."

Addison made a rolling motion with her hand for him to get on with it. He was rambling in his stories just like her father. He'd go on and on about what he had for breakfast and then running into an old friend at the Kroger pharmacy before telling you the goddamn house was on fire.

"Then who is he?"

"Well," Hayes said. "I don't exactly know."

"You don't know?" she said. "Then what the hell am I paying you for?"

"Remember when I told you McKellar Construction did work for the Department of Defense?"

"Sure," she said. "You got that from our friend Alec Dawson."

Hayes held up his hand and nodded, wanting to hook up with the story. The waitress returned with a glass of water and a cup of coffee that no one had requested.

"Mrs. McKellar," he said. "Your husband doesn't build shit. Your husband sells weapons and men to the government. You understand? He's not a building contractor. He's a military contractor with millions and millions paid out from this stupid goddamn war. When the government doesn't want to take the blame, they hire men like your husband to farm out the talent. Instead of just taking more poor kids like they did in Vietnam. They don't want to win this thing or accept the blame. Just let things simmer over there in Afghanistan."

"My husband has never been to Afghanistan."

"Maybe Dean McKellar hasn't been," he said. "But Peter Collinson flies over on a regular basis doing work for Warlock Corp."

"Wait, wait, wait," Addison said, feeling all the curses upon mankind blowing up in her face. "Dean is really Peter?"

"Dean is Peter sometimes, but we're not exactly sure who Peter is," Hayes said. "His real company, Warlock, has a hell of a paper trail. Big, big money. I've counted up nearly sixty-five million just last year."

"We don't have that kind of money."

"Peter Collinson does," Hayes said. "Mrs. McKellar, your husband isn't just operating from Memphis. He's an international player. This war has been real good to him. I think he just comes back to Memphis to hang his hat, lie low in his old foxhole. You dig? Now I need to ask you a question. How exactly did you meet this man and what all do you really know about him?"

"He said he was from Upstate New York," she said. "He doesn't have siblings and both his parents died young. He was commissioned into the army right out of college and served in the first Gulf War. He was a captain but got tired of the bullshit. He was working in Manhattan when I met him, for an investment firm, with my friend Alec Dawson. Right? He was very ambitious. He was also charming and stable and we got married way too fast. He had lots of friends in New York. Friends of my friends. Hell, I wouldn't even have met him except for Alec. I guess he screwed us both."

This was a lot for a Monday. She rested her forearms on the Formica table and dropped her head into them. Hayes remained quiet for a long while until she got herself upright and wiped her face with a napkin. He reached over for another handful from the dispenser and passed them along. "You're very good at this," Addison said.

"Seen a lot of tears in my time."

"Lots of jilted wives?"

"And husbands," he said. "And lovers. And families. No matter the size of it, a lie is just a lie. He may be your husband here in Memphis, but he's someone altogether different when he gets on that plane. You do know he has his own private plane?"

"I only know he killed a man."

"Okay," Hayes said. "That's a good place to start. Who did he kill?"

"You believe me?"

"Of course, I believe you," Hayes said. "Your husband is one of the biggest damn liars I've ever come across. I'm here to help you sort out the truth, not to doubt what you have to say."

"He killed the one-armed man."

"The one who threatened you and made that big-ass turkey sandwich?"

She nodded.

"You know the man's name?"

She shook her head.

"You know why he's here?"

"Looking for Peter Collinson," she said.

"Well, goddamn," Hayes said. "Seems like trouble always comes home to roost, Mrs. McKellar. Guess we're not the only ones searching for the truth."

Addison shook her head and reached for the coffee. It looked weak and horrible but it was hot and warmed her hands. Her lips felt very dry and cracked as she spoke. "Please don't call me that anymore. Just call me Addison."

"Addison," Hayes said. "Okay, Addison. I think your family is in danger. Any chance you might get out of town until I can straighten all this out?"

Porter Hayes advised her to pick up her kids from school and head straight to the nearest hotel. "Use cash if you can," he said. "Dean, or whoever the hell he is, is sure to be tracking your every move."

Instead, Addison got in her Escalade and drove to the nearest Starbucks, sat in the parking lot, and cried for five minutes. Once she got her shit together, she called Alec Dawson at work. He wasn't in the office, and that's exactly where an intelligent and rational woman would've left it. But not Addison. She wanted answers and damn well knew that Alec had been holding out on Porter Hayes. He knew a fuckton more than he was letting on. If it hadn't been for Alec, she'd never have met Dean, she'd never have brought him back with her to Memphis, and she'd never have settled into *Pleasantville*, raising kids and attending fundraisers with a man she obviously didn't know.

The whole thing was embarrassing as hell, like a dream she used to have repeatedly as a teen, her dream self at school completely naked and walking the halls, people pointing and snickering, and her with no place to hide, absolutely exposed to everyone.

No offense to Porter Hayes, but she needed a lot more than what would fit on a neatly typed report. Hayes was apparently an honest man, but he'd also left her with a new invoice for six hundred and twenty dollars and ninety-eight cents after the extra thousand she'd already paid him. She wasn't sure where the ninety-eight cents came from, but she was sure he had his reasons.

Addison started her Escalade again and drove toward Collierville and the house Alec shared with his daughter, Ellie. She didn't have Alec's phone number anymore, Dean long ago telling her to erase any and all messages to Alec Dawson or his ex-wife, Susan, and block their numbers. There was to be no more contact with that family. At the time, Addison thought it was a legal thing, something to do with the lawsuit, but did as she was told without a single question. Funny how that worked. Never thinking to question Dean.

She drove straight through Germantown, past the turn to her father's condo and another turn to the home where she grew up. Most everything in the quaint faux village of strip malls and little businesses looking absolutely the same. The Germantown Kroger, the Baskin-Robbins, and Our Lady of Perpetual Help, where she was confirmed and they had the funeral service for her mother.

Along the highway, you could still catch glimpses of what Germantown used to be like long ago, before she was born. Old families still clinging to their rolling acreage and farmland set between the neverending puzzle-piece subdivisions. Churchill Downs, Miller Farms, Magnolia Ridge . . .

She had a Hutch directory in her car and pulled off to find Ellie Dawson's name. She plugged the address into her Cadillac's GPS and continued her journey east, wondering how long it took Alec and Ellie to get to school every day, fighting traffic up and down Poplar. Must be an absolute mess. Addison had been to their house years ago, back when Alec and Susan had moved in. She recalled it as one of those Country French McMansions at the end of an otherwise empty cul-de-sac, surrounded by open lots and signs promising a pool and tennis club to be built soon. Alec had been the developer or one of the investors. Dean had approached her back then about selling the old house in Central Gardens for a brand-new house with more square footage and fewer headaches. But she loved that old house and never even considered the move. Besides, it was so far out of Memphis, you might as well live in another state. All the things that made Memphis, Memphis were comforting and close. Collierville was new money. Addison wasn't interested.

As she got off the highway and took some turns on a few back roads, it started to rain. She listened to the calm, soothing voice of her female navigator until she turned into a neighborhood called Rowan Oak, feeling herself smile for the first time in a while. The idea of naming a McMansion subdivision after Faulkner's antebellum house was absolutely ridiculous.

It was coming back to her now. With the current recession, the empty lots were still empty. The signs promising the pool and racquet club looked sun-faded and shabby. Earth-moving equipment stood motionless in the weedy lots as she drove into Alec's cul-de-sac, surprised that his was still the only home in the circle. His house was huge, bigger than theirs, Country French with river stone walls, a steep slanted roof, tall windows, and twin chimneys. Alec's old Jeep Wagoneer was parked out front and she pulled in behind it. Most of the landscaping was brown or leafless.

Damn, it was pouring now. She waited a few minutes to see if it would stop. When it didn't, she took a breath and ran for the front door, Nikes sloshing along the pebbled sidewalk and on up to the porch, where she furiously knocked and rang the bell. A few seconds later, Alec opened the door.

He wasn't dressed for work. He was shoeless in khaki pants and an untucked blue button-down. His eyes were bloodshot and he looked like he hadn't shaved for a few days.

"I want you to be straight with me," she said. "How did you meet Dean? And who the fuck is he?"

"What do you mean?"

"Dean McKellar, the real Dean McKellar, died in a car accident in nineteen ninety-two."

Alec held the door wide as she stepped into the foyer, dripping wet.

"How about a towel first?" Alec asked, disappearing back into the kitchen, coming back with a big white towel and pitching it to her. She ran it over her face and hair and across her damp hoodie.

"Well?" she said.

"Just how much do you know about me after I left Ole Miss?"

Alec had a fire going in the grand living room, an honest-to-God real woodburning fire, not a propane insert like what had been installed in Addison's house. The fire was warm and cozy, but the house was oddly spare and almost empty. She sat on the end of a tacky L-shaped sofa, probably a Costco special, along with two mismatched leather chairs around what appeared to be a nice antique coffee table. There was no art on the walls and only one antique rug on the hardwood floor. The only thing the house seemed to have in abundance were televisions. He had two in the main room, both above the fireplace, and another by the kitchen.

Alec noticed her staring.

"Haven't had much time to decorate after Susan left," he said. "She pretty much took everything."

"Oh, no," Addison said. "I think it looks nice."

"No, you don't," he said, smiling. "It looks like a bachelor pad, which I swear it isn't. Ellie absolutely hates it. I promised her I'd let her buy whatever she wants when she comes back home."

"I thought she was living with you."

"Susan moved back with her boyfriend and filed for joint custody," Alec said. "Tennessee law doesn't exactly favor the father in these situations."

"Even though she left you?"

"She said I was stifling."

"No offense, Alec," she said. "But Susan was a truly awful person."

"Why didn't you tell me?" Alec said, rubbing the scruff on his chin.

Addison set the towel on the arm of the sofa. "And why didn't you tell me about Dean?"

He nodded. "Fair enough."

"I want to know it all," she said. "Everything. Okay? No bullshit. You owe it to me, Alec. We were friends long before you met Dean and introduced him to me. And if there were any red flags, I damn well deserve to know. Christ, you were in our fucking wedding."

"I know."

"But he's a phony," she said. "A cheat. A liar. He's not even Dean McKellar. I don't know who the hell he is."

"Where's that coming from?" he asked. "Porter Hayes?"

She nodded.

Alec stood up and went over to poke at the fire, sparks catching and heading up the flue. God, she wanted a drink. It was so early and after the weekend she'd had and what people thought, it was probably the last thing she needed.

"Would you like a drink?" he said.

"Yes," she said. "Very much."

Alec Dawson lived so far out of Memphis, there wasn't a chance he'd even heard about the other night. The Zoo Boo fiasco, a night that would live in infamy all around the Club.

"Dean drugged me the other night," she said. "I've been drugged before. I know what it feels like. He wanted me to look like a loser in front of all our friends at a fundraiser."

"Ha," Alec said. "Friends. Those people are hyenas. They're not your friends, Addy."

"And you?" she said.

But she said it to his back as Alec turned and headed to the kitchen where—like only a man would—he had an extensive bar set up on the countertop where normal people would've served breakfast to their kids. She noticed his broad back and muscular shoulders as he poured the whiskey into two crystal glasses, the khakis fitting him nicely.

He brought back two whiskeys neat.

"Did Dean ever tell you about a man named Whitman Chambers?"

"Who the fuck is Whitman Chambers?"

"If I told you his complete résumé, you'd think I was lying," Alec said. "He was sort of like the guy on the Dos Equis ads. The most interesting man in the world. He'd been one of the very first Delta Force guys. He was part of that crazy plan to get the hostages out of Iran in 1979 that failed miserably. He fished in Nicaragua and hunted in Africa. He spoke nearly every single language and had contacts in every corner of the world. Dean and I both worked for him and we idolized him."

"You two worked for an investment firm," Addison said. "In New York."

"It was an investment firm in some ways," Alec said. "My father had a friend who had a friend. He was into all this bullshit with the Bohemian Club in California. You know about that? These rich fucking nuts who get naked every year among the sequoias and discuss world events. Anyway, I'd been out of Ole Miss about a year, working for my dad's company, and then I get an offer to help Chambers. It was still doing construction. But much different from what I was used to. I wanted to clear land and prep development; Whitman was in the business of nation-building."

"Jesus, Alec," Addison said, taking a sip of the whiskey. It felt warm and nice and spread throughout her whole aching body. "Please don't bullshit me. This sounds like complete bullshit. I promise you, I will never speak to you again if you're covering for Dean."

"I can't stand that guy," Alec said. "Okay? I wish I'd never met him. And I wish you'd never met him. As bad as you think he is, I promise you, he's worse."

"But who is he?" Addison said. "What does all this shit have to do with Dean? I'm being told his company is some type of fucking mercenaries."

"I'm a builder now and that's what I did then," Alec said. "Sometimes I did it in South America or Africa, but I was doing the same thing I do here. Bringing in the heavy equipment and doing a job. Dean is the mercenary. *Have Gun Will Travel.* You know that show?"

"My dad's second favorite."

"Dean was Whitman's right-hand man," Alec said, holding the whiskey but not drinking any. The rain pelted the hell out of the empty windows, echoing deep into the Spartan living room and open kitchen. "Chambers was a visionary. He believed that small, emerging nations would be willing to pay big money for not only infrastructure but private armies. If Chambers had lived long enough to see the Towers fall, he'd be one of the richest men on the planet. Instead, he crossed the wrong guy in Africa, and someone put a bomb on his plane."

"Jesus," Addison said. "You kept all this from me?"

"I figured once you and Dean got married, he'd told you everything," Alec said. "You guys just hit it off so damn quick, there wasn't time to warn you."

"Bullshit, Alec," she said. "Bullshit. You know me better than that. What's his real name?"

"Dean McKellar," he said. "He's always been Dean McKellar to me."

"And what did he do for this Whitman Chambers?"

"Chambers provided security and soldiers to those willing to pay," he said. "Dean ran that branch. Whatever you may think about

Dean, I promise you, in this arena, he's the real deal. He'd been Special Forces, some time at the Agency. We'd come across people in fucking Bolivia, and he'd have met them. He speaks almost as many languages as Chambers himself. Listen, I've seen him in action, Addy. You don't want to fuck with that guy."

"Terrific," she said. "He told me he'd been a captain in the first Gulf War. He got a purple heart for falling off a tank rolling into Kuwait."

"I think he might've been having some fun with you," Alec said. "Dean would never fall off a tank. And no, I know what we told you, but we were never finance bros in New York. Chambers had offices in New York and London. We made a lot of trips across the Atlantic and as young ambitious guys all over the world. Drinking at the Dorchester. The Ritz. A big time for a kid from Memphis."

Addison turned up the whiskey as fast and precise as she used to do at the bar at The Gin back in Oxford. She didn't need to explain to Alec that she could drink most any guy under the table and would never—God forbid—get drunk off one and a half glasses of goddamn wine.

"Dean killed a man the other night," Addison said. "We'd just come home from the Zoo Boo."

"How was the Zoo Boo?"

"Goddamn, Alec."

"How do you know Dean killed someone?"

"Because I fucking saw it," she said. "I was walking the path behind the house to the kitchen, and there was Dean standing inside the house with a man with one arm. I saw them clear as day through the window. He and the man were arguing, and *blam*, *blam*, *blam*, Dean shot him."

"What did you do?"

"I had been drugged and I was in shock," she said. "By the time Preston and I got into the house, he'd moved the body."

"Are you sure you saw it?" he said. "A one-armed man?"

"Alec."

"Okay, okay," he said. "I believe you. I always will believe you. And I'm sorry. Really sorry. I blame myself for all this. We were the ones who crashed your Christmas party. Where was that?"

"P.J. Clarke's," she said. "We were celebrating my stupid author hitting the list for the hundredth time."

"Right," he said. "I was late and Dean got there early."

"Yep."

"Story of my life." Alec put a hand to his temple and pressed. He looked like he was either trying to forget something or had an excruciating headache.

"Are you okay?"

"Fine."

"Why aren't you at work?"

"Late flight from Miami," he said. "Work stalled out with a development we have in Coconut Grove. Hey, do you want a refill?"

Addison nodded, and Alec disappeared again. Maybe she and the kids could stay here, taking only a couple of the endless rooms. Dean wouldn't suspect it and Alec would never tell him. He must have a hundred bedrooms in this place. Maybe Sara Caroline could finally reconnect with Ellie, be friends like they'd been as little kids, sharing a place at the little ice cream tables at Sugar Babies. Gumdrops and sprinkles. God, that was so long ago but seemed like yesterday. Alec handed her another whiskey.

"I really shouldn't be doing this," she said. "I have to pick up the kids."

Alec looked at his Rolex. "It's not even ten," he said. "You have time. Come on. Let me help you. Okay? It's going to be fine. I promise."

His smile lit up the room. The rain hit the roof and windows harder, pounding the McMansion like a fucking drum. This time Alec didn't take a seat across from her but instead moved in right beside her, stretching his arm over the couch. He didn't touch her, but he was making his presence known, in a comforting way.

"I'm sorry," he said. "I fucked up."

"I wish I'd known."

"You guys were inseparable those first few months," Alec said. "You told me you'd never been in love like that, and then all of a sudden you guys were getting married. I felt like you were happy and safe and I was happy as hell for you."

Addison sipped the whiskey, slowly this time, and allowed herself to lean back, her shoulder touching Alec's arm. "Why the hell did you both want to come back here?"

"Whitman died," he said. "We tried to keep things going for a while, but without him, the company fell apart. It was a fucking mess. Dean and I wanted out. My dad was getting older and he wanted to hand over Dawson-Gray to me. When I left, Dad had started to have some bank problems and was about to lose everything. What can I say? You and Dean had just gotten married. He told me he was done with that life. Dean stepped in with some quick and needed cash and we became partners. He was smart and charismatic, and I needed someone to step out front."

"No, you didn't."

"But I needed his money."

"And here I thought it all was fate."

"It worked for a while," Alec said. "Until 9/11 and Dean smelled all the money we could be making. We watched the Twin Towers fall on a TV in our office and everything changed from that moment. He started farming out little jobs, getting some DOD money. But then he wanted to go full out with his mercenaries, like he did with Whitman. He bought some land down in the Delta—"

"Shit," Addison said. "Shit. Shit. Shit."

"Yep," Alec said, his hand resting on her shoulder and pulling her closer. "Dean always wanted to be the lead dog. I always seemed to be a day late and a dollar short."

"Don't say that."

"I ruined your life."

"Dean ruined my life."

"A lie of omission is no less a lie," he said, leaning in to tuck her head underneath his, almost as if they were watching a movie on the couch. And she was back in the early nineties at his crummy duplex in Oxford, Alec working out "Stairway to Heaven" on his guitar. Addison in a haze of pot and cheap whiskey and laughing so hard she couldn't breathe. They had only ever kissed, and only that one night. They slept in the same bed, woke up and went to Smitty's for breakfast, and kept right on dating other people and never spoke of it again.

"I'm so damn sorry."

Addison turned to him. "It's definitely a lot."

"Can you go to the police?"

"And tell them what?" Addison said. "He has dozens of witnesses to say I'm a drunken, strung-out mess. He's seeding this whole bullshit story that I'm crazy."

"Dean wouldn't hurt you," he said. "But he'll do anything to protect himself. And whatever he's into these days."

"And what's that?"

"Nothing big," Alec said. "Just selling arms and private security across the globe to the highest bidder."

"Wonderful."

Alec lifted his head and took in a deep breath. They didn't talk for a long while, just hanging there together in that big, empty room, watching the fire. She could feel him breathing against her, and the smell of his cologne was nice and piney, and not so aggressive like Dean's aftershave.

"I'm so sorry I was late."

"For what?"

Alec turned and kissed her hard on the mouth and Addison put her arms around his neck, pulling him in as they fell into that long goddamn awful Costco sofa. There was so much kissing and not even time for Addison to take off her damn hoodie, the yoga pants pulled down to her knees, Alec ripping off his neat blue shirt, nearly tripping as he kicked out of his khakis, falling down onto the one rug in the room by the heat of the fireplace and doing stuff that she shouldn't be doing but wished she'd done so long ago. She felt all the shame of being naked and exposed, the embarrassment of living a stupid lie, just lift right off her and into their hands and mouths. She pushed Alec onto his back, feeling like she'd climbed a great hill, and straddled him, hands pressing down on his chest, and all of it so rough and intense that it happened for her over and over. Realizing that once, a long time ago, Dean had made her feel this way, too. *Dean. Oh, Jesus.* Her husband was a trained fucking killer.

After, she'd gotten up and gathered her pants up around her, pulling down her hoodie and running off in the general direction of where surely there was a bathroom. She ran the water and sat down on the toilet, goddamn crying again.

A soft knock on the door. "Are you okay?"

"No."

"You have to leave him, Addy," Alec said. "It's not safe."

25

Gaultier

Gaultier longed for the warm bed of Valerie or even his faithful wife instead of being dispensed on an errand for *Le Boucher*, Anatoliy Zub. After two days of waiting, Zub was most certainly positive that Jack Dumas was dead. Perhaps in the afterlife, Dumas had been reunited with his long-lost arm and was enjoying all the bloody steak he could eat. Living his own personal Valhalla.

Gaultier handed the keys of the car Zub had provided to a valet at the Peabody Hotel. He was happy to be back in a suitable wardrobe, plaid wool suit overlaid with a camel cashmere topcoat, after sitting around in his casino suite watching American television. Two nights in a row of *Dancing with the Stars* was enough to make him consider jumping from the window of his suite. Zub had taken away Gaultier's personal phone—but not Collinson's burner—and forbidden him from making any calls not in Zub's presence. "Anatoliy," Gaultier had said, "if you want me to reason with Peter Collinson, it must be alone and on my own terms. If not, why did you bring me to this horrible place that smells like fried fish and dirt?"

Earlier that morning, Zub was dressed as John Wayne, or perhaps Clint Eastwood, at the Sam's Town buffet bar (never in his life had he seen so much fried meat!). He tilted back his black Stetson and nodded. "I give you my word," he said. "Without his word, man is no better than animal. *Ha.* You know that line, yes? Sam Peckinpah in *Wild Bunch*. You French do love your cinema so. Peckinpah must be a god in Paris. A man without his word is animal!"

Gaultier breathed a sigh of relief as he stepped into the marble expanse of the Peabody's lobby, moving past small groupings of sofas and oversize chairs in dim light, a man in a tuxedo playing "As Time Goes By," at the piano. *Play it once, Sam. For old times' sake.*

Gaultier found a comfortable and empty sofa and ordered a Negroni from the waiter. A simple cocktail that even the most incompetent bartender could make. He was an hour early, hoping to spot any of Collinson's people before the man himself arrived. Zub had offered one of his guns, but Gaultier declined. He'd known Peter Collinson for years, and while he didn't trust him, he didn't expect Peter to shoot him in the lobby of Memphis's finest hotel.

The waiter returned with his Negroni and Gaultier took to watching the four corners of the lobby. It was early, a weekday, and besides a bustle of activity by the concierge, most of the action took place by the hotel's elevators and in and out of the gift shop. A big marble fountain, bustling with live ducks, kept everyone coming and going to take their photo. Many were families with small children dressed in embroidered sweaters and well-coiffed women in long cashmere frocks.

Gaultier set down his drink, looking up to find Collinson standing directly in front of him. Collinson removed a damp Burberry jacket and set it on a nearby chair.

"You don't look surprised," Collinson said.

"You said you would be here, my friend," Gaultier said. "And you are most often good at your word."

"Except now," Collinson said, crossing his legs. "This bullshit with Anatoliy?"

"Anatoliy isn't a man who takes offense lightly," he said. "You know this as well as anyone. Whatever game you are playing? The three-card monte, perhaps? This has caused me so many headaches, Peter. I have a life. I have my own work and no intention of being here, in your home, and speaking with you about a promise I made months ago with Zub. I offered your guarantees in my name."

Collinson had on a black turtleneck and gray wool pants. His eyes were bloodshot and his skin looked a bit craggy, even with his disheveled, boyish blond hair. When Collinson crossed his legs, Gaultier had noticed the heel on his boot must be three inches tall. Such a vain man, Peter Collinson. All the guns and insecurities of Napoleon.

The waiter appeared, and Collinson sent him away for a cup of coffee.

"Tell Anatoliy he'll get what he's owed," Collinson said. "I made a mistake."

Gaultier smiled and leaned back into the sofa. "And Jack Dumas?"

Collinson's open and boyish face dropped and turned dark. "Dumas should've never come into my house."

"Ha," Gaultier said. "Don't worry. I have no love for a man like Jack Dumas, even with his one arm and stories of battle in the Legion. He was just a pig. But you, Peter? You were always a man of honor. I will go right to the matter. Anatoliy wants to know why you traded your soul in Istanbul. He doesn't want it all, but he feels, *yes, yes*, rightly so, that you gave him pieces of junk to buy time with his money."

"Anatoliy has no idea what this is."

"Guns, ammo, power, and destruction?" Gaultier said. "No?"

"No," he said. "Why did he come here, anyway? So he can pack up his freak show of goons and fly all over the world to prove he can. I'll wire the bastard his damn money next week and all this crap will be forgotten."

"He said you left your man Jack Dumas to die," he said. "He said in his Anatoliy voice, *like a tethered goat.*"

Collinson gave him a quick glance and then looked away.

The waitress brought along the coffee and Gaultier watched as Collinson added a lot of cream and sugar to the mix. The piano player began "Somewhere Over the Rainbow." Yes, this is where Gaultier found himself this morning, on the other side of the rainbow and wanting very much to return to Paris. Zub had offered him a cut of this deal. A deal for something that may or may not have existed. Even this girl he had spoken with didn't know what her mother and Peter were working on. She said her mother was a broker of antiquities, which did seem interesting to Gaultier.

"Zub sells weapons to the Taliban."

"Yes," Gaultier said. "Of course."

"His guns kill American soldiers," Collinson said. "I can't be a part of that."

"Such a patriot, Peter," he said. "The weapons were going to Africa. To Djibouti to blow up pirates."

"That was a lie," Collinson said. "When I found out about his deal with the Taliban, I stuck him with some Chinese junk I picked up in Shanghai. Okay? Are we done here? Tell Anatoliy that if he wants his money, he'll have to leave Memphis."

"He says you have twenty-four hours," Gaultier said. "And then he's coming for you."

"He can try," Collinson said. "He might be surprised he's outmanned and outgunned here."

Oh, how this whole drama interested Gaultier. Peter Collinson, at best a bit player in the arms trade, was trying to make demands of Anatoliy Zub. He wondered what had driven him to such delusions. The young woman he had talked to didn't know what was in Pandora's box but had overheard her mother use a figure of sixty-five million American dollars. That would pay for more than Anatoliy's jet fuel and running tab at Sam's Town. But more than that, one did not insult Anatoliy Zub, or it would be *High Noon* in the Delta. The thought made Gaultier smile.

"This isn't funny," Collinson said. "He sent my former partner into my home to kill me."

"He wasn't going to kill you," Gaultier said. "He wanted to talk to you."

"When Anatoliy Zub sends someone, it's not for talk."

"And what are we doing here?" Gaultier said. "This is kind and civilized, young Peter. You and I have been friends for these last few years. I like you. That's why I have helped you in so many unfamiliar waters. But this is far too deep for you. Give Zub his gold and send him on his way. You will live another day. Nothing is worth your life."

"And that's it?" Collinson said, over the edge of his coffee mug. "That's the deal Anatoliy has offered?"

Gaultier gave his elegant Gallic shrug. He smiled and motioned to the waitress for another Negroni. It wasn't bad. The cocktails at the casino were absolutely terrible.

"Peter, Peter," Gaultier said, noticing a lovely woman in a short black dress walk by the fountain and take a photo of the ducks. "You find yourself in a corner. As your friend, perhaps even mentor, I advise you to cut Anatoliy into the deal. Perhaps apologize for the insult. Get rid of this thing quickly and send Anatoliy on his way. I understand you have a family?"

Collinson sank his head into his hands and brushed back his hair. He took in a long breath and looked directly at Gaultier and nodded.

"Zub doesn't care," Gaultier said. "He would think nothing of killing them."

Collinson didn't look away. The waiter set down Gaultier's second drink.

"I need some time," Collinson said. "I'm not selling stereo speakers in a parking lot."

"And what exactly does that mean?"

"I have to make arrangements," he said. "These items must be inspected and verified and then things will move quick."

Gaultier picked up the glass, wiping off the condensation around the rim, and mixed the ice with a plastic stick topped with a small duck. "You know what I believe?" Gaultier asked.

"What's that?"

"I think you've misplaced your little prize," Gaultier said. "And maybe in your rage, you killed a woman who was helping you find it."

Collinson's left eye twitched. Just a bit, but Gaultier knew what the girl had told him was absolutely true. Gaultier recrossed his legs and threw up his hands as he waited for a reply.

"Fuck you, Gaultier," Peter said. "You're talking out your ass."

"Is your life worth the bet?"

The arrogant little American stood up, tossed on his damp coat, and disappeared around the corner of the gift shop. So many wooden ducks, duck T-shirts, and glass duck ornaments in the display behind the glass. Gaultier watched him go, shrugged, and sipped his drink.

He reached for his new phone he'd purchased that morning and dialed the young woman's number. After three rings, she picked up.

"Can we finally meet, my dear?" Gaultier asked. "In person."

"Why in person?" she said. "This works fine by me."

"So we might discuss how to deal with this impenetrable rascal who murdered your mother," he said.

"Her name was Joanna Grayson," she said. "And you can call me Tippi."

26

Addison

The doctors weren't sure if it was related to the cancer or his failing heart, only that her father's caregiver had found him face down in the bathroom—hopefully comfortable on her mom's old fuzzy pink bathmat—and barely breathing. Branch had called her Monday afternoon, just after she'd picked up Sara Caroline early and was in line for Preston, planning on driving to Florida to stay at a sorority sister's beach condo. Following Porter Hayes's precise instructions from a phone call after she'd left Alec's house, she'd already packed her bag and bags for the kids, too, withdrawing five thousand dollars cash from the household bank account and transferring another ten into an old private account Dean couldn't touch. But her best-laid plans turned to shit with the call about her dad. Now the kids were staying at Branch and Libby's, hopefully a neutral location that Dean wouldn't challenge even though he surely knew about the money.

Sami Hassan was dying. No kidding this time. *This isn't a test.* A nice young doctor who looked all of fifteen—serious Doogie Howser vibes—confided that her father was in such bad shape that he'd probably never leave the hospital. The doctor said his big heart was now the size of a deflated balloon.

Addison imagined a sad, red party balloon while she sat in the hospital cafeteria with Preston. Branch and Libby were up on the fourth floor with Dad, trying to give her a needed break after sitting at his bedside all day and night, catching an hour or two of sleep in a pullout chair.

She'd forced herself to get a plate of eggs and bacon with some hospital coffee, while Preston was delighted to find the hospital cafeteria boasted a full-out burger bar. They were eating when Dean walked in, immaculately dressed in his bespoke plaid suit and black turtleneck, a Burberry trench up under his arm. There were flecks of rain on his shoulders and in his perfect hair.

He offered a smile and took a seat at the table, making small talk with Preston.

"That looks pretty good, partner," he said. "How about we share?"

Preston gave the same ole shuck, pretending to pull the plate close to him, Addison seeing right away how much he'd missed his father. *Who could blame him?* There weren't exactly any Disney Channel shows that covered parents who stole identities and were international killers for hire. *My Father: The Assassin* with Tim Allen and Frankie Muniz coming up next . . .

"Pres," Addison said, "Daddy and I are going to go for a short walk. Don't go anywhere."

They didn't walk far, just out the cafeteria's side door into a little outdoor dining space and meditation garden, completely abandoned as they stood under the portico with the rain coming down hard. It had grown colder and their breaths clouded in front of them.

"What do you want?"

"I'm checking on my family," he said. "Is that not okay?"

"I want a divorce," she said. "I want you to stay the hell away from me and the kids and my entire family. That goes for my ass-kissing brother, too. You don't want this to go public and get ugly."

"You made this public the other night."

"Bullshit," Addison said. "You drugged me."

"Drugged you?" he said, laughing. "Do you know how crazy that sounds? Jesus, Addison."

"And I saw everything," she said. "Absolutely everything. I don't know who that man was or what he was doing in our house, but I saw you shoot him three times in the chest. And then I know you dragged his body out to god knows where. So can we please stop with your never-ending bullshit, Dean. Or whatever your name is."

"Whatever my name is?" he said. He shook his head. "I know you're upset about Sam. I am, too. But he'll get better. He always does. In the meantime, I'll get the kids back home and we'll talk it out once everything settles down."

Addison stepped forward and raised an index finger to his face. Her heart raced and she could hear the blood rushing in her ears. "You try and take the kids and I'll tell the police everything I know and everything I've seen. How would you like that?"

"You've completely lost it," he said. "Branch always said you were emotionally fragile and would break someday. I was stupid and never believed him."

Addison shook her head and tried to compose herself. *What would Dr. Larry say?* He'd probably say don't lose your temper, Addison, as that gives the other person the upper hand. You've lost as soon as they've seen you fly into a rage. *Just walk away.* If the person won't let you, find a safe place. Addison knew she was in a safe place. Dean wouldn't touch her here. Thank you, Dr. Larry.

"My father is on the fourth floor connected to tubes and hoses and is dying," she said. "I don't know who you are or the kind of people you've brought into our lives. But if you have just one small thread of honor, you'll check yourself into a hotel and let us have some space."

A sign in the meditation garden read: "Quiet Area. Please be respectful. No smoking or profanity allowed."

Dean, stoic Dean, rubbed his stubbled jaw and readjusted the trench coat under his arm. The heavy scent of his cologne penetrated the cold and rain. It smelled overpowering and tawdry. It used to smell of woodsmoke. "If that's what you want."

"That's what I want," Addison said. "Now please get the fuck out of the way and let me take care of my real family."

Addison was upstairs now, hours later, sometime after eight o'clock, with the nurses just by for their hourly rounds, checking on her dad's vitals. She didn't ask but knew they weren't promising or offering some kind of miraculous rebound. *You know your dad's deflated old heart? We pumped it up and it's all better now!* Her father slept, tubes jammed up his nose, his right arm like a pincushion, as Sara Caroline watched an episode of *The Bachelor*. A couple in a hot tub drank champagne while Preston was entranced by *Crash Bandicoot* on the PlayStation Portable.

Her father woke up for a moment, his dark eyes drawn and haggard, cracked lips parting. "Boy," he said. "I feel like dog shit."

"I'm so sorry, Dad."

"How much longer do I have to stay in this hellhole?"

Addison felt her throat constrict and willed herself not to cry. "Not much longer," she said. "A day or two."

"Please don't let me die in this place," he said. "It smells like cat piss and cotton swabs. And don't let Kiyana go through my stuff. I know you kids like her because she's Jamaican and says funny things, but I don't trust her. I think she took one of my footballs. The one from the Alabama game."

"I don't think Kiyana cares about American football."

"She understands eBay," he said. "Just promise me."

"I promise you."

"And, Addison," he said, "once someone is gone and there's money at stake, people can get really nasty. Have you ever seen *The Treasure of the Sierra Madre*?"

"No."

"Well, you should," he said. "Your brother is just like Fred C. Dobbs. I see it in his eyes when we talk about my estate. Don't you dare let him take more than his half. Everything has been decided, fifty-fifty after the condo is sold. And I'm leaving some to the church. I hope that's okay."

"That's fine, Dad."

"And a scholarship endowment at Ole Miss," he said. "In your mom's name."

"That's nice."

He opened his palm and Addison slipped her hand into his. His big-handed squeeze was so goddamn weak that she knew it wouldn't be around a hell of a lot longer. As his eyes were about to flutter closed, he said, "How are things with Dean?"

"Fine."

"He came up to see me."

"That's nice."

"I still don't trust him."

"Me, either."

"Be happy, Addy," Sami said. "Everything else is just a lie. Time, sweetheart, is a son of a bitch."

Addison watched her father fall back asleep just before Branch showed up with a big fluffy pillow and a blanket. She barely spoke to her brother as she gathered her stuff and the kids and took the elevator down to the first floor. They crossed the lobby filled with the sick and injured, a whole class of people—night to night and day to day—that Addison had never even considered. She felt like she was inside of a bus terminal with everyone heading in different directions.

"Do you think there's television in heaven?" Preston said, saying it like something he'd thought long and hard about.

"I'm not really sure."

"I hope so," Preston said, as they walked through the pneumatic doors and out into the cold and rain. "Granddad would really hate to miss *Gunsmoke*."

They went home. Branch swore he'd call at any hour if Dad's condition changed. It was almost eleven by the time they were back in Central Gardens, the kids piling out of the Escalade, Addison relieved she didn't see Dean's Land Rover in the garage or any lights on in the house. The one-armed man was dead. At least she wouldn't have to worry about him tonight. She only needed to worry about Dean coming to take the kids. She knew what Alec had said about Dean being a dangerous man, but he'd never harm her. He'd barely ever raised his voice to her.

Addison wandered into Dean's study as the kids trundled up the big staircase. She helped herself to one of Dean's finest scotches. The bottle he only offered special guests and only once a year for a small sip.

It was still raining. A Tiffany table lamp was lit on Dean's desk.

The study was almost pleasant despite today's circumstances. She thought about turning on the fireplace, but the gas logs weren't as comforting as the real thing. Since she'd been with Alec they'd only spoken twice. She'd called him as soon as she'd gotten to the hospital and once after the run-in with Dean. He wanted to come and see her, but she made him promise that he'd keep away. For now. Until everything was sorted out. *She and the kids were safe and fine.* She had little guilt. It had happened and she was glad.

She lifted the crystal glass and toasted the awfulness of her situation and took a nice long drink as she heard footsteps along the staircase. Preston wandered into the study. "I can't sleep."

"You were sleeping in the car."

"But I wasn't really asleep," he said. "I was faking it in case you and Sara Caroline started talking about Granddad."

"I told you everything."

"I heard one of the nurses talking outside the room."

"Oh." Addison set down the scotch and walked over to where Preston was standing. After being in the hospital, the warm library was a welcome change. As she glanced down at the rug, she noticed a deep swath of something that looked like blood. Her breath caught in her throat and she felt like she might be sick.

"Do you know where we go when we die?" Preston asked.

Crap. There it was, the big question. The eternal mystery laid right out there for them to discuss on a school night, which really wasn't a school night because there was no way she was waking them up tomorrow at six. She wanted to spin Preston a tale about the pearly gates and the heavenly welcome, the clouds and the city in the sky (that she always imagined looked like Bespin from *Empire Strikes Back*), but damn, she was just so tired.

"Dad said when I got too worried about those things to pray."

"Yeah?" Addison said, taking another pull of the scotch. Damn, it was good. "Your dad would say that."

"Don't you believe Dad?"

"Things are just a little confusing now."

Preston nodded and smiled. The front of his hoodie was absolutely filthy, with greasy hamburger handprints. "Dad told me he may not come home for a while."

"That's true."

"And that if anything happened or more bad people ever showed up, to go and hide in the safe room."

Addison nodded, *sure, sure*, the secret place. The safe room. She turned and looked at her son.

"He said you guys would take us there if bad guys ever broke in or there was a tornado or something," Preston said. "Right? Dad told me to never ever talk about it. That the bad guys might hear us. Is that true?"

Addison shone the flashlight around the basement until Preston began to move some of Dean's old boxes, old electronics, and sports equipment, including two sets of golf clubs that seemed to still be in perfect condition.

"What are you looking for?" she said.

"The door."

"There isn't a door."

"Sure there is," he said.

The walls were very old brick, and the air under the house smelled like a crypt. She hated being down here, making her feel like she'd been locked away in a tomb. Preston pulled away a few more boxes and then pointed to a heavy-duty metal shelf stacked with electric saws and tools. He unlatched a corner and to Addison's surprise, it swung open like a gate. Behind the shelf was a steel door with a small keypad in the center.

"How long have you known about this?"

"I followed Dad down here this summer," he said. "I promised I wouldn't tell anyone."

A little confusion passed over his small face, not sure if he'd done the right thing. Addison touched his shoulder and said, "You're worried about me," she said. "After what happened with that man?"

"You should know," he said. "In case someone comes back."

Preston quickly punched in a code and the metal door clicked open, fluorescent lights fluttering to life as they both pushed inside. The space wasn't very large, maybe twenty by twenty feet. Someone had laid down some industrial gray carpet, added a bit of molding at the corners, making it appear like a luxury closet, and attached pegboard to one wall. Instead of tools, the pegboard was filled with dozens of rifles and handguns, small bins with clips fill of ammunition and various backpacks and belts that looked as if they'd been dragged through hell and back. A flat desk had been built into a space that looked like a small closet with six computer monitors—all on—above a brand-new Apple set up.

"Don't touch anything," she said.

"Why not?"

"This isn't a safe room," she said. "It's a damn arsenal."

Something in the ceiling caught her eye, a bauble that looked like an upside-down snow globe with a mirror surface. Addison walked up on it, transfixed, and then immediately knew it was a surveillance camera like they used in department stores. *Shit, shit, shit.*

"What's wrong?"

Addison walked back over to the computer, touched the space bar, and nine different monitors came to life. Each one of them showed a corner of her home, including the bottom left looking down right at her and Preston. Her empty pool, her kitchen, her bedroom, and the bathrooms.

"Isn't this cool?"

"This is definitely not cool," she said. "Promise me that you'll never come down here ever again."

Addison turned to flip through three different passports that lay on top of the desk. Two blue with American eagle covers. One had been issued to Dean McKellar and a second, much more worn to the touch, for Peter Frank Collinson. With trembling fingers, she'd just picked up the third passport with the gilded symbol for the United Kingdom, Jonathan Devlin, when Dean stooped down and entered the space.

"Preston," he said. "I'm very disappointed in you."

Addison set down the passport and looked to Dean. "You're the one who's disappointed?" she said. "Well, back up the truck. I have an entire fuckton of disappoint I'd like to drop on your head, Dean. Or is it Peter? Or whoever you are in London."

"Preston, go upstairs," he said. "I need to have a talk with Mommy."

27

Porter Hayes

The next morning, Darlene stopped Porter Hayes in the third-floor hallway outside his office. "You've got two men in suits waiting for you," she said, face flushed and talking fast. "They claim to be FBI agents, but I don't believe them for one hot second. One of 'em flashed their ID, but you can buy that shit on eBay. Just a couple of assholes off the street if you ask me. Kept on telling me to cooperate, give them any files we had on the McKellar case."

"Well," Hayes said, "that ain't happening."

"You think I don't know that?" she said. "This ain't my first rodeo, Buster Brown. I told them to get the hell out of our office, but they walked right past me and into your office. I was just about to call the police when I heard you coming up the steps."

Hayes nodded, removed the toothpick from his mouth, and headed straight through Darlene's outer office and into his. Two white men sat in his client chairs. One man was small, with a gaunt-looking face and slick hair; the other was chunky and wore an ill-fitting suit and a close-cropped beard. They stayed put as Hayes walked behind his desk, not even making a motion to stand up and introduce themselves.

"My secretary says you're both federal agents?"

"I'm a federal agent," said the smaller white man, making a big show about flashing his ID. Hayes made a motion to hand it over, which the agent did, and Hayes took a good, hard look. Yep, looked legit. F. Duane Bickett of the Federal Bureau of Investigation. "I'm Agent Bickett and this is Mr. Sutton with the Tennessee Department of Commerce and

Insurance. They handle the licensing of all private investigators in the state."

"Oh, I'm aware what they do," Hayes said. "I hope y'all have a good reason to bust up all into my office this morning."

"No one busted into your office, Mr. Hayes," Agent Bickett said. "Your secretary told us we could wait here until you got back from breakfast."

"Now that's a black lie," Darlene said, hanging in the doorframe. "I told them they could wait for you out here, Porter. They walked straight on in like they owned the place."

Hayes stood up and lifted a window, setting a brick in the sill to make sure it stayed put. When he sat back down, Hayes didn't say a word. He just looked to both of them, waiting to hear what kind of bullshit web they were about to spin.

"The door was open," Agent Bickett said, shrugging and spreading out his hands. "It seemed like the most convenient place to wait."

Porter Hayes was seriously beginning to dislike this motherfucker, Agent Bickett. The other man, the one called Sutton, looked embarrassed and ill at ease. His ass too big for the wooden client chair. He clasped his hands in his lap while Bickett studied Porter's wall of fame, craning his neck upward to see the mess of awards and photos earned after nearly forty years in the business.

"You really know Jerry Lee Lewis?"

"I even know why they call him The Killer."

"And why's that?"

Hayes didn't answer. He just leaned back into his office chair, waiting for them to get to the damn point before he asked them to leave. No one spoke for a long while as he smelled the roasting from the Peanut Shoppe down the street mixed with the diesel from the morning delivery trucks. "Are y'all just going door-to-door selling Girl Scout cookies, or do you have some grown-up business here?"

"You work for Dean McKellar," Bickett said.

"Nope."

"Come on," he said. "Don't get yourself in trouble by shielding a man like that. Just tell us what you know, Porter, and we'll be on our way."

"Mr. Hayes."

"Excuse me?"

"I've been working this town since well before you were sucking your momma's titty," Hayes said. "And you will call me Mr. Hayes in my goddamn office."

Agent Bickett smiled big and glanced over at Sutton. The fat bureaucrat had grown even more nervous, knowing he was nothing more than a prop brought to show-and-tell. He glanced over at Bickett and then self-consciously straightened his striped tie.

"And who exactly is Dean McKellar?" Hayes asked.

"Seriously?"

"Yeah," Hayes said. "Seriously. Is he a local guy? Criminal? What's his deal? Why are y'all looking for his ass?"

"He's not local," Bickett said.

"But where's he from?" Hayes said. "What's so important about this man?"

Bickett looked over his shoulder at Darlene still standing in the doorway and then back at Hayes. His face widened with a smug little grin that reminded Porter of a cartoon weasel.

"I'm not here for you to ask me questions."

"Is that a fact?"

"It would be a shame for Mr. Sutton to get involved," Bickett said. "He might have to put your license under review for a month or two, you know, to find out how and why you're part of a federal investigation. Trust me. That stuff can take forever and ruin a man's reputation."

Hayes leaned back farther and placed his hands behind his head. "Oh, it's like that?" Hayes said. "And here I was feeling good this fine morning. Had me a platter of biscuits and gravy down at the Bon Ton, the sun finally coming out after three days of nothing but rain. But y'all had to go and fuck things up."

Bickett tried to give Hayes a hard look that Hayes had seen done meaner and a lot better. "I need you to answer a few questions and I want that file on McKellar."

"Like I said, I don't work for any Dean McKellar, and if I did, I don't have to show y'all shit," he said. "Now y'all can go nicely, or I can call up my man Bernie Gold on speed dial. You do know Bernie Gold, right?"

Bickett shrugged and shook his head, still amused as hell with the situation. Sutton looked at Bickett and then Porter Hayes before shaking his head, too.

"Y'all haven't seen his commercial?" Hayes asked. *"When you're down and out and you need a plan. Don't you waste one minute because Bernie Gold's your man."*

"Oh, yeah," Sutton said, sitting up in the chair. "Bernie Gold and Associates. He has those big billboards with big stacks of money and gold chains and diamonds."

Sutton grinned big, like a third grader answering a teacher's question, before Bickett shot a sour look his way.

"He's gonna love meeting y'all," Hayes said. "What with y'all already trespassing and throwing around threats."

Bickett shook his head. "No one threatened you," he said. "We came to inquire about your client. Mr. McKellar is connected to two extremely dangerous foreign agents who flew into Memphis this weekend. If you don't want to answer our questions, that's fine. I can easily get a warrant to seize your files and computers."

Hayes leaned forward in his chair and looked to Agent Bickett. A swath of morning light spread across his blotter where he saw a note from Darlene to call Addison McKellar ASAP and *that means right away.* "Let me get this straight," he said. "You want me to trust the damn FBI?"

"Any reason you shouldn't?" Bickett said.

"How long you got?" he said. "How about we start with surveillance on Malcolm X, Dr. King, killing Fred Hampton. Should I go on?"

"Lots of urban legends about the old days."

"Ever hear of a little program called COINTELPRO?"

"Ancient history," Bickett said. "That doesn't have anything to do with us."

"And just where were you in sixty-eight, Junior?"

"I was born in seventy-two."

Hayes laughed and reached into his right-hand drawer for a pack of Winstons. He shook one loose and set fire to the end. He exhaled a big plume of smoke and watched the men across his desk.

"I want to know why a Russian thug named Anatoliy Zub is in my town," Bickett said. "Along with a French national who goes by the name Gaultier. He has at least thirteen different identities and is on a watch list from INTERPOL."

"How the fuck should I know?" Hayes asked. "Maybe they're all crazy about Elvis. That's all you see down on E.P. Boulevard, European folks coming to pay their respects to the King."

Bickett shook his head. He glanced over to Sutton and then back to Hayes. Darlene had disappeared back to her desk and he could hear that she was already on the phone with Bernie Gold. *A pushy federal agent's making threats against Porter and his license . . . oh, yeah? Well, he already told him to go fuck himself but that's not working.*

"This all connects to Dean McKellar."

"Y'all already sent one of your agents to follow me around town," he said. "Did you ever see me with this McKellar man?"

Bickett looked at Hayes and shook his head. "That wasn't us."

"Young fella like yourself," Hayes said. "Black man who likes mirrored shades. Drove a Ford Taurus with government plates and calls himself Carson Wells."

"Never heard of him."

Bickett stood up and placed a hand on the edge of Hayes's desk, leaning in just a little. If he was trying to look imposing, he wasn't doing a very good job. *Damn.* Times change, but Quantico keeps on churning out the same model. The same misguided attitude with a touch of white privilege like they ran the whole show and could do as they pleased.

Hayes came around the desk and Bickett took a few steps back.

Hayes walked to the door and ushered them out with his right hand. "Thanks for dropping by."

"If you're hiding or protecting Mr. McKellar in any way—"

"Why do you keep saying I work for this man?" Hayes said. "You want me to come across but won't offer me nothing but accusations."

"This morning we met with a Sergeant Jones at Memphis Police," Bickett said. "She said she knew for a fact you'd been employed by the McKellar family for the last few weeks and would want to stand up and do the right thing."

"She never said that," he said. "But it does seem like y'all lost this Dean McKellar fella. And can't find your asshole with a goddamn periscope."

Hayes drove to Nathan Bedford Forrest Park an hour later and took a seat at the edge of the bronze statue. Forrest arrogantly looked down from horseback, his saddle laden with a rifle and a saber. The inscription read: *He fought like a Titan and struck like a god, And his dust is our ashes of glory.* Before he'd been a Confederate general noted for massacring Black Union soldiers, Forrest had been a brutal slave trader in Memphis, and after the war he'd gone on to found the damned KKK. The statue was tarnished and old, the slave trader's and his wife's bones buried somewhere in the concrete pedestal.

A few minutes later, he spotted Lantana Jones getting out of her unmarked unit with the two tall coffees she'd promised. "That's too much sugar for a man your age," she said. "You trying to get diabetes?"

"Hell of a place to meet."

"I was working on a double homicide up in Smokey City and was headed back to 201," she said. "Figured this was better. I know how you hate the parking at headquarters."

"Who got killed?"

"Couple kids," she said. "One got shot last night and the other kid, the shooter, got killed early this morning still in his bed. *Drugs. Bullshit.* What else can you say? Turns your stomach. EMT got there and couldn't do a damn thing but sedate the shooter's mother, who was out of her goddamn mind with grief, running out of the house with blood on her nightgown and falling to her knees in the mud."

"I'm not gonna lie," Hayes said. "It wasn't much different when me and your daddy were on the job. But at least folks seemed to have a better reason for killing each other. What's the homicide count?"

"No too bad," she said. "Still hasn't hit a hundred this year."

"Wait till Christmas."

"I know."

"Nerves get jangled at Christmas," he said. "Too many needs and not enough money. Damn shame of it."

They sat and drank coffee. The day was unseasonably warm and Hayes had left his trench coat locked up safe in his Mercedes. Lantana had on her MPD uniform with sergeant's stripes on her shoulder and a Glock on her belt. Her nails were long and bright red, wrapping around the Starbucks cup like talons.

"Listen, Porter," she said. "I tried to call and warn you about that fed. Didn't you get my messages?"

"Not until too late," he said. "I'd been down at the Bon Ton, and when I got back found him and some man named Sutton sitting in my office."

"He didn't ask me about the McKellar case at first," she said. "He'd heard about a dead white man we'd fished out of some trees down at Riverside Park. A jogger spotted the body two days ago. We got a clean print and it came back to a former Marine sergeant named Dumas. Know anything about him?"

Hayes shook his head, taking a sip of coffee. Damn that Lantana Jones. She'd added in some of that Sweet'N Low bullshit.

"You know these feds," Jones said. "They think we work for them. Man wouldn't say jack shit about this dead guy. But I got the read on him that this man was something special to the feds. This boy, Agent Bickett, told me that Dumas was one of those military contractors, a solider for hire employed by something called the Warlock Group. What in the hell is somebody like that doing in Memphis?"

Porter sipped his coffee. "Good question."

"How's Mrs. McKellar?" she asked. "I tried her back last week and she told me her husband had come home. That it was all a misunderstanding. Her husband had been mugged in London. She seemed convinced of it, but it sounded like a bunch of bullshit to me. You sure that coffee is okay?"

"I can taste how much you love me, Lantana," he said. "Looking out for my health and all. Appreciate it."

Lantana Jones smiled even wider, a little wind kicking up by the statue, scattering an empty box of Popeyes and a few plastic bottles. As he turned, Hayes noticed someone had spray-painted *Whoop That Trick* on the horse statue's ass. Hard to take pride in a park that centered around a dead man with that kind of legacy.

"Well, I sure am glad that all is well at the McKellar house," Jones said, clicking her nails on the coffee cup. "And I guess that intruder she called about was just one of those random Memphis break-ins. Otherwise, I'd probably need to tell her that this body from the river, our dead international military contractor Jack Dumas, was missing an arm."

Porter raised an eyebrow. "Well, gotdamn."

"Only I wanted to talk to you about another missing persons report I just came across," she said. "Did you see in the paper about some old actress who had disappeared?"

"The one who worked with Elvis?"

"I'd never heard of that movie," she said. "*Easy Come, Easy Go*. Sounds fake to me. Only good movies that man made were *Viva Las Vegas* and the one where Elvis is a doctor, singing gospel and trying to get it on with that nun played by Mary Tyler Moore."

"*Change of Habit*."

"That's the one," Jones said. "Goddamn, that Elvis Presley was one handsome man. Momma would've taken good care of his ass."

Hayes shook his head, not comfortable hearing what turned on his goddaughter.

"Why'd you want to talk to me about that case?"

Lantana drank some more coffee and set the cup between them.

"See," she said, "one of our detectives went out and talked to this woman's daughter. She was sharing an apartment with her momma down off Bill Morris at Winchester."

"So."

"So," Jones said, "the daughter told my guy that her momma had been knocking boots with a man twenty years younger. Can you believe that? All that age separation, Porter Hayes?"

She picked up her coffee and knocked his knee with her leg. He smoothed down his mustache and shook his head.

"Okay. Okay," he said. "What about this woman?"

"Apparently, she'd been the real deal back in your time," Jones said. "British, blond, looked good in a teeny-weeny bikini. All that shit. The daughter said the last time she saw her mother, she was getting into a car with a white man who resembles your Dean McKellar. Only this man's name was Collinson."

"Peter Collinson?"

"Yep," she said. "Said she didn't trust this man a lick and decided to write down the tag on his Land Rover. Want to guess who that car's registered to?"

"My man Dean."

"See," Lantana said. "You may be old, Porter Hayes, but you come along real quick. Can't wait to tell Daddy you ain't dead wood after all."

28

Leslie

He was so engrossed in his story about Colonel Sanders, the parable about the man not making his first million until he turned sixty-five, that he didn't see the young Black man approach his table. Leslie had been explaining to his son-in-law Brian—second husband to his darling daughter Judy—that a man wasn't judged by his failures but rather how many times he tried. Whether it was starting your own business without two nickels to rub together or having the grit and determination of a Razorback offensive tackle. Leslie had just gotten to the gosh dang good part, the Colonel refusing to take no for an answer, when the young fella in a nice suit interrupted and said, "Leslie, me and you need to talk privately."

"Well, sir," Grimes said. "I don't mean any offense, but I don't know you from Adam's housecat and I'm having a family lunch with my son-in-law. I'm sure if you call my secretary, Rita, next—"

"I called Rita," the man said. "And truth be told, she's not worth shit."

"Excuse me, sir?"

And here it had been such a fine little lunch on the Lake Hamilton marina at Fisherman's Wharf with their old-time catfish and hush puppies, shrimp, and oysters from the Gulf. Reminded him of trips down to Panama City Beach with his family and high times on that Miracle Mile.

"Have you heard from your friend Jack Dumas lately?"

"I'm sorry," Grimes said, plucking a shrimp from his plate and dipping it into the cocktail sauce. "I don't know you or anyone named Jack Dumas."

"Big redneck with one arm and a mean disposition?" the man said. "Because he most surely knew your ass. He called you sixteen times last Thursday, Leslie, and again Friday morning."

"Well," Grimes said. "I get a great many calls from a great many people."

"How many of those folks end up dead, buck-ass nekkid, and hanging upside down from a cypress tree along the Mississippi River?"

Grimes dropped his shrimp and looked across the red-and-white-checked tablecloth at Brian. *Good gosh almighty.* What a rude man. And this restaurant had always been his little ace in the hole where he didn't have to contend with spider weavers like in Little Rock, wanting to kiss his ring and try and set up a business meeting. Here, he could pull up in his pleasure boat, tie up to the dock, and be as free as ole Huck Finn. A barefoot country boy to his core.

"Sir," Grimes said, dropping his strained smile and reaching into his jacket, "I appreciate your persistence. But this is a private lunch and a private conversation."

"I heard y'all talking," this man said. "But I'm not Colonel Sanders peddling those eleven herbs and spices in his fucking pressure cooker. I came to talk to you, Leslie. And only you. Man-to-man about a word you mostly certainly understand."

"Let me guess," Grimes said, chuckling. "Money?"

"How about the word *geniza*?" the man said. "It's a funny Hebrew word. Never heard of it until just a year or two ago. Means 'library.' Or 'hiding place.' I do have a fascinating as hell story to tell. What's your son-in-law's name?"

Leslie looked across the table at Brian, a big and sturdy—or perhaps portly, depending on your assessment—thirty-four-year-old with apple cheeks and wavy brown hair. He'd played tackle at the University of Arkansas but always made Leslie think of that fat little boy outside the Shoney's. All he needed was checkered pants and suspenders. "Brian."

"Howdy there, Brian," the man said. "I'm federal agent Carson Wells. How's that shrimp, big man?"

Brian looked to Grimes and shrugged, not sure about what to do. Which really had been Brian's entire problem from the start, unable to rise up and commit to the challenges and opportunities the Lord offered us every day. He'd rather spend his time betting on college football games or drinking dang piña coladas at the dog track in West Memphis than setting his goals.

"You're just gonna love this story, *Brian*," Wells said, sliding into an open chair beside his son-in-law. "Lots of danger and intrigue. Adventure! Excitement! It stretches all the way from ancient Afghanistan to modern Istanbul and then over to fabulous gay Paree. *Oui. Oui.* Hell, man. It's even got murder. Whole mess of them if you go back to Kabul and then those three unlucky bastards in Paris."

"That's enough," Grimes said, holding up his hand. "Give me a minute, Brian. This won't take long."

Brian shrugged and left the table without a hint of curiosity. No wonder Judy thought he was a little soft in the head. Carson Wells slid over into Brian's seat.

The hostess had them at Leslie's favorite table, in the center of the empty room decorated with nets, mounted fish, life preservers, and old diving helmets. The plate glass window offered a nice view of the marina and the speedboats crossing the glassy surface of the lake. Carson Wells plucked a hot shrimp off Brian's plate. "I'm sorry if I don't take you at your word," Grimes said, "but can you show me a badge or something?"

Wells reached into his jacket pocket and opened up an ID for Homeland Security.

"Homeland Security?" Leslie said. "I don't understand."

"I know you don't, Leslie," Wells said. "All this can be new and confusing as hell. Kind of like puberty when your dingdong first turns on and starts buzzing in your pocket. You sure want to pull on it but want to keep that control, too. Be cool about it. But this story makes a whole lot of sense if you just follow all the moving parts. See, I got access to the late Jack Dumas's phone records, and it appeared he called your ass a mess of times last week. As soon as I saw you and Dumas were working together, the whole picture show just came together. You being a man of faith, a student of history and the Bible. Not to mention the third richest motherfucker in the state of Arkansas."

"I don't know anyone named Jack Dumas."

"Yeah, you do," Wells said. "He worked for your friend Peter Collinson, or as he was sometimes known, Dean McKellar. The way I see it, Dumas has been in touch with you about this special cargo coming all the way on a slow boat from Haydarpaşa Port in Istanbul. Am I right? Or am I right, Leslie?"

Leslie had always been a good poker player, although he'd given up gambling years ago. He just leveled his gaze at the man Wells and placed his palm to the side of his face, keeping his breathing even and slow. Wells had set that hook deep and Leslie was doing his gosh darn best not to flop about. Without Dumas, what would he do now? Even Joanna was missing, according to the news, and he didn't dare to guess what had happened to that lovely but devious woman.

Grimes pushed the half-eaten shrimp plate away and crossed his arms over his chest.

"See, this whole story kicks off a long, long time ago," Wells said. "How long, you might ask? How about eight hundred years. Or you want to make it an even thousand, Leslie? A goddamn millennia."

"I don't care for that kind of talk."

"My apologies, Mr. Grimes," he said. "But we're talking history. And history isn't for those with a weak stomach. It's ugly and dirty. Unpleasant at times. Makes you study on things that you'd rather not think about."

Grimes looked out the window to see Brian at the edge of the dock, skipping stones out into the lake. He looked as unconcerned as a barefoot child. He'd never understand what Judy had seen in him.

"So there was this man, a Jewish man, in a place we never expected to find any Jews," Wells said. "A merchant on the great Silk Road who collected all kinds of things. Shipping records, personal records, poetry, even a nice copy of the Mishnah. In Hebrew, of course. That's a book of these Jewish oral traditions. Real old."

"I know what the Mishnah is."

"I knew you would, Leslie," Wells said. "Like I said, a man of God and history. I am so very, very impressed. Anyway, this man—who let's just call Yehuda ben Daniel, or Abu Nasser if you prefer his local name—kept all this stuff along with pieces of the actual Bible. We're talking the greatest hits. Jeremiah, Zechariah, and Proverbs. How my late momma sure loved that King Solomon and his words of wisdom. Abu Nasser sealed everything up in jars. Then some time later, for a reason we do not know or fully understand, he buried his collection in a cave outside Bamyan, a real nasty and rocky place in northern Afghanistan that's been overrun by warlords ever since. Now, we just call them the Taliban."

Grimes couldn't move. He was absolutely in shock, his hands gripping the edge of the table. Unable to breathe or nod, only able to continue listening to this man he'd never met tell him a tale he knew backward and forward.

"Are you following me so far?" Wells said. "Nod your head if that's a big yes."

How did this man know all this? Had Dumas told someone before he died? Had Joanna Grayson been arrested and told everything she knew? That would make the most sense. Maybe this man had threatened Joanna with prison and instead she got a little money and went on her way, people believing she'd disappeared when she was lying on a beach in the Bahamas.

Leslie Grimes nodded. He felt like a puppet with the master's hand deep up his backside.

"It's been so long, and the sands of time have covered up most of ancient Bamyan," Wells said. "Damn Genghis Khan destroyed the city in the eleventh century. The Taliban boys blew up those twin Buddhas in '01. What a damn shame. But I digress . . . one day about forty years ago, as the story has been told, a fucking goatherd was out tending to his flock, truly a nice biblical touch, and the man runs across what he believes is a wolf's den. Maybe the same damn wolf that's been picking off his goats at night? So this man does what any respectable goatherd would do, he pulls the rifle off his shoulder and wanders on in. Probably an Enfield, as I'm told so many of those were left behind by the British. He lights a torch, or maybe just a flashlight. I'd like to think it was a torch because it would heighten the drama; the flashlight's a little too modern for the story, don't you think? And while he's down in the depths of Hades, what do you think he discovers?"

"A jar."

"A jar," Wells said, clapping his hands together. "Ain't that something, Leslie? Just lying there, sticking up out of the dirt and rocks. This damn goatherd goes into a pitch-dark cave to defend his flock and makes the discovery of a lifetime. Ole Abu Nasser's personal hoard seeing the light of day after nearly a thousand years."

Grimes reached for his napkin and dabbed his forehead. His spindly white hair was receding so far back now that most of his scalp felt slick. *Abu Nasser. Bamyan.* The ancient codex and the entire *geniza.* How had this Carson Wells found all this out? How did he know about the secret books? The Mishnah? The fragments of Proverbs?

"You thought Jack Dumas was going to bring it all home for you," Wells said. "Didn't you?"

Leslie said nothing. He'd learned long ago that during a negotiation, if it was actually a negotiation, to stay quiet until the other side made their offer. Or in this case, demands.

"What do you want?"

"Can I ask a personal question?" Wells said. "Hope this doesn't come off tacky, or as the French say, *gauche.* But what exactly did you pay for all that shit to be shipped to Memphis?"

"Holy artifacts are not *shit,*" Leslie said, privately admonishing himself for repeating Wells's profanity.

"Ten million?"

Leslie swallowed. He again dabbed his brow.

"Higher?" Wells said. "Twenty-five? Thirty?"

Leslie scanned the restaurant for the waitress and then made the motion for her to bring him the bill. When he turned back to Wells, the man was smiling and shaking his head.

"Must be more," he said. "Lots more. Did you pay more than fifty mil?"

"I need to get going," Leslie said, placing his hands on the armrests to stand.

"*Ding, ding, ding,*" Wells said. "More than fifty mil. Whoa. That must be something. Can you tell me what you're gonna do with it? I read something about you starting up a big Museum of God in Little Rock. Surely you wouldn't pay all that money to just hang this stuff up in your bathroom."

"I have absolutely no idea what you're talking about."

"Game's over, Leslie," Wells said. "My job is to see to it that the geniza is shipped right on back to Afghanistan."

"Into a war zone and right into the arms of the Taliban?"

"Ever heard of the UNESCO Convention of 1970?" he said. "Some real fascinating reading. Lot of articles and subheads on international law. But to the point, it says one country can't steal culturally important shit from another country. You understand? No matter who sold it to you or how the paperwork was shuffled, you don't have the right to keep it. My main job here is to see it goes back. How much your ass gets prosecuted is up to you, Leslie."

Grimes's hand shook as he pulled out a hundred-dollar bill from his wallet and laid it on the table, unable to wait around for the check anymore.

"Oh," Wells said. "And don't bother trying your Peter Collinson. He's got troubles of his own. Seems like this little switcheroo's gonna cost him more than a pound of flesh. There's a devil just arrived down in Mississippi to get his due, and it is my professional opinion and advice for you to walk on by this shit show."

"Some things in life are worth the risk," Leslie said. "What is your life? For you are a mist that appears for a little time and then vanishes."

"Book of James."

"We all want to matter, Mr. Wells," Leslie said. "Not for decades, but millennia."

"Got you some of that Abu Nasser fever, do you?"

Leslie Grimes didn't dignify the question with a response, leaving the money on the table and walking straight out of the restaurant and onto the boat dock. Brian was seated in the captain's chair and typing on his phone. His back was to the great lake and the coppery sky over the pines. "Do you mind?" Leslie said, shooing him over. "I'll take us back to the house."

29

Addison

The stitching on her white coat said *Dr.* Marcy Bledsoe but Addison had her doubts. She seemed more like just another one of Dean's lies, the woman coming again this afternoon to the small windowless room to talk about addiction and hallucinations. She looked to be in her early sixties, half-glasses down on her nose, a jeweled chain around her neck. Her skin was a blanched white with little or no makeup, just a smear of lipstick. Her hair was cut short, man short, and had been dyed a bright coppery red not to be found in nature.

"You're awfully calm for a woman involved in a kidnapping," Addison said.

"We've covered this yesterday, Addison," Dr. Bledsoe said. "You came here voluntarily. Or don't you remember?"

"I don't know today's date or the state I'm in," Addison said. "Where am I exactly?"

"It's been a rough week for you," Dr. Bledsoe said. "Your mind and your body have been through a lot of trauma."

"You're evading the question, Marcy," Addison said. "I asked you where the fuck am I and you tell me that I've had a hard week. That's not an answer. That's you continuing to be evasive while you and my husband keep me locked up."

Dr. Bledsoe stood as Addison sat cross-legged on a single mattress covered in only a white top sheet. The room had lacquered pine walls, a few pieces of institutional furniture, and a television, the reception something horrible. She was only able to watch this awful channel called MeTV with reruns for geriatric people.

The room had a small bathroom outfitted with toiletries like you'd find in a Motel 6 and a closet with two white towels, two hand towels, and a change of blue medical scrubs she'd been forced to wear. Addison had no idea what had happened to her clothes.

"Would you like to go for a walk?" Dr. Bledsoe said.

"I'd like for you to give me back my clothes and my phone," Addison said. "I'd like to call my children and my sick father to make sure they're okay and then let them know I've been kidnapped."

"Addison, Addison," Dr. Bledsoe said. "You signed yourself in. We have you on video giving us permission to begin your treatment."

"Treatment?" Addison said. "What fucking treatment? Locking me up and taking away my rights. What part of my husband is a lying murderous sociopath don't you understand? He put me in this craphole so I'll shut up. How much did he pay you? I can pay you more. Just let me out."

Dr. Bledsoe shook her head. She pulled a penlight from her coat and flicked it on as if performing a magic act. Without asking permission, she stepped forward and checked Addison's pupils and ears and then asked for her to please open her mouth. *Say ah.* Addison didn't even think about it.

"I'm not sick and I'm not crazy," Addison said. "If you let me go, I promise not to sue the shit out of you and whatever facility I'm in."

"Magnolia Treatment Center."

"Located where?"

"I know you have a lot of questions." Dr. Bledsoe smiled again. She had such little yellow teeth, like pebbles in her mouth. "Let's get some fresh air."

They walked out of the room into a short hall lined with more lacquered pine leading to a kitchen where a skinny Black woman stirred something in a large silver pot. The woman waved, as if they were old friends, while Addison followed Dr. Bledsoe out a side door and onto the covered porch of the cabin, which faced a big lodge made of logs and topped with a green tin roof. They passed by two more cabins along a path filled with river stones. Narrow flower beds on each side of the path had only dead flowers and brown tomato plants.

"What if I make a run for it?" Addison asked.

"Be my guest," Dr. Bledsoe said. "But I wouldn't recommend it. We're located within three hundred acres along a national forest. I don't think you want to navigate the woods in this cold."

The first thing Addison remembered after Dean had caught her in the safe room was being held down on a gurney and a large Black woman tightening the straps on her wrists. A white woman, much skinnier and with a skeletal face, was probing her. She jabbed her for an IV drip. Later, the big woman made her bend over the bed while the skinny woman lubed up her hand and checked all her orifices. It was the most degrading experience of her entire life.

"Since when is violating a person considered rehab?" Addison asked. "One of your people stuck their fingers up my ass."

"Checking for contraband," Dr. Bledsoe said. "You'd be surprised how many of our patients try to bring in pills and dope. We can't take any chances that you might overdose."

Addison followed the woman toward a decent-size pond with a pier leading out to a gazebo. Beyond the pond, as promised, were the big, bad woods. As she turned in every direction, Addison only saw more woods, a single gravel road disappearing into the pines.

"How much is this setting Dean back?"

"We are a very exclusive center," Dr. Bledsoe said. "Your family is very worried about you."

"Did my husband tell you what kind of shit he put into my drink the other night?" Addison said. "I ended up in a house of mirrors at the god-damn Memphis Zoo. I thought I was coming out of my skin. I could hear the monkeys chittering up in the trees. And then that bastard dragged me through all our phony friends to make it look like I was the one with the problem. Marcy. Fucking listen to me. I saw my husband shoot a man in cold blood. I have a big stain all over my Persian rug."

"Have you tried mineral water?"

Addison took a deep breath and closed her eyes. Dr. Bledsoe was headed out into the gazebo. A sign read "Quiet Area. Please Respect Others." Addison wondered what would happen if she just started to scream at the top of her lungs, *You fucking assholes. He's fooled you. He's fooled everyone. He's a lying, devious bastard.*

In the gazebo, Addison took a seat on a bench and rubbed her forearms covered in goose bumps. Was it against regulations to loan her a damn jacket? "You don't believe me," Addison said. "Do you?"

"This is a circle of trust, Addison," Dr. Bledsoe said. "The more you accept our help, the more your world will grow. I want you to be able to leave your cabin and meet our other guests. I want you to have meetings with your husband and with your family. I know they are all pulling for you."

"Awesome." Addison looked up at her. "My father is dying."

"Yes," she said. "We know. I'm so very sorry."

"Are you a real doctor or just somebody Dean has paid?" she said. "He's done that to me before. He paid some country woman down in Southaven to act like his personal secretary."

Dr. Bledsoe placed a hand on her shoulder and smiled. "We better get you back," she said. "Your lips have turned blue."

Two days later, Sara Caroline came to visit. Addison assumed Dean was there but too chickenshit to actually come in and face her. She'd been brought into the big lodge that was starting to remind her more and more of a roadside Cracker Barrel. All it needed was some rusty iron skillets and farm equipment hung over the big stone fireplace and they'd be in business. Sara Caroline looked gaunt and absolutely drained, her blond hair pulled back tight into a ponytail. With her fresh-scrubbed face, she looked so young that Addison's heart hurt.

They hugged. They cried. They did all that business until Sara Caroline whispered in her ear, "I know what Dad did."

Addison let out a very long breath. *Oh, thank god.* A little more crying and then a glance back to see the big woman who'd held her down when she first arrived guarding the door. A dozen or so folding metal chairs had been arranged in front of the fireplace hearth. Pamphlets with the header "How to Listen to God. Overcoming Addiction through Practice of Two-Way Prayer" were laid out on each seat.

They took a seat. Addison leaned forward and held Sara Caroline's hand. The fire felt nice and warm after being stuck in the airless room all morning. It popped and crackled in the stones. Except for being held against her will and given a body cavity search, the center was homey as hell.

"Where's your father?"

"Outside," Sara Caroline said. "I know he stuck you in this place. Uncle Branch and Aunt Libby had a huge fight about it last night while I was in the kitchen. Dad says you've gone crazy and have started seeing things."

Addison held her hand tight. It felt so damn good to have someone listening to her for once and believing in her. She knew she could rely on her kids. All week she'd heard nothing but how she was an alcoholic with delusions. You hear that enough and you start to doubt your own reality. Addison reached up and patted her daughter's face. "Thank you," she said. "Thank you."

"Dad said he had to do it," Sara Caroline said. "That you gave him no choice."

"He's lying," she said. "He dropped something in my prosecco at the Zoo Boo and after I saw him shoot a man, he wanted to shut me up. Did you know he has a damn safe room up under our house with all these guns and maps? It's crazy, Sara Caroline. But it's all true. I need you and Preston to get as far away from him as you can."

"Dad said you'd say something like that," she said. "He brought over a counselor to help us all understand. I hate Dad for putting you in here. But I also understand that you gave him no choice. I know you're not thinking straight, but it's not your fault. I'm okay with it. *Really*. I want to tell you that I'm not mad at you. I just want you to get well and come home."

Addison looked back to the big woman guarding the door. Her

crossed arms were as big as smoked hams. Making a run for it wasn't going to be happening today. The thought of being held down, screaming into a pillow, and those rubbery fingers made her want to puke.

"I want you to call a man named Porter Hayes and tell him where I am," Addison said. "You can find him online or you can ask Granddad. *Porter Hayes.* Can you remember that?"

"Oh, Dad told me all about him," Sara Caroline said. "He said that guy was just some downtown con artist trying to take our money. I can't call him, Mom. Dad would kill me."

"Don't say that."

"Don't say what?"

"That Dad would kill you."

Sara Caroline just rolled her eyes and reached out and gripped her hand tighter. "It's just an expression," she said. "I understand rehab, Mom. Remember us watching that show with Marcia from *The Brady Bunch*? She said she'd once traded sex for cocaine in Malibu. You're not like that. You're a strong woman. Okay? Just don't worry about us. We've been staying with Aunt Libby and everyone is fine. Even ChaCha."

Sara Caroline smiled at her and then reached over and gave her a hug. Addison felt as still and cold as a stone. She couldn't breathe. She couldn't move.

"Mom?"

That's just when Dean timed his grand entrance in his tailored gray flannel suit with black silk tie and Italian shoes that Addison knew cost more than two thousand dollars. They'd been a Christmas gift and he'd been so proud of them, wearing them all morning with his ridiculous kimono. The Submariner on his wrist gleamed in the firelight.

"Baby," Addison said, "I'd like to speak to your father alone."

Addison prayed.

She hadn't prayed in a good long while but that afternoon and into the evening, she prayed and prayed like a goddamn nun. She got on her knees, clasped her hands together, bowed her head. The whole nine yards of what she'd learned at Our Lady of Perpetual Help. She prayed to Jesus, Mary, and Saint Charbel. She didn't remember much about Saint Charbel other than he kept on bleeding and bleeding long after he was dead. But he was Lebanese and revered by her father, and at the moment, that was enough for her. Most of her religious training as a kid amounted to the boys in her Sunday school class using their textbooks as an excuse to draw enormous penises on the saints with cartoon bubbles coming out of their mouths saying things like: "And for my next miracle . . ."

Dean had been so damn smug with her. He spoke in loud, condescending tones to make sure everyone in that lodge heard him. He used words like *understanding, faith, family*, and *trust*. He told her that she was getting the best treatment money could buy. She told him he was lying. That she had seen him shoot a man in their library. She didn't mention the rug. You'd think he would've disposed of the rug along with the man, rolled up his big one-armed ass like a burrito. The rug had been a good one, a couple thousand dollars from some antiques mall on Summer Avenue, but not worth going to prison.

Who the hell are you?

Who are you, Addison? he'd asked. *I've been with you fifteen years.*

I know you're not Dean McKellar.

If I'm not Dean McKellar, then you're not Addison McKellar. And what does that make our kids?

You drugged me and then I saw you fucking kill a guy. You told me your name was Dean McKellar, but Dean McKellar died back in nineteen ninety-two. You've lied about everything since the day I met you.

Dean shrugged. *Doesn't everybody? Don't you lie to me, Addy?*

I never lied to you.

Dean nodded. He clasped his hands together and looked at her hard. The stubble on his chin had been artfully trimmed and shaped. He'd worn the good cologne today for some reason. It always made Addison's eyes water.

He said: *I know where you've been.*

Addison knew it before he said it. But despite everything, he had the balls to actually look hurt. That's how good of a liar Dean could be. He gave her a good long stare and said, *You should've never gone to Alec Dawson about me.*

Addison was ready to run.

She knew she didn't have time to think about it or plan it. She just knew the next time that she was let out of her locked room, she'd bolt right for the fucking woods, absolutely sure neither of the women who'd held her down could keep up. Addison had been a runner most of her life. She'd run track at Hutch and had done her best to keep in shape at Ole Miss. In her New York days, she'd jogged in Central Park every chance she got, even in winter, and after Sara Caroline and Preston had been born, she had spent a lot of time in the gym. She didn't give a shit what Dr. Bledsoe had said about the retreat being so fucking remote that she'd never find her way out. What else was she supposed to do, just lie in this awful wood-paneled room with her mind churning over nothing but worry for her kids and wondering if she'd ever see her dad again? And if she were to make any legal moves against Dean, she'd have to be back in Memphis and representing herself. She could just imagine him now at the Club. *Oh, yes. Addison has pretty much hit rock bottom. We're all praying that she makes it through. But you know, substance abuse runs in her family.* So awful.

Someone knocked on the door, and before she could even respond, the dead bolt turned and the big woman entered the room with a tray. She stared at Addison as she walked past her and set the tray on top of a chest of drawers. The skinny woman who'd violated her stood in the hallway with a smile on her face, a smug look like she owned this rich bitch from Memphis. Addison stared right back.

She sat on her bed and didn't move.

The big woman opened the lid, like it was trout almondine at Arnaud's, pointing out steaming beef Stroganoff and peas. Some iced tea and coffee cake for dessert, baby. Addison would rather eat dirt.

The thing about being cooped up and told you might not see your kids again was that it could make you do things that you never even thought possible. Addison was the kind of person who tried to always do the right thing. Always said please and thank you. She was kind to animals and held doors open for old people. And said excuse me before interrupting a conversation.

So what came next felt like watching someone else.

Addison, shoeless and still dressed in the hospital scrubs, reached out for a fork as if she was hungry as could be. *Mmm. Mmm.* Brown slop and peas. She looked up at the big woman, smiled, and then stuck the fork right into the center of her hand. The woman let out a horrible howl as Addison darted, not even looking back as she ran from the room and shouldered the skinny woman to the ground. The woman floundered before Addison reached for the back of her shirt, pulled her into the room, and dead bolted the door on both of them.

They started to bang on the door just as she made it to the kitchen. A grizzled old woman wearing a WORLD'S GREATEST MAMAW T-shirt stood at the countertop. She was eating a greasy cheeseburger with a handheld radio carelessly left out of reach. Addison snatched it up, ran for the front door, and tested the lock. It was open.

She turned back to the woman and looked down at her feet. "Give me your shoes."

The woman turned her head toward the banging and then back to Addison.

"I took kickboxing for three years," Addison said. "Give me your shoes, Mamaw, or I'll punch you right in the tit."

The old woman bent down and quickly removed her ragged pair of Nikes. Addison picked them up without taking her eyes off her. They were a few sizes too large but would work fine. She slipped them on her bare feet, gripped the radio, and bolted outside into the night.

As she ran, she looked up at the big lodge. She spotted a few figures standing by the windows, so she was careful to make sure she wasn't seen as she made a run for the shadows. She crossed a gravel parking lot, ducking behind parked cars and trucks before finally deciding to head around the pond, where she tossed the radio and then ran deep into the woods.

After the first hour, guessing it had been an hour, she wished she'd at least snatched up that coffee cake from the tray or had something to drink. This was going to be a long, hard hike, and soon, her mouth felt bone dry. The moon was high and bright overhead when sometime after midnight, surely it was after midnight by then, she came to a lake. The surface shimmered a bright silver and far into the water she heard the honking of geese and flapping wings. On the opposite shore, she spotted an old farmhouse with smoke trailing from the chimney.

She closed her eyes and thanked both God and Saint Charbel. The lake was pretty damn big but she could circle it and make her way to the house.

But soon she entered a soggy marsh. She kept trying to make the loop to the house but she became trapped by stubby cypress trees and thick mud that sucked at her Nikes. At one point, she got up to her knees in sinking ooze, her body feeling nearly frozen as she tromped on ahead. *God, she was so cold.* She hadn't been so cold since that trip to Telluride three years ago. Dean had wanted to rent a fucking sleigh to a little cabin where so-called cowboys cooked steaks over an open fire. Then, like now, the cold was so bone-deep, it hurt to even take a breath. At least now there wasn't some hippie cowboy breaking out his fucking guitar and going through his catalog of Eagles songs. She could still hear his sad, spoken word rendition of "Hotel California." *Such a lovely place.*

Oh god, thinking about Telluride made the cold worse. Addison was shivering so hard now her teeth hurt.

Her breath clouded before her as she kept on trudging around the lake to the house. But as she got closer, she could hear the zooming of cars along a highway. She could take a chance at the house. But what if the asshole who lived there was Dr. Bledsoe? She'd open the door in a fuzzy robe with a coffee mug in her hand, that dumb, deadpan look on her withered face. *Addison, Addison,* she'd say. *I thought we made real progress this morning.*

Seriously, fuck that woman.

Addison headed for the road, a longer hike than she expected. She knew she looked like a crazy swamp creature with mud splattered up on her pants and across her chest and arms. She could feel the wet clumps in her hair, wild and loose across her face, and even taste the mud in her mouth.

If she'd been driving down a highway and saw a woman in hospital scrubs splattered in mud and covered with welts, she wouldn't have stopped. She'd have sped up.

Addison made it to a hill overlooking a four-lane highway. She was out of breath, resting her hands above her head to suck in some cold air. Across the road a big billboard lit up for a Kentucky Fried Chicken in nineteen miles. She did her best to wipe the dirt from her face and blood off her bare arms from the swatting branches. She had to get back to Memphis and get Dean, or whoever he was, for what he'd done. She didn't know how she'd do it. But she knew that turnabout was going to be a bitch.

Along the roadside, she jumped and waved. Car after car passed her. One big rig lit up in bright white and orange lights honked its horn but didn't stop. She tried to flag down cars for what felt like hours, although probably was just minutes. Addison was so fucking tired. She began to think about Dean taking her kids away to god knows where and that maybe she'd never see them again. Or her father. Was he still alive? Would she see him again?

She sank down to her knees and started to cry. Maybe she could just walk home. She got up and started walking again, going maybe a half mile until she saw signs for Highway 78 West, ten miles from Holly Springs. Her legs rubbery as she kept moving forward, praying again that someone would stop. If not, she would make it to Holly Springs. Soon, she was encompassed in flashing blue lights and the quick sounds of a police siren. She kept walking along the shoulder, unable to stop until she heard a man behind her asking if she was all right. "Ma'am?"

Addison turned and saw a nice man in a khaki uniform. He was an older guy with gray hair and had a friendly, pleasant face and an old-time country accent. "Looks like you've been through hell, young lady."

"Yes, sir."

"Then how about we get you out of this cold and back home?" he said. "That okay by you?"

"That would be more than okay."

The deputy opened his trunk, retrieved a thick army blanket, and spread it over her shoulders before opening the back door and gently helping her in. The blue lights continued to pulse along the roadside, lighting up the rocky shoulder.

He put the car in gear and drove off fast, soon heading up onto an overpass and then turning around the way they'd come. Addison was just about to ask him just where in the hell she was when he picked up the radio mic and called into dispatch. "This is 34," he said. "Just found that mental patient that escaped tonight. En route to take her back to the facility."

Addison reached up and gripped the cage that separated him. She shook the cage and begged him to help her. *She'd been locked away against her will. Her husband killed someone. He was the one who was crazy.*

"Oh, yes, ma'am," he said. "I'll put it all in the report."

The deputy reached down to turn up the police radio. Every word she said drowned out by static.

30

Porter Hayes

They weren't an hour out of Memphis that morning, tailing Dean McKellar's Land Rover for the second straight day, when Deacon Malone started to witness to Porter. Asking him if he's got his house in order, straight with the Lord, and that kind of thing.

"I'm good," Hayes said, driving south on I-55 past Coldwater. "But appreciate you asking."

"I don't think I could get out of bed without His help," Malone said. "I know you go to church when you can. Mainly doing it for Nina and your grandkids. Keeping up those appearances. A nice Sunday suit. Cash in the collection plate. But when you're there, are you listening?"

"You understand my situation with the Lord."

"He will ease your mind a lot more than that Rémy at night," Malone said. "I don't want to be all up in your business, Porter. But I been there before. You know, it's later than you think."

"I think I better find my client or I'm not much of a detective," Porter said. "I think that I promised to help this woman get out from her husband and then don't hear anything else from her. I knock on her door and the lying husband shuts the damn door in my face. None of this is looking real good."

"When we were up at Coletta's the other night, you just looked troubled is all," Malone said. "I wouldn't be a friend if I didn't try to share the Good News. Even knowing your position on the church."

"I don't have any position," Hayes said. He was pretty sure that

McKellar was headed down to his hunt camp in the Delta, unless he kept on truckin' on the interstate past Batesville and Grenada. The morning had started off normal, McKellar going for a five-mile jog and stopping by the Starbucks on Union before heading back to his big English Tudor. He came out thirty minutes later in dress clothes—black turtleneck, gray slacks, and camel coat—and got into his Land Rover. They expected another round at the Club or maybe lunch with his fat-cat attorney, Jimbo Hornsby. But instead, he jumped on 240 and then south on 55. It was that long leg down 55 that got Malone into preacher mode, wanting to talk about Porter's situation. "Genevieve been gone for almost twenty years, man."

"I know how long she's been gone," Hayes said. "No need to remind me."

"That woman had a strong bond with God," Malone said. "Never heard a voice so mighty. That wasn't just her gift. That came from how strong she believed."

"You know what I think?" Hayes said. "I think Dean McKellar's keeping Addison locked up down on the farm. We should've checked this place two days ago instead of following this man all around Memphis. That's why she never left her house. Because she's not in her house."

"Guess we'll find out," Malone said.

At Batesville, Dean McKellar took the second exit and headed west toward the Delta. If Porter was right about things, he'd be getting off Highway 6 in about fifteen minutes to go deeper into Quitman County.

"You know Charley Pride grew up down in Sledge?" Malone said, watching the flat landscape fly by the passenger window.

Hayes didn't answer, keeping back four or five car lengths from Dean McKellar. But the farther they got on into the Delta, so damn big, empty, and treeless, it would be a hell of a lot harder not to be spotted. He figured if McKellar made the turn Porter thought he'd be making, then they'd just pull over for a few minutes and drive straight to the property listed on the deed.

"Preacher said you can't spell life without *if*," Malone said. "*If* stands for both a choice and a chance. Make a choice or take a chance with the Lord. You know what I'm saying?"

"Sure thing, man," Hayes said. "Hey. You mind checking in my glove box?"

Malone leaned his big ass forward, grunting, and opened up the glove box, pulling out some speed loaders for his .38. "This what you're looking for?"

"This man will shoot our Black asses dead and then drop us in the river without a thought," Hayes said. "I known folks like him back in Nam. Fellas like him don't kill for their country. They kill 'cause they like watching shit burn."

"You ever think this may be the final days of our story?"

"All the time," Hayes said. "*Live each day as if it were your last, without frenzy, without apathy, without pretense.*"

"Don't think I know that verse."

"It's not a Bible verse," Hayes said. "It's Marcus Aurelius."

Hayes watched the taillights of the Land Rover cross a rusted bridge over the Tallahatchie and then approach a country crossroads, where Mc-Kellar turned left and headed south just as he expected. Hayes pulled off onto the shoulder and let down his window for some fresh air.

"You a hard man, Porter Hayes."

"Not hard," he said. "Just realistic. I'm too old for some bedtime stories."

"What happened to Genevieve wasn't about you," Malone said. "He had greater plans for that woman. We can't even understand how this whole big story fits together."

"Appreciate you, Deacon," Hayes said. "You're a good man and a better friend. And I thank you for witnessing to me today. But once we go on down into the Delta, some shit's gonna fly and I need you to be on it. You got your big-ass gun?"

"Always do."

"Good," Hayes said. "Because I'm not going back to Memphis without my client. Some things just aren't done."

Deacon hadn't spoken since they'd pulled off on the side of the road and then continued on five minutes later. He only called out the country roads where Porter was supposed to turn, keeping to the map of north Mississippi they'd brought from the office.

"Should be about five miles down the road."

"Might have a gate," Hayes said. "White folks love to have their property sealed off with cattle gates. Maybe some No Trespass signs and Rebel flags."

"Since when has that stopped us?"

"Never."

"You know you saying that losing a client just wasn't done had me thinking on that old movie with Bogart."

"*The Maltese Falcon.*"

"Yeah," Malone said. "I don't recall much about that movie other than Bogart saying that you can't allow anyone to kill your damn partner. You think you'll say that if I hike my Black ass into a hunt lodge to find some white woman?"

"You mean, would I avenge you?"

"That's right," Malone said. "Avenge me."

"Maybe," Hayes said, following a big curve of road under a canopy of oak trees, leaves falling down brown and dead across the windshield. "I never took on a partner. But I'll see what I can do if you get yourself killed."

"That must be it," Malone said, pointing to a big log house with a green metal roof. A dirt road led straight to the main house with an open gate along the highway. There were a few cabins and neat trailers set up on the land and, as expected, a lot of No Trespassing signs and fences topped with barbed wire. Dean McKellar's Land Rover and an old truck seemed to be the only vehicles. "Place looks like a goddamn Cracker Barrel."

Hayes found a spot down the road to pull off where they were far enough away not to be seen but could still check on the house with some binoculars.

"You think he's trying to get her to change her mind about what she's seen?"

"Probably."

"You think he was a goddamn secret agent, superspy motherfucker?"

"Back in Nam I came across a few folks in that Phoenix program," Hayes said. "Counterintelligence against the Vietcong by any means necessary. He's way too young, but McKellar got the same air about him. You just know he's an any-means-necessary motherfucker."

Malone folded his arms over his big stomach. "That don't scare me," he said. "What are we waiting on?"

"Make sure we know what we're up against," Hayes said. "I want to make sure when we go in, we know the entire situation."

Malone lowered the binoculars. "Well," he said. "We won't have to worry about McKellar. He's headed back out now."

Hayes took the binoculars from Malone—suddenly struck with the memory of April 1968, watching the Lorraine Motel from the back of Fire Station No. 2. Dr. King dressed in a crisp dark suit, standing over the railing, facing the parking lot. Porter now focused his binoculars and followed the Land Rover as it headed back out the dirt road, kicking up a plume of dust on its way to the highway, where it turned north back the way it came.

"Long drive to stay for a few minutes," Malone said.

"Woman's got to eat."

"Like I said," Malone said. "What are we waiting on?"

They drove through the open gate, dust flying up around Porter's Mercedes, making hell of the detail he'd just gotten. He parked behind the old red truck, a Chevy, and they both got out of the car and headed up the path to the wraparound porch. Porter decided he'd approach the situation same as a wellness call, two ex-cops making an appearance to check on a client. If McKellar or his people wanted to get the local law involved, fine. He just wanted to make sure Addison was safe, and if she was locked up in this place, get her free and get Dean McKellar's ass charged with kidnapping.

He knocked on the door, and after they didn't hear a creature stirring, drifted around to the side of the property. Porter figured maybe the truck was just some old beater that McKellar kept on the land.

From the creaky porch, Hayes got a good view of the open property. There were two other cabins and three small trailers, a decent-size pond with a pier, what looked like a gun range, and a thick batch of pines and cypress trees bordering the land.

"Redneck heaven," Malone said, pointing out a collection of ATVs parked in an open metal garage.

Hayes picked a door lock, deciding just to press on, better to ask for forgiveness instead of permission, and walked inside, calling out for Addison. The lights were off and no one answered, the building open and empty. A big stone fireplace dominated the center of the house, flanked by mounted ducks and animal heads.

They checked out several bedrooms in the big lodge, which weren't fancy, more like bunkhouses with shellacked pine walls and adjoining bathrooms. They met up by the fireplace and the open kitchen, which was the size of a small diner with a long bar to seat at least a dozen or so folks. There was a big-ass Viking range and two oversize stainless-steel sinks with pulldown nozzles. Everything was commercial grade, right down to the steel door of a walk-in freezer where they probably kept the duck, rabbit, hogs, and deer.

They looked at the walk-in and then to each other, both having the same bad thought. The big steel door was padlocked. "Got a crowbar in the trunk," Hayes said, tossing the big man his keys.

Malone returned a minute or so later with the crowbar, pressing it behind the padlock and straining until the screws popped free and the door opened with a hiss. Hayes walked in while Deacon waited by the door and peered inside. Sides of beef, pork, and maybe venison hung up on hooks, covered in plastic sheeting.

"I think I'm gonna be sick," Deacon said.

"You never acted like that until you got off the pork."

"It's unclean, man."

"Where's it say that?"

"What have I been trying to say," Malone said. "The Bible."

"Same thing that says you can't eat any catfish."

"Bottom feeders," he said. "It's all unclean."

"Says who?"

"Says the Lord," Malone said. "Damn, Porter. That's a lot of blood on that floor."

Hayes looked down, barely noticing that he'd stepped into a pool of sticky half-frozen blood, his good Italian boots making tracks across the metal floor.

He walked down the rows of meat, each marked with dates, enough sides of beef to feed an army, until he came up onto something that damn near took his breath way.

"Deacon," he said. "Come on up and see this."

"Nah," he said. "I'm good."

"Deacon," he said. "Goddamn it. Bring the camera."

Porter felt like all the air had left his body, a heavy weight falling onto his shoulders as he saw the legs sticking out below the sheeting. So this is how it all worked. The man had killed Addison and then brought her here to cool out until he could make sense of things. Porter had seen dead bodies before, many more than he ever wanted, but he'd never been okay with it. The same broadside loss and emptiness fell over him as he took out his pocketknife and slashed the plastic in front of the distorted face.

Deacon was back, out of breath, and at his side holding the camera. "Gotdamn, Porter," he said. "That Mrs. McKellar?"

Porter Hayes stepped back and studied the woman's empty face. The eyes half open and mouth wide in horror. Her skin was bluish white, her lips still coated in garish lipstick.

"I saw this woman in the newspaper," Porter Hayes said. "Some kind of actress that made pictures with Elvis."

"What in the fuck is she doing in this man's meat cooler?"

Hayes didn't answer. He just turned away from the dead woman and shook his head. Addison sure was swimming in a river of trouble.

"Like the old song says," Deacon said. "Don't let the devil ride."

31

Tippi

Her mother had always been attracted to rich, dangerous men. Or at least men who pretended to be rich and dangerous. One of Joanna's last boyfriends had been a man named Richie Valentino who liked to hold court at the Sinatra booth at La Dolce Vita on Santa Monica Boulevard. He'd drop little hints that he was connected with a "family" back in New York, always with the shiny suits and cologne. He said he dabbled in trucking and the movie business, but when Tippi would try to pin him down at one of his long dinners (what movies have you actually made?), he'd wave his hand away and her mother would admonish her for asking Mr. Valentino too many questions. He was going to produce her life story for Lifetime. He had a top writer on it and had already talked about casting. But Valentino soon disappeared, leaving her mother with the tab for at least six dinners at La Dolce Vita along with a grimy toothbrush, a half-used bottle of Brut, and four pairs of black silk Jockey shorts. *Ah, Joanna. You never did learn.*

As Tippi sat on a concrete bench in front of the Graceland Welcome Center, her friend Mark looming somewhere nearby in case of trouble, she wanted so much to believe her mother was still alive. Joanna Grayson could talk her way in or out of most anything. They'd gone from absolutely broke to somewhat comfortable in L.A., Joanna trading on her relationships with old movie has-beens to a decent job at an antiques store in West Hollywood, or what Joanna called the edge of Beverly Hills. She and this Peter Collinson were probably planning to run off somewhere,

Peter being the new bit of danger and excitement, and soon she'd get a cryptic postcard from Martinique or Cancun mentioning a specific hotel or bar to find her. After all, it had happened twice before.

But now Tippi had to look out for Tippi—Joanna would most certainly understand—and if she could trade this latest cargo container full of priceless junk for enough cash to get the hell out of Memphis, all the better. She glanced back over her shoulder to see Mark sorting through a CD bin in one of the souvenir shops, his greasy black hair glistening in the fluorescent light.

The allotted meeting time came and went, Tippi figuring on giving up the whole thing, when a striking older man with a prominent nose and closely cropped hair turned the corner between the shops and Elvis's airplanes. He wore a dark, slim-fitting suit with a silk pocket handkerchief and elegant cuff links. He cut through the crowd of elderly people in sweatshirts and Crocs like a knife, glancing about until he locked eyes with Tippi and offered a confident smile. He was very handsome in an aggressively European way.

"Even without the red scarf, I would've known you."

"How's that?" Tippi asked.

"You have the most beautiful voice," he said. "And the most beautiful face."

"That's nice."

He introduced himself as *Monsieur Gaultier* and then lifted her hand to kiss it.

"No need for all that," she said, snatching her hand away. "And don't think about any funny business. You're being watched."

"Oh?" Gaultier smiled and took a seat beside her. He smiled as if he owned everything around him, precise with all his little movements and not-so-subtle flirting.

"Why would you ever get involved with Peter Collinson?"

"Oh, no," she said. "Not me. I thought he was a short little twit. Like I said on the phone, he and my mother. She thought he hung the moon."

"Collinson is not a good man."

Tippi knew her mother had gotten herself into some real trouble this time. If she'd wanted to flee Memphis with Collinson, Joanna would've at least warned Tippi. Instead, she had gone out with a kiss on the cheek as Tippi lay on the couch watching *American Idol* and told her she'd be back by midnight.

"Can you tell me what this is all about?"

"I thought you would know," Gaultier said. "Of course, you must know what it is that we are bargaining for?"

"I know it's worth a lot of money."

"No doubt."

"And it is very old," she said. "Old and rare. And for the right price, I can lead you right to it, Monsieur Gaultier. Now let's cut the bullshit and talk cold, hard cash."

The man smiled and placed a hand on her thigh. What bothered her most was that the gesture didn't offend her in the least. There was something almost comforting about it, like he would be the one who would solve all her problems and fetch her mother back right away.

"Do you know where he is?"

"Collinson?" Gaultier said. "I assume he is at home with his family and his dog. Waiting for the right moment to collect this prize."

Tippi took in a deep breath, watching the passenger vans line up along the welcome center, the Elvis faithful walking along the red carpet fiddling with headphones. "He can't collect what he can't find," she said. "Only my mother knew, and she wouldn't tell him unless she'd been paid."

"And the last time you saw her was with him."

Tippi nodded.

Gaultier took in a deep breath, removed his hand from her thigh, and crossed his arms over his chest. He turned to her and nodded. "I'm sorry," he said. "As I said, if she didn't tell Peter what he wanted to know, she is most surely dead."

Tippi already knew. She'd known since Joanna hadn't come home that night. But to hear the man say it struck her with a rotten, cold feeling. She looked at the goose bumps raised on her arm before turning back to see if she could spot Mark. "What you're looking for is locked up with customs," she said. "You'll need me for the manifest. Without the manifest, you are stuck in Shit City, monsieur."

"Shit City?"

"I guess this all depends on what this old crap is worth to you," she said. "Peter Collinson is absolutely useless."

Gaultier reached out to straighten the shirt cuffs peeking from his suit. She stared at his white cuff links shaped like skulls, and he shrugged. "A gift from my father. It's a rather fascinating story . . ."

"I don't have long," she said. "How much?"

"When I was very young, I used to watch a lot of American television shows," he said. "There was this one we called *Faisons Un Marché.* 'Let Us Make a Deal.' You know this one? You are offering me a prize that is in the box without telling me what I may find."

"It was valuable enough that Collinson killed two people."

"Perhaps more," Gaultier said. "I know of at least three in Paris."

Gaultier shrugged and crossed his legs, looking across the street at the Graceland mansion perched on the hill.

"Is that your friend?" Gaultier said, pointing to Mark, who was talking to one of the security guards.

"Why do you say that?"

"Because he won't stop staring at us."

"Am I really beautiful?"

"You are, my dear," he said. "You remind me of a young Jane Birkin."

"Oh?"

"She and Serge Gainsbourg were like gods in France. Do you know 'Je T'aime Moi Non Plus.' You know. 'I Love You. Me Neither.' It is a very practical song. Birkin breathing so incredibly sexy. It is nearly orgasmic. Gainsbourg is like Elvis to us."

"I don't give a shit about Elvis," she said. "Or goddamn Gainsbourg."

"No?"

"I only care about you giving me a goddamn price," she said.

Gaultier let out a long breath and rubbed the cleft of his chin. He nodded and then turned back to her. "I will need to discuss this with my people."

"There are more of you?"

"There is an awful man who insisted I come to Memphis to straighten out a very messy situation," he said. "All the way from Dubai. Which I didn't really mind. I don't really care for Dubai."

"And does he know what he's in for?"

"All he knows is that Peter Collinson cheated him, and he wants whatever it was that Peter traded for his money." Gaultier looked over at Mark and gave him a friendly wave. Mark looked away, running a hand over his pompadour, and turned his back. His jean jacket was airbrushed with a scene from the '68 Comeback Special. "This is your boyfriend?"

"Just a friend."

"Have you ever been to Paris?" Gaultier said. "To walk along the Seine at night is absolute magic, my dear. You should be there and not here."

This man had a confidence about him that was far more than arrogance. He smiled at her again, so self-assured, and placed his hand back on her knee.

"That's far enough," Tippi said, removing his hand.

"A woman like you deserves so much more," he said. "I think I have an idea to make sure that you have it all."

"You should know there is another buyer," she said. "Some rich weirdo in Arkansas who would kill his own mother to have this."

"Then why involve me?"

"You said you can get us through customs."

"Ah," he said. "Are you asking for a partnership?"

She looked at Gaultier, a little wind blowing down Elvis Presley Boulevard and ruffling her hair. "I don't know you," she said. "I don't trust you. I want my money up front. If you want me to connect you to this man, that will cost extra."

"Don't worry, darling Tippi," he said. "I will make you a very happy woman."

32

Porter Hayes

Branch and Libby Hassan lived in a two-story yellow brick house in Chickasaw Gardens that had to be worth close to a million bucks if not more. Hayes had parked across the street. It was hard to go unnoticed as a Black man in that neighborhood, but the Mercedes seemed to keep the private security satisfied. The guard truck passed him by twice with only a tip to his ball cap as Hayes read the sports section of the *CA*. He'd been sitting there a little more than an hour when a black G-Wagen pulled into the driveway. Hayes stepped out of his car, stretched, and reached for his leather jacket, sliding it on and approaching Libby Hassan as she passed a few sacks of groceries on to one of two boys.

She hadn't seemed to take any notice until he was about five feet away. "You boys go ahead in," she said. "I'll be right there."

"Mrs. Hassan, I'm—"

"I know who you are," she said. "And my lawyer told me not to speak to you."

"Your lawyer or your husband?"

"Both." Libby lifted two more full paper sacks in one of her arms, reaching for the hatch. Hayes stepped up and closed it for her. "What does it matter?"

"Might matter a lot to Addison," he said. "She's been missing for several days now."

"Addison isn't missing."

"You want to bet her life on that?"

"She's been sick," Libby said. "She has the flu. Dean's been helping with the kids. Why are you trying to make trouble for them? Weren't you already paid?"

Hayes nodded, reached into his coat for his Winstons, and fumbled around in his trouser pockets for his Zippo.

"I really wish you wouldn't."

Hayes placed the Zippo back in his pants but let the Winston hang loose from the corner of his mouth. The little white security truck showed up again and the guard let down the window, staring out at them. "Everything okay, Mrs. Hassan?"

She looked at Porter for a long moment and said, "It's fine," she said. After the truck rolled on past, Libby turned back. "Dean told me that you've been trying to extort money from him."

"Not true."

"He said you made up a bunch of stuff," she said. "Maybe to black-mail the family."

"Also not true. Your friend Addison knew it wasn't made-up."

"He said you were deceitful, money-hungry downtown riffraff."

"Riffraff?" Hayes said. "Damn. Hadn't heard that word in a while. But yeah. That part may be true. I am indeed some downtown riffraff."

She set the grocery bags on the hood. Everything about the house and the lawn symmetrical and perfect. The hedges and bushes looked to have been cut by a barber's steady hands, the lawn starting to brown but without a weed.

"Where is Addison, Mrs. Hassan?"

Libby was a small woman with fine features and shoulder-length bleached hair. She had the gaunt look that middle-aged women get when they exercise too much and barely eat anything. Her clothes looked like they'd been bought at the same place Addison shopped. Black cashmere hoodie and tight leggings. Running shoes and a black ball cap.

"She trusted you."

Hayes nodded.

"She said you'd found out that Dean wasn't Dean," she said. "That he owned some kind of mercenary firm and had been selling soldiers and guns overseas."

"Yes, ma'am."

Libby placed her hands in her pockets and turned back to the house's window. One of her twin boys peeked out from a curtain and then quickly disappeared. "Dean put her in rehab," she said. "My husband helped and supported him. Something happened at this party and Addison got wasted."

"Dean drugged her."

"Why?"

"To make her look bad in front of y'all's rich-ass friends," he said. "I'd just passed along a file that told her a hell of a lot of nasty truths about the man she'd married. Oh, and I'm pretty damn sure besides shooting a man in his living room, he killed a woman named Joanna Grayson. I found her body earlier today at Dean's farm down in the Delta. Let's cut to it, Mrs. Hassan. I'm worried as hell about Addison."

Libby's face softened and she looked down at the ground as if embarrassed to keep eye contact with Porter. "I am, too."

"Then how about you help me?"

"I really fucked this up," she said. "Addison won't ever forgive me."

"Where is she, Libby?"

"I don't know," she said. "Branch won't tell me anything."

"Would Branch tell his father?"

"Maybe," she said. "I don't know."

Hayes reached into his jacket and handed her his business card. She took it and quickly placed it into the pouch of her hoodie. "Call me if you learn anything that might help Addison."

"Mr. Hayes?" she said. "Addison's father isn't at home. He's at Saint Francis. They're about to release him into hospice."

"Hospice," he said, shaking his head. "Damn. Didn't know it had gotten that bad."

"Four-oh-eight in a private room," she said. "God. I feel like I might puke. Branch has made me feel so guilty and stupid whenever I take up for Addy. I guess he's a real son of a bitch, too."

Hayes nodded. "Yes, ma'am," he said. "Lots of that going around."

"How you doing, Sam?"

"I wake up coughing and go to bed coughing," he said. "I got a tube jacked up my pecker and it takes a dozen horse pills every few hours to keep me hanging on. But you know. I can't complain."

Hayes pulled up a sturdy wooden chair to Sam's hospital bed. He'd found Sami Hassan asleep and sat in a nearby couch until a nurse came in to check his vitals and offered him a paper cup of pills. When Sam turned to look out the window, he'd spotted Porter and smiled. "Well, I'll be a son of a bitch. Porter Hayes."

Hayes made a gun with his thumb and forefinger and pointed at his old friend.

"Is Addy with you?" Sam asked, lips dry and cracked.

Hayes shook his head, sad to see all the tubes plugging into Sam's arms and up his damn nose. "Hoping you could help me find her."

"Find her?" he said. "I thought you were looking for her worthless husband."

"Well," Hayes said. "You know, I did find his ass."

"I knew you would," Sam said. "Hey. Why don't you ever stop by the restaurant? I'll serve you up a mess of pork that would make you slap your momma."

"I'd never slap my momma."

"I remember her," he said. "Momma Hayes was a pistol. When did she pass?"

"June," Hayes said. "Nineteen seventy-nine."

"What year is it now?" Sam said. His eyes were glassy and unfocused. But he knew Porter and knew that he'd been working with Addison. That was something.

"Two thousand ten."

"Shit," Hassan said. "Ain't time a motherfucker?"

"You know it," Hayes said. "It's like the record's just about over and you and me are just spinning on those last empty grooves. Listen, Sam. I need to talk to you about Addison."

"I'm glad you found her husband," he said. "And nailed his ass. I told her you were the best. Nobody better in Memphis than Porter Hayes."

"Did you know Dean put her in rehab?"

"Rehab?" he said. "For what? Drinking too much white wine with those rich ladies at the Club? Come on."

"Remember Dago?"

"'Course I remember Dago," he said. "We got his ass sent straight to Brushy Mountain."

"Your son-in-law makes Dago Tiller seem like Chatty Cathy, man," he said. "Killing folks ain't just an aside, it's his main business. He hires thugs and guns for hire all over the globe. He's not who he says he is. The real Dean McKellar died nearly twenty years back. I don't even know if his marriage to Addison is legal."

Sam the Sham tried to sit up, not realizing where he was or that he'd been filled with so many tubes. Porter caught him and eased him back down to the pillow. "Easy, friend."

"Not married?"

"He's a bad dude," Hayes said. "I gave Addison a full report and she went missing a short time later. When I went searching for her, I found a woman named Joanna Grayson dead at Dean's place down in the Delta. Do you know why he'd be hooked up with her?"

"Never heard of her."

"She was an actress," Hayes said. "Made a movie with Elvis back in the day."

"He killed this woman?" Sam reached out a giant hand and grabbed Hayes, but there was no iron left in his grip. "What did this cocksucker do to my daughter, Porter?"

"I figured when Addison called Dean on his bullshit, he went to making her look to be unfit," Hayes said. "He and your son got her put into a rehab center."

"Where?"

"That's what I hope you'd help me with."

"Son of a bitch," Sam said. His voice so drawn and tired. He was white-whiskered with bloodshot eyes. "Get me my pants. Come on. I'll go with you. I'll kill the bastard."

"Sam," Hayes said, resting his hand on Sam's big forearm. "Settle down. I got this. You rest."

"He was just here," Sam said. "With my grandkids. He said Addison had the flu."

"He lied," Porter said. "He drugged her to make her look bad in public. If you can find out where she is, I promise I'll get her out."

Sam started to speak but then launched into a bad coughing fit. It was so awful that a nurse ran in from the hall and raised his bed up a foot higher. She gave him a glass of water and helped him calm down before leaving the room.

Hayes hated like hell to see Sam in that condition. He'd always been larger than life, holding that old Louisville Slugger behind his old bar—the Domino Club on Madison—like Babe Ruth, no one crossing him without the retribution he deserved. Now he couldn't walk to the bathroom without help and was soon headed down that last road in hospice. No food. No medicine. They just let you lie back and die.

"They're sending me home."

"I heard."

"It's a hospice-type deal."

"Yeah," Hayes said. "I got some experience with hospice."

"I know you do," Sam said. "Genevieve was a lovely person. How long's she been gone?"

"Long time, Sam."

"Time doesn't make a lot of sense to me right now," he said. "Clocks might as well be broken and upside down. Everything seems the same. Addison was twelve years old yesterday on her little pink bike with a banana seat and now this. How the fuck does that happen?"

There was a knock on the door and a middle-aged man with Sam's face but not his stature walked into the room. He grinned as he held two Styrofoam cups in his hands. When he saw Porter, the grin dropped.

"Branch," Sam said. "My son."

Porter stood up and Branch set down the coffees on a hospital tray. He was dressed like most white men in East Memphis, pressed checkered shirt and khakis with a fuzzy fleece vest. He had dark hair neatly barbered and combed to the side like a teenager from the sixties.

"Where's Addy, Branch?" Sam asked.

"At home," he said, trying to regain that smug grin. "I told you already that she has a flu."

"Mr. Hayes here said you and Dean put her in rehab."

Branch Hassan took a wide stance, put one hand in his pocket, and looked to his father and then over to Porter Hayes. "I don't see how that's any of his business," he said. "We didn't want to worry you, Dad."

"Consider me worried."

"She made a real scene at the zoo last week," Branch said. "She nearly fell into the lion's cage on the way out. Dean had to carry her out while everyone was watching."

"He drugged her, son," Porter Hayes said.

"Oh, come on," Branch said. From a distance, Branch Hassan would look just like a teenager except for the wrinkles and dark five o'clock shadow. The man hadn't inherited any of his father's physicality, at just under five foot eight, and probably didn't weigh much over a hundred pounds.

Sam lifted up his right hand and ushered Branch to his bedside. He looked to Porter and Porter nodded in Sam's direction. Branch walked slowly to the hospital bed and then leaned down toward his father's face. His dad took a breath, oxygen going up into his nose, and then motioned for him to come in closer.

Branch came closer.

Sam whispered something in his ear. Porter's hearing wasn't what it used to be, but he could make out something about money, the barbecue restaurant, and changing his will. Branch Hassan's face went completely bloodless, white as a goddamn sheet, as he straightened himself back up.

"How about you and me step out for some fresh air, son?" Hayes said. "It's time for you to get on the right side of things."

"You want me to side with this guy over my own brother-in-law?" Branch asked Sam.

"It's not just about Addison," Hayes said. "I understand your niece and nephew are still with Dean."

"Why wouldn't they be with their father?"

"Because he's a stone-cold killer," Hayes said. "You need to get with the goddamn program, Branch. Your whole family is in some serious shit."

33

Gaultier

t had been a week of boredom and so much idiocy, being stuck inside the Sam's Town casino hotel at Tunica with Anatoliy Zub and his barbarians. All they did was watch television (country music videos and pornography), graze at the endless buffet, and gamble. Poker, blackjack, roulette. One day they forced Gaultier to drive out into a cotton field to watch them shoot AR15s into a rusting pickup truck. There were drugs and whores brought down from Memphis— of course there were, after all it was Anatoliy Zub—and late-night games of Texas Hold 'Em with Zub wearing sunglasses and his ten-gallon hat, a prostitute perched in his lap. *Ivan the Terrible Comes to Dodge City.* Gaultier was given an unlimited expense account at the hotel and frequently asked to join in Zub's little American vacation. *Hamburgers, hand jobs, and champagne in the jacuzzi.* Finally, now they were on the move and on their way for what they'd flown thousands of miles to recover. Gaultier had spoken to Tippi and Tippi had supplied a routing number for a bank in the Bahamas. Funds were transferred and a manifest with shipping container numbers faxed to Sam's Town. Gaultier had arranged every single step.

Now it was past midnight, a caravan of Anatoliy Zub's SUVs driving north along the Mississippi River past great oil containers and refineries belching fire and dark smoke.

"Peter Collinson," Zub said. "So slick and clever to try and cheat Anatoliy Zub. But you, my friend, helped me to fuck this man in the asshole. His prize will be locked up and back in Murmansk in a week. I will sell these weapons for twice as much as Collinson owed me. Debts will be squared. I might even spare his life."

"You will be disappointed, Anatoliy," he said. "Peter stole your money. But he took a lot more from the Taliban. I think this is something quite old and rare."

"Better than guns?" he said. "Better than missiles?"

"Yes, Anatoliy," Gaultier said, putting a fist to his yawn. So very late. "When they realized they'd been tricked, the Taliban sent three men to kill him in Paris."

"And?"

"Collinson killed them all," he said. "There was a lot of blood and flies in his flat. Such a fine flat, too. On the Haussmann."

"When I was a boy, I had no interest in Paris," Zub said. "I only wanted to come to America. I went to the cinema to watch cowboy movies every week. The faces of John Wayne and Gary Cooper so very big, the size of a Lana truck. John Wayne in the doorway in *The Searchers*. Amazing. Just amazing. But there was one film that meant very much to me. *The Magnificent 7*. Pure poetry, Gaultier."

"I know it."

"Yes, yes," he said. "But do you know it? The code of men. How to live and how to die. How to make your way with a gun. No home. No family."

"No enemies."

"Ha ha," Zub said. "*None alive.* Yes, yes. Robert Vaughn. Napoleon Solo. So I get my gold and go home. You will be compensated, of course. I knew you would help. Apologies for that little trick we pulled in Dubai. You must understand how it was necessary. Like ushering a goat into a cave."

Gaultier wasn't exactly thrilled about being compared to a goat. "And now you will fly me to Paris?"

"Not my plane," Zub said. "I have business elsewhere. But I fly you home. Okay? Business class. Not coach. I would not wish that on even you. Crying babies and fat Americans breaking wind."

"You are a prince, Anatoliy."

"Yes," Zub said, tilting the brim of his cowboy hat as they drove through a never-ending labyrinth of warehouses and shipping containers. "I am."

The driver of the SUV slowed at the gate to one such facility and said something to Zub in Russian. Zub admonished him and pointed to the gate. Zub punched up a number on his phone and the gates rolled back. Soon their SUV was deep inside the big maze of shipping containers, walls of red, blue, and green, battered and rusted from months at sea.

"This is it," Zub said. "Christmas morning as a boy. Wooden toys and *Krasnaya Shapochka* candy in my stocking. Maybe a knife from my father. He liked to present me and my brother with many knives. Did you know I killed my first man when I was eight? What a delight. A delight, I tell you. He'd come to rob my family while my father was away. Steal our television. I stuck the knife deep into his right eye and twisted it like a clockmaker."

Zub's SUVs lined up together, lighting the side of a battered yellow Conex.

Zub opened his door and walked out to join his men, who were smoking cigarettes around the back of the container. A nervous-looking American in dirty coveralls waited alongside with a bolt cutter. One of Zub's men stepped forward and handed the man an envelope that was surely stuffed with cash. The man peeked inside the envelope, licked his lips, and walked up to the lock. Zub stood back, hands on hips, his men muttering in Russian and blowing smoke up into the wind. Overhead there were big cranes for unloading Mississippi River barges and loading containers onto trucks or onto railcars. They had passed over railroad tracks just before coming into the gates of this place. Gaultier could not see the river but could smell it, metallic and cold.

The man in coveralls cut the lock and swung the doors open, headlights illuminating the empty, open space of the container. Zub walked inside and then began to yell Russian obscenities. Gaultier did not speak Russian, but he knew the words. *Mu'dak. Blin.* And also: fuck, asshole.

"Empty," Zub said. "Is empty."

Zub emerged from the container and threw his black cowboy hat to the ground. He looked at the man holding the bolt cutters and swore more to him in Russian. His face had turned a bright crimson, a slight sheen of sweat across his face and chest. Zub walked up to Gaultier and thumped him on the chest. "What is this?" he said. "You want to fuck me, too? Straight in asshole?"

"Maybe you made a mistake, Anatoliy."

Zub spoke Russian to one of the bears. The man they called Lukyan was just as bald and stubble-faced as the rest. Nearly indistinguishable. He closed one of the large doors and pointed to the numbers and then opened a sheet of paper in his hands. He shrugged and then pointed to the painted numbers, nodding.

Gaultier stepped back. Two of the men walked toward him. Gaultier lifted his hands as one of the bears knocked out his legs with the butt of an AR15. Gaultier tried to get to his feet as the bears kicked him to his back. Zub was over him now with a silver pistol, a very fanciful and vain gun with a pearl handle. He had flashed it to Gaultier many times after buying it from a gun shop in Tunica, saying it was exactly like John Wayne had carried in *True Grit. Fill your hand. You son of a bitch. Ha ha.*

"This," Gaultier said, "is not my fault."

Zub didn't answer. Gaultier believed he heard the slight clicking of the revolver. More Russian obscenities in his ear. The bears stepping back, surely thinking they were about to be sprayed with blood. He heard the crack of Zub's pistol, deafening in Gaultier's ears, his heart pumping fast, waiting for that minute when everything was over and then what? Who knew, but Gaultier tried desperately to recall a prayer from his childhood.

The American with the bolt cutters fell into a heap, blood spreading on the dusty ground. Lukyan walked over to him, kicked at his boots, and nodded to Zub.

Then the little American flopped onto his back, a pistol in hand, and shot Lukyan in the chest. The bear fell like a giant oak.

Every single Russian, including Zub, unloaded their clips into the American. The man's body danced off the asphalt like a marionette.

One of the bears reached under Lukyan's arms and began to drag him toward the river.

"No time," Zub said. "We must leave him. Get in truck."

Zub's English was even worse when he was agitated.

The Russians left Lukyan and the dead American and started the SUVs, circling out of the container facilities. No one spoke for a long time. The driver fiddled with the heater, hot air blowing through the front seats and back to where Gaultier had sweated through his finest shirt. Zub sat behind him, creasing the crown of his dirty black hat.

"I want Collinson's family," Zub said. "I take them. He will have no choice."

"May I speak freely, Anatoliy?"

"What is it?" he said. "What do you want?"

"You don't understand a man like Collinson," he said. "But I do. He obviously knew a lot more than we thought. But to take his family? To kidnap his children? That is very dramatic, but it won't work. A man like Peter Collinson will simply move on, change his name again, and start over. Whatever he has in this city is nothing more than a facade. You would be the star of your own Western movie, just fiddling with empty props."

"Props?"

"His children, his wife," Gaultier said. "They mean nothing to him."

"What do you suggest, Monsieur Gaultier?"

"You must dig his grave," Gaultier said. "And show it to him. Make him understand, like a Western, that this is the end of his line."

"Good," he said. "Yes. Very good. You bring him to us."

"If you want Collinson, I will need five of your best men."

"Why five?"

"Because in Paris," Gaultier said, shrugging, "three were not enough."

Zub placed the cowboy hat on his head, ejected two spent cartridges from his six-shooter, and tossed them from the moving car. "I will come, too," he said. "It will be like showdown."

34

Sara Caroline

The thing about having your mother in rehab was it gave Sara Caroline more freedom than she'd ever had in her life. After her dad had picked up her and Preston from Aunt Libby's and brought them home, she'd barely seen him. She and Preston were living wild and free. The only adult in their life right now was some big dude named Mr. Chad, who'd drive them to school and then back home in his ridiculous black Hummer. *So embarrassing!* Dad called him a work friend, but she noticed that Mr. Chad did a lot more than just driving. He'd stay outside their house most nights, smoking cigarettes and walking around the pool and the fence line. Some other guy, who looked almost exactly like Mr. Chad, muscled and ugly with a bushy beard and hunting clothes, would sometimes replace him. She wasn't sure where her dad went during the day and most of the night, but he left her a credit card. She and Preston ordered takeout like fiends and stayed up late watching R rated movies (all four *Fast & Furious*!) and a few Disney shows to even things out. She may be fourteen but still loved watching *Kim Possible* and the show with the Jonas brothers.

She got out the cereal in the morning and even made pancakes for Preston. She did the dishes, watched TV, and listened to her iPod while snooping around their big, empty house. Since the summer she'd really been into Katy Perry. She loved "Teenage Dream" and "California Gurls" and how Katy Perry seemed to just not give a shit and really loved life. She was completely outrageous with the blue hair and cherry cupcake bra. She was a hell of a lot better than that boring, sad-ass music her parents liked. The Dave Matthews Band? Please.

That afternoon, she was surprised to spot her dad's Land Rover in the line to pick her up at Hutch. He hadn't said a word about Mom since they'd visited her down in Mississippi. She had looked so weak and vulnerable, but Sara Caroline knew that was all part of the process. Her boyfriend Russell's mother had a friend who went to a rehab center in Vail after being addicted to sleeping pills. He said she came back completely clean but now was hooked on cigarettes and black coffee, talking about Jesus all the time.

She opened the rear hatch and tossed in her lacrosse gear and jumped up front in the passenger seat. He had some of his dad music playing loud, one of his favorites. Hootie and the Blowfish, "Hold My Hand." She looked back at the girls waiting in line as he drove off. She hoped like hell none of them had heard that corny-ass song.

"I'm sorry, but some stuff has come up," he said. "You need to tell your friend Russell he can't come over tonight."

"Why?"

She'd been planning a fun Friday night with Russell all week. They were going to watch *Harry Potter and the Half-Blood Prince*. And if her luck held out, she'd send Preston upstairs to bed early and maybe they could make out a little. She'd been so used to having her freedom and running the house that she'd never thought anything would change. Did she want her mom back? Sure she did. But rehab took time. Right?

"Mr. Chad and Mr. Bob will be helping us out tonight," he said.

"Who's Mr. Bob?"

"The man who's been driving you to school all week."

"I thought that was Chad."

"I guess they are very similar," he said, cutting through traffic up to Poplar. A light rain starting to fall.

"I don't like either of them," she said. "They smell like cigarettes and crappy hamburgers."

"Life is hard and unfair, Sara Caroline," he said, eyes fixed on something far ahead. "My father told me that when I was about your age. And you need to know that now."

"Oh, I know."

"Do you?" he said, giving a short little laugh. "You and Preston grew up a lot different from me. You don't have to worry about anything."

"I worry all the time," she said, annoyed her father would say such a thing to her. Like she lived a charmed life or something. Her mother was a drunk and she was practically raising her little brother. "When is Mom coming home?"

"Not for a while," he said. "But I want to keep you both safe. And that may involve us leaving Memphis for a while. Is that okay?"

"Like vacation?"

"Sort of," he said. "There are bad people who'd like to see some harm come to me and my family. But I won't let that happen. That's why Mr. Bob and Mr. Chad have been around. They're the best of the best and have worked with me for a long time."

"Building things?" she asked. "Like, they do your construction projects?"

Her father didn't answer and took a hard turn onto Poplar, turning on his lights and the windshield wipers. His car stereo still going, rolling onto something new from his playlist. "Crash into Me." Such shitty, sad sack music.

"Was it hard?"

"What's that?" he said.

"Growing up."

"Yeah," he said. "I've been on my own since I was Preston's age."

"You never told me that."

"Your mother and I didn't want you to worry," he said. "But your mother has made a real mess of things lately. She's not fit to look after you and that's why it's best to leave for a little while. You've never really traveled abroad. I think it would be good for you to see other countries."

"Like in Europe?"

"Have you ever wanted to see the United Arab Emirates?" he said. "Dubai?"

"Not really."

"It's a very modern city," he said. "They have indoor surf pools and indoor snow skiing. I think you'd have a ball."

"I thought it was just like nightclubs and whores and stuff."

"There is a private school there," he said. "For American children. It's a great opportunity."

Sara Caroline couldn't breathe for a moment. School in Dubai? And leaving her mother in that awful place in Mississippi. She wanted to speak up, say something, but it was like the words wouldn't form in her mouth. She held on to the armrest as her father darted up and around cars faster than she'd ever seen him drive, fucking Dave Matthews Band blaring from the speakers.

"I won't leave Mom."

"You don't have a choice."

"You can't make me."

"Of course I can," he said "I'm your father."

"This is awful," she said. "Mom was right."

Her father quickly pulled off Poplar into a little neighborhood and slammed on the brakes, nearly throwing Sara Caroline into the windshield. But she caught herself against the dash, her pulse racing like a maniac. Her hair scattered across her face and she couldn't breathe for a moment. Just choking sounds in her throat.

"About what?" her father said. "What did Mom tell you?"

"She said you were a liar."

"What else did she say?"

"I don't know," she said. "That's it. You're going to be late to pick up Preston. Quit it. Just stop talking to me."

Her father reached out and grabbed her arm, nearly yanking her from the seat, and looked at her hard. "Don't lie to me."

"You're hurting me."

"What did your mother say about me?"

"Nothing," she said, pulling her arm away and staring straight ahead. She hated her father more at that moment than anything. "But you're being a fucking asshole and I hate your shitty music. Dave Matthews sucks balls."

Her father shook his head and let out a long breath, slamming the SUV back in drive and turning around in someone's driveway. It was a nice little house, one story, with picture windows framed by green shutters and rosebushes out front. It looked like a quiet, simple place to live without so much empty space and big closets and a dirty, dark basement that seemed to go on forever.

Her father turned onto Poplar and turned up the music. Dave Matthews wailed on.

Sara Caroline told Russell that tonight wasn't going to happen. Russell acted all gloomy and ridiculous about it, making it seem like it had something to do with that one time he tried to go up her shirt. He'd attempted to unlatch her bra and she'd slapped his face.

"Russell," she said. "Shut up and listen to me. My dad is going to make us leave Memphis . . ."

There was a knock on the door and her dad peered inside. "Dinner."

That was all he said. No apologies. Just "dinner." Like she was some kind of dog, and he was rattling the bowl down in the kitchen. *Whatever.* She pulled on a hoodie, tucked her head inside, and trudged down the great, dramatic staircase to their brand-new and finally finished kitchen—although in all honesty it looked the same as the old one—where she saw Chad and Bob sitting on opposite sides of the family table helping themselves to giant cartons of coleslaw and beans and an aluminum tray stacked with ribs. From the nearby sacks, she could see they'd stopped off at Granddad's Bluff City Barbecue for a free meal. Sara Caroline thought the gesture was gross and tacky considering Granddad's current condition.

"I'm not hungry."

"Sit down," her father said. "We eat as a family."

"A family?" she said, watching as Preston snatched a rib off the pile along with a mountain of white bread. "Whose family?"

"I already talked to Preston," he said. "I want both of you to pack tonight. We leave first thing in the morning. Don't bring anything along that you can live without. Okay? Two pieces of luggage. No more."

Preston beamed. "We're going on a trip, S.C.!"

"No shit," she said. "To the fucking desert."

The sound of Chad and Bob eating the ribs made her sick to her stomach, so much sucking, slurping, and smacking. One of the men—Chadbob—wiped his greasy beard on his forearm tattooed with *We the People* in cursive. Set alongside his chair was a very big, black gun.

The man followed her eyes and then continued to slurp the meat off the bone, taking a second to wink at Sara Caroline.

She cried herself to sleep and awoke to the sound of men yelling and glass breaking. Her dad was downstairs somewhere barking orders. She heard gunshots—a long, loud stream of shots—coming from outside. Like in her backyard. She jumped to her bare feet and ran into Preston's room. Her brother shivered on the floor with his hands over his ears. She grabbed him by his pajama top and pulled him into the closet. He whispered: "Dad says they've come for us."

"Who?"

"I don't know," he said. "He said for me to stay in my room."

"JesusfuckingChrist."

ChaCha ran in and began to lick Sara Caroline's face. She smoothed down his curly hair and hugged the dog close. "We have to go," Preston said.

"Go where?" she said. "You just said we have to stay."

"Did Dad tell you about the safe room?"

"What the hell are you talking about, Preston? People are shooting at our house."

"Come on," he said. "Don't panic."

"I'm not panicking," she said. "How can I panic when I already peed my pants?"

Sara Caroline and Preston, ChaCha hot on their heels, ran down the hall and the great staircase into the entryway, her father and Bob and Chad yelling about securing the house, locking down the perimeter. It all sounded like something from one of Granddad's old Westerns, saving the house from a tribe of wild Apache. None of it seemed real until there was more shooting and the windows cracked apart in the living room. ChaCha barked like crazy as her father screamed at her and Preston, telling them to go back upstairs and then Preston said something about the safe room. Her father said "go" and they ran to the cellar door and pulled it open to head down into the darkness. Just then Bob—or was it Chad?—made a giant *oof*ing sound and pirouetted from behind the kitchen island, landing flat on his back, blood coming from his mouth.

She tackled her brother to the ground, lying flat across his back like she did when he misbehaved and she threatened to lick his cheek. Her heart was racing, and her ears felt like they were filled with cotton as the back of the kitchen—all that detail trim work and paint that her mom had gone on and on about—just shattered into a million pieces. Her father fell down beside her and reloaded a handgun. For a few seconds, she could hear absolutely nothing. That's when she noticed her feet were bleeding and smearing blood all over the newly sealed floors.

"It's the fucking Russians," her dad said.

Russians? What fucking Russians? she wanted to ask. But there wasn't time. They hurriedly stood up and Sara Caroline followed Preston and ChaCha down the creaky old steps and past the laundry room and into the doorway that separated the new from the creepy old space that smelled like decaying bricks and earth and where all great toys went to die. "What are you doing?" she said. "We need to help Dad."

"Come on," he said. "I'll show you."

And then he did, running past a cluttered stack of Barbie Dreamhouses and Thomas train tables, toward a far wall where a heavy metal shelf had been pulled out, revealing a half-open door, bright white light spilling from behind it. She was out of breath, wincing at the sharp pain of glass in her feet. More gunshots and heavy steps came from above. Inside, a row of monitors lined the wall. Open folders and stacks of different-colored money lay on top of a computer desk. "What in the hell is this?"

"Dad is a hero," Preston said.

"Dad is a liar."

"No, he's not," Preston said. "He's saving us."

She grabbed Preston by the shoulders and then pressed her hands against his red cheeks, sandwiching his sweaty little face. "No. You saved us, Preston," she said. "Dad nearly got us killed. Mom was right. Mom knew everything. Everything she said about him was true."

Preston walked back to the steel door, pulled the tool rack back in front of the doorway, and then shut the secured door behind them. She heard the hiss of a lock and the lights went dim for a moment. ChaCha made it his duty to sniff around all four corners of the safe room. "What did Mom say about him?"

"What is this place?"

"Dad calls it the safe room," he said. "But Mom said it's a fucking arsenal."

"Maybe it's both."

"I'm sorry I cussed," he said.

There was an odd quiet for a few moments and then more footsteps above them, sounding like an entire football team tramping on the floor above in game cleats. They heard one muffled shot—both of them clutching each other and recoiling with the sound. And then another. The men upstairs yelling, but not in English.

Preston started to cry. She hugged him tighter. ChaCha pushed his wet nose between them.

They stayed down there for what felt like forever until the footsteps and the heavy guttural talk stopped. The house had been fully silent for a good twenty minutes when she asked Preston to open the door.

"What if they're still here?"

"I want to check on Dad."

"He's dead, S.C.," he said. "You know he's dead."

"Stay here," she said. "Don't open the door for anyone else but me."

Sara Caroline walked back out into the cellar and then to the laundry room, listening for the smallest creak in the ceiling above her.

She silently moved up the steps and into the kitchen to find a complete mess. Mom's so-called dream kitchen full of holes, cabinets hanging loose by one hinge, and her beloved subway tile shattered behind the new stove. The man Bob or Chad—Sara Caroline didn't feel bad that she hadn't cared enough to learn his name—lay face down by the oven. A sign by the door read "God Bless This Family."

This was seriously fucked-up. *What else could you say?* Damn, her feet were really bleeding. Mom was going to be pissed.

"Dad?" Sara Caroline said, calling out. "Dad."

She found another body in the living room, half-hidden under their enormous flat-screen TV. Same military-style pants and same laced boots as her dad. She clutched her hand over her mouth and stooped down to pull the TV off him. A huge sigh escaped her when she saw it was the other one. *Bob. Yes, it was Bob.* Bob had the scar on his cheek. Or maybe they both had scars? Either way, it wasn't her father.

She had moved on to the library and the entry hall when she heard the sirens. From the open front door she saw the flashing blue lights of police cars lined up along sleepy Belvedere Avenue. Cops crouched behind the hoods, aiming guns up the hill to the McKellar house.

She took a hard swallow. *Holy shit. Holy shit. Holy shit.* Her fucking house was destroyed and now the cops were coming to get her.

"S.C.," Preston said, yelling from the stairwell. "Can I come out now?"

"Hold on," she said. "Everything is fine. Just close your eyes and trust me."

35

Addison

This time last year, Dean had flown the whole family to Mustique to celebrate her thirty-ninth birthday. He'd rented a private plane and a private villa built on the ruins of an old fortress overlooking the Caribbean. The villa came with 24/7 staff and two golf carts to run down to the beach for snorkeling or scuba or over to the Cotton House for one of their amazing dinners. The decision to make each day was to either get a massage at the spa or head to their own private lagoon. *Sea turtles. Galloping horses along the beach.* One night at the island's artfully shabby bar, Dean had arrived in all his silly-ass white linen glory, complete with huarache sandals and a new straw hat, wanting her to meet their new neighbors.

She recalled the man being French, Dean calling him just Gaultier, no idea if that was a first or last name. She'd tried to shake hands, but the man brought her hand up to his lips as Dean asked if she might show Monsieur Gaultier's beautiful female friend their villa. The men had some kind of business to discuss. The woman had shrugged, seemingly used to it, and rode along in the golf cart into the hills.

She'd thought, that was Dean. Always working. But now, lying on her single bed and staring up at the ceiling in rehab, she knew the whole fucking thing was odd. The family vacation had been an afterthought to his own goddamn business.

She'd been pretty drunk that night at Mustique, Dean not finding any problems with her drinking back then, as she wound the narrow little roads in her golf cart, headlights scattering over the palms and large boulders. The woman—so pretty and so quiet—rode beside Addison. The only thing Addison could think to ask was "Are you two married?"

The question brought a smile to the woman's face. She was small boned, with delicate features and the most beautiful brown curly hair. Short and stylish. Addison told her it was so lovely and that she herself could never pull it off. The woman turned to her and said: *But it is perhaps your husband's gaze that you worry about?*

Back at the villa, Addison opened up a new bottle of wine from a whole cellar of the stuff, and they sat out on the wide stone deck overlooking the water. She couldn't remember the woman's name or where she was from, only that the woman seemed annoyed that she'd been left with some stupid American.

"Matt Damon was at the bar tonight," Addison said. "He's super short."

"In this place, you learn not to care," she said. "Prince William arrived a few months ago. So much security and the roads being closed. I saw him later at the Cotton House. It looks as if his royal hair has started to thin."

"Would you like more wine?"

The woman had smiled. "It is with wine that our lives become slightly more tolerable."

The woman stared out at the water and Addison had gone inside the villa to check on Preston and Sara Caroline, both of them acting exactly the same as they would back in Memphis. Never mind the gorgeous private island with the stars and the moon and the fucking lovely beach. Sara Caroline was on her bed texting and Preston was watching a car chase on a giant television.

She walked back out to the patio and found the young Frenchwoman still staring out at the endless black Caribbean. She was crying.

"Are you okay?"

"It's just so endless," she said. "This life. This money is like chains."

Addison knew she was drunk or high. So incredibly dramatic. She had been about to ask what she meant when Dean had showed back up with Gaultier. When Addison asked them to please stay, the man had shook his head and smiled. "We are already quite late for dinner. I think it is the lobster tonight. No?"

After they disappeared, Addison had asked, "And what exactly does he do?"

"Like most people here," he said. "Spends money as fast as he earns it."

"And you just met him today?"

"Never saw him before in my life."

Addison heard her doorknob rattle and tossed a beaten paperback onto the floor. She knew it was night but had absolutely no idea of the time. They'd already brought in her grilled chicken, French green beans, and two soft white rolls and had even come back for the tray. Maybe it was Dr. Bledsoe making the late rounds, wanting to know why—*yet again*—Addison didn't want to participate with her group. *Being open and honest is your path to sobriety.* Addison looked down at herself, dressed for bed in a flowery hospital gown that tied twice at the back. After her escape, they hadn't even offered her any flip-flops.

The door opened and some huge Black guy burst into the room. He had on navy coveralls and carried a big spray canister like she used on her rosebushes back home.

"You better do a good job," she said. "This place is crawling with roaches."

The big man set down the canister and walked toward her. He looked to be only a little younger than her dad, with graying hair and a broad grin. "My name is Deacon Malone," he said, trying to catch his breath. "I've come to get you the hell out of here."

Addison propped herself up on the bed and stared at him, running the words back in her mind. He tossed a duffel bag down at her feet and nodded toward it.

"Who are you?"

"Deacon Malone," he said.

"Okay?"

"Porter Hayes sent me."

"Porter Hayes," she said. "Jesus Christ. Why didn't you just say so?"

Porter Hayes, Obi Wan. Deacon Malone, Luke Skywalker. It was all fine by her and she stood up and unzipped the bag. "Porter packed a few things for you to change into. Can't be walking the halls like that."

"And how the hell did you get in?"

"Strolled in with some tools and roach spray," he said. "Nobody paid me any mind."

"Fair enough."

"Come on," he said. "We don't have much time. These folks changing shifts now."

They slipped out of the cabin with no problem. Pepper and Salt, as Addison had named the big Black woman and her skinny country cousin who kept her locked up, were nowhere to be seen. As she followed Malone outside and down the pebbled paths, she saw the big Cracker Barrel lodge completely lit up by some kind of event going on in the main room.

Hayes had packed her some old gray sweatpants and a Grizzlies sweatshirt along with a pair of Chuck Taylors that were two sizes too big. But she wasn't complaining as she flopped down the path feeling like Ronald Fucking McDonald. She was getting out of this place and back home to confront Dean's sorry ass and save her children from that psycho. She wasn't fucking around anymore. She was going straight to the Memphis police or the feds. She was going to get a mean-ass attorney. She was going to quadruple Porter Hayes's daily rate and they were going to find out exactly who this son of a bitch really was . . . *the real Dean McKellar was a dead man. She was married to a dead man.*

She felt as if she was almost home when she saw Dr. Bledsoe step into the lighted path. The wind whipped the white coat around her as two men in matching black polo shirts joined the doctor to block their way. One of the men had his hand on a gun.

"Oh, Addison," Dr. Bledsoe said, shaking her head. "Who is this man? I thought we'd come to such a wonderful understanding today."

"I have no idea," she said. "I just gave him a hand job so he'd give me a pint of vodka in his car."

That really threw Bledsoe, and she looked to one of the guards. The man reached for his gun and Deacon Malone—*what a name!*—held up his hands. Addison could hear the cold, brisk wind high up in the pines and then the hard snick of what sounded like a shotgun.

"On your knees, Doc," someone in the dark said. "Or you gonna be pickin' buckshot out your asshole."

Dr. Bledsoe froze. She looked to the guards and nodded. The guards turned and came toward Addison before someone came out of the dark and knocked one of them to the ground. The other man looked over at Bledsoe, licked his lips, and then carefully got down on his knees and laced his hands behind his head. "Y'all don't pay me enough to get my head blowed off."

"And you, too, lady."

The voice became a man and the man stepped from the shadows. It was Porter Hayes, dressed in his brown leather trench coat and carrying a shotgun, long cigarette bobbing from his lips. "What the damn hell?" he said. "Are we going to have a failure to communicate, Doctor? Get on your goddamn knees."

Dr. Bledsoe, pasty-faced with her dyed red hair and white coat, slowly dropped to one knee and then two. She winced with pain as Deacon Malone took handguns off the two guards. Hayes glanced up at Addison and motioned with his head back behind him.

Addison didn't hesitate and ran flat out to the parking area, where they found Porter's old black Mercedes with the lights on and engine running. Addison scooted in back and Malone hopped behind the wheel and made a big sweeping U-turn, kicking up gravel and dirt. They skidded to a stop near where Hayes held the doctor and the guards at the end of his shotgun. Malone leaned over the console and opened the passenger door. Hayes jumped inside and Malone floored the accelerator.

"You okay?" Hayes asked.

"What day is it?"

Hayes told her.

"Oh god," she said. "Oh god. Where are my kids?"

"Everything is fine," he said. "Everything is fine. There was some trouble back in Memphis. But your children are doing real good."

"What kind of trouble?"

"Well," Hayes said, lowering the window to blow out some smoke, "y'all might want to check into a hotel. Apparently, your house has got a few holes in it."

36

Porter Hayes

The McKellar house was pretty fucked-up. Everything looked fine from the street but once you headed inside to the living room and kitchen, the place was shot to shit. Broken glass, old books turned to confetti, all that new kitchen cabinetry looking like Swiss cheese. Addison hadn't seemed to care one damn bit, impatient to get to her kids. Hayes stood in the shot-up kitchen with Sergeant Lantana Jones, who was doing her best to get a statement. But Addison kept repeating over and over: "I have no fucking idea who did this. I don't even know my husband's real name. Okay? Can I go now?"

"But you just spoke with him?" Jones asked.

"He called Mr. Hayes on our way back to Memphis," Addison said. "Looking for me."

"Where had you been, ma'am?" Sergeant Jones asked.

"That's a long story."

"I got a long time," Jones said. "Folks in Central Gardens aren't going to be happy about a fine old historic home like this turning into the damn OK Corral. Do you see that blood on the floor? That belonged to the two dead men we just hauled out of here."

"Who were they?" she said.

"Your daughter says they worked for your husband," Jones said. "Some kind of private security."

"Please don't call him my husband," Addison said. "I don't know who that man is."

Addison looked to Porter and Porter nodded. He had told her to play it straight with cops, no reason to hold anything back about the man she'd known as Dean McKellar. They'd need the police reports and records of the danger he'd put her in before she headed on into court.

"This sounds crazy," Addison said. "But everyone thinks I'm crazy anyway. Before Dean hung up, he told me he'd been kidnapped by some Russians. He said they were going to torture and kill him unless I could help him."

"Help him do what?"

"I don't know," Addison said. "He was screaming and yelling before we got disconnected. I have to be honest. He didn't make much sense and I kind of quit listening."

"Russians?" Jones said. "In Memphis?"

"I know," Addison said. "That's all he said and then the phone went dead as I was trying to find out what happened to Preston and Sara Caroline."

"The kids are with your sister-in-law," Jones said. "Just released them about thirty minutes ago. They're smart children, Mrs. McKellar. You got to be proud. When the shooting went down, they headed straight into that old basement and hid. They were scared but unharmed. You okay?"

Addison nodded and wiped her face with the sleeve of her sweat-shirt. The clothes had been some of Nina's old stuff she'd left at Porter's house.

"One more thing," Jones said. "What's your husband have to do with Russians?"

"I don't know."

"Why would someone want to kill him?"

Addison smiled. "I don't know," she said. "But I definitely understand."

"Russians," Porter Hayes said.

"In Memphis," Jones said, raising her eyebrows. "Ain't that some shit?"

Jones assigned two uniform cops to run Addison over to her brother's house in Chickasaw Gardens before Hayes and Jones walked outside the big front door. It was busted wide open, letting in all that cold air as they stooped under the yellow crime scene tape. He spotted that little fed, Duane Bickett, with two of his boys around the side of the house. They were all wearing those dumbass FBI windbreakers they loved so much. Bickett stared in Hayes's direction, and Hayes turned his back to him. "Come on," Hayes said to Lantana Jones. "I ain't got the time."

"They rolled up right before you."

"How about we roll on?" Hayes said.

"Fine by me," she said. "Me and you need to talk private anyway."

They were in Jones's unmarked unit and headed back downtown toward 201 and Hayes's office. He rode shotgun as Lantana raced along Union past the UT medical center and the old Scottish Rite Temple. "What if I told you this was the second time I heard about Russians this week?" she asked.

"Even if I weren't the best goddamn detective in the city, I'd say that just might be a clue."

"Best goddamn detective?" she said. "Shit. Maybe back in the day of the Disco Fucking Duck."

"Talk to me, Lantana," he said. "What do you know?"

"Yesterday morning, we got a call on two bodies found down by South Port," she said, navigating Union with her left hand. "A couple men on the daylight shift found the bodies along a private road. Took some doing, but we IDed one of them as this man named Davies, a river rat broker, working on getting containers off the ships and onto trucks."

"And the other was Russian?"

"Get this," she said, hitting a little bump as they passed Sun Records, Hayes's ass leaving the seat and then slamming back down. "Dmitri Sokolov."

"That's a name you don't hear much in Orange Mound."

"Flew into Memphis on a private jet with a bunch of other Russians," she said. "Once we got that, the feds took the whole thing over and I was glad as hell to clear my plate."

"Do you know what they were looking for?" Hayes said, lowering the window and firing up a Winston. The cold wind felt good on his face as they passed the *Commercial Appeal* building and drove on toward downtown.

"It was Agent Bickett who was in charge," Jones said. "A first-class motherfucker."

"Come on now, Sergeant Jones," Hayes said. "You giving that man way too much credit. You know his momma don't love him that much."

Jones couldn't help but grin and they rode for a while in silence as they headed deeper into downtown. Hayes checked his phone and saw a text from Deacon Malone that he'd changed out Hayes's car for his own and left the keys in the office. He'd get the vehicle situation straight and then roll back to Central Gardens to check on Addison. That shithole they'd found her in down in Marshall County wasn't any five-star hotel. Addison looked mad as hell but also fragile, pale, and half-starved.

"Followed up on that tip you gave me," Jones said. "I rode with the Quitman County sheriff to that hunt club and checked the freezer and the whole damn property down there."

"But you couldn't find that dead woman."

"We didn't find shit," she said. "Not that I trust any of those folks down in Quitman County. I planned on taking some prints, brought down one of our lab folks, but that place had been cleaned out. The whole damn house smelled of nothing but bleach and Pine-Sol. Must've moved that body right after you left. Wish you'd stuck around."

"Had to find my client."

"Ain't that just like you," she said. "Porter Hayes."

They drove past AutoZone Park and the Peabody Hotel before turning up Third and on over to Madison. She slowed and parked behind Porter's Mercedes, keeping the engine running. He reached out for the door handle.

"I don't know what those feds are looking at," she said. "But I can tell you they don't know shit about Memphis."

Hayes let go of the handle and turned to her.

"Two of my detectives worked that scene at the port before the feds took over," she said. "Looked to them like those two dead men had been arguing over something that came out of a shipping container."

"Okay."

"An empty shipping container."

"Someone else beat them there?"

"Maybe you are as good as you think," she said. "That dock was a secured site and we got video of the vehicles coming and going from the gate, although we didn't catch nothing on the shooting itself. Just those three trucks heading out. Feds following up on all that mess."

"What was in the container?"

Lantana Jones smiled. "Either the feds already knew or just didn't care."

"You gonna tell or you gonna make me beg?" he said.

"Security had called into dispatch two hours before the Russians got there about a break-in at the compound and folks looting containers along their docks."

"*Memphis.*"

"Yeah," she said. "Those boys killed each other over something that someone else had stolen two hours before."

"Any idea who?"

"No," she said, tapping her long red nails against the wheel. "But I got some folks I like. If I were working this thing, not the feds, I'd be headed down to talk to Hotbox."

"Deonte Taylor in on this?"

She nodded. "Stolen shit from the port?" she said. "What do you think? Doesn't he owe you a thing or two?"

"Actually, I owe him."

"He'll talk quicker to you than me," she said. "Might be worth a ride down to Washington Heights."

37

Gaultier

He tried to talk his way out of it.

Collinson, so very arrogant, believed he could talk his way out of anything. But not with Anatoliy Zub. Zub hadn't flown all the way from Dubai with six of his best men, now noticeably five, to return to Russia empty-handed, Zub reminding everyone within earshot that his private plane was fueled up and ready once the business was concluded.

Gaultier watched all the action unfold from a sofa in the high-roller suite of the Sam's Town Casino. Zub had rented the entire top floor.

Collinson screamed as Zub started to chop off his ring finger with a very large knife. Zub claimed it was an authentic Bowie knife, like the American hero. *The man who died at the Alamo. You know this movie with John Wayne as the Davy Crockett? So much excitement for me in the Moscow theater.*

More screaming. The finger was free from Collinson. Gaultier looked up from a copy of the faux leatherbound book listing the so-called amenities of the hotel. Things had gotten so terrible, he contemplated ordering a hamburger from room service and turning in for the night. *Why not?* With all of Anatoliy's recklessness, the police would be breaking down the doors any minute.

Zub's men had gathered around a poker table, Collinson's blood all over the green felt. His finger lay by a pile of playing cards. Zub stood and nodded to one of his men to bring a fresh towel. "So very messy, Peter," he said. "You bleed like a sticky pig."

"You're wasting your time," Gaultier said. "He doesn't have it."

"What good are you?" Zub said. "You did nothing but talk. This is the only way to deal with a man like Collinson. He lies as freely as he breathes. Would you like a drink?"

"Of course," Gaultier said. "Why spoil such a pleasant evening?"

Two of Zub's men had been wounded at Collinson's house and Collinson, poor Peter, looked terrible. He had been beaten very badly, Zub never what you might call a patient man. Gaultier had heard stories, just rumors really, of Zub's rudimentary dental work with pliers and silver scaler to drive down to the nerve. The situation could have been so much worse than a useless finger. Not even the one he used to shoot.

"Ask Gaultier," Collinson said, wavering on his feet like a boxer in a later round. "He knows I didn't take it. How could I?"

Zub looked over to Gaultier. Gaultier, legs crossed, leaned back into the deep cushions and flipped a page. He was now looking at the catfish plate. Gaultier had never had catfish, but it was promised to be fried a deep, golden brown and served with frites. "I told you, Anatoliy. He can't find it. He has lost his own treasure."

"And how would you know this?" Zub asked.

"He murdered two people trying to find it," he said. "Yes, Collinson has a very rich buyer, but nothing to sell."

"No," Zub said, slamming his fist onto the table. All the cards, poker chips, and the still warm, bloody finger bounced up off the felt. "He has it. He has hidden it up his anus. Who else would know?"

Collinson was seated in a wooden chair with a bloody hotel towel wrapping his hand, his face completely white and eyes dead. "There is a man named Wells who works for the US government but also for an Israeli art dealer named Wolfe. I've heard that he's in Memphis. He must have paid off a woman I trusted and got to the container before us."

"Trusted a woman?" Zub asked. "You? This I do not believe."

Gaultier stood up, laid down the in-room menu, and placed a hand in his right pocket. He looked to poor Peter and then back to Zub. "I know this man Wells," Gaultier said. "Sounds like his doing."

Zub smiled at Gaultier. "We are friends, yes? Like Bowie and Crockett."

"Which one am I?" Gaultier said.

"Who is the one with big knife?" Zub said. He laughed and flashed the blade. "I am Bowie, of course. Of course. Do you wish to see?"

Zub pivoted fast and threw the knife overhanded and hard. The knife stuck perfectly into the wall by a cheap oil painting of a vase of flowers. Everything in the suite festooned with flowers, the sofas, the settées, the bedspreads. Zub walked over and placed his arm around Collinson. "Oh, Peter," he said. "My old friend. What was in this box that was worth so much that you screwed Anatoliy Zub? I came here for weapons. Maybe a special bomb that I would have sold to Taliban. *Boom.* And now I am hearing of antiques? Now you are a man of culture? What is it, Peter? Rare sculpture? The treasures of the pharaohs? King Tut's mummified penis?"

Peter Collinson turned his head and spit blood onto the floor. His face was very tight with pain. "It's a Bible," Collinson said.

Zub looked to his men and then over to Gaultier before he doubled over with laughter. He laughed for a long while until he righted himself and thumped Collinson hard in the back of the head. "You are a funny guy," he said. "But this is no joke. If you make me laugh more, I send your penis back to your mistress in Paris. Or is it your mistress, Gaultier? I hear they are very much the same."

Gaultier shrugged. Valerie could do as she wished. He did not own her or she him.

"It's a very rare and very old Bible," Collinson said, trying to catch his breath. "There's a man here who is ready to pay millions for it. He's crazy for this kind of thing. If you can get to this man Carson Wells, you'll get it back and we can sell it and be done."

"And who is this Israeli he works for?"

"It doesn't matter," Gaultier said. "If Wells has it, it's probably halfway back to Tel Aviv by now. You're all wasting your time. This is nothing but a *secousse de cercle.*"

"What is that?" Zub said, walking over to pick up his black cowboy hat. The Russian placed it upon Collinson's sweaty head. "What does that mean?"

Gaultier made a stroking-off motion with his left hand. "It means you are shit out of luck, Anatoliy," he said. "Either let this man go or kill him. But this game of yours is over."

"Can this man Wells be reasoned with?" Zub asked.

"No," Gaultier said, scratching at his cheek. "But he can be bought."

Zub nodded, knowing and appreciating that kind of animal, and took the cowboy hat back and placed it on his own head. He started to pace. "*You see, in this world there two kinds of people, my friend,*" he said. "*The ones with loaded guns and those who dig. You dig.* Ha ha. Eastwood so great. I joke with you. But seriously, you must find this man Wells and bring him to me. I like this idea of this Bible. Perhaps I give it to my mother. She very religious and pray for me for many years."

"This isn't the kind of Bible you read," Gaultier said. "This is a very, very first edition. The kind you put in a museum."

"And worth so much trouble?"

"More than fifty million," Gaultier said. "Easy."

38

Porter Hayes

The two-story brick building had been a lot of things over the years. A grocery store, a pool hall, and most recently a blues club called the Hard Luck Café. A mural of Isaac Hayes in all his Hot Buttered Soul glory faced the parking lot. Now, Deonte Taylor, who most folks knew as Hotbox, did his business up on the second floor, running drugs from down on the Gulf Coast on up to Chicago. He'd taken over this little slice after Craig Petties went to jail, Petties running pretty much all of Memphis before he skipped town to hide out with the Beltrán-Leyva cartel in Mexico.

Three of Deonte's boys were playing pool when Hayes walked in. A CD jukebox was pumping out some of that Memphis crunk. All that bullshit about hustling money, pimpin' hos, and drinking champagne. It wasn't exactly Johnnie Taylor singing "Party Life" but damn, not much was. Hayes reached into his coat, shook out a Winston, and lit up. "Came to see Deonte."

"Deonte ain't here," one of the young men said.

"Yeah, he is," Hayes said. "His ride's parked out front."

"And what's it to you, Pops?" asked another.

"Pops?" Hayes said. "Damn."

Hayes staggered his feet and placed his hands in the leather jacket, feeling the grip of his .38 in his right hand. "Okay. Wait a minute. Who's your momma, young man?"

"What the fuck you say?"

"Your momma Juanita Brooks?" Hayes asked. "I used to see you at

St. James AME church on Sundays. You used to stand up during the sermon, looking over everyone's head to follow that golden collection plate with your eyes. All that cash sure held some interest for you."

"And who the hell are you?"

"Tell Deonte that Porter Hayes wants to see him."

One of the young men shooting pool looked up from the table. He exchanged a look with a kid in an Oakland Raiders cap. The kid with the cap stopped what he was doing, racked the cue, and headed up a set of side stairs. Okay. Now he was about to get a little respect.

"Wait here," Juanita Brooks's son said.

"Sorry to hear about your momma," Hayes said. "Gone too soon. She was a sweet young lady."

The kid just stood there, face drawn, not sure what to make of this old man in his leather jacket who knew his momma back in the day. What Porter wanted to tell the kid was that he knew his granddaddy, too; one of his brother's people running with the Invaders when Hayes had been a cop just back from Nam. His granddaddy had been as tough as he was stupid. Ended up selling out Porter's brother Marvin to the feds for that thirty pieces of silver.

The kid in the Raiders cap rambled down the old rickety steps and pointed upstairs. "Hotbox said you were cool."

"Boys," Hayes said, blowing out smoke and tossing down the butt, "y'all ain't got no idea."

Deonte's upstairs office wasn't really an office at all, mainly a storeroom filled with boxes full of Nikes and Panasonic TVs, pyramids of STP oil, Beautiful Textures Tangle Taming shampoo, and cases and cases of Courvoisier and Mickey's Big Mouth. Deonte Taylor hung loose in the middle of it all, dressed in some saggy-ass black jeans and a Raiders jersey. A braided gold chain around his neck.

"Damn, Deonte," Hayes said. "Looks like goddamn Kmart in here."

"Porter Hayes," he said. He looked to one of his lieutenants. "Listen, man. This old *Superfly* motherfucker used to own this town. I heard ladies used to hand you their panties when you were out on a job. Even in church."

Hayes grinned and shrugged. He reached up and smoothed down the mustache.

"You need a TV?" Taylor asked. "Some of them burner phones with big-ass numbers you can see without your glasses? What they call those things. Jitterbugs?"

Hayes walked on into the crowded space. The room was dark and airless, smelling like man funk and weed. He could hear more crunk from downstairs shaking the floor and old plaster walls. Pinups of naked women, most of them pornographic, had been shellacked between the bricked-in windows. The tops of the windows were rounded with some fancy plaster molding, Hayes had heard something about this place, way back when, being a dance hall. Or was it a whorehouse?

"Your boy Randy produced that," he said. "That damn Project Pat. 'This Ain't No Game.'"

"Project Pat? Okay, then," Hayes said. "Listen, Deonte. I need your help."

"You don't want a TV?" Deonte asked. "I got forty-inch Panasonics with Dolby sound. I bet you still got one of those old box televisions with the rabbit ears, watching reruns for Don Cornelius running that *Soul Train* line. *Confunkshun, Ohio Players.* Damn *Midnight Star.* I tell you, man. You watch an old down-and-dirty flick on this motherfucker and it gonna make that peepee hard again."

"I don't have a TV," Hayes said. "And my peepee doing just fine."

"I bet," Taylor said. "Some of that John the Conquer root?"

"Centrum Silver."

"You really don't have a TV?"

"House got broken into last Christmas," Hayes said. "Nearly cleaned me out. Along with my stereo and collection of Luther Vandross albums."

"Oh, damn," he said. "Luther. Rest in peace. 'A House Is Not a Home' reminds me of my grandmomma."

"Fine woman," Hayes said. "She had the most incredible Sunday hats I ever saw. Sometimes, I think I may get older, but the past is never past. You know who said that?"

"Run DMC."

Hayes laughed. He looked over at the boxes of TVs as if he was interested and then turned back to Deonte and his two boys. "Someone's been hitting containers down at the port," Hayes said. "I don't care who or why. I just want to get back something that's been lost."

"What is it?"

"Don't know."

"How big of a container?"

"One of those big-ass Conexes," Hayes said. "This just happened two nights ago. Two units were hit and whoever did it got away clean."

Deonte shrugged. He nodded to one of his boys and the boy headed on back downstairs. Hayes didn't know if he was headed down to make some calls or about to rouse the boys from downstairs to start some trouble. Hayes wasn't worried. Deacon Malone would've walked in by now, scoping out the situation and ready to react if necessary.

"I don't mess with the port," Deonte said. "Or anything along the river. You got the cops and those folks from US Customs. I don't need or want any federal charges on my ass."

"But you know who it might be," Hayes said. "Because they'd come to you about moving what they stole."

"This shit that you don't know what it is?"

"Well," Hayes said. "I don't think it's Jordans or flat-screens, if that's any help."

"Then who gives a good goddamn?"

"Exactly," Hayes said. "I'd like to check it out and make an offer if I see what I like."

"Drugs?"

"I don't believe so," Hayes said. "But haven't ruled it out."

"Guns?"

"Maybe," Hayes said.

"If it were guns," Deonte said. "I'd already have them."

"True."

"I can check around for you," Deonte Taylor said. "But you'd owe me twice after I got that mixing board back for Randy. That wasn't no easy favor. Got Crips all up by his studio. One of my boys got shot getting it back."

Hayes shrugged. "He lived."

"You a hard man, Porter Hayes."

"Don't know any other way to be."

Hayes shook Deonte "Hotbox" Taylor's hand before taking the old rickety steps down to the first floor and janky-ass poolroom. He found Deacon Malone flipping albums on the jukebox. He had on his long wool coat that he liked to wear on Sundays. Hayes knew he had two sawed-off shotguns hung from inside like smoked meats.

Malone pressed a few buttons and looked up from the hot neon. The three young guns in the pool hall studied the big man as if he were a brand-new rhino brought into the Memphis Zoo. Soon the crunk shut off and they heard the sweet melodic voice of Reverend Al Green take over. "Take Me to the River." Charles Hodges on organ. *Yes, yes, yes.* Now that was music.

"Get what you need?" Malone said, pushing out through a side door. The morning light shone into the darkened room behind them.

"Don't know," Porter Hayes said. "Time will tell."

Two hours later, Hayes doubled back from downtown, driving south on Highway 61 to the Third Street Flea Market. Deonte had come through with the name Miss Ricky Swearengen, who got his start with drag shows at the J Wags disco but now sold shit out back of his specialized Ford Econoline van. Deonte said Miss Ricky's crew had been hitting containers up and down the river for the last few weeks. They'd been the one he'd been reading about in the *Commercial Appeal* who drove off with a truck full of Nikes coming in from South Korea. Deonte said wasn't no need to rush since Ricky only had one leg and did business from his wheelchair. Deonte's people had seen him out earlier that morning hustling Oriental rugs out behind the old Southwest Twin Drive-In. *Does that sound like what you're looking for?*

Hayes pulled his Mercedes into what used to be the parking lot for the old theater. The movie screens were now rusted to hell, the projector room looking like a spaceship perched on top of what had been the concessions building. Hayes walked through where folks had set up for the Saturday market on the back of pickup trucks, card tables, or just laid out on the asphalt over bedsheets. Kids sold their music on CDs they burned. An old woman bundled up in a red coat and an Atlanta Falcons ski hat sold dozens of porcelain figurines of little white children playing games and dressed up as animals. A fat man in overalls sold fishing equipment from the back of a busted-ass truck. There were used power tools, TVs, and stereos. All of it likely stolen. One young man hocked vinyl records stored in milk crates from the back of a rusted-out Toyota. Hayes thought about checking to see if the man had any of his Luther.

Hayes strolled through line after line of hustlers with what looked to be hot merchandise. At least two of the cars were selling Nikes that surely had been part of the big Nike heist he'd read about. One handmade sign read "Jenuine Jordans." It didn't take him too long to find a man in a wheelchair who sure as hell looked like his name would be Miss Ricky. Hayes couldn't tell how old he was, but he looked eaten up with drugs or some illness. The man didn't have any facial hair or eyebrows and wore a satin turban over what Hayes assumed was a bald head. His skin was the color of an old penny and his eyes looked almost yellow.

The man was slumped into the chair and Hayes wasn't sure if he was dead or alive.

"You Ricky Swearengen?"

"Every inch," Ricky said. "And I know you. You're a goddamn cop."

"Used to be," Hayes said. "But not for a long while."

"You looking for some rugs?" Ricky asked. "Check this shit out. You ain't never seen nothing like what I got. What size you looking for? You being a fine man of taste and distinction."

"What else you got in that van?"

"Some real old vases, brass lamps, and old guns and shit," Miss Ricky said. "I bought this whole damn truckload from the estate of a nice old Turkish woman. Said she'd had all this in her family for years. I could put all this up on eBay but I figured I'd bring it out to market this fine November morning. Check out the quality of them rugs. This ain't no Sears and Roebuck bullshit. Tell me what catches your eye, young man."

"Young man?" he said. "Me and you look like we made about the same trips around the sun."

"Maybe," he said. "Okay, then. What's your game, Porter Hayes?"

"You know who I am."

"Hotbox told me you'd be coming," he said. "Told me to play it straight with you."

"Then you know I know that all this old, dusty shit didn't come from some ole dead Turkish lady or drop off a damn truck," Hayes said. "And I'm sure when you opened up that container, this wasn't exactly the shit you were hoping to find?"

Miss Ricky giggled. It was high-pitched and annoying and he covered his mouth with a thin hand. He wore a fuchsia muumuu, his right foot showing off a brand-new high-top Jordan.

"Is this everything?" Hayes asked.

"Maybe."

"Everything from that Conex y'all busted into?"

"Go ahead and tell Momma what it is you're looking for."

"I got to be honest, Miss Ricky," Hayes said. "I ain't exactly sure. Mind if I take a look at the merchandise?"

Ricky tossed a dismissive hand over his shoulder, staring right ahead at the rusted movie screen. Someone had set up a backyard grill from behind an old Crown Vic, grilling out hot dogs and selling Kool-Aid.

Hayes searched in the high pile of rugs and inspected pieces of pottery that had been laid on a card table. There were maps, swords, old coins, and brass containers that looked like spittoons. But damn. For the life of him, Hayes didn't see a thing that was worth killing over. But who knew? Maybe these old rugs were priceless. Maybe these were the finest goddamn rugs ever made. Maybe those old gold urns held the ashes of Alexander the Great. After about twenty minutes, he gave up and walked back to Miss Ricky. Ricky had a cheap Mexican blanket up over his lap.

"I think you're holding back."

"Miss Ricky ain't hold nothing," he said, giggling. "Well. Except for one big thing."

"How much do you want for the whole lot?" he said. "I mean every damn thing y'all pulled out of that container. And I mean everything."

"That's interesting to Miss Ricky," Ricky said. "Is this the part when you say you know so-and-so who work for the police and then if I don't come across, you're gonna have them bust my ass? They been working that bullshit since Starsky and Hutch got to cornholin' Huggy Bear."

"Something's missing here."

"Ain't nothing missing."

"Nothing?"

"Maybe a few things," Ricky said. "Some cheap-ass blankets, and a few plastic tubes filled with old maps and shit. Nothing but yellowed paper, not thick enough to wipe your ass. Man, I got to move this shit. Everybody love them old rugs. Those old knives and shit make a man look as big and bold as Sho'nuff from *The Last Dragon*. I figure you can have it all if you want it. But you know how it work. Remember Bob Barker stepping up with that long, thin microphone. *All this shit can be yours, motherfucker, if that price is goddamn right.*"

"I don't think that's what Bob said."

"Oh, no?" Ricky raised his nonexistent eyebrows, his skin looking like melted caramel. "Well. That's what I heard."

"Give me a price."

Ricky put his index finger to his lips, pursed them, and then gave him a price that made Hayes nearly crack a rib from laughter. Hayes just shook his head and sized up what all Ricky had laid out and what kind of truck he'd need to move it. "How 'bout we spin that big wheel one more time?"

Ricky looked up at the gray sky and then back at Porter Hayes. He shuffled the Mexican blanket over his one leg and then looked back at Hayes.

"You and I both know if you try and pass this off out on Summer Avenue, cops gonna be all over your ass," Hayes said. "This shit belongs to my client, and my client is willing to offer a fair price for its return. Call it a finder's fee."

"Three grand?" Ricky said. "That's fair as hell. I mean look at all this stuff. A treasure for the goddamn ages. Look at the workmanship on those rugs, Porter Hayes. Got a better weave on them than half the women in Memphis."

"I think we can make a deal here," he said. "But I need to make a call and check in with my financial backers."

"Sound like I'm not the only one spinning some bullshit today."

Hayes stepped away from Miss Ricky's Econoline and walked out to the old movie screen while he dialed up Addison. She picked up after three rings.

"I think I found what Dean was searching for," he said. "Figured you might be interested?"

"Why?"

"Insurance policy," he said. "Or to save your husband's life. Even if he is a motherfucker. Excuse my French."

Addison didn't answer. Her silence lasted so long he thought they might've been disconnected.

"How much?" Addison asked.

Hayes told her. She agreed the cash wouldn't be a problem.

"What if I told you that I didn't care what happened to him?" she said. "That's on him."

"Ma'am," Hayes said, "I'd say that every day you are sounding more and more like your old man."

"Let's get it anyway," Addison said. "What could it hurt?"

39

Addison

You're a short, pathetic asshole and I'm embarrassed we're even related."

"Wow," Branch said. "Just wow. There are two sides to this, Addison. You really want to be pissed at me for taking care of your kids while you and Dean work through all your bullshit?"

"All our bullshit?" Addison said, stabbing her finger into Branch's skinny chest. "Dean kidnapped me and locked me up in some hellhole in Mississippi. I may have never gotten out of there thanks to you. All you did was facilitate his lies about me being a drunk and a pill popper. You put my children in danger. I know you and Dean are good butt buddies, with your stupid matching Land Rovers and your little bro getaways. But Dad taught us one thing, and you goddamn well know it."

Branch didn't say anything, but he knew the answer: family always came first. They were standing on the front stoop of his little colonial in Chickasaw Gardens, a house that neither he nor Libby could really afford. Addison knew her brother was in debt up to his eyeballs and had been cooking more than the ribs at Bluff City Barbecue. He'd been taking money out of the equity her dad had built up over the years just to pretend he was a big shot.

"You were out of control," Branch said. "I was doing what I thought was best."

Branch crossed his arms over his chest, eyes wide like a scared little bitch. Branch could never ever take criticism. Addison loved her late mother dearly, but she had committed the cardinal sin of many mothers of sons and made Branch grow up thinking he was truly special and unique. Branch Hassan was about the most average person she'd ever known. Medium size. Medium intellect. Never worked hard for anything or appreciated how hard their father had worked to give them a solid and stable life.

"People were killed in my home," she said. "In my fucking home, Branch. *With my children there.*"

"I know," Branch said, looking her in the face. "Are you blaming me for that, too?"

"Forget it," Addison said, pushing past him and heading back into the house. "We're out of here. *Kids. Kids!* Pack up. Get your stuff. We're leaving. Your uncle can go fuck himself."

Preston was laid out on the couch watching ESPN *GameDay* with his twin cousins. Sara Caroline had run upstairs with her aunt Libby as soon as Addison confronted Branch about siding with a con artist and a killer over his own damn sister. *What is the one family rule?* Maybe he didn't even know anymore. Dean wasn't family. He wasn't anything. He was a goddamn sperm donor.

Preston didn't complain, already used to moving from house to house, and bounded up the steps to get his gym bag and video games. Sara Caroline was another story, looking down from the banister. "I'm not going," she said. "I'm fine here. With Aunt Libby."

Addison had pretty much reached her ultimate damn limit. All the wonderful, compassionate advice from Dr. Larry was sent to her mental incinerator. She walked halfway up the steps, leveled her finger at her daughter, and said, "I said, right fucking now."

Libby put her arm around Sara Caroline. "She's fine here, Addy," she said. "No trouble at all."

That's Libby, all smiles and manners while the world turns to shit. A Southern woman to her core who'd never talk about a problem straight on. Asking *How'd you like your coffee?* while the damn kitchen was on fire.

"Libby, thank you for finally getting your head out of your ass and telling Mr. Hayes where to find me," she said. "But when it comes to my own kids, you can politely fuck right off. I'm not staying another minute with people who stabbed me in the back for no good reason."

"Addy."

Addison waited with her keys in the foyer. Preston and Sara Caroline wandered down a few minutes later with their backpacks and duffel bags. Addison had slept hard on their couch until sunup and hadn't quite organized her thoughts when Branch had wandered in and offered to make breakfast, acting like absolutely nothing had happened and all was right in the world.

"Addison," Branch said, speaking to her now from the living room. He couldn't look her in the eyes. "I didn't know. How the hell could I have known?"

"They held me down, Branch," she said, wiping her eyes. "They strip-searched me and locked me in a room. Is that what you wanted? Was I such a threat with my chardonnay that you had to step in? Jesus. Fuck off, Branch. I can't even stand to look at your stupid face. Dad would be so fucking ashamed of you."

Addison slammed the heavy old front door so hard that she heard a picture fall off the wall, the glass shattering.

Preston was in the back seat. Sara Caroline in the passenger seat. Addison started the Escalade and backed out of the driveway, circling back and then out of Chickasaw Gardens.

"Great," Sara Caroline said. "Just awesome, Mom. Now we have no place to sleep."

"Maybe we can get a hotel," Preston said. "With a heated pool."

"No," Addison said, tired. So fucking tired. "We're going somewhere safe with an old family friend."

God love him. Alec Dawson had prepared for their arrival.

He'd bought Zapps chips, Tostitos, and Cokes for Preston and hummus, pita chips, and a little crudité platter for Sara Caroline. He said if they wanted dinner, they could order pizzas or go out (although none of them felt like going out). He'd put Sara Caroline up in Ellie's room and gave Preston a large guest bedroom downstairs. The room was unfurnished except for an inflatable mattress and a flat-screen television. Alec bragged to Preston that he got every single channel available including all the different ESPN and movie channels. "Just don't go all the way up into the five hundreds, some of those movies might be inappropriate," he said.

"How inappropriate?" Preston asked. Excited.

"Keep to the cartoons, bud," Addison said.

Alec closed the door to the room and walked with Addison into the open living room of the somewhat empty McMansion. The fire was going again, a cozy contrast to the dark gray day outside. While Alec went out to the woodpile, Addison helped herself to a nice bottle of cab that Alec had bought for her. After all the bullshit she'd endured in her faux rehab and then finding her home shot to shit, she believed she deserved a drink.

She kicked off her running shoes, her ridiculous Louis Vuitton luggage still by the front door. The television was off and the room wonderfully silent. No more talking or the draining fear that she'd never see her kids again. No more threats and intimidations from Dean. Dean was stuck in whatever mess he'd made. He could have gotten their kids killed. She might've been locked away in that shithole for years. If it hadn't been for Porter Hayes, things could have gotten much worse.

Alec appeared and set down an armload of wood by the stone fireplace. He had on a black cashmere sweater and tan cords with a pair of worn-in hunting boots. It struck her that she'd never heard Dean ever mention duck hunting until he'd moved to Memphis with Addison. And then he became obsessed, later acting as if he'd been born in the marsh, shooting ducks with his father. All of it a lie, but she'd never called him on it. She thought he was inventing memories for a man that Dean had told her in his weaker moments that he hated. *I hated my father. He was the most cruel man I've ever known.*

"Is that wine okay?"

"Best wine I've ever had."

"You're kidding."

"After what I've been through, I would've settled for Boone's Farm."

Alec smiled and came over to the big L-shaped couch and took a seat by Addison. He wrapped an arm around her and pulled her in. God, he smelled good, like woodsmoke and old leather. Susan must've been as horrible as Addison had heard. The guy had gone grocery shopping for her kids. He had offered them his home. Last night, they'd been in a safe room with Russian killers coming to get her husband. Her husband. The thought of that cruel little shit made her face flush.

"Porter didn't want me to come over here," she said. "He wanted to put us up at a Radisson in Olive Branch."

"I can't imagine why you didn't take him up on that offer."

"Sounded great to Preston," she said. "He heard it had a pool."

"I'm glad y'all came over."

"I didn't know who else to call," she said. "My brother is a fucking dick."

"Yes," Alec said. "He is."

Alec leaned over and kissed Addison on the forehead. The thought that she had ever been intimate with Dean made her physically ill. Being with Alec made her feel less dirty somehow, less the absolute idiot she'd been for the last fifteen years of her life.

"Do you remember that time you pushed me down frat row in a shopping cart someone had stolen from the Big Star?" Addison asked.

"We'd stolen a bunch of crawfish from the Sig Ep house and you were tossing the tails at people like Mardi Gras beads."

"How did things get so fucking crazy?"

"We grew up."

"Did we?" Addison said. "Really? Maybe I'm older, but I feel the same. How the hell did I get mixed up with a guy like Dean? Or whatever the fuck his name really is."

Alec just smiled and looked at her empty glass. "More?"

She nodded. Alec got up, got the bottle, and refilled the glass. He walked over to the fire and stoked it a bit before standing up and looking at his phone. Alec turned to the bank of windows facing the rear of his property, which looked out on cleared space for a neighboring house that had never been built. "I'm afraid it's going to rain all night."

"I don't want to go anywhere," Addison said. "I want to sleep for a week."

"You're safe here," he said, taking a seat beside her. He reached his arm around her and pulled her in close. "You all are safe."

Alec had ordered pizzas and the kids had eaten at the dinner table as Addison lay on the couch. Michael Caine was on TV, tied to a chair and being forced to watch a psychedelic slide show. *You will forget everything about the* Ipcress File. *You have forgotten your name.* Between the rain, the fire, and the wine, she'd fallen asleep only to awake sometime later with most of the house dark. Her head was in Alec's lap and he was stroking her hair.

She shot upright.

"What time is it?"

"Almost ten," he said. "Ready for bed?"

She was wearing blue jeans and an old Disney World sweatshirt he'd let her borrow. She stood up and walked over to the kitchen. Her kids, being her kids, hadn't even thought about cleaning up the mess they'd made. Open boxes of pizza with not much left but the crust. She was so hungry, sleeping through most of the day, that she picked up a few stray crusts and two last pieces of pizza.

"I was thinking," she said.

"I'll sleep on the couch," he said. "It's cool. You can have my bedroom."

"You don't need to do that," she said. "I obviously can sleep fine on the couch."

Alec's hair was kind of tousled and wild. His smile so big and pleasant that she just reached out and hugged him, a slice of pepperoni in her right hand. When she looked up at Alec, he moved in and kissed her full on the mouth. But then his eyes shot up and he pulled away, Addison turning to find Sara Caroline in the hallway. "Okay," her daughter said, wandering off.

"Well," Addison said. "She already suspected it."

"This has to be a lot on her," Alec said.

"The Russian murder squad, the dead bodyguards, or us kissing?"

"There's two extra pizzas," he said. "Want me to heat one up?"

"Please."

"I have both a . . ."

"Don't care," she said, taking a seat on a barstool. "All pizza is good pizza."

Alec turned on the oven and stood opposite her, across the bar. He reached out and touched her hand. "You can stay as long as you like."

"Be careful of what you offer," she said. "You should see my gorgeous kitchen. I'd finally gotten it updated. Fifty thousand bucks. All marble counters. Walnut cabinets. Viking range."

"What are you going to do, Addison?" he said. "About Dean?"

Addison took a breath and watched as he slid a pizza box into the oven. She was so damn hungry, she would've settled for just the marinara-stained box.

"There's something I haven't told you."

Alec waited.

"When Dean called me, he said those Russians had kidnapped him," she said. "And that he'd call me later about wiring money to some account in the Bahamas. He said someone had stolen something very valuable from him and the Russians were holding him accountable."

"Okay."

"I had no idea what he was talking about until later," Addison said. "Porter Hayes found out Dean has been waiting for some container shipped in from Turkey to arrive in Memphis. It was filled with all kinds of antique rugs and lamps. I don't know why. But it was important enough that Dean said it could save his life."

"How'd you know what was in it?"

"Mr. Hayes found the people who'd looted it down at the port," she said. "He told me what he'd found. I had to pay some man named Miss Ricky three thousand dollars."

"Miss Ricky?"

"Yep," she said. "That's what he calls himself."

"And this stuff might save Dean's life?"

Addison shrugged. "Would you think I'm a heartless bitch if I said I honestly don't give a shit?" she said. "Dean nearly got my kids killed."

"I can't say I blame you."

"You know when something like this happens, you try to figure out the person you are and the person you want to be," Addison said. "I kept on thinking about who I was before I met Dean. Who was I as a kid and when you and I first met each other? What would I be like without Dean in my life? I'm pretty damn sure I've lost myself. I'm the woman Dean wanted me to be. Do you know that piece of shit luggage by the door cost three grand? I spend ungodly amounts every month on my hair, my nails, Botox. For what?"

"So, you're not going to give this stuff back to Dean?"

"Fuck 'im."

"Aren't you curious?" Alec said. "Don't you want to know why all these people are after him?"

"Mr. Hayes expected it to be a bunch of guns but it's only some rugs and crap," she said. "He said the rugs are really nice and there are some old pottery pieces."

"Looted from Afghanistan."

"Probably."

"I mean it's all so crazy," Alec said. "None of this would have happened if Dean hadn't fucked up somehow on this deal. Would you mind if I take a look at the stuff? I'm no expert, but we've both bought a lot of antiques over the years. Maybe we might notice something that Porter Hayes wouldn't recognize."

"I doubt it."

Alec walked over to the oven, deep in thought, and walked back with a hot box of pizza. He nearly burned his hands and slid it fast right in front of her. He blew on his fingers. "Where is it?"

"Mr. Hayes has it at some warehouse downtown," she said. "He rented a truck."

"Well, I'm game if you are."

"Tonight?" Addison asked. "No way."

"The curiosity is really killing me, Addy."

"Be careful of how you say that," she said. "Do you think the kids will be safe?"

"I don't think Dean is ever coming back," Alec said. "I hate to say it, even after all he put you through, but he's probably dead."

"Okay," she said. "You're right. Let's go. I'll call Porter to meet us there."

They didn't talk much on the way into downtown. The rain had come on heavy, hammering the windshield as they merged onto 240 from the expressway and went farther into Memphis, where Alec drove past Elmwood Cemetery. The streetlights shining down onto the thousands of headstones and mausoleums matching the depressing, cold night. "My dad will be buried there," she said. "He bought four plots a long time ago. He said it was the wisest investment he ever made."

"How close is he?"

"It's bad," Addison said. "I get to see him tomorrow."

"Cancer is ruthless," Alec said. "I'm so sorry, Addy."

"So how do you think you can help me with this crap I bought?"

"I learned a lot from Susan's spending sprees," he said. "Before she cleaned out pretty much everything I owned, I'd spent nearly a million bucks in antiques. I know a good and authentic rug. I'd like to believe I could spot a fake when I see one."

"But let's say these are the finest rugs ever made," she said. "Hand-woven by fairies and kissed by the gods. That's not what Dean does. Dean sells guns and men. Right? Isn't that his entire business model?"

"Pretty much."

Addison watched as they continued past the cemetery, thinking about that wet, cold ground, peering across the headstones to maybe see into that far corner where her mother was buried and her father soon would be. A matching set of the Hassans. Preston and Sara Caroline would go through a parent in rehab, a parent possibly dead, and then the loss of a grandparent. Her father was the last of the family now that Branch was pretty much dead to her.

"What's that address again?" Alec said, checking out the street signs.

Addison told him.

"Once you get this all settled, I think you and the kids deserve a vacation."

"Anywhere in particular?"

"Where's your favorite spot?"

"Dean used to take the family to Mustique," she said. "I really liked it there. But I don't think I'd like it anymore."

"Why's that?"

"I know how Dean paid for it," she said. "Blood money. Dirty deals. Everything I have feels gross. I don't want any of it anymore. I want to sell the house, give away my ridiculous jewelry, and I want Dean, if he's alive, to go to prison for the rest of his life."

"Damn, I'm sorry, Addison," Alec said. "This whole situation sucks."

"Why are you sorry?"

"It's all my fault," he said. "I could have warned you."

"You can pay me back with your keen eye for antiques," she said. "Or maybe you could use some fine rugs around your place. Not to hurt your feelings, but your house looks pretty sad. One cheap sofa and a dining room table. Just a bunch of TVs and a refrigerator for all your wine."

"Like I said, Susan didn't leave me with much."

"I'll make you a good deal," Addison said. "If you see something you like."

Alec laughed as two old brick warehouses came into view along Crump Boulevard. The security gate was rolled back and open. Porter had beaten them there, the lights already on inside one of the six-story towers.

Alec parked and they both got out. He opened his umbrella and covered Addison's head as they made their way to a loading dock and up inside the building. The first floor was a huge, open space with a U-Haul truck parked in the center of the concrete floor. It was quiet and cold in the building, the rain sweeping across the dock as they walked farther inside, industrial lights shining overhead. She called out to Porter but didn't hear anything. Their feet echoed off the brick walls as they got closer to the truck. The back of the truck was closed and padlocked.

"Mr. Hayes?" she said, calling out. "Porter?"

Four big white men with shaved heads walked around from behind the truck. They all had guns.

"Addison," a voice called from the open doors to the loading dock.

She turned. Goddamn, it was Dean. He was walking like an old man with his left hand cradled against his chest. A granite-faced man in a black cowboy hat and duster prodded him along with the end of a rifle. Dean looked dirty and disheveled. His dress shirt was covered in blood.

"Alec," she said, softly.

He didn't answer.

"Alec," she said again.

He didn't answer.

"What did you do?" she said.

Alec wouldn't look at her, turning away as Dean walked closer with the strange man in the cowboy hat. The man had a brushy mustache and very pale blue eyes. "You have good wife, Peter," the man said in a thick Russian accent. "She look like Camilla Sparv. You know this film *Mackenna's Gold*? So very good. Omar Sharif tries to kill Gregory Peck with tomahawk."

Dean looked over to Alec and nodded. Alec nodded back.

"I'm out," Alec said.

"You're out?" Addison said, launching into Alec with her fists. "You fucking asshole. All of you are fucking assholes."

"I didn't mean to hurt you, Addy," Alec said as she hit him with both her fists, pummeling his chest. "I have to look out for Ellie. The IRS has taken almost everything. I could go to jail."

Dean grabbed Addison by her waist and dragged her back. The Russian man reached into his duster and pulled out a very long silver pistol. Addison stopped fighting and froze in place. The man took the pistol, looking like a relic from the Old West, and pressed it to Alec's temple.

"Wait," Alec said. "We had a deal. You already transferred the money. I brought you Collinson's wife. We're done here."

"No," said the ugly Russian in the cowboy hat. "You are done here."

The Russian pulled the trigger and a big chunk of Alec's head blew off, gorgeous hair and all, and some of the blood and brains ended up in Addison's face and eyes. She dropped to the floor screaming, and Dean let her go. She began to sob, her ears full of the sound of gunshots, kneeling and screaming on the filthy warehouse floor.

When she thought she was hollowed out, the Russian cowboy walked up and looked down at her. "You are finished?"

Addison didn't answer and the Russian stepped over her to accept a pair of bolt cutters. He walked over to the U-Haul, snipped off the lock, and raised the cargo door.

Addison shook with cold fear, feeling as if she might choke. Flecks of Alec's blood and brains all over her. *Jesus. Jesus. Jesus.*

"*Ole turkey buzzard flying high*," the Russian cowboy sang. His men pulled out rolled-up rugs and tall golden urns. "Theme to *Mackenna's Gold*. So very good. It's like poetry. No?"

"You're crazy," Addison said, pushing up to her feet. Alec was dead and crumpled on the floor. He'd been so handsome, good, and decent. Right? That had happened. Or none of this had really happened. She was sleepwalking, watching something on television with Michael Caine watching a psychedelic screen. Entirely too much wine. *You are not Addison McKellar. You have no name.*

Dean leaned into her ear and said, "Shut your damn mouth for once, Addison, and maybe we'll get through this."

40

Porter Hayes

Porter picked up Deacon Malone at the Dixie Queen on Belle-vue before heading to the United Warehouse where he'd parked and locked up the U-Haul. Malone left his ride and piled into Porter's Mercedes, the stereo playing "Woman Across the River" from the *Who's Making Love* Album. Malone had a half-finished cheeseburger in his hand, embarrassed that Porter had caught him out breaking his damn diet at ten o'clock at night. "We're going where and for who?"

"Mrs. McKellar decided to have a show-and-tell in the middle of the night."

"Why would she do a fool thing like that?"

"Says her new boyfriend understands antiques," Hayes said. "And might be able to help us figure shit out."

"You did your job, man," he said. "This some white people problems. Let them go on that *Antiques Roadshow* and make things happen. You sure you ain't hungry?"

"Got some Pirtle's on the way home," Hayes said. "I was soaking my bad ankle and watching this Michael Caine movie on TCM. Michael Caine is this spy who likes to cook and listen to classical music. But he used to be a thief, too, and his boss sends him in undercover to see who's kidnapping the best scientists in England."

"Don't sound like *Truck Turner* to me."

"I don't like Addison stepping out like this," Hayes said. "I already told her she didn't need to be staying over at the house of her husband's ex–business partner. Those two got some bad blood, and if this Dean McKellar busted loose, that'd be a place he might check. I don't trust any of those motherfuckers."

"What did she say?"

"Wouldn't listen to any of it," Hayes said. "Said she was sick and tired of men telling her what to do. And so I backed off. I told her to call me if she needed me."

"And so she called you to take a look at that shit you bought off Miss Ricky," Malone said. "Don't you know he used to shoot Ping-Pong balls under his tuck up at J. Wags? Heard he could make 'em fly twenty feet. Now that's some talent."

It was almost eleven and Hayes drove on toward the warehouse where he'd been storing a lot of his family stuff over the years. Still had some furniture of his momma's, lots of records of Genevieve's, even some of her masters, and several old file cabinets with billing and case files going back to 1971. His old friend Sawyer told him that one day he needed to write a damn book about all he'd been through, from Dr. King to Elvis to that time Cybill Shepherd got blackmailed.

"I thought y'all were going to turn over all this shit to the feds?" Malone said.

"Been thinking about it," Hayes said. "Problem is I don't trust them, either."

"So you just decided to hide it deep in that old warehouse."

"Not my call," Hayes said. "That's Mrs. McKellar's business."

"Might be time we stop calling her that."

"When she decided not to negotiate with the folks who took her husband, I thought we might start calling her Sam the Sham Jr."

"Now I like that," Malone said.

Hayes sped up the windshield wipers, the rain blowing sideways over Crump. They passed a few all-night gas stations and convenience stores, the new Budweiser distributor. Up ahead, beyond the tall twin warehouses, stood two billboards. One read GOD SO LOVED MEMPHIS John 3:16. Porter was not sure if the Lord had Memphis in mind when he sent down his son. The other was hustling Project

Pat's latest album, *Real Recognize Real*. The rapper had on sunglasses and pointed two guns down into Crump Boulevard.

"Is that them?" Malone said, pointing to an old Jeep Wagoneer parked by the loading docks.

"Yeah," Hayes said. "But nobody in their right mind would keep that gate unlocked at night."

Hayes rolled past the twin warehouses and pulled into a vacant lot to the west. The undercarriage of his Mercedes hit the uneven busted concrete as he wheeled around and shone his headlights to the area out back of the warehouses. Two black SUVS were parked behind the fencing.

"Okay now," Malone said. "This is when we phone that shit in and circle back to the Dixie Queen. You ever had that fried fish plate? Comes with slaw and those sweet Hawaiian rolls. You let the white people deal with their white people shit, and it's on me."

Hayes made a U-turn, nose toward the street, and cut off the engine and lights. Johnnie Taylor was still playing on the stereo. "Hold on This Time" . . . He could hear Genevieve backing Taylor up on vocals, speaking to him from nineteen sixty-eight. Nobody, no one, not even Aretha, had a voice like that.

"Stay here," Hayes said.

"Don't you worry," Malone said. "I ain't going nowhere."

Hayes walked quick and with purpose, trying to not think about the ankle giving him trouble, as he headed past the twin warehouses. He had his hands in his jacket, head down as he darted into the shadows by the open fence. The rain was coming down harder now, pinging the puddles in the lot, not a soul around. As he headed up the slanted entry at the loading dock, he heard folks talking and walked up to the first floor to see the U-Haul truck parked in the big open space where he'd left it. Locked up tight. Or so he thought while he'd been resting his damn foot and enjoying a movie.

From where he stood, he spotted Addison and that man Alec Dawson. And then there were four, maybe five other white men. And then someone who looked a hell of a lot like Dean McKellar. *Son of a damn bitch.*

A long time ago, back in the boonies with his unit, they came across two American soldiers held by the Vietcong. The VC had a big fire going, washing clothes or making some soup or something, sixteen, twenty Charlie walking that perimeter. Hayes's unit was only eight men strong, but they came up with something that evened out the goddamn odds. Only took one man stepping up and ducking in and his Zippo lighter did all the rest. *Poof* went that grass hut and sent Charlie scattering in every direction.

What they needed was a damn distraction.

Malone got behind the wheel of the Mercedes with Porter beside him as he loaded both his guns. Hayes had his trusty old .38 and brand-new seventeen-shot Glock he kept for special occasions. Malone headed east on Crump and then made a big U-turn, driving back to the warehouse, turning off the lights and moving slow through the chain-link gates, parking beside the Jeep Wagoneer.

Hayes got out and grabbed a concrete block to set down beside the driver's door. Malone had the window down, rain pinging the arm of his jacket as he studied the block. "That's your plan?" he said. "Come on now. I'm tight with Jesus. But not that tight."

"Be ready."

"You gonna give me a signal or something?" he said. "Make the sound of a sparrow?"

"Don't worry about that, man," Hayes said. "You'll know."

Hayes reached into his pocket for a small flashlight and used it to find his way to a side loading ramp where the two SUVs had parked. That door was open, and he walked up the steps and inside, hearing a lot of yelling and what sure sounded like Russian. He'd been expecting Russian, but of course he didn't know Russian from Ukrainian or Polish. Maybe they were Czechs. Whoever or whatever they were, they had Addison and her male friend and were about to take all that shit Hayes had gotten off Miss Ricky back to Moscow.

Hayes pulled out the new Glock from his jacket and got ready. One of the Russians turned his head, maybe hearing Deacon driving up into the opposite loading dock. He turned to another Russian and whispered into his ear. Addison was yelling now. She was mad as hell and Alec Dawson raised his hands as a white man in a cowboy hat came up into his face. Then the black-hatted Russian shot Dawson's head off, spraying blood all over Addison.

She screamed and screamed.

Two of the Russians ran toward the front loading dock just as Porter's beautiful black Mercedes sedan with leather seats, a sunroof, and Blaupunkt stereo shot through the center of the building, scattering everyone the hell out of the way until it almost T-boned the U-Haul, but instead ran flat ass into a big brick wall. The crash was something horrible, even worse than the gunshot into that man's head, and there was cracking glass and the acrid sweet smell of burning oil and antifreeze.

Malone, who had set the concrete block on the accelerator and let it rip, started firing from the front dock. Hayes started firing from the rear dock to pinch them in. Dean McKellar jumped up into the U-Haul with the man in the cowboy hat jumping into the passenger side, started the truck, and drove off. Hayes ran into the side of the building to Addison, trying to pull her up onto her feet as the last of the Russians ran out to their SUVs behind the warehouse. The U-Haul rambled down the front dock and disappeared.

"He was going to kill me."

"He sure was."

"They killed Alec," she said. "Oh my god. Oh my god. His brains are all over me."

Addison was white-faced and in shock as Deacon Malone wandered around the warehouse, shotgun up and ready as he checked the big space. His feet sounded like big patting drumbeats until he got up close to where the Mercedes had done battle with the brick wall. He inspected what was left of Porter Hayes's ride.

"Hope you up on your insurance."

"We need to get her the hell out of here."

Malone nodded. He headed on over to the open metal door at the rear of the building. He turned back and nodded to Hayes and Addison. She was shaking but let go of him and walked to the Mercedes, set her hand on the trunk, and threw up onto the concrete floor.

"It may not play your Johnnie Taylor tape," Malone said, walking back into the warehouse. "But one of those boys left a truck for us."

"Keys in it?"

"What's that got to do with nothing?" Malone said, as he walked outside into the rain.

Hayes walked over to help Addison. His car was a mess, antifreeze and oil spilling out everywhere. Alec Dawson looked even worse, lying crooked on the floor, half his goddamn head gone. Addison pushed herself away from the Mercedes and walked toward the dead man.

Hayes wanted to pull her back and help her out. She didn't need to be studying on such a god-awful mess.

An engine started outside. Malone honked the horn.

"Come on," Hayes said. "We need to get you out of here. I'll call the cops after we're gone to clean up all this shit. I'm real sorry about your friend."

Addison's face was completely blank as she walked up on Alec Dawson, turned back for a moment to Porter, and then surprised him by kicking the hell out of the dead man.

"I let them take it," she said.

"They can have it."

"I am so fucking stupid," Addison said. "Jesus God, Mr. Hayes."

"Porter," he said, pulling her toward the back entrance. "Just Porter is fine, Miss Hassan."

"What was all that stuff?"

"Don't know," Hayes said. "But I promise you one damn thing. That's all on them now. And that karma can be a bitch."

41

Tippi

D amn if you don't look just like your momma," Carson Wells said.

"You knew my mother?" Tippi asked, knowing not to believe a word this man was saying. He wore a slim-fitting electric blue suit over a black T-shirt and had on a pair of well-made tasseled loafers, also black. Even though it was dark and raining, the man insisted on wearing sunglasses. He either thought he looked dynamite with the shades or had bad eyes. The glasses were so dark that Tippi couldn't really tell.

"Of course I did," Wells said. "Last time I saw her was after her book signing at Graceland. *One Night with You: The Joanna Grayson Story.* She and I had a little heart-to-heart over a club sandwich and milkshake. Promised to be in touch if she found out anything new about Peter Collinson and all his down and dirty business."

Tippi had contacted Wells on behalf of Monsieur Gaultier, meeting him in the lobby of the Peabody early that morning. Workers on ladders were decking the halls with garland from the second-floor railing and putting up a very tall artificial Christmas tree. It was raining outside and a bit cold and somehow all the holiday frivolity made her think of Mother. She had on a black rain jacket knotted over her pencil skirt and white silk top. The jacket had belonged to Joanna. She'd made a picture in it during her time with Hammer. Something to do with lesbian vampires.

"Monsieur Gaultier said you were a con man."

"Oh, come on now," Wells said. "That just hurts."

A waitress came over, set down cocktail menus, and asked if they were ready to order. She and Wells both said no at the same time and the woman shrugged and turned right back around to the bar.

"You don't trust me."

"I heard you were a federal agent," she said. "Is that true?"

"Maybe," he said. "I like to keep all my bases covered."

"You worked for Homeland Security after 9/11," she said. "Caught a bunch of soldiers sending museum pieces back to the States. And then you went on to work for a man named Wolfe who sells antiquities on the black market."

Wells leveled a hard look at her and crossed his legs. He put a very long index finger to his lips. *Shh.*

"Gaultier has an offer for you."

"Oh, okay," he said. "Do tell, baby."

Tippi explained everything exactly as Gaultier had told her. *No more. No less.* The waitress came back around, impatient to get their order, the lobby growing crowded with tourists to see the grand duck walk. A lot of restless kids behind velvet ropes. A doorman in his red jacket with epaulets and fancy hat held up a cane announcing the big event would happen promptly at eleven.

"This is happening later today," she said.

"Today?" Wells said. "Shit. I can't knock the dominoes over that damn fast. This is going to take some phone calls and smooth persuasion. You understand? All these people, my government contacts, can be mistrustful as hell."

"I'll tell Gaultier."

"Wait," Wells said. "Wait. I didn't say I couldn't do it. I just said it would be difficult."

"Have them there at exactly five o'clock," Tippi said. "If you don't, the geniza will be lost forever."

"How the fuck do you know about the damn geniza?" Wells said. "Nobody knows about the geniza."

Tippi stood up and offered her delicate and manicured hand. Wells craned his neck behind him and then looked about the ornate lobby, worried someone was watching them. He finally stood up, too, and stared at her open hand. "Does it have to be today?" he asked.

"Monsieur Gaultier has every confidence you'll make this happen," she said. "His current situation is untenable."

"Untenable," Wells said. "Well, shit. Ain't everybody's."

42

Leslie

Today was truly a blessed day.

Leslie had been praying on it long and hard. He'd been asking Jesus why the geniza hadn't been delivered into his care yet. And the one word that came back to him was *humility*. Just the word *humility*, banging around in his old gray head, thinking about his appearances on cable news and those op-eds in the *Democrat-Gazette* about America becoming a godless country. Were his impassioned pieces about bringing God back into the classroom really about exalting Him, or had Leslie been talking for his own glory? He and Roberta had a long discussion about humility and service unto Him as they watched the sunset at the lake house, figuring that maybe the International Museum of the Bible would never happen.

But then early this morning—before first light—came the phone call, and all the worry and fretting had just melted away. God is good, and he answers the prayers of the righteous. The geniza would finally be his and would be a centerpiece to the multimedia center on the banks of the Arkansas River, a beacon to the world of the ancient, modern, and living history of the Word of God. Like he told folks time and again when they asked, Leslie Grimes wasn't a collector. He was a storyteller of history, without the interference of high-tower academics and those left-wing atheists. The museum would demonstrate that the Bible had always been the pure, unadulterated Word of God and hadn't changed a lick in thousands of years. It was the record of God's lips to the human ear. *This was his role in history. Even to be just a footnote to God's Word sure would be something.*

"What was that, Mr. Grimes?" asked his son-in-law, Brian. He and Brian were in the back of this big cargo van he'd taken from the Tomes and Treasures warehouse that afternoon. "I can't hardly hear back here."

"I said the Bible is the record of God's lips to the human ear," Grimes said.

"Are we gonna eat supper at the casino?" Brian said. "I sure am hungry. Heard they have a fancy steakhouse down there."

Leslie shook his head. *Quick to hear. Slow to speak. Slow to anger.*

Up front and behind the wheel, Leslie had brought along Bubba Kinkaid, a retired state trooper and a member of his Baptist church Bible study. There wasn't a tougher man alive to watch his back before he authorized the transfer of funds, the payment on delivery after all the money he'd paid up front. Absolutely no foolishness with Bubba around. And sitting up in the shotgun seat was the man who would validate the true and authentic geniza. Ole Ronnie Scott himself, a true-life evangelical Indiana Jones who'd traveled the globe searching for lost artifacts of the Bible. He'd searched the world for everything from Noah's Ark to the Lost Ark of the Covenant. Ronnie even wore one of those Aussie flop hats and a leather jacket when he'd met them at the tarmac that morning. Leslie immediately flew him from Dallas on his private plane for the big occasion. "Wouldn't miss it," Scott said, tipping the brim of his hat.

Leslie wasn't too thrilled about having an exchange of such holy artifacts at a den of iniquity like the Sam's Town Resort and Casino. But Peter Collinson said his new business partners had insisted on it. Leslie didn't like the sound of new folks being involved but trusted that once he could get in the room with Peter and his people, he could handle the negotiations.

Bubba Kinkaid parked the cargo van in the casino lot and walked around to open up the sliding door for Leslie and Brian. Kinkaid popped open an umbrella over him as they walked, the big red neon sign for the casino shining in the gray, rainy day.

"I sure don't like this, Mr. Grimes," Ronnie Scott said, the rain beading on the brim of his flop hat. "Collinson promised to be an adviser on *Deeper Devotion* and help us find some army folks who worked with those missionaries in Iraq. I swear I could never get that man on the phone."

"Peter Collinson is a player on the international stage," Grimes said. "But he still has time for his family and his faith. I trust him."

"But the money—"

"I know," Grimes said, dodging the puddles in the parking lot. He now held the umbrella, Brian and Bubba trailing behind them. "I know. But if I didn't do something, everything would've been destroyed. The Taliban would've rolled those holy tracts and used them to smoke their hashish and opium."

Leslie was in full CEO mode that morning with his navy power suit, lavender dress shirt, and blue-and-white striped tie. As he walked into the lobby of Sam's Town, he pulled off his gold glasses and dried them with the show hankie. A miniature western town had been constructed above the lobby, ringing it with a dry goods store, livery stable, dance hall, and even a little church. Bubba Kinkaid watched every bit of the lobby like a gosh dang hawk.

The lobby was abuzz that morning, phones ringing at the welcome desk, men with walkie-talkies running to and fro. Leslie figured there must be some trouble in the casino. *Someone had surely been overserved at the blackjack tables.* They kept walking toward the elevators, security folks running past them, winding their way around two new Chevy trucks advertising "The Big Holiday Giveaway."

Bubba Kinkaid punched the button for the fifth floor, up to what Peter Collinson had called the high roller suite. As Bubba reached across, Leslie saw the butt of a big pistol he kept holstered under his black blazer.

"You want me to get us a table?" Brian asked. "Down at the steakhouse?"

Leslie pinched his nose, closed his eyes, and took a deep breath. He'd already been through all this with Brian. He was there because he was a former Razorback offensive lineman with a behind larger than a steer. They needed him to look tough.

"We're not here to eat, Brian," Leslie said, folding his silk hankie and placing it back in his breast pocket. "We're here to pick up one of the most important archaeological finds of the twenty-first century. Does your gosh dang gullet have a problem with that?"

Brian didn't say a word and the men crammed into the elevator for the short ride up to the penthouse floor.

"I didn't mean nothin' by it," Brian said to no one in particular.

Leslie's heart nearly skipped a beat; a kid at Christmastime couldn't compete with what he was feeling as they exited the elevator. He couldn't wait to have all the pieces of the geniza safe in the cargo van, hightailing it back over the river to Arkansas. He would soon be able to touch the Word of God from only a century after the death of Christ.

The four men walked the long hallway, only to see the suite door was wide open. Bubba Kinkaid looked to Grimes and Grimes nodded, ole Bubba pushing his way inside. Leslie followed and walked into a large living space with tall gold lamps, big plushy couches, and even a baby grand piano by a plate glass window looking out onto the rain-swept Delta and Mississippi River.

And then there were all the dead men.

Several dead men splayed out all over the floor and into the hallway back to the bedroom.

Leslie Grimes couldn't speak. Bubba Kinkaid pulled his gun.

Brian just walked out of the room, a confused look on his big, dumb face, and ole Ronnie Scott took off his adventurer's hat and started to make retching sounds.

"Good god almighty," Bubba said. "Better get you out of here, Mr. Grimes."

Through a second window facing the parking lot, Grimes could see a circus train of police cars with flashing blue lights headed south toward them on Highway 61.

Bubba touched Grimes's elbow, and Grimes shook him away.

"It's here," he said. "Damn it. It's here. Help me find it."

Bubba Kinkaid said something about looking out for his best interests, but Leslie Grimes didn't hear a word of it. The words sounded as if they were both underwater, mumbling really, his legs feeling like he was walking through jelly from dead man to dead man. Two of them had on blue windbreakers, Bubba toeing one over to his stomach to see "FBI" written in yellow letters. The other men wore fancy blue jeans and high-necked sweaters, with expensive pointy-toe cowboy boots. They looked as large as gorillas at the zoo, weightlifter types with shaved heads and goatees.

"Check the bedroom," Grimes said. "He promised two large boxes. Small enough for us to carry out of here."

"Nothing's here."

Grimes walked into a bedroom, finding mirrored walls and a huge circular bed for the depraved. Another dead man at the foot of a mirrored wall. He checked the closets and the bathrooms and Bubba ran into the room yelling, "Security is here, Mr. Grimes," he said. "We need to get gone. Someone called in gunshots."

The man in the bedroom (a third federal agent), shuddered a bit, not quite dead, like an old engine trying to sputter to life or one of those plastic divers he'd had as a kid, the wind-up mechanism about petered out. Grimes stooped down onto one knee and then the other, pressing his right ear to the man's mouth. Grimes was praying silently to himself, please let him find the geniza. *Please, dear God. I am your servant.*

"Fuck that," Bubba Kinkaid said. "We're gonna be cornholed five ways from Sunday if I don't get you out of here. This is a goddamn bloodbath."

Grimes shooed him away, glaring at him for using such language.

"Where's Peter Collinson, son?" Grimes said. "Where is Peter?"

"He fucked us," the agent said. His eyes glassy, blood all over his chest and down his leg. There was a pistol not six inches away from his right hand.

"Who?" Leslie Grimes said. "Who did this?"

"Everything was a lie," the man said. "All of it."

And then the man slumped over, maybe dead, maybe not, and Grimes didn't have a moment to say a good word or two for his immortal soul. Bubba Kinkaid was already at the entry door to the suite ushering him out with his hand. Grimes could hear the police sirens, wondering what had happened to the great adventurer Ronnie Scott, as he followed Bubba as fast as his spindly old legs would go. Leslie's heart was racing something awful, sweat rolling down from his old gray head into his eyes, running down metal steps faster than he'd moved in decades.

Bubba opened the fire exit to the lobby, and the men ran out as the EMTs and police ran in. They slowed a bit, trying to walk real casual past the Great Christmas Giveaway trucks and cardboard standups with ladies in red bikinis promising "A Winner Born Every Minute at Sam's Town. Come on. What Do You Have to Lose?"

Grimes glanced back and saw that either he or Bubba Kinkaid had been tracking blood through the lobby. Two policemen stopped them as they tried to bust out the door and back to the van—Brian and his T-bone dinner be damned—and asked them to hold up for a moment.

Leslie Grimes swallowed and bent over to catch his breath, his tie flopping down to the floor. All he could think about was how his momma sure would be disappointed in this whole damn mess. "Hold on a minute, Officers," Grimes said. "Can we all just take a moment to pray?"

43

Addison

L *ater...*

Her father died three days before Thanksgiving, and the extended family descended on her dad's town house like worker bees. Uncle Frank and Aunt Adel stoked the kitchen for forty-eight hours, filling the house with the smell of kibbeh, baba ghanoush, and cabbage rolls. Sara Caroline made stuffed grape leaves for the first time in her life and Preston learned to love baklava. So many of Daddy's old friends from Central High and Ole Miss—even the retired chancellor—driving up to the service at Our Lady of Perpetual Help. A poster board photo of Sami Hassan in his Rebel football uniform, looking tough and focused as he ran toward the camera, flanked his casket. They wept, prayed, and ate. Many remembered her mother's quiet contributions and sacrifices. Aunt Adel sat on the tiny brick patio to share a cigarette and drink some arak, which tasted like chilled old licorice and made Addison wince a little. "When they were first married and you weren't yet born, your father lost everything. He lost his bar and your parents had to sell their home. Your father wouldn't take money from me or his brother. He started selling cars and worked at nights at Anderton's, cooking steaks and fish. He was so tired. He'd fall asleep at Mass on your mother's shoulder. I hope that's where he is now. Your father could never rest. His entire life."

And now it was Thanksgiving Day, many of the family and friends already come to pay their respects. It was just immediate family and the best of Sami's friends at the graveside at Elmwood. The rain and clouds had gone away that morning and Addison was sure someone would tell her the sun peeking out from a cloud was her father letting them know everything would be all right. And sure enough, when the sun shone bright on the casket, Aunt Adel looked up and smiled at her, nodding. *Yes, Yes. A sign from above.* Addison glanced in the other direction to Porter Hayes in his serious pin-striped suit. He'd looked up at the sun and then back at Addison and shrugged.

She and the kids had been staying at a Marriott Courtyard on Germantown Road. They'd soon clear out her father's town house and live there until the Central Gardens home sold. Their realtor called Addison minutes after her father took his last breath wondering if she'd be okay with getting a contractor to fix the kitchen and the bullet holes in the ceiling.

A priest finished his reading at the graveside. Uncle Frank stepped up and read something in Arabic. A few close friends from the Cedars Club dabbed their eyes. They lowered the casket and Addison looked around the rolling grass hills of thousands and thousands of headstones, obelisks, and concrete angels. The cemetery a beautiful fucking downer despite the sunshine. Her father's name now on the same marble slab as her mother's. Story over. Turn the page and move on. That would be a hell of a lot easier if she knew even a little more about the man who'd fathered her children and shared her bed for fifteen years.

Now Dean McKellar—whoever he was—was a man on the run. The police, the FBI, and Homeland Security had all paid her a visit after a big shooting at a casino in Tunica. For a week, she'd kept the kids out of school, but it had been her father who'd told her to hold her head up and just keep walking. Let them throw their stones and talk behind your back. Nothing will hurt you if you and the children keep walking. *Don't look back, Addy. Ever.*

Addison held Preston's hand as she made her way through the headstones of decades and decades of dead Memphians. Politicians, soldiers, blues singers, even a famous madam who helped the sick and dying during the yellow fever epidemic. Somewhere was Boss Crump. And over the hill was Ma Rainey. It was black, white, enslaved, and slave owner. And now the grounds held a white woman from the Delta and the son of a man who came to this country with nothing, barely able to speak English. Down the hill and on the winding road through the headstones and the trees, she spotted Porter Hayes. He was standing next to the brand-new Mercedes sedan she'd insisted on buying him. At first, he wouldn't take it, but it was his straight-talking secretary Darlene who called him a bullheaded fool if he didn't.

Hayes had on a long black coat over his suit and leather gloves. In the weeks since Dean's disappearance, he and a CPA he trusted had walked her through the files they'd found in Dean's secret room. The good news was that Dean had put a massive amount of his holdings in Addison's name to hide it away over the years. It wasn't the kind of money Porter said he hoped to find, but it would "keep the kids in private school and pay those country club dues."

But she dropped the Club. She was selling the big Central Gardens house. She didn't want any of it—the jewelry (except for what had been her mother's), most of the clothes, the cars, the photos of the outrageous family vacations. The thought of what Dean had done for all that expensive garbage, killing people or having people killed, made her want to puke. If she and Libby were speaking, she'd invite her over for a big bonfire of all Dean's junk. His hunting clothes and bespoke suits and six pairs of cowboy boots with outrageously tall heels. What a vain little prick.

"I think ole Sam would've liked the service," Hayes said. "I don't speak Arabic, but it sounded real nice."

Addison introduced Preston to him. Sara Caroline was saying goodbye to her aunt and uncle. Addison had planned the funeral without their input—her shrewd father had made her executor of his estate.

"You don't think he opened up the heavens with the sun?" she asked.

"Miss Hassan," Hayes said, peering up at the beams shooting from the clouds, "I been on this earth nearly seventy years. What I've learned is that nobody knows nothing."

Addison looked down the rows of cars on the crooked road out of the cemetery. Libby with the twins and goddamn Branch. She waved to Addison and Addison nodded back.

"You got somewhere to go after this?" Hayes said.

"My brother invited us over for Thanksgiving dinner," she said. "With some family who flew in."

"Glad to hear you patched things up."

"I wouldn't go that far," Addison said. "I may drop off the kids. But I'm not going. Libby hires the worst caterers in the business. Everything looks pretty, but it doesn't have any flavor."

Porter Hayes stood in the open door of his new Mercedes. The polished hood and modern headlights suited him. "Y'all like turkey necks?"

"Excuse me?"

"Smoked turkey necks," he said. "In gravy. Candied yams. Mac and cheese. Collard greens. That type of thing."

Preston tugged at the sleeve of her dress. She looked down at her son, seeing so much of her father in his face. Preston seemed interested in Porter's offer. Sara Caroline walked slowly toward them. Some of the cars and SUVs pulled out on the narrow blacktop and headed out the Elmwood's ornate metal gates. "Change of plans," Addison said.

"Again?" Sara Caroline said. "Awesome."

They ate a big buffet meal at a place called the Gay Hawk over on Danny Thomas. Her father would've liked that. He had a lot of love and respect for the late entertainer as he'd also been Lebanese. Her father attributed a lot of his success to looking up to Danny Thomas as a kid. She could still hear him: *His real name was Amos Kairouz. From Detroit but came here for St. Jude. That man did so much good, Addy.*

Hayes pulled a few tables together in a back room decorated with a big painting of Martin Luther King Jr. Soon they were joined by his son, Randy, and daughter, Nina. Nina had two boys, teenagers, but they ate up front by the cash registers with some cousins. One of the young boys looked almost identical to his grandfather. His name was Porter, too.

The cinder block building was short and squat, only a few blocks over from the housing projects. On the way in, Hayes gave a homeless man five dollars to watch his new car in the parking lot. Addison didn't feel like eating. She felt hollowed out. But she picked at the turkey necks and a few candied yams. She would've killed for a glass of white wine but even thinking about it made her feel absolutely ridiculous.

When Preston got up for seconds and Sara Caroline was engaged in a conversation with Nina, Porter leaned over and asked, "You hearing anything on your ex?"

"I still don't know who he was," she said. "Really."

"Does it matter now?"

"Would be nice to know a name."

"But you know the man," Hayes said. "His character."

"What character?"

Hayes got up from the table, announcing that Mr. Bobo was putting out some banana pudding. "Hadn't you had enough, Daddy?" Nina said, smirking. "You know this isn't a competition."

Nina looked over at Addison and smiled. Addison felt good being among Porter Hayes's family, knowing that he'd meant so much to her father. She figured maybe she'd work things out with Libby. Damn, it was hard to stay mad at Libby. But Branch? That was an altogether different issue. What apology could he possibly offer? Not that he had even tried. *Sorry, Addison, I helped your fraud of a husband kidnap you and put you in an abusive rehab, if it even was real rehab at all, and I helped him spread the word that you were crazy. My bad.*

"You ready?" Hayes asked, looking at Addison as he leaned down and kissed his daughter on the cheek.

Hayes drove them back to the funeral home in Germantown where she'd parked her car. As she got out, Hayes reached up to the visor and handed her a CD. "My son burned this for you," he said. "Figured you might like to hear some of the tracks my late wife sang on. Back in the day."

Sara Caroline opened up the Escalade's passenger door and Preston followed, lying down in the seat behind her. Addison had done her best to shield her kids from the worst about Dean but they definitely knew. She just kept trying to move ahead like she'd promised her dad. Keep moving. Don't ever look back, or the bastards will catch you.

Addison offered her hand to Porter Hayes. "Are you ever going to send me your final invoice?"

"You're kidding, right?"

"Paid in full?"

Hayes looked at his shiny new Mercedes and nodded. "And then some. Here, take a few business cards. You know. For your rich-ass friends."

She pocketed the cards, hugged the man tight, and walked back to the Escalade. Addison watched as Hayes headed west toward downtown, and then she headed east back to her father's town house. It would take her weeks to make that place livable, but at least she'd be free of all things Dean. There had been almost as many questions about Alec Dawson from the detectives as there had been about her stupid-ass husband. She'd found out Alec no longer owned his house and that Dawson-Gray had gone into bankruptcy nine months ago. *Poor Ellie. Poor sweet Ellie.*

As they drove, Sara Caroline studied the CD Porter had given her—no label or markings—and turned on the stereo. "I Only Want to Be with You" started to blare from the speakers. *Jesus God.* Addison didn't say a word, driving with her left hand as she punched eject with her right. Hootie and the Blowfish spit out of the stereo, and she caught the disc in her hand, let down her window, and tossed it out.

"That's littering," Sara Caroline said.

"Is it?"

Sara Caroline put in Porter's CD and Addison heard the smooth, silky voice of a man singing. *But now I'm as different as sunshine is to rain.* Porter Hayes's wife, Genevieve, singing the chorus. *Not like I used to be. Not like I used be.*

44

Gaultier

He had no regret or remorse for taking the geniza. Anatoliy Zub and Peter Collinson had been so very distracted with the police knocking on the door of the suite to even notice. He'd simply rolled the items, metal bins stacked and stored on a luggage trolley, onto a service elevator and out to Carson Wells waiting in a white van. Wells had even been good enough to drop Gaultier at the Memphis Airport, where he'd caught a plane to Atlanta and then on to Paris. He had to sit in economy class but the thought of all the money he'd made on the American expedition had lulled him to sleep. The only thing that he hadn't expected, never even contemplated, was that Zub and Peter Collinson would get away, too. Ostensibly on Zub's private aircraft, flying back to wherever fit Zub's fancy.

To those in the know, those in the arms trade, Collinson was quite dead. Zub had supposedly bragged at a trade show in Frankfurt that Collinson had been dropped in the Atlantic, halfway across the pond. Gaultier had offered the geniza to Monsieur Wolfe through his emissary, Carson Wells. (Wolfe was already brokering a new deal with the Israeli national library.) And if the millions Peter had counted on to buy his own life from Zub came to Gaultier instead, well, such is life. *What do such things matter to a dead man?*

Many weeks later in early spring Tippi joined him in Paris. They were walking together now along the Seine at sunset and in the shadow of the Musée D'Orsay. Tippi had adopted a look of fuzzy sweaters with scarves, dark jeans with knee-high leather boots. Her hair was pulled back into a tight bun with very red lips as was the fashion with Parisian women.

"Do you have any remorse?" she had asked. It had been the first time she'd brought up Peter since arriving in Paris.

"Why would I?" he said. "I tried to save his life many times. Turnabout is more than fair."

"He was a bastard."

"Very much so."

"I wonder what he did with my mother."

"It is best not to think on such things, my dear," he said. "Let's find a quiet café and have dinner. Have you been to the Lipp? I like good and hardy Alsace food. Despite all the old women and their pampered dogs."

"I have other plans," Tippi said. "But thank you."

Gaultier shrugged. Tippi had made it quite clear that she never wanted to be anyone's mistress and certainly not his second or third, but she would work for him in some capacity. What she called a Girl Friday. She was very intelligent and spoke passable French. Even if she said no to him now, he hoped that one day she would say yes. Since his return Valerie had become such a bore. Telling him that she'd grown to hate the smell of cigars and that she had already taken another lover. A Corsican named Philippe.

As they crossed the Pont Neuf, Tippi allowed Gaultier to hook his arm in hers. An older man and a much younger woman not exactly scandalous in Paris. The evening had taken on that lovely glow, a quality of light that he only knew in his wonderful city. Tippi saying no to dinner but yes to one drink at Le Fumoir.

He stopped for a moment to allow Tippi to admire Notre Dame at its golden hour. A pleasure boat passed under the bridge, the music from a band echoing beneath their feet.

"Just one drink."

"Of course," Gaultier said.

She sat outside with him on the large, comfortable chairs of the café. She smoked a few skinny cigarettes while he enjoyed a Liga Privada with his cognac. Tomorrow he would be back in Sète with his wife and his children. Apparently, his son had grown obstinate in his absence and their aging mansion needed a new roof. His wife was sometimes more demanding and forceful than Zub.

"Pick you up at eight?" Tippi asked.

He nodded.

"Gare de Lyon?"

He nodded again.

"Oh," she said. "I bought a present for your wife today. I will give it to you in the morning."

"Was it expensive?"

"Extremely."

They didn't speak for a while, Gaultier burning the cigar down to a nub. He stood up and kissed her on both cheeks, telling her that he'd see her in the morning. Being in such close proximity to a wonderful young woman had put him in a melancholy mood. He walked the streets alone, stopping off at two more cafés before finding himself crossing the Champs- Elysées and over to Le Balzac. A line had formed outside on the brick streets. A fitting turnout for a retrospective of Melville.

He bought a ticket to *Le Samouraï* and sat in the rear of the theater, sleeping on and off, once spotting a man who looked so very familiar in the other row. With the dull head of tobacco and cognac, he believed for a moment it was Peter Collinson. The man back from the dead and swimming across half the ocean to get his money. Such paranoia and stupidity.

Gaultier knew he'd had too much to drink and needed to get back to his flat and pack. Morning would come very early. He excused himself and walked over past several people before pushing the cinema doors wide out to the street.

The air had grown cooler that evening, as he slid into his suit jacket in the glow of Le Balzac's marquee. He lit a fresh cigar and walked along the narrow one-way street back up to the Avenue Friedland, where he'd kept the same flat for twenty years.

As he was about to cross the street, he spotted Tippi standing by the entrance to the apartments. She held up something in her hand and Gaultier immediately knew he'd left his father's lighter at Le Fumoir. He nodded and smiled, walking quickly across the road to join her. But instead of handing him the lighter, she pressed tight against him and gave him a most wonderful kiss.

"Why?" he said.

"The boy I met bored me," she said. "I heard you know things."

Gaultier held up both of his hands. "Me?"

"This double snake thing?" she said. "My mother said Collinson learned it all from your mistress."

"It is a dragon," he said. "A double-crested dragon."

Tippi kissed him again and soon they were up in his flat, Gaultier's oft-neglected bird, LouLou (his housekeeper was paid well for its care), squawking with welcome. Clothes were shed and bodies intertwined. There was much gasping and some screaming, Gaultier very proud of himself after they finished. The dragon not so much a trick as a wondrous performance of stamina and strength.

He offered Tippi a cigarette. But instead, she took the silk sheet around her (so very modest) and went into the bathroom. Gaultier opened a window and lit up the rest of the cigar, happy but still very melancholy about returning home, the admonishment of his wife so loud in his ears.

He was already thinking of tomorrow when he barely heard the tight little click in the other room. LouLou began squawking. He reached for the gun on his nightstand only to recall he'd left it in his travel bag in the bath. Tippi was running the water in the bathroom now. He stood up, completely naked, streetlights cutting through the shadows, as Peter Collinson entered with a gun.

Peter didn't say a word. He looked at Gaultier, so naked and vulnerable, while he moved like the sweeping hand of the clock with his back to the bathroom door. The water had stopped and all was quiet. Gaultier could hear his own breathing, thinking to himself. *Well, this is how it happens. But if so, are you not very happy?*

Collinson told him to turn around, get on his knees, and face the window. Gaultier had few options and did as he was told. Collinson was dressed in black pants and a black sweater, looking very much like the killer he was rumored to be.

"You talked your way out from Zub?"

"Zub is dead," Collinson said.

Gaultier nodded. Collinson told him again to turn around. He'd want the spray of blood away from him and onto the bed, nice, compact and professional.

"May I ask your true name?"

Collinson knocked him hard across his temple and Gaultier stumbled, finally getting down onto his knees and seeing the smoke rising from the ashtray and the lights across the street. The sounds of zooming traffic and an ambulance from far off. He took a deep breath and closed his eyes. *Was it too late for prayer?* He was trying to remember the last prayer he had made when he heard the gunshot and a heavy thud behind him.

He turned, his head bleeding over his one eye and down his cheek and saw the blurry vision of Tippi, still clutching the silk sheet around her, holding the pistol he'd packed with his shaving kit in her right hand.

There were no words.

Gaultier shook his head as she walked closer to him and handed him back the warm gun. She wrapped her arms around him and took in a deep breath before standing back as if suddenly wondering if Collinson was truly dead.

He watched her staring at the man's body. And then she turned her wonderful face to him. The bright eyes and perfect profile of a star of classic cinema. He nodded. "Yes, my dear," he said. "It is over."

Tippi took in a deep breath. "*Easy Come,*" she said. "*Easy Go.*"